"What the unnamed New England island at the heart of Elizabeth Winthrop's evocative new novel lacks in size it more than makes up for with intrigue. Thanks to richly drawn characters and Winthrop's talent for suspenseful storytelling, the reader can't help but succumb to the undertow." —*People* magazine

"Filled . . . with life and personality . . . emotionally complex . . . [a] satisfying plot . . . *Island Justice* is the kind of book that used to be called a 'good read'— there's nothing better." —*The New York Times Book Review*

"Winthrop packs onto her small island adventure, romance, mystery and humor. Besides being a good yarn, the story captures the feel of an island. We hear the bell buoy, the foghorn, the gulls . . . I was sorry when I finished this wonderful, rich book." —*Book Page*

"Winthrop delivers an illuminating story of a crisis of community." —*Publishers Weekly,* starred review

"A warmly satisfying story that vividly depicts scenes both natural and human." —*Library Journal*

"Sam is a naturalist, deeply engaged in studying the island's natural ecology. But he is also Maggie's guide to the human ecology of the island, a system that surely and silently takes care of its own. With its thorny characters and suspenseful plot, *Island Justice* creates an appealing setting for a small-town story that is full of incident." —*The Boston Globe*

"A highly readable book that has many facets and never panders . . . a fine novel." —Knoxville *News-Sentinel*

ALSO BY ELIZABETH WINTHROP

In My Mother's House

ISLAND

JUSTICE

A Novel

ELIZABETH WINTHROP

Quill / William Morrow / New York

Copyright © 1998 by Elizabeth Winthrop

Excerpt from "Wild Geese" reprinted from *Dream Work* by Mary Oliver,
copyright © 1986 by Mary Oliver. Used by permission of Grove/Atlantic, Inc.

It is the policy of William Morrow and Company, Inc., and
its imprints and affiliates, recognizing the importance of preserving what has
been written, to print the books we publish on acid-free paper, and we exert
our best efforts to that end.

The Library of Congress has cataloged a previous edition of this title.

Library of Congress Cataloging-in-Publication Data

Winthrop, Elizabeth.
    Island justice / by Elizabeth Winthrop.
        p.   cm.
    ISBN 0-688-15920-6
    I. Title.
PS3573.I56I85   1998
813'.54—dc21   97-36566
                                                        CIP

Paperback ISBN 0-688-16968-6

Printed in the United States of America

First Quill Edition 1999

    2   3   4   5   6   7   8   9   10

BOOK DESIGN BY DEBBIE GLASSERMAN

www.williammorrow.com

TO JASON,
FOR THIS JOURNEY, THIS LOVE

AND IN MEMORY OF KASHA
1981–1997

Acknowledgments

In the creation of the world of this book, I have called on many people for their expertise. I wish to thank them here.

Carl Richey, a well-known dog handler and trainer, for introducing me to vizslas and for showing me a small corner of the complicated and fascinating world of pointing dogs

Barbara Roberts for invaluable information about furniture conservation

Naturalists David Fermoile and Ed Horning, who introduced me to the yellow spotted salamander, "herp fanatics," and the rich and varied world of island coastal ecology

Bill Keogh for his knowledge of construction materials and methods

Starling Lawrence for talking to me about guns, shoots, and pheasants

Rosanna DeVergiles for her information on the breeding and training of vizslas

Ted Harrington for his knowledge of fishing

In researching this novel, I have talked to many inhabitants of islands up and down the coast of New England. Island people by nature tend to be cautious and reclusive. Many who helped me with information for this book specifically asked not to be named. I would simply like to thank them here for their generosity, their willingness to answer questions, and their enthusiasm for this project.

I am grateful to the Virginia Center for the Creative Arts for award-
ing me a residency at a crucial time during the writing of this book.

Thanks to the people in my life who uphold, support, and nurture
me either by listening or reading or simply by enduring the ebb and
flow of confidence that accompanies any artist in the midst of the
creative process: Eliza, Andrew, Anneski, Margot, Linda, Billy, Raymond, Margaret, Betsy, Candy, Tish, and Jason.

And finally, to Alison, without whom I shudder to think.

Meanwhile the wild geese, high in the clean blue air,
are heading home again.
Whoever you are, no matter how lonely,
the world offers itself to your imagination,
calls to you like the wild geese, harsh and exciting—
over and over announcing your place
in the family of things.

—Mary Oliver
"Wild Geese"

ISLAND JUSTICE

One

NAN DIED LATE IN JUNE up on the island. They found her at the bottom of the porch steps, her hand resting on her throat, as it always did when she was contemplating something.

"She went without pain," Maggie's mother said when she called her in London to tell her the news. "The doctor says her heart gave out. Just like that."

"But she was only seventy-three. So young," Maggie whispered.

"A year older than me," her mother said. "And I expected her to outlast me. She seemed so strong, toughing it out up there right through those grim winters." There was a delay, a transatlantic hiccup on the line, and they both started to talk at once. Her mother prevailed and Maggie heard, "They'll have a service on Saturday. Up on the island of course. She'll be buried there."

Sitting cross-legged on the bed in her hotel in London, Maggie could still believe that Nan was waiting for her on the other side of the Atlantic as she always had before. It was seven A.M. in the States. Surely she was out on the porch this very morning in her favorite wicker chair with that old moth-eaten blanket still wrapped around her knees. Any minute now she'd hoist herself to her feet and go down the steps to the perennial garden where she would putter about, adjusting a stake here, snapping a dead blossom off there. And later in the day, after lunch and a nap, she would make her way down through the apple trees to the narrow stony beach where she and Maggie swam every afternoon in the summer, their feet stuffed into white rubber shoes because the rocks were slimy with algae and unpredictable. In the long evenings, they'd set up a round table in the corner of the porch for raucous sunset dinners with all the misfits on the island, both summer and winter people mixed. Nan had been a year-rounder for over twenty years and served as a bridge between the two worlds. The day began and ended with the porch. Nan belonged there. And Maggie belonged there too, but only with her. Only with Nan alive.

MAGGIE'S LAST VISIT to the island had been cut short by a call from a private dealer in London who asked her to come over and survey a collection of eighteenth-century furniture. If he purchased the lot, he would want her to oversee the conservation work on the pieces.

"But you've only been here five days," Nan had said over their usual morning tea on the porch. Fog was rolling up the hill from the ocean, and Maggie had wrapped an extra blanket around Nan's knees. "You're barely over jet lag from the Madrid trip. Poor Kasha. You just got her here and now you're going to haul her back down to Philadelphia and throw her in that kennel again."

At the sound of her name, the Siberian husky lifted her head and eyed Maggie. Her leash was tied to the porch railing.

"Don't be so dramatic, Nan," Maggie said. She was sitting on the railing looking out over the orchard where Nan's daffodils had just begun to bloom. "She doesn't stay in a kennel. My friend Susan takes her. She loves Kasha. Besides, this is big. The first job I've gotten with this collector, and he'll pass my name along if I do good work for him."

"It's always a big job, Maggie." Nan lowered her teacup to the glass-topped table. "You've been on the go constantly since last fall. The business is well established by now. You can surely afford to turn down one or two projects."

"I know I can. But if there's work out there for me, why turn it down?"

"Ah, youth, " Nan said. " At your age, I was always on the run too. Look at your foot. It hasn't stopped jiggling since you got here. Last night, it made the china rattle at dinner. I kept thinking one of the legs of that old table had come unglued."

"Knowing the way you treat your furniture, it probably has," Maggie said. She glanced down and stilled her foot. "I hadn't noticed."

"Of course you hadn't. I never did either. If I have one regret in life, it's that I didn't learn to be still earlier on."

"When did you learn?"

"Not till I was in my fifties. When I moved up here full time. Island living has a way of slowing you down." Nan laughed and pointed. "Look, your foot's started up again."

At that, Maggie had stood up and cleared away their tea things.

SHE FLEW BACK for the service, a quick round trip between London and a museum meeting in Amsterdam. Nan's two nephews and their wives were there. One of them had put together a lunch at the house.

"You'll come, I hope," the woman said. Her name was Jane, and Maggie had only met her once or twice. The nephews rarely came to visit Nan on the island. Nobody in her family ever understood why she had moved up there full time. "You know all the people out here better than we do."

Maggie had been hoping to avoid the house. She glanced at her watch. "I have to catch a plane first thing tomorrow out of Logan for Europe."

"It won't be long, I promise you. The four of us have reservations on the afternoon ferry."

"All right, just for a minute."

Maggie refused to walk through the house, but went around the side to the porch where sandwiches and iced tea had been set out on two long tables. The whole island had come, some to honor Nan and others for the free lunch. Lots of people pushed through the crowd to greet Maggie. Although they knew she was only the god-daughter, they thought of her as the real family. She had spent her childhood summers with Nan, and in the twenty years since then, had come back three or four times a year. Most of the faces were familiar to her, but they blurred together as she shook one hand after another. People murmured their condolences, and all the while Maggie kept pointing to her watch and explaining about her trans-atlantic flight. After an hour, she managed to hitch a ride with a departing guest to the tiny island airfield.

When the small plane banked into a left turn above the shoreline, Maggie had a clear view of Nan's house crowning the hill above the little inlet. Three stories high, with the porch all along the front and the kitchen wing sprawling over to the side. All the years Maggie had come to visit, the house had never felt large to her, but now, looking down on it from the air, she wondered at Nan rattling around in that enormous place all by herself, year after year.

Would she ever see it again? she wondered. Probably not. Without Nan, there would be no reason to come to the island. She closed her eyes. An overnight in Boston and then on the plane to Amsterdam tomorrow. She couldn't let herself think about Nan now. Not yet. Later on she'd make herself face it. When she had more time.

Two weeks later Maggie was house-sitting at a friend's flat in London when her mother called again.

"You've got something here from a Matthew Bunker, Esquire, up on the island. I think he must be Nan's lawyer. Do you want me to open it?"

"I guess you'd better."

There was a pause and Maggie could hear the rustling of papers. "It's the will," her mother said. "With a letter. Oh, boy."

"What does it say?"

"It seems she's left you the house."

"To me? Not the two nephews? Are you sure?"

"That's what the letter says. Apparently she rewrote her will at the end of April."

"I was there in April and she never mentioned it to me," Maggie said.

"It does make a certain amount of sense. You were her goddaughter, after all."

Maggie was silent, her hand over her mouth.

"It's a huge present, Maggie. The house is probably worth quite a bit."

"Yes, I know."

"If you're intending to sell it, summer's the only time."

"I can't talk about it now. I've got so much going on here. I'll deal with it later. Thanks, Mother."

She remembered how large the house had looked from the air. It loomed in her mind, pressed against her with its weight. What was she going to do with a house? Nothing right now, she decided. Later. She would think about it later.

She managed to put it off until the end of the summer. Once she had finished up the job in London and the one after that in Amsterdam, she was scheduled to do a major survey of the furniture collection at the National Museum in Prague, but they called her early in September to reschedule. The funds had not all been secured yet. This kind of thing was routine in her business, but it always threw her off. It meant she had no work lined up for the fall. There was nothing to keep her from going home. She would have to deal with Nan's house. There was no more avoiding it.

"It's going to be a hard sell now, Miss Hammond," the real estate agent told her when she called him from Philadelphia the first of October. "Summer people have all gone home."

"Well, I'm headed up there to put the place in some sort of shape."

"Do you want me to begin showing it right away?"

She imagined strangers pushing open Nan's front door, poking through the closets, tramping out onto the porch. "Not quite yet," she said after a pause. "I'll call you when I'm ready."

The next day, she packed a couple of bags, loaded Kasha into the backseat of the car, and headed up the interstate.

EVEN THOUGH SHE was a good forty minutes early for the three-thirty ferry, the crew member in charge of parking decided to put Maggie's car on the boat right away. It meant she'd be first on, last off, but she didn't care. In early October, there wouldn't be more than two or three cars going over. If that.

The man rapped sharply on the hood of the car.

"Don't turn around," he said. "Just keep looking at me."

She nodded. She always forgot. If you'd been to the island before, you understood that you were to stare straight ahead at the ferry-parker as the car rolled backward, make minute adjustments to the steering wheel, depending on whether the man pointed left or right with one casually lifted index finger. You were not to glance in the rearview mirror or turn around and look behind you. You were to trust him completely. In the summer, he parked as many as twenty vehicles per boat, five times a day, ten if you counted round-trips.

He tapped the back window when her bumper touched the bumper of another car that looked as if it might have died in the hold of the boat some years before. The man stopped beside the passenger window to peer in at her.

"Don't forget to set the emergency brake," he said, but she knew it was just an excuse to get a closer look at her. Kasha distracted him.

"Geez, big dog. That a wolf?"

"No," she said for probably the thousandth time. "Siberian husky."

"Pretty dog, but I bet he's got teeth."

"She does," Maggie said. "Big ones."

LATER, STANDING UP on the deck, with Kasha pressed close to her side, she watched another driver, a man who kept turning and checking for himself that his dark-green Mercedes wasn't going to hit something. Finally, the ferry-parker walked around, opened the door on the driver's side, and motioned him out with a contemptuous jerk of his thumb.

"What do you mean?" the stranger demanded.

"I'll put your car on. Chuck," he called out in the direction of the freight office. "Come over here and help me, will you?"

"I'd rather you didn't drive this car."

"Either you let me back your precious car on this boat, buddy, or you can drive it right back onto the mainland and park it there for the winter." The ferry-parker shrugged. "I couldn't care less either way. It's up to you."

Maggie recognized Chuck when he came out of the office. He was the one who'd been keeping an eye on the house for her all summer, a thin man with thinning hair and a slight limp. She didn't remember him working on the ferry before.

Down below, they all stood around while the stranger took his time getting out from behind the wheel. The crew members barely waited for him to move out of the way before they went about their business, this time Chuck pointing his index finger, the other fellow doing the steering while the man walked along behind, watching. Maggie knew that for any island person, they would have left the car sitting by itself in the middle of the deck. But to teach this fellow a lesson, they would park him as close as possible to the starboard bow, where the white paint of the metal hull threatened the sleek green door of his fancy car.

The man looked like a summer person. Maggie wondered what he was doing, coming onto the island this time of year. He could be here to check on some repair to his house or to bring some business friends over for a day of golf or fishing. But he seemed to be alone.

She slid onto the bench on the port side, which gave her the afternoon sun warm on her face and the view of the lighthouse on their way out of the harbor. Kasha loved tight places. She crawled in under the bench and curled into a circle between the cabin wall and Maggie's feet.

Maggie leaned her head back. Water slapped against the side of the boat, and in the distance, a bell clanged, signaling the arrival of a train from the west. It sounded like a kid hammering on a tin plate. In the summer, the boat waited for the train, but there was no point on a Wednesday afternoon in the fall. Across the way, people were fishing off the dock. In all the years of sitting here waiting for the ferry to leave, she had never seen them pull in anything. She'd heard the river mouth was badly polluted, and you wouldn't want to eat your catch.

A few feet above her, a seagull landed softly on the piling. It stalked once around its tin-topped perch and surveyed the scene. She saw the red eye, the red dot at the end of its beak where Nan once told her the baby gull tapped so the mother would regurgitate its food. In the old days, Kasha would have been straining at the end of her leash and barking, but now she didn't lift her head, lulled as she was by the rocking of the boat and the warm sun.

"NICE OUT HERE," said the man with the foreign car. "Mind if I sit?"

Maggie shook her head. I was wrong, she thought. This man was not an owner. Someone used to the island ways would probably have sat alone, would certainly never have asked permission. She slipped her hand under the bench and rested it briefly on Kasha's head to let her know it was all right.

"You've been to the island before?" he asked in an accent. Irish, she thought.

"Mmm."

"This is my first trip. But I'll be staying the winter. I'm the new doctor, Dennis Lacey."

Yes, definitely Irish. "Maggie Hammond," she said.

Beneath them, the engines began to rumble, and the man on deck watch trotted past to lift the hawser off the piling.

"Do you live here year-round?" he asked.

"No," she said. "But I've been coming to the island since I was a child."

He was a stocky, barrel-chested man, who sat with legs spread, his hands hanging between his knees. Once or twice, when the breeze disturbed his graying hair, he settled it back into place with a quick brush of his hand. A silver tube lay between them on the bench. Fishing rod, she figured.

The ferry picked up speed as it left the harbor. Kasha scrabbled out from her hiding place and lifted her nose to sniff the air. Maggie kept two fingers curled around her collar, but Kasha seemed more interested in the sensations of the boat under her feet than this man. The doctor put out his hand for the dog to sniff, but she ignored it.

"So, what's this island like?" he asked.

"Pretty deserted in the winter."

"Seems odd since it's only forty minutes from the mainland."

She shrugged.

"How are the natives?"

"Prickly," she said. "Good neighbors in a disaster and distant much of the rest of the time. I assume you've been warned that there are no amenities," she said. "None."

"What do you mean by none?"

"No drugstore, no movie theater during the winter, no bank, no barbershop, no—"

He put up his hand to stop her.

"Why don't you tell me what there is," he said.

"Two grocery stores, one open in the morning, that's where you buy the paper, and the other in the afternoon. A hardware store, a video store next door, a post office, a gift shop open on the weekends, a library three afternoons a week and Saturday mornings, a coffee shop for breakfast and lunch if you like a lot of grease with your french fries, a real estate agent." She stopped. "That's about it. Wednesdays you get round-trip for the price of a one-way ticket. Busy day on the ferry in the winter. I'm surprised we don't have a bigger crowd today."

"What's the population?"

"About three thousand in the summer, three hundred in the winter."

He shaded his eyes and looked out over the water, but it was too early to see land. "How big is it?"

"It's about twelve miles long and three miles wide. There's a paved road that runs up the center, but out at the eastern end it turns to dirt." She stood up and wrapped Kasha's leash twice around her hand. "Time to buy our tickets."

"How long are you staying?" he asked.

"Only a few weeks. I'm cleaning out a house so I can sell it."

"That's a tough job." He began to gather up his fishing rod and briefcase.

"You can leave those out here. Nobody'll take them."

"Of course," he said, as he followed her inside. "Big-city habits die hard. I should remember. I grew up on an island myself. Off the western coast of Ireland."

"Then you should do fine here."

"I doubt my wife will like it much. We've kept our apartment in the city."

A wife, Maggie thought. Funny. She hadn't pegged him as a married man.

IN THE CABIN of the boat, the regular winter passengers had taken up their usual positions. The islanders who were coming home from their day jobs on the mainland hunched over the stiff piece of cardboard balanced on their knees for their running poker games. Five or six teenagers from the island commuted over to the high school on the mainland because their parents thought it was better than the island school. They staked out the same territory every day in the winter, lounging against the sea-smudged windows, smoking cigarettes. There were parents on the mainland who sent their kids to the island school because they were impressed with the small student-teacher ratio. This same ferry had just taken the mainland kids home on its earlier run. When any of them got out of hand, Chuck Montclair settled them down. He manned the ticket window for the afternoon run in the winters. He liked the job. It gave him a chance to talk to people.

Miss Yola, with her soft-brimmed cotton hat and her aluminum cane, was waiting for him when he opened up. Her face was round and the skin smooth. She looked much younger than her sixty-five years. She went over to the mainland every other week to see the physical therapist.

"How's the hip?" he asked.

"Better, I suppose," she said. "I'm out walking a bit more. Made it all the way to church last Sunday. Now give me a minute to find my ticket."

"No rush."

Miss Yola came to the island years ago as a maid to an eccentric old lady named Esther Mansfield. When Miss Mansfield died, she left everything to Miss Yola—the house, her clothes, the little white dog, and enough money to keep up the place it seemed, because Miss Yola never worked another day in her life. In the beginning, everybody was outraged. A black woman owning a house like that. Somebody's maid. But over time, people got used to her.

"You've got two extra customers today," she said as she slipped him the blue round-trip ticket.

"That's right. One must be the new doctor."

"How do you know that?"

"The MD on the license plate of that fancy new car of his. He's Irish. Still got an accent."

"You are the most noticing sort of person, Mr. Montclair. And I see Maggie Hammond's come back. She wasn't here all summer, was she?"

"Nope. I've been keeping an eye on the house for her."

"No word on John Burling yet, is there?" she asked.

"Not that I've heard," Chuck said. "Al Craven and Randy Baker, some of the others, spent all last night out there with the Coast Guard looking for him."

"If I ever want to know anything about the comings and goings on this island, you're the man to talk to." Miss Yola fussed with her purse, a beat-up black leather thing with a gold snap. She probably inherited it from Miss Mansfield right along with the house, Chuck thought.

"That storm came up so sudden," Miss Yola said. "No warning. Except for the auk."

"What?"

"I saw Sam in the post office yesterday. He told me he found a dead auk in the rocks on White Beach. That's an ocean-going bird. Never comes to shore except when there's bad weather out at sea."

Chuck shrugged. "John Burling was in such bad shape that day he wouldn't have paid any attention to a hurricane warning, never mind a dead bird. He was on the afternoon ferry."

"The casino again?" Miss Yola asked. She didn't bother to lower her voice. Everybody listening already knew about Burling and his gambling.

He nodded. "Had to lend him money because he'd lost his ticket, and the boss man said two weeks ago that I couldn't take anymore IOUs from him." The note was right there by his shoulder, tacked up on his bulletin board next to a couple of bad checks from summer people and a note about a missing dog. "Then I heard he dropped in at the Lounge and put down a few more beers before he went out in the boat. Everybody tried to stop him, but it didn't do any good."

ONCE MISS YOLA had moved away, Chuck flicked the switch on the loudspeaker to make the announcement that the ticket window was closing, when the two extras came in from the starboard deck.

"Round-trip?" he asked just to be ornery.

Both shook their heads.

"I expect I'll be here for a while," said the man in a low voice. "I'm the new doctor. Dennis Lacey." He put his hand through the ticket window and Chuck nodded, without shaking it.

"That'll be four-fifty, off-season fare."

"Would you know anything about the fishing on the island?" the doctor asked as he thumbed through his wallet.

"I've done some," Chuck said.

"I was going to try fly fishing for blues."

"I stick to spinners myself."

"Hello there, miss," he said, when the doctor made room for Maggie at the window.

"No charge for the dog is there, Mr. Montclair?"

Chuck was pleased. Most of the summer people didn't bother to learn your name, and when they went off-island they forgot it.

"So you've still got Kasha, then?" he asked, leaning out the ticket window and dropping his hand. The husky sniffed out of politeness and gave him an offhand, lazy lick. "She looks pretty good."

"She is, for an old-timer. Thirteen in December."

"We missed you this summer," he said.

"I just came back that one time. For Nan's service."

He nodded. He'd seen her there in the cemetery standing by the grave all alone when everybody else had dropped away to talk among themselves. She'd folded her arms across her chest, he remembered now, and rocked back and forth on her feet like a child trying to comfort herself without making any noise. He had skipped the lunch afterward. She'd come and gone the same day on one of those little planes that made the trip from the mainland in eight minutes.

"Still roaming around the world?" he asked. "London, Spain, and places like that, I hear."

"Did Nan tell you?"

He shrugged by way of answering and took some time counting out the change for her twenty. Wasn't Nan Phipps actually. It was

Anna Craven who worked in the post office three mornings a week and believed that reading postcards didn't count as a federal offense.

"Thanks for all your work on the house."

"Just doing my job. When Henry Willard retired, I went over to Craven Construction, and Mrs. Phipps switched the house to them last year. Said she couldn't imagine anybody but me fussing with the old place."

"So, how are you doing?" Maggie asked and sounded as if she really cared.

"Fine." He shrugged. "Got a bum knee so I had to give up the heavy work. I drive the mail up from the boat some mornings, take a ride over and back in the afternoons, do some work with Anna Craven's hunting dogs. One thing and another."

Maggie grinned and he remembered that she had fine white teeth. She was in her late thirties, he figured. She had a thin face and brown eyes and dark red hair all wild and curly. She was wearing one of those long, swirly, foreign-looking skirts that seemed dangerously full, the kind that got caught in car doors or bicycle wheels.

"Are you staying a while?" he asked.

"A couple of weeks at the most. I've got to get the place cleaned up so I can put it on the market."

"You're going to sell it? Gee, that's too bad. I can't imagine somebody else owning it after all these years."

"Me neither. But I don't have much choice." She sounded defensive. "I don't honestly know why she left it to me."

"Well, those nephews of hers never visited but once or twice," Chuck said. "You were the one who came all the time."

"It's going to feel strange in that house without her." Maggie's voice dropped away. "I don't like to think about it."

"I know what you mean." He didn't tell her that he'd been the one to find Mrs. Phipps that day in June. When he first saw her lying at the bottom of the porch steps, with her eyes closed and her legs stretched out in front of her, she looked as if she were taking a nap. He'd actually said out loud, "You might be more comfortable in a chair, Mrs. P." "I'm just resting my eyes," was what he had expected her to reply, the way she had so many other times. When she didn't answer, he knew absolutely clearly, in that one instant, that she was gone. He had knelt beside her and lifted the upper half of her body into his lap and cradled her for a while like a baby. He was glad he had that time to say his own good-bye to her before he went inside to phone for help.

The silence between them drew on. Around the cabin, people looked up briefly from their books and their card games. They'd been listening all along, of course.

"I hope you have some time in the next few weeks," Maggie said at last. "I need to go over some things with you. The place will need painting, of course, and probably some work on that roof outside my room. I remember Nan was worrying about it when I was here in April."

"Oh, I'll be around," he said. "You call me any time. I have to show you how to work that new hot water heater, anyway."

"Where are the keys?"

"Same place she always keeps them. On that shelf by the phone. But you won't need them. The door's open."

MAGGIE MADE HER way out the front of the cabin, urging Kasha over the metal doorsill. The wind had picked up. Even on a summer afternoon, it could be cold out here on the bow, but it was Maggie's favorite place to stand watch as the island began to show itself across the expanse of gray water. Without turning around, she knew that behind them, the mainland had disappeared, and up ahead, she could already pick out the low brick buildings of the old naval base, the stony beach out beyond the little airport, the red buoy housing the bell that rang day and night, its tempo increasing when the swells were high with a westerly wind on an incoming tide. The pilings that lined the edge of the channel looked to her like soldiers at attention, and now she could see the tumble of thick reddish undergrowth where it spilled down over a line of bleached round rocks.

She crossed the bow. Nan's house stood at the top of the hill above the tennis club. From this distance, she could just make out the long porch, the dormer windows on the third floor reflecting back the afternoon sun, the shingled roof, the orchard sliding down the hill, and at the bottom, the rocky beach. She dug in her bag for glasses; on the porch, a jumbled disarray of wicker furniture came into focus, and on the kitchen side of the house, the overgrown vegetable garden.

Behind her, the horn blew, a long insistent noise that made the deck vibrate under her feet. Now they were close enough for her to see for certain the sight she had been putting off all summer; that Nan was not standing on the dock, one foot up on a freight flat, and one hand waving her big straw hat back and forth. Maggie knew from all those years of watching her wave in other guests that Nan started that windmill motion with her arm long before she could possibly have made out Maggie's shape on the deck of the boat. It was as if she never left the dock between Maggie's visits, as if she stood there waving Maggie home the entire time she was away.

Maggie gave Kasha's leash a warning tug and the dog stopped sniffing at a piece of squashed gum.

"Let's go inside," she said. "It's too cold out here."

Two

THE HARBOR LOUNGE was owned by Lila Keller, a beefy woman with blond hair going gray. Somewhere along the road of life, she'd hooked up with Jim Sullivan, a skinny blue-eyed man who appeared behind the bar one night. Nobody remembered seeing him get off the ferry, so behind Lila's back, people said she found him washed up on the beach and just picked him up and carried him home. The two of them never got married, but he didn't leave either. Everybody knew Lila and everybody knew not to cross her or they wouldn't get served the next night. The Harbor Lounge was the only game in town in the winters, except for bingo on Wednesday nights in the basement of the Catholic church, and bowling Saturday nights, and the occasional party down at the community center. Lila opened up her place even on holidays because as she said, you needed a drink after being cooped up with your relatives all day.

That evening, when Chuck stopped in, everybody was keeping Al Craven company before he went out again to look for his father-in-law.

"The old fool's either pulled in somewhere and found a bar or he's smashed that boat up on the rocks," Al said, and the patrons lined up along the bar nodded agreement. Most of them had one foot up on the rail, one hand on a cold bottle of Bud. Ellie, Randy Baker's girlfriend, was the only one perched on a stool with both feet tucked under her.

"It true they were going to repossess his boat?" someone yelled from down at the end.

"The man doesn't have anything else," Al said. "If it weren't for my Anna, he would have starved to death years ago. She's always going around behind his back paying off the man's debts. What can you do? He's her father. You know what they say. Blood is thicker than water."

"Maybe he took it down deliberately so the bank wouldn't get it," Randy Baker said quietly. "He sure did love that boat."

"Enough of this mournful talk," Lila said with a thump on the bar. "So, come on, Chuck, what about Maggie Hammond. How much is she going to ask for that house?"

"Maybe she won't sell it," Chuck said.

"That's not what I hear. Bob Wright said she's just about ready to list the place."

Chuck shrugged. "People change their minds."

"What does she need money for?" Al asked. "She's the Wharton grandchild."

"My place?" Randy Baker asked. He was the caretaker for a big estate halfway up the island on the sound side. Some people named Kitteredge owned it now, but it had always been known as the Wharton estate.

"That's right," Lila said. "But the girl never knew her grandparents. The Whartons cut her mother out of the will when she married that man Hammond. And then the creep walked out on his wife and kids right after the grandparents died. When it was too late to change the will."

"How come you know so much about it?" Randy asked.

"Nan Phipps and I got to be friends back in the early seventies, when she first moved on the island full time," Lila said. "Maggie Hammond was a cute little thing back then. Not as skinny as she is now. All those bright red curls."

"She's the girl with that wolf," Al Craven said. "Billy and I saw her coming off the boat when we picked up the lumber for the Davidson job."

"It's a Siberian husky," Chuck said.

"Well, excuse me, your lordship," Al said down the bar. "It looks like a goddamn wolf to me."

Chuck's ears burned. It amazed him how little Al knew about animals, considering his wife trained hunting dogs.

"So, how long's she staying?"

Chuck took a long drink and said nothing. He liked keeping information to himself. The men didn't pay much attention to what he had to say anyway because he wasn't like most of them. Kept to himself, didn't drive around with a gun and a snarling dog in the back of his truck, didn't gamble, not even lottery tickets. Was always puttering around with his camera. The black-and-white photo on the front cover of the monthly paper, the *Island News,* usually had his name running along the bottom. The captions read "The Island after the January snowstorm" or "Sunset over White Beach."

"That new doctor's got some weird accent," Billy muttered. "I heard him asking directions." Billy Slade was Al's sidekick, a short wiry man who always wore a Red Sox baseball cap pulled down low over his eyes.

"Irish," Chuck volunteered.

"Did you see those pointy cowboy boots he's wearing?" Randy asked. "Dumb-looking things. I just about asked him if he brought his horse on the ferry or was it swimming over later?"

The crowd laughed. A couple of bottles hit the bar with a thump. Randy Baker, a tall man with thick blond hair, looked like a transplanted Californian. Lila liked to say that Randy went through women like a hot knife through butter. Ellie, the latest one, was a surprise. Twenty-two years old if that, a daughter of one of the summer families. She had three earrings in her left ear and smoked filterless cigarettes, the way an actress in a play might do, picking the odd piece of tobacco off her lip with an elaborate pinch of her long manicured fingers. Nobody expected her to last very long once the cold weather hit.

"So where'd you see him, Randy?" someone asked.

"I helped him carry a load of stuff into the house from his car. A lot more painting supplies and fishing gear than medical stuff, if you ask me. Has an easel. Asked me about fly fishing for blues."

A ripple of laughter ran up and down the line of drinkers.

Nothing on this island is sacred, Chuck thought, as he put his money down on the bar and pushed off his stool.

"You're leaving so soon?" Lila said. She didn't necessarily care. It was just something to say.

He shrugged without answering.

"Hey, Chuck," Al called out. "I hear Anna wants you up to my place first thing in the morning. There's field work to be done with those vizslas."

"Yep," Chuck said. My place. It's her place too, he thought. Al never said our. Everything was always mine in his book.

"My wife is one hell of a dog trainer," Al said to the air, and the air murmured general agreement.

"You watch yourself, Chuck, with those Hungarian bitches," Al said to the audience. "They can go right out of their heads when they see a big man like yourself coming at them."

The crowd laughed, but they shifted uneasily on their stools. Chuck walked out the door with the blood pounding in his ears. Al Craven was a jealous man, and he was the sheriff on the island. Everybody knew not to mess with Al or any of his possessions, meaning his guns or his fishing rod or his money or his wife because he had this streak of meanness in him. Plenty on the island had seen it over the years.

Men like Al Craven had been taunting Chuck his whole damn life. He was sick to death of walking away from it and sick to death of popping antacids for his ulcer.

WHEN MAGGIE PULLED the car into the small driveway next to the kitchen, she sat for a long time staring at the side of the house without moving. Kasha circled and whined and finally drove her out of the car with a series of sharp inquisitive barks. She pushed the front door open and marched straight up the stairs to her old bedroom, the one she and Nan had painted navy blue on a whim one weekend.

She dropped her bags in the middle of the room and turned slowly around taking it in. The dark walls had always reminded her of a cave in contrast to the billowing white curtains and the steady western light that reflected off the water. As usual, everything had been left ready for her, but Maggie saw a few changes. Nan had moved their favorite dollhouse up here and set it on a table next to the north window. Maggie hunkered down to look. They had spent one whole summer filling the rooms of this three-story house with bent twig furniture. Maggie had drawn the tiny pictures on the wall and Nan had framed them. Painted clay vegetables lined the shelves in the kitchen. They had intended to donate the house and its contents to the library raffle, but in the end they couldn't bear to part with it, and Nan set it out on a table in the living room. She must have moved it upstairs to make way for this year's furniture project.

A vase stuffed with dried sea lavender had been placed on the marble-topped bureau. Three seashell necklaces that Maggie had strung the summer she was ten dangled from one of the finials next to the oval mirror. The top bureau drawer held the summer diary from her fifteenth year. The two postcards of the Cascade mountains that her father had mailed her that summer were still tucked inside the front cover. In the closet she found clothes she hadn't seen in years, faded blue overalls, a floppy straw hat she wore in the sun, a flowered cotton dress Nan made her put on for birthday parties. She buried her nose in the soft material that had grown shiny with wear and age, and smelled sea air, mildew, and a distant delicate hint of perfume.

Kasha padded into the room, her nose to the floor.

"Same place, old girl," Maggie said out loud. She needed to hear her own voice, to try and drown out what she wouldn't be hearing, Nan calling from the foot of the stairs that tea was ready on the porch, or would she please bring down an extra towel when she came, or did she want to go blackberry picking?

The house was already starting to ambush her. She would have to keep herself focused on the job at hand. She went to bed early with a pad of paper and began to make lists of the essential work that had to be done. All the rugs should be taken out and cleaned, the floors polished. She'd get Mr. Montclair to check that leak in the corner of her bedroom and the other one in the bathroom. Spot painting here and there would spruce the place up. As for the clutter, she'd simply have to be ruthless.

Nan's cleaning lady had continued to come over from the mainland twice a week all through the summer. So the house at least was clean, as clean as it ever could get because the tables were covered with rocks and feathers and shells that Nan picked up on her beach walks, and the Victorian hat stand was overflowing with hats perched every which way on its pleading brass arms, and the same porcelain mug sat by the phone in the front hall. It was filled with a paintbrush, four pens that had long since run out of ink, and an old toothbrush used to clean the silver.

How could you have misjudged me so badly, Nan? Maggie wondered as she dropped the pad on the floor by her bed and flipped off the light. I need my life to be as unfettered as possible, and you've dragged me back and weighed me down with all this baggage of yours. If it was money you wanted to give me, there must have been an easier way.

She'd left the window open, and across the water, she could hear the muffled clang of the buoy bell off Stony Point. The soothing, familiar sound lulled her to sleep as it always had, and to her surprise, she did not open her eyes again until the gulls woke her at first light.

SHE CARRIED HER breakfast tray to the front porch, where she could turn her back on the house for a while and lose herself in the long view of the clear, uncluttered sea. Her breath billowed out in the air, and she was grateful for the hot steam that rose from her tea. Kasha was tied up to the porch railing, where she alternately sat and then jumped up at the whiff of rabbit or some stirring in the bushes. She strained, she barked, she looked longingly at Maggie, then settled her aching haunches back onto the peeling floorboards. It was always this way their first few days on the island.

"You know if I let you go, you'll never come back," Maggie said in a stern voice. "Act your age. The time for chasing rabbits is over."

A movement on the side lawn caught her eye and she turned to see a dark-haired man watching something in one of the apple trees through a pair of binoculars. She followed the line of his gaze, but saw nothing in particular. He lowered the binoculars so they dangled on the string around his neck, consulted a book, and made some notes. Then he stretched, yawned, and surveyed the view from the rise of the hill. Down below, the gray morning sea was rippled by a light wind. Under a bank of lowering clouds, a strip of pale light edged the distant mainland. She wondered how long he would stand there before he noticed her. She felt like a voyeur and yet, she was reluctant to disturb him.

Finally Kasha got to her feet and trotted out to the end of her line to investigate. She barked once and the man turned.

"Good morning," Maggie called.

He waved and made his way through the grass toward her.

"I hope I didn't disturb you," he said from the bottom of the porch steps. "My name's Sam."

"I'm Maggie Hammond. Would you like some tea?"

"Sure."

He waited out on the porch while she boiled more water. When she returned, he had fixed his binoculars on the overgrown garden. Kasha was sniffing at his boots.

"Anything interesting?" She set down the tray and they settled into two of the wicker chairs.

"A flicker. I was hoping to see the blue-winged teal. Chuck Montclair told me he thought he saw one when he was over checking on the house. It's a migratory bird. None's been recorded on the island for five years."

She handed him a mug of tea and pushed the sugar bowl his way. "Is birdwatching a job or a hobby?" she asked as she settled her back against the creaky wicker.

"Both. I'm the naturalist on the island. I also teach science at the school. In fact, I was planning to bring some classes over to Mrs. Phipps's beach this afternoon. We're doing a unit on shoreline ecology. I hope you don't mind."

This was merely a formality. Maggie knew the rules of the island after Labor Day. The year-rounders toured through houses, played the golf course, and walked along the private beaches, all the places that were considered off-limits in the summer. Nobody stopped them or cared to.

"That's fine with me. There's a path down through the orchard."

"Yes, I know it," he said, but not in a patronizing way. Just a simple fact. He had a strong face, blue eyes, and thick black hair that shined in the light. "I honestly didn't expect to find anybody here."

"I just arrived yesterday. I'm cleaning out the house."

"Are you Mrs. Phipps's daughter?"

"Her goddaughter." This man had the ease and confidence of a long-time resident, but he clearly didn't keep up with island business as well as most locals. Everybody knew that Nan had no children. "Have you lived here long?" she asked.

"Six years last month."

"I can't imagine it full time."

"I can't imagine living anywhere else now," he said. There was a pause. She watched him wrap the string around the dripping tea-bag, squeeze the last drops into his mug, and then lay it on top of his spoon on the broad white arm of the wicker chair. His thoughtful, considered pace made her edgy. "Mrs. Phipps loved it here," he added.

"She did. It wouldn't suit me. I'm just fixing up the house to sell it. Do you happen to know anybody who'd like to buy a wonderful Victorian with a view of the sea and the setting sun? The real estate agent has been discouraging about my chances this late in the season."

"I'll keep my ears open, but the year-round people don't usually have the kind of money you could get for a place like this. You might be able to rent it through the winter and put it on the market next spring. Is it heated?"

"Yes. That's not a bad idea. So tell me, what grades do you teach?"she asked.

"The whole school. First grade through high school. Of course, that's only sixty-eight kids."

"Including the ones they bring in from the mainland?"

"Including them." He glanced at Kasha over the edge of his mug. "Nice-looking dog. Huskies are prettier when they age. When they're young, they remind me of raccoons, with those black circles around their eyes."

The dog lifted her white face, stared at the stranger, then watchfully settled her head back onto her paws.

"You're going to keep her on a leash the whole time?"

"Probably," Maggie said with a shrug. "Kasha's a city dog. Up here with all the smells, she's acting like a two-year-old. If I let her run wild, I doubt I'd ever see her again."

"She'd find her way back when she got hungry enough. After all it's an island, and huskies don't like water, do they?"

"Hate it," she said. She took another sip of tea. "What does it mean to be the island naturalist?"

"I run the museum. I'm doing a comprehensive study on the flora and fauna of the island. Under a grant. And we also participate in a statewide survey on the reptiles and amphibians." Although his tone of voice was polite, he kept one eye on the lawn and the orchard and the sea beyond to make sure he didn't miss anything that flew by.

"Snakes?" she asked.

"Snakes, salamanders, toads, frogs. This time of year, most of them are beginning to hibernate, so I concentrate on the birds. Migration time."

"That's a lot to keep track of."

"Almost everybody on this island helps. They report their findings to me and I enter everything on the new computer we just got. A donation from a generous summer resident. Hopefully it means I'll be keeping the records in a less haphazard fashion than I have before, although I'm not promising anything. I'd much rather be out in the field than hunkered down inside staring at a screen."

She nodded and drained the last sweet drops in her cup.

"I'd better get going. My first class starts in twenty minutes." He got to his feet. Kasha stood up too and strained at the leash.

"How long will you be staying?" he asked.

"A couple of weeks at the most," she said. "If I can get it all done by then. It's not just the house. I have to make up my mind about the furniture too."

"Are you going to sell it furnished?"

"Partially. I'll have to see. Nan has some beautiful pieces, but they're in terrible shape because of the moisture from the ocean. I'm a furniture conservator, so it would probably make sense for me to take the best pieces with me to restore. "

"You could get a lot of work on this island," he said. "From what I hear. I don't get inside the big houses much."

"Nan used to tell me that. But I work mostly with museums and collectors."

"Well, call me if you need anything. I'm in the phone book. Sam Matera."

"You're Italian." Of course. The dark hair, a five o'clock shadow by noon probably. It was the bright blue eyes that had thrown her off. The men she had met in Italy had dark eyes, almost black. "From what part of the country?" she asked.

"My father's family was from the north. Parma. But I grew up in Maine."

"Have you ever been to Italy?"

"No," he said. "I should, I suppose. If you can't remember the last name, I'm right before Chuck Montclair in the book. No other Materas around."

She nodded thanks.

"On island you just dial the last four digits."

"Yes, I know."

"Of course. If it's all right with you, I'll bring the kids around three this afternoon. Tide is low then. Mrs. Phipps's beach pulls in the best specimens. It's because of the curve of the shore and the narrow inlet."

"Sure, no problem."

"You're welcome to join us."

"Thanks. I'll see how much I've gotten done. I might want a break from all this dust and clutter by then."

My beach now, she thought much later when she was touring the real estate agent around the property.

Three

Lauren Root, the nurse on the island, always let herself into the clinic early on the first day with the new doctor. She liked to check the medicine chest and straighten out the clinic rooms long before he came through the waiting room from his house next door. It never hurt to make a good impression, and she figured the two of them were going to be in harness until June, and if they didn't hit it off, they had a long grim time ahead.

During the winter Lauren served as the hairdresser and manicurist on the island. The weekend before she had treated herself to French tips and a strawberry-blond rinse, and she appraised her new look in the bathroom mirror while she was sponging out the sink. A man was a man after all, she thought as she tucked a loose curl behind her ear. Even if he was married. And Randy Baker told her this morning that the doctor had arrived without his wife.

She heard him moving around in his living room on the other side of the thin wall and wondered what the fancy doctor from New York thought of that musty little house with the wall-to-wall carpeting and the fake pine paneling and the frilly strawberry-chintz sofa covers. Years ago, she'd made those covers herself and the curtains that matched, but she'd read enough decorating magazines since then to know how tacky the place looked.

When she was ready for him, she slammed the file drawers a couple of times to let him know she was open for business. Sure enough, the doorknob rattled a few minutes later and the chime rang in the waiting room when he stepped through.

"Good morning," he said. The voice was deep, low, with just the slightest accent. She liked it.

"Hello," she said, and offered her hand. "Dr. Lacey, I'm your nurse. Lauren Root."

His skin felt soft. She took in the shy brown eyes, the black hair just going gray swept straight back off the high forehead, the stocky figure. He was not a tall man, an inch or two under six feet.

"I'm very glad to meet you. I expect I'll need to rely on you a lot, especially in these first few weeks."

"That's why I'm here," she said. "The coffee's all made. I usually start it when I come in."

"I drink tea, actually. I'm an early riser. I'll make myself a pot in my kitchen. It's quite a change for me to have my house next door to my office. In New York, they were twenty blocks apart."

Tea, of course. The Irishman.

"Did you find everything you needed next door?" she asked.

"Oh, yes. I was surprised by all the food. Did you do that?"

She smiled. "We always stock the kitchen for the winter doctor the first week. Courtesy of the Island Health Committee."

"I was very glad to find it. I didn't realize the store would be closed when I got in. One other thing. Is there any place to get my shirts done?"

"I'll talk to Annie Slocum. She takes in extra laundry for people in the summer. I'm sure she wouldn't mind."

"Thanks. So where do we start?"

Businesslike fellow. All right then, she'd show him she knew her job.

"Clinic hours are nine to twelve and Mondays four to six. Two hours off for lunch, and in the afternoons, you make house calls and respond to emergencies, which usually means the sprained ankle that someone didn't get around to during clinic hours." She handed him a portable radio out of the desk drawer. "I respond to Portable One. You're Port Two."

"How many people have these?"

"About twelve who've been trained as EMTs. They double as ambulance drivers. The fire chief. The sheriff."

He checked out the radio, flipped the talk switch on and off. "Doesn't look too complicated," he said.

"No. Be sure to keep that around you all the time. Even on the golf course."

"I don't play golf," he said quickly. "Not all doctors play golf."

"But you're a fisherman," she said.

"Yes. How did you know?"

"Randy Baker told me down at the Rocky Point. Local coffee shop. He said you were asking about fishing."

"Word gets around quickly," he said.

"Oh, yes, hard to keep a secret on this place."

"That will be a change from the city," he said. "I drove myself out to the eastern end of the island this morning. To get the lay of the land. 'Tis a beautiful place."

She smiled at the " 'tis." Wait till Anna Craven heard this man speak. With all of her craziness about Ireland, she'd die.

"Yes, it is," she said, and she had to be careful not to pick up his accent and imitate it. She had a gift for that, a useful thing when they needed her for one of the extra parts in the school plays, but she didn't want him to think she was making fun of him.

"Any cases I should know about?"

"You'll find out soon enough. There's old Wilfred Hines who's got a bad heart. His daughter calls us up at all hours of the day and night if she thinks he's breathing funny. Some kids with asthma, one or two with eczema, a couple of ulcers. Mostly you'll be dealing with accidents and colds and splinters and babies. Although right now, we have a man missing off a boat."

"How long ago? "

"Monday night. So today's the third day. The Coast Guard and some of the island men have been out looking for him. We had a big storm out at sea that night."

The doctor had closed his eyes for a moment. He opened them when she stopped speaking.

"Go on," he said.

"The man's name is John Burling. He's a gambler and a heavy drinker and he's done stuff like this before. Taken the boat up the coast and holed up in some harbor until whatever trouble he's in blows over. He comes crawling back when his daughter has paid off the creditors. But he hasn't called in yet and he was pretty well tanked when he left."

The bell rang in the waiting room.

"Guess we're open for business," she said.

ANNA CRAVEN WAS pleased with the way Shooter had performed with the guns in the morning, so she took him with her when she went downtown to do her errands. His owner had gotten sloppy and let the vizsla ride in the car with the kids all summer, so she put his cage in the back of the station wagon and ordered him to kennel. He hopped right in and curled up. "Good dog," she said. "Getting your manners back."

She took the road by White Beach, the one that ran along the edge of the smaller golf course. The colors were muted now, chicory faded like washed-out jeans, yellow ragweed, and everywhere the shiny brown-red leaves of sumac. At the bend in the road, she rolled the window down and breathed in the smell of the dried grasses and the salt air. She reminded herself of her dogs, their noses always cocked for the scent of game. In the back, Shooter was barking, short, sharp reminders that there were birds out there, and he was not being allowed to do his job.

"Quiet," she called, but her tone was lazy and half-hearted, so he kept it up.

Her husband, Al, had come in at three o'clock in the morning and dropped like a stone into the bed beside her.

"Any sign?" she'd asked.

"Nothing," he mumbled into his pillow. "I don't know, Anna. Your old man might really have done something to himself this time."

She had lain awake for a while mulling over this possibility. Ever since her mother had died when she was twelve, Anna had been taking care of John Burling. She'd cooked for him, dragged him up to his bed when he came home drunk, hidden money from him so he couldn't gamble it away, paid his debts.

"He might be dead," Anna said out loud, simply to test the word on her tongue. The strange tone in her voice silenced Shooter in the back. How would she feel if it were true? Relief, she had to admit. In the beginning, there would simply be relief. One less person to worry about.

She slowed the truck for a woman walking toward her with a dog on a leash. This must be Maggie Hammond. Chuck had said something to her about a husky when they were out in the field working the vizslas this morning.

Anna poked her head out the window.

"What's her name?"

"Kasha," the woman said.

"You should let her off the leash."

"She'd run away."

"She must not have been properly trained then," Anna said.

The woman shrugged. Kasha was briefly distracted by Shooter, barking in the back of the station wagon, but she seemed much more excited by the smells in the high grass. Anna rolled the station wagon slowly along beside them on the wrong side of the road.

"She's a beautiful dog. About thirteen?"

"In December. Good guess."

"Bet people think she's younger," Anna said. "She acts like a puppy."

The husky was diving into the thick sedge, straining on the leash. Her tail was curled up tight and her back haunches were trembling.

"The arthritis is pretty bad, isn't it?"

"It comes and goes. In the city she's much calmer."

"Lots to smell. My dogs scent the pheasant. She goes for rabbit, I expect."

"My name is Maggie Hammond."

"Sorry. I'm Anna Craven. As you can see I'm better with dogs than people. Welcome to the island." With a quick tap on her horn, Anna sped off.

LATER THAT AFTERNOON, Maggie was standing in the side yard surveying the tangle of Nan's neglected perennials when she heard the noise of a group of children moving up the road toward her and Sam's voice rising above their chatter.

"Left, right, left, right. Hup one, two, three, four. Back in line, Slade. Arms by your side. Attention. About face. At ease." A pause. "All right, regiment, this is our destination. Danny, it's your turn to carry the supply pack. We will go down through the orchard quietly please, because the house is occupied. In fact, the lady who now owns it may decide to join us."

She let herself out through the gate as if on cue and waved. "All set," she said.

"Maggie Hammond, this is the fifth, sixth, and seventh grades of the Island School." She was glad he didn't throw a lot of names at her. She'd never been particularly good with children and she didn't want the added responsibility of trying to put names with faces. The boys were darting about, boxing each other on the arm, and two of the girls, hand in hand, were looking solemnly at her as if she were some new and strange specimen of adult.

"I have cookies and lemonade for everybody," she said in a low voice to Sam as she fell into step next to him. Two boys heard her and begged to eat first, but he silenced them by simply waiting until the clamor died down.

"Afterward," he said. "We'll miss the tide."

"Sorry about that," she said.

"No problem. They're just blowing off steam. They'll be fine once we get down to the beach."

They set off along the path through the orchard. The kids swarmed around them and some of the boys dashed ahead.

"So how are you doing with the house?" he asked.

"It's hard to know where to start. The real estate agent came over and took a look around."

"What did he think?"

"That I'll get a lot more for the place if I do some basic work on it. Clear away the clutter, fix the roof, paint, do the floors. He didn't think I should rent it. He thought it was more important to get it ready to put on the market."

"He's probably right. I've been thinking about it and I couldn't come up with anybody who needs a rental this winter."

"Mr. Montclair was over too. Nan didn't do such a bad job with the major repairs. There's a new hot water heater and she rewired one wing of the house about five years ago. But there's furniture to be restored and floors to be sanded." She looked around the orchard. "Even the apple trees need pruning. I've never owned a house before. I guess you can tell."

He smiled. Kasha barked twice from the porch. "Thanks for leaving her up at the house," he said. "It would have been too distracting."

Two girls came up beside Maggie and one squeezed in between her and Sam.

"Is that a wolf?" she asked.

"No," the other one replied. "It's a Siberian husky. I know all about dogs."

"This is Erin Craven," Sam said with a hand on the girl's shoulder.

"And I'm Katie Morrison. I live on the mainland."

"She's my best friend," Erin said. "Is your hair naturally curly?"

"Yes," Maggie said, wondering if this was Anna Craven's daughter. If so, plain speaking and direct questions seemed to run in the family. "I like your braids."

"I did them," Katie said. "I put in the flowers."

"Purple asters," Sam said.

"It must be fun going on these field trips with Mr. Matera," Maggie said.

"We call him Mr. M.," Katie said.

"I'm his assistant at the museum on Saturdays," Erin said.

"He's the nicest teacher in the whole school," Katie said.

Maggie looked at Sam and he shrugged. "I pay them off," he said. "I'd better keep an eye on those boys." With that, he broke into a smooth jog down the hill, his knees bent, his body leaning back loose and easy.

"What do you do at the museum?" Maggie asked Erin.

The girl prattled on. Maggie half listened. Six years Sam had been living on the island. Funny their paths had never crossed.

When they reached the bottom of the hill, he was straddling two rocks at the end of the path, handing out white plastic bags. The rest of the group had already spread out along the beach, searching for treasures.

The girls wandered off together.

"Would you like a bag?" he asked Maggie.

"Certainly. It reminds me of Easter egg hunts. Tell me what I'm looking for."

"Anything that helps me teach the unit on the ecology of the shoreline. Whatever the sea has decided to toss our way today. Feathers, shells, rocks."

"I'm an old beach scavenger from way back. Nan and I were down here most afternoons. For sea glass and those good-luck rocks. The ones with a line around them." Her breath left her for a minute. This was the first time she'd been to the beach since the summer before and she had a sudden clear image of Nan picking her way along the rocks, her old robe hanging open, the belt dangling below.

He was watching her face.

"Mr. M., I found a bird bone," called one of the boys, and he went off to examine it.

Maggie made her way to the farthest end of the beach, near the big rocks, slimy with seaweed and bird droppings and the endless years of sea washings. She knew from experience that this was where things got caught in the little pools between the rocks.

She rolled up the legs of her khakis and hunched down just like the kids. The surface was calm and the tide low, so that between each rock there lay a small distinct underwater world, safe for the next hour or so until the sea rolled over the rocks to suck back its treasures. She collected a green fuzzy sea urchin and the battered back shell of a blue crab and mussels torn loose from their home rocks. From nooks and crannies, she pulled out hermit crabs and gull feathers and a small sample of seaweed, the color of army camouflage. Something large was caught between two rocks further out from the shore, and she straightened up to get a better look. It looked like a black plastic bag, and she was furious that some careless boat owner had just hurled his trash into the ocean. But she was wrong. Black plastic would reflect the sun. The surface of this dark form was dull, and it billowed out, responding to each small motion of the sea the way clothes did when you went swimming in them. It was a body.

She rested her collection on the top of a large flat rock and looked behind her. Erin and Katie were moving her way.

"Girls," she called as casually as possible. "Go back down the beach, will you?"

"Why?" they asked.

"I want you to tell Mr. M. to come over here. Just tell him. None of the kids. Will you go do that right now, please. It's important." She put her finger to her lips and waved them off. They hesitated, whispered to each other, then turned back.

"Mr. M.," she heard them calling as she clambered over the last two rocks between her and the body. She would have to touch it, turn it over, because there was a chance this person was still alive. The water was deeper here. She dropped one foot down, searching for the bottom, and the frigid water shot up to her knee before her sneaker found a flat rock that would hold her. She took two handfuls of his green shirt, knew now by the bulk of him that this was a man, and with her other leg braced, she flipped the body. It happened smoothly, the sea assisted her, and now the form floated on its back, face exposed, eyes popped open. She knew instantly that this man was dead, probably had been for a while. The skin was a patchwork, blue white in some places and blotchy pink in others, as if someone had applied rouge where it didn't belong. The flesh looked fragile, at the very edge of disintegration. If you touched it, it would pull apart easily. She screamed, and at the same moment, her foot gave way and she slid in up to her waist.

Two hands slipped in under her arms. "I've got you," Sam said. She nodded, unable to speak. "Hold on, I'll pull you up onto the rock behind you." Amazingly enough, he did, although she had no idea how he could get enough leverage. Her legs, bare at the ankles, scraped on the rough surface, but she didn't care. Someone was here. He would see. This was a dead body. She was not crazy.

"Oh, God," he said, his breath tickling her ear. "It's John Burling."

THE KIDS HAD trailed along behind him and were gathering at the edge of the rocks, Erin in front.

"Mr. M., what is it?" one of them called. "Can we come see?"

"Erin," he said, in a stronger voice than anybody had ever heard him use. "I want you to lead everybody back up the orchard path. Wait for me on Miss Hammond's porch. Right now."

"What is it?" Erin said.

"Erin." Erin wondered why he sounded so angry with her. She hadn't done anything. She saw something bumping up against the rocks. It looked like a garbage bag with a white thing tied to one end of it. "Erin," he said again. "Do as I say right now. All of you follow her."

And they did, slowly, reluctantly, with many glances over their shoulders to try and figure out why the red-haired lady was sitting on the rock with wet pants and her hands over her face and why Mr. M. was glaring at them so intently.

"Maybe they're in love and he wants to be alone with her," Katie said to Erin.

"Don't be dumb," Erin said. "He just met her."

"There's something down there in the water," Liz Slocum said. "It looks like a pile of garbage."

"I think it's a dead whale," said a sixth-grader.

"I don't think it's garbage or a whale," Jimmy Slade said in his nasty, spooky voice. "I think it's a dead body."

"It doesn't matter what it is, Jimmy," Erin said. She concentrated on speaking each word separately, the way she thought a grown-up would talk in a crisis. "We just have to go sit up on the porch and wait for them."

"I'm not getting anywhere near that wolf," said Danny Slocum. He was only in the fifth grade, and he'd been bitten by a dog when he was six years old. You could still see the long scar down the side of his nose. One hundred and fifteen stitches, he liked to tell anybody who asked.

"It's not a wolf," Erin said. "It's a Siberian husky. And you don't need to worry. I know how to handle dogs." Erin was surprised at the confidence in her own voice. She liked the way she sounded.

Four

MAGGIE HAD BEGUN to shake.

"Take a couple of deep breaths," he said from behind. He was rubbing her arms.

"Who is John Burling?" She was still staring at the white up-turned face. The man looked as if he were floating in a quiet pond on a summer afternoon, gazing at the sky.

"A fisherman and a drunk. He's Erin Craven's grandfather. Put out to sea three days ago in the middle of a bad storm and he's been missing ever since. If you can climb down now, we'd better get moving. I don't want the kids to come back."

"We're just going to leave him here?'

He put up his hand to help her as she started sliding down the slick round rock. Her legs felt numb with the cold.

"I don't think he'll float out again," he said. His hand felt warm, incredibly warm. "The tide has turned, but just a little while ago. I've got to get up to the house and start calling people."

Of course he was right. They could hardly carry this large man up the hill themselves.

"I'll need you to keep the kids distracted while I'm on the phone," he said, halfway up the orchard path. Her whole body was shaking now and even with her hand holding tight to his, she found it hard to keep her legs moving. "I'd use the portable radio," he went on, talking half to himself. "But I'd rather not, in case Anna Craven is near one. It's better she hear about her father from another human being, not in some general message." The cold had sunk down into her bones. Her legs slowed to a stop, and he turned to look at her.

"I'm sorry," she said. "I'm just shaking so hard. I can't seem to control it."

He took off his shirt and wrapped it around her. Then he slid an arm along her back and pulled her in close. "Lean against me," he said. "Go ahead. I've got you." The last half of the path, with his arm supporting her, her feet barely touched the ground.

"You better change into dry clothes as soon as you can. You don't want to get pneumonia. I've had it. It's no fun."

She nodded. She didn't trust herself to speak at that moment. She didn't want him to move away. His body next to hers was the only thing keeping her warm.

"Was John like that when you found him?"

"No," she managed to say. "Face down."

"You turned him over?"

"I figured I had to. The person might still be alive and you were at the other end of the beach."

He stared at her for a minute. "You were right."

THE CHILDREN WERE draped in various positions over the ancient wicker couches at the far end of the porch. Erin was sitting right next to Kasha, rubbing the dog behind her ears.

They all started talking as soon as they saw Mr. M.

"What's going on?"

"Can we go back to the beach now?"

He put up his hand for silence. "I have to make some phone calls," he said. "Erin, you take everybody in the kitchen and pass out the lemonade and cookies. Miss Hammond needs to change into dry clothes."

"It's a body, isn't it?" Jimmy Slade said.

"We're not sure what we're dealing with yet," Sam said. "The phone?" he asked as the children started to trail after Erin.

"Go through there into the study," she said. "They won't be able to hear you there."

"Dry clothes," he ordered.

She took Kasha by the collar and locked her in the back room behind the laundry. With all these people milling about, the dog could be unpredictable. In the dryer Maggie found a towel and a pair of jeans and changed her clothes behind the pantry door. An old cardigan of Nan's from the laundry basket fit her fine.

Back in the kitchen, the children milled around Erin, who was passing out cookies. For once, Maggie was grateful for Nan's regular ransacking of the island thrift shop because there were enough glasses for everyone. She put on the kettle and warmed her hands over another gas burner. The children came to rest, some two to a chair, some leaning against walls and doors. Above their heads, dried herbs and strings of garlic from last year hung next to a collection of copper pots, large and small, battered and dull with tarnish. The wooden table was scarred here and there by burn marks from hot pots left too long on the surface.

"Last year, a dead porpoise washed up on White Beach," one little boy said.

"And remember the Portuguese man-of-war," said another.

"What's that?" Katie asked.

"A big huge blue jellyfish," said Erin. "It was gross. Danny's father found it."

"Down by the ferry dock," Danny said.

"Mr. M put it in a bucket and brought it into school."

"How about the turtle?" Katie said. "I saw pictures of that."

"It was a leatherback sea turtle," said a child who took her thumb out of her mouth to speak. She seemed too old to be sucking her thumb, Maggie thought.

The sudden whistle of the kettle startled her.

SAM CALLED THE DOCTOR's office first. Lauren answered.

"We've found John Burling," he said without a hello. "His body washed up on Mrs. Phipps's beach."

"Oh, God," said Lauren. "No hope?"

"None. Is the doctor there?"

"No. I'll get him on the radio. But what about Anna? Someone should be with her when she gets the news."

"That's why I used the phone," Sam said. "You decide, Lauren. We're going to need some help getting the body out of the water and up the hill. And the tide is coming in. Not a lot of time before it floats back out again. Besides that I've got twenty kids here huddled in Miss Hammond's kitchen. Erin Craven too."

"Does she know it's her grandfather?"

"Not yet."

"Okay. I'll get right on it."

BAD NEWS ON an island this small always spread fast. The fire whistle blew moments after Sam's call to Lauren, and in five minutes the cars and trucks were beginning to pile up along the road outside of Maggie Hammond's house.

Anna was in her kitchen when she heard the whistle. She picked up the phone and called the doctor's office.

"Is it Pop?" she asked.

"Yes," Lauren said.

"Where?"

"Mrs. Phipps's place."

"I'm leaving now," Anna said, and hung up.

She didn't even ask how her father was, Lauren thought after she put down the phone. Maybe she thought he was still alive. I should call her back, she thought, but before she had a chance the phone rang again. Anna would find out when she got there. Soon enough.

THE DOCTOR HAD TAKEN some time off to explore the other end of the island and was a mile or so from his car at the easternmost point when the portable radio squawked at him.

"Port One to Port Two. Come in, Doctor." It was Lauren's voice. His first call. First emergency.

"Port Two to Port One," he said, feeling a little foolish. All up and down the island, the portable radios were tuned to this frequency.

"We have a body down on the Phipps's beach."

"Which house is that?"

"Where are you now?"

"Other end of the island. By the lighthouse."

There was a pause and he knew they were all wondering what in hell he was doing up there. She gave him directions and he tried to visualize the left hand turn across from the fire department.

"Port Five to Port Two. Don't worry, Doc," chimed in a man's voice. "Just follow the cars. The whole island will be there. You'll find it."

"Right," the doctor said, and hooked the radio on his belt before he jogged back across the marsh to his car.

He drove recklessly down the road, hitting sixty on the straight section by the driving range. By the time he found the Phipps's house, the main road was almost totally blocked by cars pointing in every direction with some of the doors standing wide open. It looked as if the drivers had barely taken the time to slam their gearshifts into park before they jumped out and ran to the scene.

RANDY BAKER AND Billy Slade were two of the first to arrive. With Maggie's permission, they lifted one of the green louvered shutters off the side porch along with some rope.

"Can you handle the kids?" Sam handed Maggie his tea mug, still half full. "I've got to go back down there with them."

"Yes, I'm fine. Here's your shirt."

"Thanks. And I'll need a sheet. Something to cover him with."

"They're kept up on the third floor. Go around to the side of the house. I'll toss one down to you out the window."

He stood still for a minute, ignoring the commotion all around them. "Your lips still look blue. Are you warm enough?"

"I'm getting there," she said. "I promise."

A SMALL CROWD HAD gathered by the side of the house, talking in low tones to each other. Al Craven pulled his truck right up onto Maggie's lawn and trotted down the hill after the others without a word to anybody.

Despite Maggie's efforts to keep them entertained inside, the children had slipped out of the house and were watching too, hoping the grown-ups wouldn't notice them and shoo them back in. More people arrived. They took up positions on the lawn and all along the railing of the front porch and stared down at the sea. The three-thirty ferry was making its way across the horizon, and in the distance, they heard the usual two blasts of the horn as the boat approached the dock. The ferry crew would be mystified that nobody was there to meet them. The boy who drove the grocery truck wondered how long it would take for the afternoon delivery of milk to sour in the sun. But he didn't move. After all it wasn't every day that a dead body washed up on the shore of the island. He was curious to see what it would look like. Word had gone around already that it was John Burling. Gossip flew from one mouth to another about his debts, his last gambling spree on the mainland, the news that his boat was going to be repossessed. People wondered where Anna was.

When Anna arrived, she parked her car down by the club away from the crowd. She knew the back way up to Mrs. Phipps's from behind the tennis courts. As a child she used to sneak around those bushes in the summertime, watching the rich kids in their white shorts slam the ball back and forth across the red rectangle of dirt. She'd been fascinated by their concentration, their complete dedication to the angle of the ball, the way it hit the strings, their rage and frustration when they missed it.

She stationed herself at the edge of the path through the orchard. Nobody up at the house could see her waiting there. Whatever came up the hill, she had bought herself some privacy.

The doctor was forced to park down by the club too. As he trotted up the hill, he saw a woman skirting the courts and ducking through the trees, but he didn't follow her. He took the road and pushed through the crowds at the house until he came up behind Maggie Hammond, who was standing apart, leaning against her porch railing with people ranged along it on either side of her.

"Hello again," he said. "Quite a crowd."

"Yes, here I thought I was inheriting a quiet little place by the sea."

"What a view you have," he said. "What's happening?"

"Some of the men are down at the beach bringing him up."

"It's that man who's been missing?"

"Yes." She closed her eyes. Sam was back down there. She couldn't imagine having to look again at the flabby, uncertain skin of the dead man's face.

"I'd better join them." He sounded reluctant.

"You might as well wait. There's nothing you can do for him," she said. "They'll bring him up soon enough."

"It's one of the island men, isn't it?" he asked, remembering all the way back to Omey Island, to the day they brought his father's body in. Maggie was looking at him. He forced himself to concentrate. "I would be considered an interloper, I expect."

"I think so."

He pointed over to the orchard. "There's a woman standing there in the trees. Can you see her?"

Maggie shaded her eyes. "I don't have my glasses, but I'm pretty sure that's Anna Craven. It's her father they're bringing up."

"Who found him?"

"I did. Face down between two rocks." Her knees began to tremble slightly and she leaned against the railing to still them.

To her surprise, he put his arm around her shoulders and squeezed once, very hard. "Brave," was all he said before he moved away to stand by himself at the place where the path met the lawn.

Suddenly, she felt a hand slip into hers. It was Erin Craven.

Maggie dropped down next to her as much to steady herself as to comfort the girl. "Are you all right?" she asked.

"I heard people talking. It's my grandfather, isn't it?"

"Yes, it is," Maggie said.

Erin's eyes were wide and staring, but she wasn't crying. "You found him?" she asked.

"Yes. He looked peaceful. He looked as if he were rocking to sleep on the waves."

"That's why Mr. M yelled at me to get away, wasn't it? He didn't want me to see."

"That's right, Erin. I think your mother is over there in the trees."

Maggie squeezed Erin's hand once, expecting her to slip away, but the girl didn't move. Maggie pulled herself to a standing position. They waited with the others.

DOWN AT THE shoreline it took the men a good while to maneuver the body over the rocks to the makeshift stretcher. John Burling had never been a small man, the rocks were slimy, and the tide was rolling back in. Without saying much to each other, the men were carefully trying to avoid touching any exposed piece of body. It was obvious to all of them that even though the skin had not yet begun to disintegrate, it was on the verge. If it scraped against a rock or even the rough surface of a man's workpants, it could fall apart, open up maybe even as far down as the bone. Salt water could preserve, but only for so long.

"Poor bastard," Randy Baker said. His long blond hair had fallen over his face, and his hands weren't free to push it back.

"I hope to God he went quickly," Al said, staring down into his father-in-law's bloated face. "Drowning's a slow and ugly way to die."

"Don't look at him anymore, Al," Billy said.

"Is Anna up there?" Randy asked.

"Guess so. Lauren probably phoned her. I think she's been expecting this," Al said. "He's been nothing but trouble to her."

Sam stayed silent. He had been on the island for six years, and in his professional capacity, he had been accepted, even welcomed, but he knew to stay out of any long-term island business. He hoped that by now, Anna Craven had found Erin and had prepared her for what was coming up the hill.

They spread the sheet over the body and looped the rope loosely around it just enough to keep the dead weight from rolling back and forth.

"One, two, three," Al counted. The men crouched down. "Lift," he said. They all rose together. Al and Billy were both under six feet, and even though the four had arranged themselves carefully with the shorter men at the front, their movements were jagged and sloppy. With the steep slant of the hill and the uneven footing, this would not be easy.

"Take it slow," Randy said. "He's sliding this way."

"We could have waited for the stretcher," Billy said. "Thayer should be back pretty soon."

"Where is he?" Randy asked.

"He took the ambulance to the mainland to get that oil leak fixed. He was coming back on the three-thirty."

"Someone should have gotten Lauren to bring over one of those extra stretchers from the back closet at the clinic," Al said. He reached under to get a tighter hold on his corner of the shutter. There was precious little to hang on to, and the ancient green paint was flaking off in their hands. "That doctor won't be here for a while. Sounds like he was up island admiring the scenery."

"We don't really need him anyway," Randy said. "The man is dead."

They stopped for a minute to catch their breath. "The ferry's docked. Want to put him down and wait for the stretcher?" Billy asked.

Al shook his head. "Might as well get him up the hill. Everybody's waiting."

Nobody argued with him. If they lowered John Burling to the ground here, he was liable to slide back down the hill, shutter and all.

Anna stepped out of the bushes as they approached her. The other men looked to Al to see if they should set her father's body down and give her a moment alone with him, but he kept putting one foot in front of the other. She fell into step next to him.

"Does he look bad?" she asked.

"No, he looks peaceful enough. He went the way he wanted to, you know. With the boat."

"Is there any sign of the boat?"

"Not that we could see. Are you all right, honey?"

She nodded. It was impossible for the other men not to listen, and they were always surprised by the softness in Al's voice when he spoke to his wife in public. Sometimes it was hard to remember that this was the same Al they saw thumping the bar down at the Lounge or haggling over his last bet at their regular Wednesday night poker games.

"Where is Erin?" Al asked.

She didn't answer. To her horror, she hadn't thought once about Erin.

"She's up at the house with the other kids," Sam said from the back. "Maggie Hammond is keeping an eye on them." Anna glanced over her shoulder at Sam. "Erin didn't see him, Anna. We made sure none of the kids saw."

"Thanks, Sam."

"Better get on up there," Al said. "It's no time for her to be with strangers." Anna moved on a little ahead of them and broke out into the clearing first. The crowd stirred and some people stepped forward to comfort her.

"Where is Erin?" she asked.

"Up on the porch with that Hammond woman," Lauren said.

"Let her stay there," Anna said. "No reason for her to see this."

"This is Dr. Lacey," Lauren said, and a stranger stepped out of the crowd. He nodded at Anna and took her hand in both of his. This intimate gesture from a stranger in front of a crowd of people she had known all her life made Anna feel shy. The island people were not touchers. She couldn't remember the last time someone had held her hand this way, especially in public.

"I'm sorry for your loss," he said with that lilt of an accent. "Very, very sorry." He sounded deeply sad and for a moment, Anna felt as if he were more in need of comfort than she.

"Thank you," she managed to say while behind her, the four men lowered the body slowly to the level ground.

"You must be the doctor," Al said from behind her, and Anna sucked in her breath just the slightest bit. It was always this way when Al met someone new, she realized, in this odd moment when everything seemed to be happening in slow motion. She cringed and waited.

"Yes," the man said. "Dennis Lacey. "

"I'm Al Craven, the sheriff here."

"I'm glad to meet you."

"There's not much you can do for him now, Doc."

The doctor hunkered down and lifted the sheet. Anna noticed the man was wearing cowboy boots, and then beyond that, she saw her father's blank eyes staring up at her the way he always did, as if somehow he were waiting for her to fix this problem too. The doctor used his thumb and forefinger to close the eyes, then dropped the sheet back down over the face. Paul Thayer had finally arrived with the ambulance, and the men gathered around to lift the shutter and lower it on top of the stretcher he'd brought. It seemed more dignified that way. There would be no need to roll the waterlogged body from one surface to another.

There was talk of death certificates and transporting the body to the mainland on the ambulance boat. Al took charge, ordered people here and there, designated Paul Thayer as the driver, then decided to go with him. Anna moved away and climbed the porch steps. Later on, she would have to call her brother Dave on the mainland and see what he wanted to do about a funeral. She wondered if they'd be able to find Frank, the youngest. Nobody had heard from him in two years.

When she found Erin in the crowd, she gathered the child into her arms and rocked her back and forth. The people on the porch stood at a respectful distance, but they could see how, through it all, Erin kept holding on to Maggie Hammond's hand.

EVEN AFTER THE BODY was gone, people didn't want to leave. They lingered on the porch, talking to one another, offering help to Maggie. They asked how long she was staying, dredged up all their memories of Nan Phipps, settled down in the wicker chairs as the sun lowered in the sky. Maggie wondered which of these people had sat on Nan's porch before. Crises like this blurred the lines between summer and winter people. But then Nan had never paid much attention to those lines anyway.

It feels like a wake, Maggie thought. They must consider me rude. I should be putting out food, offering drinks. But now that the lemonade and cookies were gone, there was only enough food in the house to feed one person with a limited appetite. Jack Riley, the last and most serious of Maggie's affairs, used to tell her that she ate to live. He was an excellent cook and lived to eat.

"This is like the old days," one plump woman said. "With television and VCRs, we never get together the way we used to."

"It's not exactly a happy reason for a get-together," answered another.

"Well, I didn't mean it that way," said the first, and others leaning against the porch railing joined in, and they went on talking about the potluck suppers they used to have, and the dance parties in each other's houses.

Maggie was curled up on the battered canvas seat cushion of the wicker couch, listening as the words washed back and forth around her. She picked up news of the island that normally would have taken her months to learn, that in the summer she might never have known at all. Stories of accidents and unpaid debts and fights between old friends. Either they had forgotten she was there or, because of her role in this disaster, they had, for the moment, accepted her as one of their own.

Finally, as dinnertime approached, the hangers-on gathered themselves together. Maggie made feeble attempts to get up. Her legs felt as if twenty-pound weights had been tied to them, and she was thinking of spending the night on this uncomfortable cushion simply because climbing the stairs to her bedroom loomed as an impossible task. People urged her to stay seated, patted her on the shoulder as they left. She heard the slamming of car doors, the roll of tires over gravel, and then headlights, one after another, swept briefly across the lawn and she was left alone in merciful silence.

She stood up and tottered to the back room, where Kasha was lying on her side, sleeping. For a horrifying moment, she wondered whether she was dead too, but the old dog lifted her head, then scrambled stiffly to her feet.

"Hello, Kash. Hungry?"

She fed her, then tied her up with a long lead to the porch railing.

"I'll just lie here for one more minute," she said to the air as she sank back down onto the wicker couch. It had come to feel like home.

Inside the house, the phone rang, but she didn't move. The ringing stopped for five minutes, then started again, but still she sat. She had begun to shake, a gentle tremble down in her legs that moved up through her body. She breathed deeply, trying to still her limbs, but it was uncontrollable, this bone-knocking, jackhammer shaking. She had never felt anything like this before. The front door slammed and somebody was walking through the house. Kasha barked.

"Are you all right?" the voice asked, and she looked up to see Mr. Montclair. Kasha was growling at him. Had he come to show her the hot water heater?

"I-I'm so c-c-c-old," she managed to say.

"Quiet, girl," he said to the dog, and Kasha settled down.

He got Maggie up and walked her to the little sofa in front of the fireplace. Once he'd made a fire, he rubbed her legs and arms with rough, blood-stirring motions. When the shaking had eased, he rattled around in the kitchen for a while and returned with some hot chowder and toast. He brought her Kleenex when she started to cry, then went back to the rubbing as if it were the most natural thing in the world that he should be taking care of her like this.

"I'm so sorry, Mr. Montclair. This doesn't usually happen to me."

"Have you ever touched a dead body before?" he asked.

"I guess not."

"Then I suppose you're allowed to fall apart."

"Do you think his ghost is going to haunt the place?" she asked.

"John Burling? He doesn't have the time to mess with you. He'll be over at the bank, harassing the mortgage people who foreclosed on him. Or he'll be sitting at the bottom of his ocean in that ramshackle boat of his, swilling down another glass of gin."

Maggie managed a small smile.

"That's better," he said. "Hold on, I'll bring in the dog."

Kasha bounded into the room, and when she found Maggie prone on the couch, she stuck her nose in her face and tried to lick.

Maggie gave her a rub behind the ears. " Good girl. Go sit."

Finally the dog settled herself near the fire.

"I never had the shakes like that before."

"Post-traumatic shock," Chuck said. "I used to see it all the time in Korea. Never knew when it would hit. Sometimes days after the boys went through something they'd start to shake. I hear you were down there with Sam and his class."

"That's right."

"If you had to go through something like this with someone, I can't imagine a better man."

"The kids seem to be crazy about him."

"He's crazy about this island. Don't get in between him and some animal he's trying to save."

"What do you mean?"

"Last spring, for example, he found a seal washed up on the beach with a bullet hole in its head. Well, we thought he'd go nuts. He borrowed some leaky old motorboat from Jerry Slocum and floated around the seal breeding ground in Shell Harbor for most of a week with a rifle across his knees. Swore he was going to shoot anybody who got too near them."

"Did he catch anyone?" Maggie pulled herself to a sitting position and tucked a blanket around her knees.

"Nope. A couple of us went out there one rainy night and persuaded him that it must have been some maniac passing in a trawler that did it and we hauled him back in. He damn near died of pneumonia. Another time, I found him in the bushes up by the old fort, digging around for a half-dead striper. Some crows were tormenting the female osprey and she had dropped the fish from her nest. Sam found it and left it out on a rock and sure enough, she came back for it." Chuck shook his head. "The man is driven. Wait till the salamander walk."

"What's that?"

"Sam organizes it every spring, around the end of March. There's some kind of salamander that lives on one side of the road and breeds on the other. It's on the endangered list. We all go out and make sure they don't get run over when they cross."

"Guess I'll have to miss that. I'll be long gone by then," she said.

Chuck shrugged. "It might be worth coming back just to see it."

"Is there a woman in Sam's life?"

"There was a teacher he spent some time with when he first got here, but she left after a year. Nobody since that I know of. Sam's a loner. A lot of us are. The island teaches you how to do that. It's not necessarily a good thing."

You don't need to live on an island to be a loner, Maggie thought.

He got up to take her dishes into the kitchen.

"I can do that now, Mr. Montclair," she said as she pushed the blanket off her lap.

"You get yourself up to bed," he said. "I'll just rinse these off and head home. As long as you feel okay."

"Yes, thank you. I'm fine now. Just tired."

He shrugged. "Not every evening I have good company like this. A lot more interesting than the Harbor Lounge or my darkroom. Do you think you could get used to calling me Chuck? It makes me feel old to be called Mr. Montclair."

"Of course. One other thing. When do you think you might be able to start on that roof?"

"Soon enough. Don't you worry."

"You know there's no use in my getting those rooms painted if we haven't—"

He put up his hands to cut her off. "I know, I know. Off to bed with you."

"All right. Can you be sure the front door locks behind you?" she called as he disappeared down the dark hallway to the kitchen.

"No problem."

She locked the other doors and walked slowly up the stairs to her bedroom with Kasha at her heels. She heard the buoy bell out at the point, as it rocked back and forth with the waves. The night was clear. Standing at the window, she saw the thin band of lights blinking at her from the mainland. It was only a short ferry ride away, but between here and there lay the black, black sea, and all that it held in its wide liquid lap.

Was it only yesterday that she'd arrived on the island? She felt as if she'd been here for weeks.

Five

THE CLEAR FALL days lingered on. Down at the post office in the mornings, people congratulated one another over the weather as if they were personally responsible for it. Most of the migratory birds had already passed through, although out on the eastern end of the island, a late wandering warbler had been spotted. In the fields, the delicate rusty foliage of beardgrass and the yellow-brown switchgrass alternated with the purple asters, which took longer than usual to dry and fade. Somebody left a bunch of them on John Burling's grave in the cemetery across the road from the chapel. It was not Anna, and when she came for her first visit after the stone had been put in place, she wondered who might have done it.

IN ONE OF her restless inventories of the house, Maggie discovered that Nan had filled a side attic with furniture she had never seen before.

"Where did this all come from?" Maggie asked Chuck.

"She's been collecting it for a while. Some of it came over on the boat and some of it from the thrift shop. Mrs. P. was a real pack rat."

"You don't need to tell me, Chuck." Maggie shined the flashlight slowly around the room. "Some of these pieces look pretty good. Nan had an eye."

"Maybe she was collecting them for you. So you'd have something to work on up here."

"You mean while I wait for you to get to that roof?"

Chuck shrugged. "It's on my list. But Al Craven's put me on the Davidson job full time. If you'd let me know you were coming up, Miss Hammond, I would have cleared my schedule."

"Don't Miss Hammond me, Mr. Montclair," she said as she dragged one of the tables into the light. "How's your knee?"

"Not so bad today. No rain coming. Why?"

"Can you help me get some of these down into the study? I want to give them a good look and see if they're worth restoring."

"This one's kind of pretty," Chuck said as they were maneuvering it around the last landing on the stairs.

"It's a good example of an eighteenth-century Pembroke table."

They cleared some space in the middle of the room, then carried down one chair and another table.

"That should do it." Maggie clapped the dust off her hands. "I've got my work cut out for me."

"You sound kind of happy about it."

She didn't answer. She was walking around the table.

"See you," he said. "I've got to get going."

She squatted down and tapped the inlay on each of the legs with her fingernail. Some lifting, she thought. But not too bad. Better than she had expected, considering the humidity up here. She'd mark the worst places with masking tape.

She heard the front door close before she realized Chuck had even left the room.

LAST DECEMBER ANNA Craven had ordered a black cowboy hat from a Western catalog. It was a spur of the moment decision, the kind of thing she had dreamed of before, but had never done. She was working in the post office the day the package arrived, and she managed to slip it into the back of her station wagon before anybody else saw the large cardboard box from some mail-order place in Oregon. She took it home and put it on. It fit well, the brim not too wide, the black oval a perfect frame for her serious face, with its heavy eyebrows and the coarse dark hair going gray around her temples. The thin rattlesnake strap and the feather added a touch of bravado, a sense of a woman who didn't mind what people thought of her.

She hid the hat in the attic where Al and Erin would never find it, and every few weeks when she remembered it, she would sneak upstairs and try it on, admiring her reflection in the mirror left up there from Erin's dress-up days. She knew it was a ridiculous purchase and even thought of sending it back, but time went on and she didn't.

On the day of her father's funeral, with Al in the station wagon sitting on the horn and yelling at her to hurry up, she came downstairs wearing the hat.

"What in God's name is that thing?" Al said.

"A black hat," she said. "For the funeral." Erin was leaning over the front seat trying to look at herself in the rearview mirror. Her body grew still.

Al revved the engine, but didn't slip the car into gear.

"We'd better go, Al. I don't want to be late for my own father's funeral."

"You look ridiculous. Take that thing off."

She did. She rested the hat in her lap, then when he reached for it, she deftly slid it down out of reach beside her right leg.

"Come on, Al, stop it. It's just a hat. Please let's go."

"I don't want my wife walking around looking like a damn fool," he muttered as he finally shifted the car into gear. "Next thing you'll show up in cowboy boots like that idiot doctor. Don't you dare wear that thing in public. People'll be asking where you parked your horse."

"I like it, Mom," Erin said quietly.

"Nobody asked your opinion," Al said.

"Thanks, Erin," Anna said. "I like it too."

Erin pressed her forehead against the back window and counted to herself by tens. She always did this when the three of them drove somewhere. It helped the time go by.

Anna didn't wear the hat to the funeral, but she put it on the next day when she and Chuck went out with the dogs.

"Nice hat," he said.

"It looks great on you," Lauren said when they met in the grocery store. "You look as if you were born out West somewhere."

"Maybe in a former life," Anna said.

"It's a whole new you," Miss Yola said one day when they ran into each other on the beach.

"I'm different somehow," Anna said. "For one thing, I'm an orphan."

"Child, you always were an orphan."

Anna and Miss Yola had this kind of blunt conversation when they were alone together. It started years ago. The Burlings' garage backed up on Miss Yola's house and Anna would come visiting just to get some woman talk. With two brothers and a father in her own house, grunts and curses seemed to be most of what passed for conversation.

Anna started to wear the hat all the time. People on the island recognized each other by their vehicles and by the shape of a person's head behind the windshield. Soon they incorporated Anna's new hat into her profile and looked twice if she had forgotten to put it on, had left it on the front seat of the car by mistake. She could smash it down in a high wind, and there was room enough around the brim to fit a scarf underneath it on the bitter days. But still she was careful to take it off whenever she saw Al's truck coming toward her on the road. At night, she hid it on the top shelf of the cupboard in the dog pen.

ONE EVENING WHEN they were coming in from a walk, Kasha began to bark wildly as soon as Maggie opened the front door. A small dark animal lay on the floor of the front hall, chattering at them. Maggie grabbed Kasha's collar and backed away.

"I think it's a bat," she said to Kasha, who was pulling on the leash, trying to get inside again. She tied the dog up to the porch railing and let herself in through the kitchen. She had planned to call Chuck, but when she saw Matera right above Montclair she dialed Sam's number instead.

Ten minutes later he knocked on the kitchen door. His face popped up out of the darkness when she flicked on the porch light, and she smiled through the glass at him.

"I figured you'd be the right man for this job," she said when she saw the gloves and the large glass jar he was carrying.

"You couldn't have called at a better time. I need something to show the first- and second-graders tomorrow. This will be much more interesting than the stuffed beaver in the museum. They've seen it before and besides that, it's getting a little moth-eaten."

The bat was just where she'd left it. It opened its mouth and hissed at Sam as he approached.

"There, there," he said in a low voice as he closed one large gloved hand over the top of the animal and scooped it up. "Interesting. This isn't what I expected. Want to see?"

She nodded.

He held the animal gently but firmly in both hands while he slowly exposed the upper section of its body. The bat chittered at them, its pointed teeth bared. The tiny, perfectly formed features of its face seemed strangely out of proportion to the large ears. Silvery fur covered its nose and cheeks. Maggie felt as if a miniature wild dog were staring up at her.

"What did you expect to find?" she asked as she unscrewed the top of the jar.

He released the bat inside and slipped the lid back on. Air holes had been punched in the metal surface. "The little brown bat," he said as he carried the jar into the front workroom where he could study the animal under the light. "You can often find a cluster of them hanging upside down behind your shutters. Now this has the same silvery hair as the hoary bat except this one has a black throat. Hoary bats have buff-colored throats."

The bat stretched one wing up along the glass. It looked eerily like a human arm draped in a translucent cape.

"Dracula," Maggie said. "Do you think he's got any friends around? I'd just as soon not wake up to a gaggle of bats in my bedroom."

Sam had lifted the jar and was turning it slowly. "You know what? I think it may be a silver-haired bat." His voice rose with excitement. He glanced over at her. "This is a real find. We've never recorded one of these on the island."

She had to smile. He looked so happy. "Sam, do you think he's got any buddies in the house?"

"I doubt it. They're due to start hibernating any time now, so you shouldn't have a problem. This guy was probably left behind."

"Will you let him go?"

"Sure. Tomorrow night after his viewing at school." He lowered the jar to the surface of the desk where she had spread out her tools. "I see you found some furniture to work on. These things look like they belong in a surgeon's office."

"That's true. They do look strange. They're the tools I use for repairing wood. I use different ones when I'm working with carved wood, brass or tortoise shell."

"What are they called?"

"That's a maul, three gouges, two firmer chisels, two double-angle gouges, a couple of rifflers."

"Great name."

"You need those to finish places that are hard to get at. Clamps for gluing, microspatulas. Side-cutters for removing nails. And some of my own inventions. I persuaded my dentist to let me have this one." She lifted a tiny silver pick.

He took it out of her hand and turned it over. "It looks as if it would be good for getting meat out of lobster claws," he said. "And this came from your doctor, I expect. He pointed to a syringe. "Or your local drug addict."

"I use that to inject water under veneer to soften the old glue. And the second one to smear the fresh glue. I'll need to get some more things the next time I go home. I have some small saws and hammers that I didn't bring up. Of course, I had no idea there'd be so much work to do."

"So you'll be staying a while?"

"Maybe. Hold on a second. I want to let the dog in."

Kasha bounded up to where Sam was hunched down in front of one of the tables and greeted him with a short eager bark. Sam reached out and dug his fingers into the dog's thick ruff to scratch. "Nice piece," he said, nodding at one of the tables.

"That one's almost done. I had to replace most of the inlay on the legs."

"Listen, I meant to warn you. Did a Mr. Woodworth call you?"

"A couple of days ago. He said something about an architectural survey of the island. That was your idea?"

By this time, he had slid down to the floor and Kasha had curled up next to him. He moved his hand behind her ears. Maggie settled into a chair. " It was," he said. "The museum has received a grant to do a study on all the structures of architectural significance on the island. I thought you might be interested in the project."

"I took courses in architectural preservation in graduate school but that was ten, twelve years ago. It's not really the same thing."

"Well, you're certainly more qualified than any graduate student we could get. And you're here."

"For the moment," she reminded him. "Who's Mr. Woodworth?"

"Head of the board of the museum. He lives in Boston year round. Very generous with his time. He's the one who gave us his old computer."

Maggie hadn't liked the man on the phone. He'd said something about her grandfather, Fred Wharton, and what a good friend he'd been. "I never met my grandfather," Maggie had replied and turned the conversation back to business.

"What does this study entail?" she asked now.

"It's quite simple. There's a form to fill out on each structure. I did the preliminary work last summer with an architect so I can give you a list of the places that have to be done. You go through each house, take documentary photographs, fill out some basic data. The whole thing will be compiled into a report. The draft is due in May. Do you have a camera with a zoom and a wide-angle lens?"

"Yes. I use one all the time in my work. How many places on this list?"

"Forty or so. Plus some public buildings like the post office and the library."

"I told Woodworth I'd think about it, but don't get your hopes up. It means I'd have to stay here much longer than I'd planned."

"You seem pretty well ensconced for now." Sam glanced around.

She was. So many of the jobs she was called in on now involved clean-up after a flood or a fire, or the assessment of a collection that had been improperly stored. Hazard mitigation, they called it. She was expected to survey the damage, estimate the size of the project, and direct the local people in the recovery work. It had been a long time since she'd been able to do the actual work on the furniture herself. Conservation involved a meticulous step-by-step process on each piece, and over the years she had developed a rhythm that allowed her to work on more than one project at a time. The glue on new corner blocks for a chair seat might be drying while she lifted a strip of inlay from a table leg. Now that she had the chance, she spent long hours in the workroom. The fall was slipping away from her and yet, as each day passed, she felt less inclined to leave. She'd agreed to let Susan, her neighbor in Philadelphia, move into her house on Walnut Street while hers was being renovated. A curator had tracked her down two days ago, and to her own surprise, Maggie had put him off at least until after Christmas.

Sam stretched his legs out in front of him and Kasha flopped her head into his lap. "I seem to have made a friend."

"I hope you're not allergic to dog hair. She sheds terribly." They were silent for a moment. A sudden wind blew up and a screen door slammed by the kitchen. It was darker on the island than anywhere else Maggie had ever been. The houses all around Nan's were owned by summer people who had closed them down for the season.

"How does a naturalist get involved in preserving buildings?" she asked.

"On this island you have to be a jack-of-all-trades. I think of myself as a conservationist."

"Of wildlife."

"Of the island. And everything on it. The land, the birds and animals who make their home here, the houses, the people."

"You sound fierce," she said.

"I am. This island is one small ecosystem. Everything is woven together, every bit of life either supports or destroys something else in the pattern, and it's under constant threat. Whenever the boat arrives, it can bring trouble. A species that will threaten the others."

"You mean some stray moth?"

"Exactly. Or a virus. Or developers. People who come to destroy instead of build up."

"And from what I understand you're not a man to tangle with."

"Who's been talking?" he asked.

"Chuck."

"In this business, it's easy to fall into despair. Action keeps me from it." He lifted his leg slowly to warn Kasha. She sat up. "Guess it's time to take my silver bat home." He got to his feet.

"Would you like coffee? Something to eat?"

"No, thanks. I'd better go. I have papers to correct." When he picked up the glass bottle, Kasha scrabbled to her feet and lifted her nose to sniff at it. The bat was curled up in a corner.

"You're a busy man." She flicked on the dim overhead light as she led him out into the hallway.

"Have you been to the museum yet?"

"No. Not this visit." She smiled. "To be honest, not since I was about twelve."

"Why don't you come in Saturday afternoon? I'll give you a tour."

"Fine." He had stopped in the front yard to look at the sky. Maggie joined him.

"So many more stars here than in the city." She turned slowly around. "At least it seems that way."

"No reflected light." Their breath made little clouds in the air and Maggie shivered. "I hope you didn't have any nightmares about John Burling," he said. "That was a pretty terrible thing for you to go through."

"I think about that face sometimes. Staring up at the sky, just the way we are now."

"At least the man is in some kind of peace. He rarely was when he was here." He touched her quickly on the cheek with the tips of his fingers. "Good night, then," he said before he disappeared into the darkness. The headlights of his truck swept onto the road. He hit the horn once and lifted his hand from the steering wheel as he sped past.

Six

ISABELLE ARRIVED ON a Friday afternoon boat with a group of hunters. When Dennis Lacey caught sight of his wife at the rail, she was chatting with two young men who had gun cases slung over their shoulders. To his surprise, his wife was carrying his waders. Their green tops rested against her jacket. He had asked for his rubber boots, the everyday ones for bad weather, but she must have gotten confused. Always before she had refused to have anything to do with his fishing . He lifted his arm to wave to her and put it down again before anybody saw. Isabelle was too caught up in her conversation to look for him on the dock.

Even now, as the boat backed delicately toward the dock, he could see the light glinting off her dark sleek hair, like water off the back of a seal. The hunters seemed to be entranced by her as she tossed her head and laughed and put a finger up to her chin. He knew each of her coy mannerisms by heart, and they seemed out of place here, more appropriate for Mrs. Bigelow's dinner parties on Fifth Avenue. She had seated him next to Isabelle at one of those dinners four years ago, when the old lady had decided he would be useful as an extra man. Isabelle, he learned later, had just been left by her rich English boyfriend, and Dennis, with his Irish accent, must have felt to her like an echo of him. They were engaged in a matter of months and married soon after that in the Catholic church even though neither one of them had attended Mass for years, except on Christmas and Easter. Isabelle was an important part of the life he thought he wanted. It included a rich private practice in New York, an upper East Side address, a fancy car. And nobody had ever been so beguiled by what she called his dark Irish melancholia. Deep down he always suspected that he was nothing to her but a figment of her imagination, a way to wipe the Englishman off her slate.

She doesn't belong on this island, he thought when at last she caught sight of him and held the waders up above the boat rail to be sure he saw. They both knew that. His morbid love of the sea and the Irish melancholia that had once entranced her now seemed ridiculous and overwrought, as she had told him when he first decided to take this job.

LATER THAT NIGHT over the chicken dinner that he managed to cook for her in the ancient electric oven, she told him officially.

"You cannot be surprised, Dennis. You never did believe I would come out here to live. I do not see how even you can possibly stand this house for very long." She had spent a year furnishing their apartment on Seventy-fourth Street. She'd covered an entire wall of the study with framed prints of various species of trout, and he spent most of his time in that room. The rest of the apartment reminded him of a small but sumptuous hotel on the Left Bank. He often felt like a guest in his own house.

"You will redo this place, won't you?" she asked.

"I was waiting for you to come and take over, my dear."

She raised her eyebrows and for once was silent. He had always gotten along perfectly well without paying much attention to his physical surroundings. "I suppose I thought we could live apart for a year and see how things went," he said.

"That's not possible, Dennis."

"You know I was forced to take that leave from the hospital. This job gave me the time I needed to sort things out." He could tell she wasn't listening. "There's already somebody else, isn't there?"

"Yes. You do not know him. An art dealer."

"It's up to you, Isabelle. It always has been." Sitting back in the wooden kitchen chair, he knew he would go through the end of this marriage with the same distant courtesy he had always adopted in his relationships with women. Perhaps it was an Irish trait, he thought, remembering the older men from Omey Island huddled over their stout in the pub in Clifden, so many of them unmarried, still living at home with Mum.

"I'm sorry, Dennis," she said and reached across the table to touch his hand. "I really am. You are a sweet man—"

He raised that same hand to stop her. "Please, Isabelle, no explanations, no obits. Let's just leave it the way it is."

It had become his ritual to take a walk along the beach every night after dinner. He asked her to join him.

"At this hour?" she asked. "In November? You must be mad."

When he came in much later, his hair damp from the sea air, he crawled into bed next to her and slid his fingers along the upturned bone of her hip. She didn't move. To his own surprise, he rolled her over and took her quickly, angrily, claiming her body one last time. When he was done, he lifted himself off her, without speaking.

"Dennis," she whispered into the darkness. "Where did you learn to make love like that?"

He didn't answer.

"Will you come back to New York with me?"

"No," he said. "I am sick and tired of the city. I like it here."

"It must remind you of your childhood by the desolate Irish sea."

"Perhaps."

"So neither one of us will change our minds."

"No. I suppose not."

They said no more about it.

"I WOULD LOVE to meet your wife," Lauren said to him in the clinic the next morning. "I understand she came on the boat yesterday."

"Do we have any Polytrim?" He didn't look up from the chart in his hand. "Danny Slocum has conjunctivitis."

"Right here." Lauren swung herself around her desk to the glass-fronted cupboard.

"She's French?"

"Mmm. The gossip mill has been working well, I see." He closed the metal-backed chart with a snap and handed it to her. "Please show Annie how to put in the drops. He should come back to see me in three days. I'll take the next patient in my office."

Lauren was undaunted. She didn't let people's moods get her down. The French wife was probably still asleep in the double bed with the lumpy mattress on the other side of the wall beside Lauren's desk. Lauren knew that bed well.

Randy Baker had told her yesterday that this woman would never last ten minutes on the island.

"Why?" Lauren had asked.

"Too fancy. She pulled a fur coat out of the backseat of her car. Now where is she going to use that, I'd like to know."

"At the Wednesday night bingo games." Lauren grinned. "We've all decided it's time to tone them up."

"Besides that, she's got no luggage. One little bag, that's all."

Dr. Lacey closed the clinic early with no explanation, but it didn't take a genius to figure out where he was headed, Lauren said to herself as she spent a few extra minutes pounding the dust out of the ancient pillows on the sofa in the waiting room. Sure enough, the front door of the house opened and closed, and through the picture window, Lauren could see the man walking his wife to the car. A thin woman as reported, in blue jeans and high-heeled boots. He put his hand under her elbow to steady her on the uneven cement walk, but it looked to Lauren more like the gesture of a well-brought-up man than that of a loving husband. She glanced up at the clock. They'd just make the twelve-fifteen boat.

SATURDAYS DURING HUNTING season, Anna got up before dawn and went out to the kennels to start cleaning the pens before Chuck arrived to help her take the dogs up island.

The men who came for the weekend hunt were always eager to be in the field early, before the frost burned off. This was the time when all her training and hard work were put to the test, and it was also the time that she hated the most. She loved to train the dogs, and she loved it when they worked well. But each season the hunting itself seemed to bother her more. Often, with her fingers resting lightly on the dog's head, and the men's guns to their shoulders, she closed her eyes so she did not see the pheasant cut down with a shot just as it beat its way to the open sky.

The weekend hunters were a varied group, the older men relaxed and happy to be out in the cool morning air, taking pleasure in watching the dogs work. If they killed a bird, fine. If they didn't, well, that was fine too. But the group this Saturday was young and aggressive. Chuck had put out their twenty-five birds the beginning of the week, and if these men didn't bring in twenty-five, they would consider the shoot to have been a failure.

Anna never slept well the night before a shoot, and the dogs picked up her excitement as soon as they smelled her. Some of them were already pacing in their pens when she pushed open the sliding door of the kennel. She had twelve of them now, six in training, six boarding. Eight were vizslas, the copper-colored Hungarian pointing dogs that she liked the best. They were small, short-haired, wiry dogs with thin, elegant faces, eager to please, easy to train if you got them early enough. They strained and whined at the sound of her voice, noses up to the wire of their pens as she walked down the line. They were anxious to be out in the field today. In early November, after the first hard frosts the scent of game was ripe. She put her fingers through the wire mesh and touched each of them as she went by.

It was always a full house in the fall. The owners started bringing them back in early September so that Anna could brush up their training. It was a big job. In March she'd had the dogs all winter. The older ones were steady to wing and shot, they'd lock on point and hold it for an hour if she let them. But most of the owners took them off after the hunting season was over and treated them like house pets, and the dogs came back to her in terrible shape. This year, her best retriever had been allowed to play tug-of-war with the kids in the family so she'd developed a hard mouth. If Anna couldn't break her of it, she'd mangle the birds when she brought them back to hand.

She went down the row, letting two of them at a time out in the training yard while she scrubbed their pens with disinfectant. When they heard Chuck's truck turn in the driveway, they started barking, one after another down the row. Chuck told her it always reminded him of prisoners in a long line of cells banging on the bars with their tin cups to make trouble.

He came to the door. "Your timing is perfect," she called over the noise. "I just finished the pens."

He said something in reply, but she couldn't hear him.

"Quiet," she shouted. The barking subsided for a moment, then started up again. She unhooked the spray bottle from her belt. The dogs took one look and dropped into silent watchful positions. They hated the water sprayed in their faces, and they knew from experience that she'd do it if she had to.

"It's only Chuck, ladies and gentlemen," she said. "Calm yourselves."

"Are we ready?" he asked from the door.

"Ready as we'll ever be."

"I've got coffee."

"Great. I could use it." They drank their coffee the same way, light with sugar. Saturday mornings he usually brought a thermos and something for her to eat so she didn't wake her household moving around in the kitchen.

"Who's on today?" he asked in a low voice even though they were much too far from the house to wake anyone.

"Whistler and Shooter."

"Where?"

"Up by the ninth hole in that stand of woods next to the Brady house. We'll start there. With this group, we'll be at it all day," she said grimly.

"Who is it again?"

"Whistler's owner. The guy from Virginia. Ben Murch. He's bringing that doctor friend of his from last year and two others."

"Christ" was all Chuck said. Murch was on the board of the country club and was the only member who'd voted against year-rounders using the golf course off-season. He was an ass. It would be a long day.

Erin woke to the distant yipping of the dogs and the click of small rocks as her mother's station wagon made its way out of the driveway. She buried her head under the pillow and slept again until her father's voice stirred her two hours later.

"Up you get, lazybones," he called from the bottom of the stairs.

Saturday mornings in the hunting season, her father cooked breakfast. He put on her mother's apron and whirled around the kitchen making pancakes and eggs and grits and toast. By the time Erin got downstairs, there was a big plateful of food waiting for her. She'd heard him talk about how skinny she was, how she needed to put on weight and get strong. She'd heard the arguments between her mother and father about her asthma and the way her mother babied her.

She dressed quickly. She wanted to get the breakfast ordeal over with because then she was free to spend the rest of the day at the museum with Mr. M. Sometimes he bought her lunch and they sat on the bench outside Island Foods where everybody could see them.

"Here you go," her father said, and put the plate down with a flourish. "Something to fatten up my little girl, slap some meat on her bones."

"Daddy, I hate the fried eggs on top of the pancakes."

"Don't whine, Erin. It's good that way. That's the way I always eat it." Then he leaned across the table and before she could stop him, he poured syrup over the whole pile. Everything mixed together like that. It was disgusting. Her mother would never make her eat it that way.

"I can't finish all this," she said in a small voice.

"Now don't start that nonsense," her father said. "Dig in." He settled down in front of his plate, tucked his napkin into the neck of his shirt, and divided his pancake into sections. "And stop fooling with your hair."

She slid her hand down off her head and glanced at the clock. Nine-fifteen. The museum opened at ten and she liked to be there first, waiting on the steps for Mr. M. She pushed the eggs over to the side and started on the pancakes. In the background she could hear the constant low chatter of the weather channel coming from the radio on the shelf above the sink. The dogs who had been left behind in the kennel got stirred up about something and started with their barking. The ragged chorus rose to a crescendo, peaked, then subsided.

"Damn dogs," her father muttered. "They bark at anything. So," he said, pointing at her plate with a syrupy knife, "how is it?"

"It's good, Daddy," she said. "You make good pancakes."

"You bet I do. Not many fathers like me, I tell you."

"I can't eat all this, though. It's as much as you have and you're bigger than me." She'd tried this ploy before, but maybe he'd forgotten.

"We've got to fatten you up, girl." He caught her wrist in his hand. "You're nothing but a bag of bones. That's why the asthma gets you so bad in the cold weather. You don't have anything to fight it with."

"Nina Malloy is really fat and she gets asthma too."

"Is that Dan Malloy's kid?"

"Yes."

Her father rolled his eyes. "That whole family is sickly. I remember Dan when he was in school with me. Always coughing or hacking away with one thing or another. His mother babied him. She would come running over from her classrom, you know she taught the third grade, with Kleenex and cough medicine. It was pathetic."

Erin took another bite. Her throat was beginning to close up. This usually happened to her right at this point, about halfway through the pile. Sometimes her father lost interest in this project and she could scoop the rest into the garbage under something else. But he didn't seem in a rush today. When he got up to pour himself another cup of coffee, she managed to slide a gooey chunk of pancake into the open napkin on her lap before he settled down at the table again.

"What are you doing today, Daddy?"

"Work. What else? All those summer people have got one problem or another. The Keiths want their gutters cleaned, the Murrays have a stopped-up toilet and so on. And we're behind on the Davidson house. But the hell with them all. I might go fishing with Randy off Stony Point this afternoon. He's still got his boat in the water even though there's not much left out there this late in the season. What are you hiding under there?"

"Nothing," she said quickly as she rolled her napkin up in a ball.

"Yes, you are." He walked around to her side of the table and put out his hand. "Come on, what is it?"

"Nothing."

He uncurled her fingers and emptied the contents of the napkin back on the plate. "Now you're going to eat that. I can't stand it when you waste food. Come on, stop dawdling. I have work to do."

"Mr. M. likes me at the museum by ten," she said. "I can't eat anymore, Daddy."

When he finally let her go, he'd put the last bites in the refrigerator for her to eat later. She'd have to stay away until after her mother got home. Her mother would never make her eat that cold, wadded up, egg-covered food. Her stomach felt heavy and roily and she was careful to steer her bike around the places on the main road where last winter's frost had pushed the macadam up into miniature hills.

"You're late today, Erin," Mr. M. said. "Everything all right?"

She nodded with her head down.

"I'm used to you sitting on the step waiting for me. We've actually had one visitor already."

"Who?"

"Somebody over from the mainland for the day. He was interested in our osprey count. They had very low figures over there last summer too. He thinks it's because the flounder has been fished out in the sound. Over here, it may be the cormorants that are fishing the freshwater ponds." He pushed open the door. "I bought the supplies for that poster I want you to make about the ospreys."

Erin loved the way Mr. M. talked to her as if she knew as much as he did about this stuff. He treated all the kids that way. Even when little Sally Thayer brought her dumb beach glass collection to him, he put it out on a special discovery table by the front door as if it were some rare and important treasure.

"Do you want me to work on—" but she couldn't even finish the sentence before she had to run for the bathroom. She didn't make it. The sight of undigested pancake on the floor made her retch again and the rest of it came up.

She wanted to die. He made her lie down on a bench in the back room with a bucket next to her while he cleaned it all up. When he came back to check on her, she was curled on her side with her back to him. She never wanted to see him again. She wanted to disappear.

"Feel better?"

"I'm sorry," she whispered. "I'm so sorry."

"What for? You can't help it. I've cleaned up worse things in my life. I won't describe them to you right now, though. Probably wouldn't be a good idea."

The nicer he was, the worse she felt about it. "My father cooks me breakfast on Saturday mornings," she said.

"That's nice."

"Mom's out with the hunters today."

"Right. I saw the signs posted up island yesterday."

"He gives me too much food. I can't eat all that in the mornings. It makes me feel sick."

He patted her on the shoulder. "It's all right, Erin. You just lie here for a while and then I'll drive you home."

"No," she said. "No, I don't want to go home. Nobody's there anyway. I'll be all right."

"Okay. You rest. I'll be in the front room if you need me. I've put on the fan to air things out."

That was his nice way of saying that her throw up smelled. She knew that everybody's throw-up smelled, but that didn't help.

She didn't throw up again, in fact, was well enough to sit up next to him on the bench at Island Foods and have a snack and drink warm Coke. He said that settled an upset stomach. People stopped and talked to him about the weather, the birds they'd seen, how their kid was doing in his science class, and all the time, he sat next to her and ate potato chips out of the same bag as if they were best friends or partners or something. She was so happy to get out the door this morning away from her father and the soggy pancakes that she'd forgotten to bring her backpack with her wallet in it, but it didn't really matter because Mr. M. usually bought her lunch anyway. If only Katie Morrison could see her now. She decided she would call Katie up later on and tell her all about it.

But after their lunch was over, he started talking again about taking her home.

"My mother is going to be out all day with the dogs," she said. "And my father is fishing with Mr. Baker on his boat."

"You sure you want to hang around with me?" he asked. "I have a meeting with Miss Hammond this afternoon."

"That's fine," Erin said. "I won't be any trouble, I promise." She had been watching for the red-haired woman ever since the day her grandfather's body washed up on the beach, but she never saw her. Once Erin even biked up to her house, but the door had been locked and nobody had answered when she knocked.

MAGGIE BROUGHT KASHA to the museum that afternoon. "I'll tie her up outside," she said.

"No, you can leave her with me," Erin said. "I'll watch her."

"That would be great."

"Erin, are you through with the cards for the herp survey?" Mr. M. asked.

"Almost."

"Herp survey," Maggie said. "What's that?"

"Erin can tell you."

"We're part of a state survey," Erin said. "We have to list every single reptile and amphibian we find and mail it in to the main office. I'm just checking the cards to make sure they're filled out right before we send them."

"Can I see?" Maggie asked. When she leaned over, her curly red hair fell like a curtain down the side of Erin's face. Erin reached out and touched a strand. "What's a Rana sylvatica?"

"Wood frog."

"Ambystoma maculatum?"

"Spotted salamander."

"You're really good at this, Erin," Maggie said.

"She is. Once you're finished, Erin, why don't you work on that poster we talked about," Mr. M. said.

"All right."

"Come see our new computer."

"What an invitation," Maggie said with a laugh, then the two of them went off to the back room. At first they kept the door open, and Erin heard them talking low, then sometimes laughing again. She wished she could hear what they were saying. She wished she could be in there with them, but Kasha wandered around sniffing under everything, and when she tried to go in to that back room, Miss Hammond said, "No, Kasha, go see Erin," and one of them closed the door.

When Erin finished filling out the survey cards, she started working on a big poster about the fishing habits of the osprey. They were planning to display it with the photographs Mr. M. had taken last summer of the birds' regular nesting sites.

Erin was proud of her block printing, but what with keeping an eye on Kasha, who kept going to the front door and whining, the letters went up on a slant when she wasn't paying attention. She propped the poster up on a table against the wall to see how it looked. She squinted and tilted her head. Bad. No matter how you looked at it. She'd have to start again, get more poster board. That was all right. She got money out of the petty cash drawer and put the leash on Kasha. She'd show both of them how grown-up she was. By the time they'd finished their meeting, she'd have the poster all done and Kasha wouldn't be whining and scratching at the door anymore because of her walk to the store.

Kasha was thin and wiry, but Erin knew she was strong, so she kept her hand wrapped tightly around the loop of the leash.

"Good dog," she said in a firm voice. She'd never walked a dog on a leash before. She liked it. It made her feel like a grown-up city woman. Kasha seemed eager to trot along, stopping every so often to sniff the bushes. They took the shortcut to the store, along the edge of the bird sanctuary.

A truck came up behind them on the narrow road and slowed. She waved at Jerry Slocum, proud that he could see what she was doing. And then with no warning, when she wasn't watching, there was a jerk on her arm, and she yelled, but Kasha had burrowed into the underbrush, the red cloth leash trailing along behind her.

Mr. Slocum stopped his truck and leaned out the window. "Everything okay?"

"Oh, sure," she said rubbing her arm. "No problem. Kasha loves to go exploring."

So he drove on and she pushed her way after Kasha, yelling her name, but not too loud because she didn't want Mr. M. and Maggie to hear.

The paths were overgrown, and the leaves underfoot black and slimy. Erin didn't know the sanctuary. She'd only been in there once with Mr. M. on a bird walk, but she hadn't paid any attention to where they were going.

"Kasha," she called. "Kasha, come back here now." But there was no sign of the dog, not any barking or scrabbling in the underbrush. Erin was getting all scratched where the branches poked out at her. She began to wheeze.

"This is not happening to me," she said out loud in as calm a voice as she could find.

She stopped in the middle of a clearing and tried to breathe very simply and easily the way other people did, the way she'd been breathing just a few minutes ago. But that old panic came up when she reached the pool of murky stuff at the bottom of each breath, and her heart began to pound as the bottom started getting closer to the top, and she felt as if she had no room left to push the air in. In the distance she heard Kasha barking and she wanted to call her back again, but she was scared to waste even the tiniest bit of air.

She lowered herself onto a wet log and tried to sit up very straight and imagine the air going in and out of her body. Her inhaler was in the backpack that she had left behind that morning. She hated the inhaler. When she sprayed it in the back of her throat, it tasted like some kind of weird chemical gas, but now she wished she had it. She wished she had anything that would make some room in her chest.

"Erin?" It was Mr. M.'s voice calling to her from behind the museum.

"Erin?" Now Maggie Hammond's voice.

"I'm here," Erin said, but she knew it wasn't loud enough for anyone to hear. She was sitting next to some dried-out ragweed, so she got up and moved very slowly to the other side of the clearing with her shoulders hunched in and pulled together and settled back down on a rock. She should try to walk out, she thought, but walking took a lot of energy, a lot of air waste, more than she was willing to spare right now. She had to concentrate completely on breathing. When the attacks were as bad as this one, she knew that was all she could afford to do.

"Where could she have gone?" Maggie's voice rose in panic. "Kasha is much stronger than she looks. I hope she doesn't pull Erin over. You know, if she smells a rabbit she takes off. You really have to be prepared for that."

They jumped in Sam's truck and headed first for the store, but nobody had seen her there. Nobody was home at her house either or at Maggie's. Jerry Slocum flagged them down on the way back into town. The two trucks stopped in the middle of the road.

"I saw Erin Craven walking that dog of yours," he called across Sam to Maggie in the passenger seat. "You still got her on that leash?"

"Where?" Sam asked sharply.

"The back road by the Lewis sanctuary. Some problem?"

"I hope not," Sam said as he gunned the truck.

By the time they found her, still sitting on the rock, back upright, she had begun to panic. It hurt now to breathe and the noises coming up out of her chest were wild and ragged. She had never sounded like that before. The skin in that little hollow at the bottom of her neck got sucked so far in every time she tried to take a breath.

Mr. M. leaned over and picked her up as if she were a bag of books, nothing much to carry at all.

"It's okay, Erin," he said. "We'll go right to the doctor."

She tried to say how sorry she was, that she was sure Kasha was right around somewhere, but he shook his head. "Don't worry. Save your breath, just breathe," and there was such a look of panic in his face at the sounds coming out of her chest that she stopped trying to talk. Behind her, Maggie was calling wildly for Kasha, and she wanted to put her fingers in her ears because she was sure Kasha was dead or drowned or something, and it was all her fault and nobody would ever speak to her again.

"Shall I come with you?" Maggie asked.

Sam shook his head. "You look for the dog. I'll get Lauren on the radio from the truck so she can track down the doctor. These attacks sound worse than they are."

Erin thought, this is the worst ever, but she didn't try to tell him that. I like the way he smells, she thought and for a minute she forgot how much it hurt to breathe because of how easily he carried her, how safe she felt in his arms.

On Saturday afternoons, Lauren ran an informal beauty salon in her living room. She was working on Miss Yola's left hand when the call came in. She had been telling Miss Yola all about the Frenchwoman's clothes, and as usual she had done a certain amount of embroidering with the truth because she figured everybody on the island had come to expect that of her. It added spice to a story.

"Portable seven to Port one," a voice crackled from the kitchen.

"Damn," she muttered. "Can't a person have at least one day off without the world coming to an end? Don't move, Miss Yola. I've just got to do the final coat on that thumbnail."

"Erin Craven," she said as she lowered herself back down into the folding chair in front of the typing desk she used as a manicure table. "One of her asthma attacks. The doctor's coming in from somewhere. That man sure does like to roam around on his time off."

Miss Yola chose to veer away from that subject. "Poor little Erin," she said. "She looks so scrawny and anxious all the time."

There was a silence between them as Lauren concentrated on the thumbnail. "More going on there than meets the eye," Lauren said with her head still down.

"Yes," Miss Yola said. "I expect there is. At least Anna has finally gotten some peace from that father of hers."

They both paused again at the brink of some disclosure. Miss Yola knew more because she lived right on the other side of the little inlet from the Cravens' house. Voices carried across water, particularly in the summer when the wind was still and everybody left their doors and windows wide open. She also knew more because ever since Anna was a little girl, she had trusted Miss Yola to keep her secrets and Miss Yola had. It was the ones Anna kept from herself Miss Yola worried about. Sometimes the only way a person could get up each morning and live through another day was if she didn't look too closely at things.

"Do you have to go in to help with Erin?" Miss Yola asked. "I can just sit here till they dry."

"No. She probably needs a shot. The doctor knows where I keep the medicine. Sam is bringing her in to the office in his truck. I could hear her wheezing in the background. Sounds worse than usual."

"Ragweed season should be just about over by now. That's what gets her going."

"Nobody home at the Cravens'. Anna's up island with a bunch of hunters. I think Chuck's there with them, but I can't raise him on the radio."

"Anna likes him to leave his radio in the car," Miss Yola said. "The noise throws off the dogs while they're hunting."

"I'll try again in a while."

Miss Yola spread her fingers out to admire them. "I like this light color. It reminds me of those pink mallows by the edge of the pond. The ones that come out in August."

"It looks good against your dark skin," Lauren said as she screwed the tops on the little bottles. Every single session Lauren worked in some comment about the color of Miss Yola's skin. Miss Yola found it amusing that after all these years a person still couldn't get over it. "Funny about Sam," Lauren went on. "First John Burling's body and now this. For a man who generally keeps to himself, he seems to be getting into his share of trouble."

Miss Yola knew that Lauren had made a big play for Sam Matera when he first came to the island. She forgave him easily enough for choosing that mousy high school teacher over her, but she still didn't understand why he wouldn't even come to her bed for comfort when at the end of the school year, the woman took off for good. It wasn't natural for a man to "go without" like that for so long. She didn't exactly say Sam was queer, but whenever his name came up in conversation, she left the idea lying around like an old unwashed plate.

Seven

SAM SETTLED ERIN in his lap in the waiting room of the clinic. He counted slowly, starting over each time Erin began a new breath to convince her that she was still breathing separate ones. It helped him as much as the girl. He had never heard oxygen take such a long noisy time to get where it needed to go. Erin sounded as if she were drowning.

A car pulled up outside and the doctor walked in. He took one look. "Don't move," he said to Sam. "I'll give her the Theophylline while she's in your lap."

In the next room, they heard the sound of running water, then the doctor came back, still dressed in his fishing vest. He must have been out on the beach. His hair was damp.

"Who do we have here?" he asked, hunkering down in front of them with the needle behind him, out of her line of sight.

"Erin Craven," Sam said.

"Erin. One of my favorite names."

"It's Irish," she said at the top of a breath.

"So 'tis," the doctor said, turning up his accent just a bit. "And so am I."

"You were fishing," she said.

"Smart girl," he answered. "Off the rocks at Stony Point."

"Catch anything?" Sam asked, to keep her from wasting her breath talking. They all knew she was trying to stall.

"A couple of big hits, but I couldn't bring them in. 'Tis going to be too cold out there soon."

"My father's fishing," Erin gasped. "On a boat."

"Is he now? Well, I hope he has better luck than me. Now, Erin, you've had these shots before, haven't you?"

She nodded. "I hate them," she whispered.

"I don't blame you one bit. But they work faster than the inhaler. We've got to open up those bronchial passages and get you some breathing room in there."

He talked to her the way Mr. M. did, as if she were a grown-up. She liked his voice. It went up and down like music.

"No need to watch," he said. "Just look the other way."

She buried her head in Mr. M's chest, against the scratchy wool shirt he was wearing and he whispered to her that it would be okay and stroked her hair, then the jab came and she cried out once and stiffened.

"It burns," she said.

"It does. But the worst is over." The doctor wiped her arm with a cool wet pad. "Sam, will you carry her into the back room. Might as well give her a quick check up while she's here. Just put her in the big stuffed chair. It's easier for her to breathe sitting up."

Erin reached out for Sam's hand once he lowered her into the chair.

"He can stay, Erin," the doctor said. "I promise I'm not going to hurt you."

And he didn't. Once as her breath began to calm, he just did all the normal things doctors do, listening to her chest and poking things into her ears, and the stick down her throat. He ran his fingers around her neck and down her arm.

"How'd you get this bump?" he asked.

"What bump?"

"This one here. On your arm. It's pretty nasty looking."

"I fell off the monkey bars," she said. "Last week."

They were all too old to play on the monkey bars anymore, but sometimes with the classes all mixed up together at recess, the seventh-graders started horsing around like little kids again.

The doctor rolled up her sleeve and spent a long time looking at the bruise, poking around it with his fingers, asking if this hurt and that hurt.

"No broken bones anyway."

What a dumb doctor, she thought. She would have told someone if she'd had a broken arm. She closed her eyes. Suddenly she felt really tired. She wasn't sure she could walk back to Mr. M.'s truck right now. Maybe later, after a nap.

"Is ANYBODY HOME at her house?" the doctor asked Sam.

"Not yet. Her father's gone out fishing with Randy Baker. We might be able to raise them on the radio, but it doesn't seem worth it." Sam lowered his voice. "I think she had a fight with him this morning."

The doctor nodded toward the next room and they tiptoed away. "We could move her into one of the beds, but I think it's better for her to sit up. What kind of fight? Her father's Al Craven, the sheriff?"

Sam explained as much as he knew. "The kid is thin, but Al seems to think she should eat like a grown man."

"Has she had the asthma a long time?"

"I've only been here six years, but at least as long as that. She gets colds easily. I know that because she misses a lot of school."

"That's a nasty bruise she's got on her arm. You don't know anything about that, do you?"

"No." He remembered that Maggie was out looking for Kasha. "Listen, Lauren is trying to raise Erin's mother, who's up island with the hunters. Could I leave Erin here with you? Maggie Hammond's dog got away and I should go try to help find her."

"That husky on the leash?"

"That's what started all this. Erin was trying to walk her and Kasha took after something. The dog is old and stubborn and has never been off the leash. Maggie thinks she won't come back."

"Go on," the doctor said. "The fish weren't biting anyway."

ANNA WAS PROUD of the dogs. For the first shoot of the season, they had behaved well, particularly Whistler, Ben Murch's vizsla, who'd only come back to Anna from Virginia three weeks ago. She wondered whether Murch even noticed. All he cared about were numbers. They'd bagged sixteen pheasants and a couple of wild quail, and his friends were pleading with him to go in for the day. They were all ready for a good shot of whiskey by the fire.

The men were standing around having a smoke when Chuck came up next to her. "Lauren just called in on the radio. She's been trying to reach us for a while. Sam had to take Erin in to the doctor's office. She's had a pretty bad asthma attack."

"Damn," she muttered, and Chuck knew what she was thinking. If only it weren't this asshole, Murch.

"Use the dogs," he said. "After all, the men want to go out again tomorrow, don't they?"

"Mr. Murch." She strode toward him with Shooter at her side. "I think it's time to take the dogs in. They've worked hard all day and you want them to have some spark for tomorrow."

"Whistler can go all night, if he has to," Murch said. "Can't you, boy?"

The dog wagged his tail at the sound of his name. He looked to Anna for an order and got none so he held his position.

"Ben, come on, it's four o'clock," called one of the other men. "In another half hour we won't be able to see anything anyway."

There was a pause and finally the man ground his cigarette out underfoot. "Okay. But let's start good and early tomorrow, Mrs. Craven. We're still owed nine birds."

"Use my truck," Chuck said as she made the turn into her driveway, wheels squealing. "I'll take care of the dogs and meet you at the doctor's office."

She grabbed the keys from him. "Thanks," she whispered and bolted.

"Drive carefully," he called after her, but he knew she couldn't possibly hear him over the noise of the dogs barking and the rev of the engine. And he knew it was a foolish thing to say to a mother rushing toward a sick child.

Anna threw open the door to the clinic.

"Erin," she called as soon as she was inside. "Erin."

Dr. Lacey stopped her in the narrow hallway, his finger to his lips. "She's fine," he said. "She's sleeping."

"Where?"

He led her back to the chair where he had propped a pillow under Erin's head so she would not wake with a stiff neck. Anna leaned over and listened to her daughter's chest. She heard the deep wheeze. It must have been a bad attack.

She followed him into his office and he shut the door so their conversation wouldn't wake Erin.

"I gave her a shot of Theophylline," he said.

"It must have been pretty bad, then. She hasn't needed that since last winter. Usually she just uses the inhaler." Anna was talking very fast.

"She didn't seem to have it with her."

"It's in her backpack. She probably went off without it this morning. Lauren says Sam brought her in."

Dennis said nothing for a moment, hoping the pause would give her time to slow down. When he spoke again, his words came out slowly and deliberately.

"Yes, I found them here. He was very good with her. She seems to trust him."

Anna mulled over that comment. Erin did seem to love her Saturdays at the museum. She must remember to thank Sam.

"What happened?" she asked.

Dr. Lacey gave her as much of the story as he knew and watched Anna carefully as she took it in. She had a round sensible face and straight black hair with the slightest touch of gray at her temples. There was a fierceness about her that he'd seen before in mothers of sickly children.

"Apparently she threw up this morning. Erin told Sam she'd had some kind of fight with her father."

"A fight? What do you mean?"

"An argument over breakfast."

"He always cooks her breakfast on the mornings I have to take out hunters."

Dennis backed off. "I've been looking through her charts," he said. "She's been sick a lot."

"It's the asthma. It comes down from my husband's side of the family. He had it when he was little." Dennis already knew that. During the hour he'd been waiting for her to pick up Erin, he'd gone back and looked through the charts on both sides, Craven and Burling. The medical records were detailed and often included editorial notes from the nurse. Al Craven had asthma and eczema as a child. His younger sister died of meningitis when Al was six. When he was eight he was bitten on the hand by a neighbor's German shepherd. As for Anna Craven, née Burling, he knew already that she was the daughter of a German woman who died when Anna was twelve, that John Burling was a drunk, that as a child, Anna herself seemed to have been as healthy as a horse except for a couple of odd incidents when she was taken over to the mainland, once with a broken arm and another time with an unexplained burn on her thigh. Later on, Anna had two miscarriages and an ectopic pregnancy, so Erin must have felt to her mother like a miracle child. No wonder she felt so fierce about her.

"That's the tough thing with asthma," he said gently. "Every little cold can get so complicated. However, they've made considerable advances in the treatment of asthma in the last few years. I'd like to teach her how to use a Peak Flow Meter which will give her some control over her own situation."

"Is it complicated?"

"Not at all. The machine itself is a simple plastic device. Looks like a baby bottle. It will allow her to test the rate at which the air leaves her lungs so she'll get a warning long before she experiences any other symptoms. That's the time for her to start the inhaler. I'll order one and you can bring her in Monday after school so we can show her how to use it. What is she using now?"

"Proventil."

"How often?"

"Twice a day. More when she has an attack."

"I want her to use it four times a day as a preventative. Then I'm going to add Intal. It's another inhaler. She can take it at the same time as the Proventil." He was writing on her chart while he was speaking.

Anna nodded. Al wouldn't like the extra expense. Never mind. She'd pay for it herself. It would be easier than fighting with him about it.

"One other thing. Have you noticed the bruise on her arm?"

"Yes," she said. "She fell off the monkey bars."

"That's what she told me too."

"You sound like you don't believe it."

He shrugged. "It's just an odd place for that big a bruise. There's no fracture in the bone. I checked."

"I'm sure, Dr. Lacey, that I would notice if my only daughter had a broken arm." She doesn't like me, he thought. She's lumped me in with the fancy summer doctors who fit the patients in around their golf games.

"I'm sure you would, Mrs. Craven. But it's my job to consider all possibilities." He took a deep breath and tried one more time. "How does she get along with her father?"

"Fine," Anna said quickly.

She'd stand up now and walk out, Dennis thought. She knew exactly what I've been driving at. But she didn't move. Instead, she leaned back in the chair and closed her eyes for a minute. The muscles around her mouth went slack and her face grew softer, fuller. He expected it wasn't often that she was able to let down her guard.

"Erin is an Irish name," he said quietly. "I have a cousin named Erin."

"My grandmother took me to Ireland when I was a kid," she said. "Only time I've ever been out of the country. Practically the only time I've been off this island."

"I grew up on an island. Off the western coast. Near a little town called Clifden. Omey Island."

"I don't think we went there." Her eyes were still closed, as if it weren't possible to have this kind of conversation with your eyes open.

"Nobody does. It's a tidal island."

"What does that mean?"

"We were an island when the tide was in and part of the mainland when the tide was out. Spent a lot of my teenage years driving at high speed across the wet sand with water up to the gunwales of Tom Walsh's car."

The picture seemed to amuse her, and her mouth stayed soft and easy. He tried to think what else he could say to keep it that way.

"Boys will be boys," she said. "Especially on islands. I know. I have two brothers. Any stores on your island?"

"A sweet shop, a pub naturally, a church naturally, a little place where you could buy cigarettes and last week's newspapers and a few groceries, and a graveyard." He paused. "Naturally."

She opened her eyes then, but didn't speak.

"My father was lost at sea too," he said, his voice gentle. "A storm took our whole fishing fleet. Twenty-seven men from Omey and the two nearest towns. Our family was considered one of the lucky ones because the sea gave us back a body to bury. Lots of crosses in the graveyard from that storm, but only four bodies in the ground."

She sat up suddenly. "Were you the one who left those flowers on my father's grave?"

"Yes. I hope you don't mind. I haven't been home to Omey in ten years. When they brought in your father's body, it took me back."

"I don't mind." The tension had come back to her jaw.

She would leave soon if he didn't think of something more to say. He liked talking to her, especially today, the day his thin French wife had strolled away from him onto the metal deck of the ferry boat and waved only once before she went inside to buy her ticket.

"Living on an island can be hard," he said. "People have romantic ideas about it. But they don't really know."

"Erin is always saying that to her new friend Katie. Katie commutes over to the school from the mainland."

"I was almost born in a rowboat because my mother was putting up preserves and thought she could last till the tide dropped."

Anna put her head back again and listened while he told her about his odd birth in the living room of the first house on the mainland and the time his uncle swam across at high tide and walked into the house dripping wet. He heard the bell jingle at the clinic door, but he was in the middle of a story so he kept talking.

"Anna," called a man's voice outside the door, and she started up, her eyes wide and frightened and answered "I'm in here, Al," just as he threw open the door.

"What's going on?" he said.

"Shh, Erin's asleep," she whispered.

"Mommy?" Erin called.

"Coming," she called back and brushed past her husband to the child.

"Your daughter had a bad asthma attack." Dennis got to his feet. Al Craven was a thin wiry man and not tall, but something about him made Dennis feel better standing up. "I had to give her a shot of Theophylline."

"Jesus, must have been bad. She hasn't had one of those for a year or so."

"Good crop of ragweed this fall."

"My wife gets a little nutty over this." Craven didn't bother to lower his voice. In the next room, Anna and Erin could hear him. "I tell her you've got to stop babying the kid. She's growing out of the asthma now. That's what the doctor in the hospital over on the mainland told us last year."

"Actually, it was Sam Matera who brought her in," Dennis said quickly. "Erin was out in the woods." He explained about the dog getting away.

"That husky?" Anna asked from the doorway. Erin was on her feet now, leaning against her mother.

"It wasn't my fault, Mom. Kasha just pulled away in the one second that I wasn't looking."

"We'd better get you home," Al said, and to everybody's surprise, he slipped his hands around Erin's waist and lifted her from behind.

"Daddy, stop it," Erin cried, her feet swinging two inches above the floor.

"Light as a feather," he said.

"Al, put her down," Anna said. "She's not a baby."

Al ignored his wife. Erin squirmed out of her father's grasp and pulled her sweater back down over the top of her pants.

"Didn't I see you fishing off the point this afternoon?" Al asked.

"You did. Two strikes, but I didn't catch anything."

"Always wanted to try that flyfishing. Must be damn hard to cast with no weight on the line."

"It's practically impossible. But I'd be glad to show you." He didn't like this man, but he didn't want him to know it.

"Let's go," Al said, and followed Erin out to the car.

Anna lingered for a moment. She looked embarassed. "He thinks she's still a little girl."

"Hope I didn't bore you." He leaned against the door jamb. "You've heard about the Irish gift of gab."

"I have."

"Bring her back on Monday and I'll show her how to use the meter. She should keep the inhaler handy, especially tonight."

"I know."

"Don't hesitate to call if it starts up again."

He was sure she heard him, but she didn't answer. From outside, Al was yelling at her to hurry up.

AL HAD HIS truck parked at the end of the driveway with the motor running when Anna came out of the doctor's office.

She opened the door on Erin's side. "Honey, you ride with me in Chuck's truck. I haven't seen you all day."

Al reached across Erin and pulled the door shut again.

"Anna, will you quit it? Let's just get home before the whole damn island knows our business. Let the girl be."

Erin squeezed her eyes shut at times like these as if she were trying to wipe out the world, and Anna hated to see it. She felt as if she were losing her daughter faster than she ever thought was possible, as if whole days were slipping by now when she couldn't seem to get time alone with Erin, and she didn't know what she was thinking anymore or who she was. On the ride home behind her husband and her daughter, she studied the backs of their heads and she wondered how many secrets Erin was keeping from her.

Chuck flagged her down just before their driveway, and they pulled off into Miss Yola's place to switch.

"She okay?" he asked, and she loved him suddenly for the concern in his face. What a nice man Chuck Montclair was. Why didn't she take the time to notice that more often? Why didn't he ever get married?

"She's fine. Doctor had to give her a shot so it must have been pretty bad. Maggie Hammond's husky ran off while Erin was walking her somewhere. I didn't really get the whole story."

"Oh, God, that's bad. The girl's pretty crazy about that dog."

"I know you, Chuck Montclair. You're going to go right down now and see if you can help her," Anna teased.

"Yes, I am, Mrs. Craven." He popped the black cowboy hat on her head before he got into the cab of his truck. She heard the Mrs. loud and clear and wished irrationally that she could switch places with Chuck. She would rather tramp through the cold November woods looking for a lost dog if it meant that afterward she could go home to his simple third floor apartment down in one of the fort houses, and fall asleep all alone in his narrow single bed. And he could cook Al dinner and deal with everything that would come before, during, and after that simple event.

"Well, you'll probably have dog-hunting company," she said. "I expect Sam's out there too."

"Yours are all bedded down for the night. Figured you didn't need to fuss with them."

"Thanks, Chuck."

He took off, his tires spitting gravel. From inside the house, the little white dog started yapping, but when Miss Yola came to the door, Anna just waved and drove away. Al was mad enough as it was. She didn't have time now to stay and chat.

Just before she turned into her driveway, she took off the hat and stuffed it back under the front seat of the car.

Eight

MAGGIE WOULDN'T COME IN, and Sam figured he'd better not suggest it again even though it was already dark and they'd tramped up and down every path in the sanctuary at least three times. Her voice sounded hoarse from calling, and she hadn't spoken to him for a while. When he handed her one of the flashlights he'd found in the supply closet up at the museum, she stared at him with a stunned look in her eyes.

"We'll find her, Maggie," he said, and she nodded, but he couldn't be sure she'd heard.

Finally, he managed to convince her that the dog might have found her way home, so they got in Maggie's car and drove slowly down the road calling Kasha's name, over and over, first his low voice from the passenger side and then her higher one from the driver's side. Chuck Montclair's truck was parked outside her house and when they made their way onto the dark porch, they heard him calling for Kasha down through the orchard and then out along the little beach.

"Sweet man," Maggie said as they leaned against the railing. "I wonder how he found out."

"The doctor, probably," Sam said.

He was thinking that the last time they'd found something on that beach it was a body, and he hoped that didn't happen this time. This was an old dog. If she had a heart attack chasing some rabbit, she'd die in the bushes and they might never find her. And Maggie would decide the island was a bad-luck place and she'd leave, and he'd miss laughing with a pretty woman over something the way he and she had been doing just this afternoon, although right now, he couldn't remember for the life of him what it had been.

"A penny for your thoughts," she said in a weary voice.

"Too many of them. They'd cost you more than that."

"I guess we've got to stop and eat something."

"Good idea," he said. "It will give us the energy to go out again later."

She cupped her hands around her mouth and yelled, "Chuck" with what was left of her voice.

Chuck accepted her invitation to join them for dinner.

"I don't know what there is to eat," she said.

"I'll figure something out," Sam said. "You sit."

"I'll get the two six-packs out of my truck," Chuck said.

She curled up in a big overstuffed chair and watched Sam moving around the kitchen. Her eyes followed him, but her thoughts seemed far away. He pulled open all the drawers and left them that way so he could find what he needed without bothering her. From what he saw in the refrigerator, he could tell that she wasn't a cook. The cupboards were stuffed with cans and packages that looked as if they'd been there since Mrs. Phipps's time. He'd been to one of her famous porch lunches the first summer he'd come on the island. She was a creative, messy cook, he remembered, and luckily she kept a well-stocked larder. Six boxes of his favorite brand of pasta lined the top shelf. He found good olive oil and hot red-pepper flakes in among the spices. And yes, the head of garlic in the fridge was drying out, but he could salvage the four cloves he needed. With a loaf of bread and the two packages of spinach in the freezer, he was in business. Thank you, Mrs. Phipps, he said to himself as he set about chopping.

Chuck handed out three bottles and put the rest in the fridge. He and Sam kept up a running patter of island small talk. Sam glanced over at Maggie from time to time. He didn't think she was listening, but the background noise of their voices might comfort her the way the sound of a radio made a house feel less empty.

"Is it supposed to rain tonight?" she asked suddenly in the middle of one of their sentences.

"Nope. Clear for a couple of days," Chuck said. "She'll be all right. A dog like that was born to live in the wild. When she comes back, she may turn her nose up at regular dog food. Hell, I bet she'll only eat live rabbit after this."

Sam didn't think Chuck was helping much even though he meant well. The pasta was boiling and the smell of garlic filled the kitchen.

"Can a dog turn wild that quickly?" Maggie asked. "In a few days? Maybe she'll come back and circle the house, snarling at me."

"Oh, come on, I didn't mean that," Chuck said.

"I wouldn't blame her," Maggie went on. "After all, I've kept her on that leash and I've been traveling so much and I altered her so she couldn't have puppies. I wouldn't blame her at all."

This wasn't just about the dog, Sam thought as he dished out the pasta. "It's time to eat," he said. He set out the plates along with a bowl of the grated Parmesan he'd found in the freezer, the hunk of heated bread, and a small jar of Dijon mustard to spread on his spinach.

HE WAS GLAD to see that she ate hungrily and took seconds when he offered them. "I can't believe you made something that tastes this good from what I had in this kitchen," she said.

"It looks as if Mrs. Phipps knew how to stock her larder."

"Sam's a famous cook on the island," Chuck said. "Wait till you taste his pies at the Thanksgiving Day dinner. If you're lucky, he'll do pecan and deep-dish apple. Crust to melt in your mouth."

"I pay him too," Sam said, and that at least made her smile.

"Is Erin all right?" she asked.

"Fine." Sam cleared the dishes and put the kettle on. "Doctor seems to be a good man. He was very gentle with Erin."

"That poor kid belongs in Arizona," Chuck said. "This climate is terrible for her. She's such a skinny little thing too."

"She says her father's trying to fatten her up. She threw up in the museum this morning, all the pancakes he'd gotten down her."

Chuck took another swig from his beer and set it down a little too heavily on the table. He'd been back to the refrigerator twice. Sam and Maggie were still nursing their first. "Don't get me on the subject of Al Craven," he said.

Maggie and Sam exchanged glances. "Feel free," Sam said. "Get on the subject."

Chuck shook his head as if trying to resist temptation.

"There's good coffee in the freezer," Maggie said when she heard the water boiling. "I brought it up with me from Philadelphia. The filters are in the cabinet—"

"Found them," Sam said. "Stay put." He measured out the coffee. "The doctor was asking her about a bruise on her arm this afternoon. Nasty-looking thing. Erin said she fell off the monkey bars.

You don't think she's getting hit at home, do you, Chuck? Al wouldn't do that, would he?"

"I wouldn't put anything past Al."

"Shit," said Maggie.

There was a silence while the three of them mulled over this possibility.

"Did Al grow up here?" Maggie asked.

Chuck nodded. "Yup. Born and bred and both his parents before him. He's a rich man, Al is. Doesn't do shit with it. Buys lottery tickets every week as if he needs more."

"Rich from what?"

"Construction work on the island. Cheating people."

"He came in at a pretty good price on the community center," Sam said.

Chuck shrugged. "Maybe. No way we're going to be in there by Thanksgiving."

"We're not? He's still saying he can make it."

"He's got me and Billy Slade working full time up island on that Davidson house. We haven't even touched the community center since August."

"But that's not cheating people," Maggie said. "It's just missing deadlines. I've done that myself."

Chuck tipped his bottle all the way up and drained it. " Every time Al Craven goes to fix a toilet or sends me to do it, he makes those summer people pay through the nose. What can they do? They're off on the mainland somewhere. They're stuck. And the other thing you got to remember about a job from Craven Construction is you better buy your own materials. God knows where Al gets some of that stuff he uses. Right off the boat from Taiwan or something."

"My bills haven't been too bad," Maggie said.

"That's because I didn't let on how often I came by," Chuck said. "Al doesn't know it, but I'm the one who told Mrs. Phipps to order that new hot water heater direct from the mainland, and I told her where she could get a good deal. She said if I didn't do right by her, she'd come back to haunt me."

Sam saw Maggie stiffen. Liquor made Chuck foolish. With the dog gone, Maggie didn't need to be reminded of Nan right now. "Did Al go to school here?" he asked.

"Yep. He and Anna were high school sweethearts. Everybody knew they were going to get married from the beginning. But Al went into the navy first."

"Was he in Vietnam?"

"Nope, somehow he got out of that. Came home in sixty-seven. Said he never wanted to see a boat again. I think he gets seasick pretty easy."

"What about his parents?"

Chuck leaned back in his chair and ran his hands through his thinning hair. "Kept to themselves. Old Will Craven was a pretty hard drinker and I think he slapped his wife around some. I know he hit Al."

"And Anna?" Maggie asked. "The only time I talked to her, she seemed pretty tough."

"Anna Craven is a real peach," said Chuck, and Sam thought it wasn't the liquor that made his eyes shine. "Rare woman. Smart, really good at what she does. Al has no idea how lucky he is. No idea." He pursed his lips. "You've got me talking too much. I have to be up island at six A.M. tomorrow morning. Another day with the hunters."

He stood up and steadied himself with a hand on the tabletop.

"You okay, Chuck?" Sam asked. "Want me to take you home?"

"Hell, no. Good-bye to you both. Nice to have your company. Don't worry about that dog. She'll be waiting on the porch in the morning, I bet you that."

"I hope so," Maggie said.

AFTER CHUCK LEFT, she asked Sam to drive around with her one more time. Their breath made clouds in the air and their rhythmic calling out the two sides of the car reminded her of the fog horn on nights when the weather socked them in.

"Let's try White Beach," he said. "I brought the flashlight."

"Good idea. I've taken her down there for walks. Maybe she remembered."

They parked the car. He took her hand to help her across the line of round white rocks to the hard-packed sand. The night felt so much darker than in the summers, Maggie thought. So many of the houses were closed up for the winter. They stood out like missing teeth in a jack-o'-lantern, constantly reminding you that you had been left behind. Saturday night. On the mainland, the shore lights glowed, a cluster to indicate a town, then a strip of darkness, and another cluster for the neighboring town. She had a sudden sharp stab of envy for the bustle and life of those places. Not so long ago, on a Saturday night, she was in London, out at the theater with friends. What was she doing here?

"Don't you ever feel like leaving this place?" she asked Sam.

"Sometimes. I usually go out west for some camping and hiking with a friend in June when all the summer people first arrive."

"I mean for good."

"Nope. Not yet."

They could see the froth of the surf. Like white ribbons against a dark cloth, the waves rolled in one after another up to their feet. The wind off the water felt damp and cold. Maggie turned up the collar of her jacket. Sam walked ahead of her toward the beach grass, calling Kasha's name. The flashlight swept back and forth across the sand in a wide arc.

She waited by the edge of the water while he covered the length of the beach and then came back again.

"She's not here," Maggie said. "We'd better give up for tonight."

"I'll drive."

"The keys are under the seat."

"There are things a dog knows how to do," he said as he started up the car. "We forget. They're better equipped to spend the night out in the wild than we would ever be. She's got the hearing, the sense of smell, the intuition."

"I think of all the times I've gone away," Maggie said. "Now I know what it feels like to be left behind."

He didn't answer, and she was grateful for his silence.

"Where did you park?" she asked when he pulled up outside the house.

"My truck's still at the museum. It's all right. I'll walk down to get it."

They sat in the car without moving. "Sam, I don't think I want to be in the house alone tonight."

"I'll stay if you want."

"There are exactly"—she closed her eyes and counted in her head—"four bedrooms on the second floor and two on the third. You're welcome to any one of them except for the one at the top of the stairs on the right. That's where I sleep. How's that sound?"

"It sounds fine to me."

HE CHOSE TO sleep in the room next to hers on the second floor. Sometime in the night he woke to the sound of crying and sat bolt upright. He held himself absolutely still, listening, but he didn't hear it again. The wind had come up, and throughout the house, the doors, hanging loose in their frames, rattled irregularly. Rain started slowly, one drop, then two or three in a row on the roof outside his window. The erratic beat reminded him of a moth banging against a lampshade. He heard Maggie's bedroom door open and close, then her step on the stair. He pulled on his jeans and went out to stand on the landing.

"Are you all right?" he called.

"Oh, God," she said. "You scared me. I'm just going down to check the porch."

He waited. Through his open window, he heard her calling for Kasha. Then, the porch door slammed and the lock was flipped. It was an odd sound. He had not locked the doors of his house since his first night on the island.

She came back up. She was dressed in a long gray T-shirt, and from the way the hall light hit her, he could see her nipples pressing against the thin cotton material. Her hair was tangled and there was a wadded up bunch of Kleenex in her hand.

"Chuck was wrong," she said. "It's raining. Kasha hates the rain."

"Have you slept at all?"

"A little. I keep hearing things."

He took a step toward her and she put up her hand. "Please, Sam. Please, I'll be okay."

"All right," he said. "Just knock on the wall if you need me."

"I will. I promise."

He waited at the top of the landing until her door closed. " 'Night," he said to the empty hallway.

He didn't sleep well, knowing more, as he now did, about the shape of the body lying on the other side of the wall.

When Anna got home, she found that Erin had shut herself up in her room.

Anna knocked quietly at the door.

"I'm fine, Mom," Erin said. She was lying on her bed. "I need to do my homework."

"Have you got your inhaler?"

"Yes," she answered with a roll of her eyes. These exaggerated gestures were a new development. Hormones probably.

"All right, sweetie, I'll call you when dinner's ready." As Anna made her way downstairs, she realized that she'd been whispering. Al was in the living room watching television. She always knew exactly where he was in the house, and she tiptoed around him. Last week at bingo, Annie Slocum said her Jerry was like a bear when he was hungry. She just stayed out of his way. Anna laughed at that. She had started to say something about Al being like a bear when he was hungry, thirsty, hot, cold, but she'd stopped herself. It sounded ridiculous.

She even kept her voice low on the phone. Whenever Lauren called, she complained she couldn't hear Anna. "I don't know how you manage to train those dogs with that tiny little voice of yours," she'd said just the other day. "It's disappearing on you."

"The better a dog is trained, the less you need to raise your voice," Anna had replied.

The kitchen sink was full of breakfast dishes, the griddle sticky with spilled syrup. She closed her eyes for a moment, imagined herself into one big, simply furnished room where the light flooded in through a wall of windows and there was nobody but herself to feed.

"When's dinner?" Al called. "I'm starving."

"Coming," she said. Coming, coming, coming.

They had leftover roast chicken, carrots, and mashed potatoes. But everything took longer than usual because once Anna had peeled the potatoes and dropped them in the pot of water, she forgot to turn on the burner. She was thinking about the doctor, his tales of the Irish island, the soothing sound of his voice. Remembering the time in his office, she realized how incredibly rude she had been. Whenever something happened to Erin, Anna shot into action, and afterward, when the crisis had passed, she felt limp and lifeless. But she didn't remember ever doing that before, putting back her head and closing her eyes when somebody was talking to her. Luckily it didn't seem to bother him. He seemed to like telling her about his father and the storm and the sweet shop. Such a funny name. Sweet shop. It must mean a candy store.

"Anna, what in God's name's going on here?" Al said, throwing himself into one of the kitchen chairs. "Did you have to go out and kill the bird?"

"Sorry. I guess I'm just tired. It's been a long day."

"Don't talk to me about tired. First I had to deal with Erin's nonsense about breakfast. The way she looks when I try to feed her, you'd think I was asking her to eat a goddamn bar of soap. "

Anna took a deep breath. They'd been through this before. "Her stomach is very small, Al. It's better if she eats lots of little meals during the day."

"That's a load of crap," he said, snapping the newspaper and folding it. "She's got to eat three meals a day like everybody else. She's not going to have her mother following her around with spoonfuls of cereal for the rest of her life."

He was talking about one time, just one time when Erin was six months old, and Anna was a young, nervous mother. She'd crawled around behind the baby on the back porch trying to get her to finish her oatmeal. Al took a picture of it. Whenever he started thinking about Erin and her eating, he brought up the porch scene again. Anna had read in magazines about teenage girls getting phobias about eating. All the experts told you not to make food an issue. But the more she tried to convince Al to lay off, the crazier he got about it.

Anna was relieved to see that Erin actually seemed hungry, and the three of them ate for a long while without talking. Al was still looking at the paper and every so often, he read something out loud about the nuclear sub base across the way or the joke of the week, which Anna laughed at, but didn't find funny.

"Do you want more?" she asked as soon as he put his fork down.

"Sure do. I'm hungry as a horse."

When she took his plate, his fork and knife slid off onto the floor.

"Now your mother would never get a job as a waitress, Erin."

"I don't want her to be a waitress," Erin said.

"That's good, because she'd be fired the first day for dropping things." Anna filled his plate with food and put it back down in front of him. He lifted it and handed it to her. "Now let's try that again, Mrs. Craven," he said. "You don't slam a plate down in front of a person. You lower it."

"Come on, Al, I'm exhausted."

"No, I mean it. If those hunters ever get sick of coming up here and killing those tame birds, you may have to get a job down at the Rocky Point. So you'd better start practicing."

It was always easier to go along with him than fight, yet she hated for Erin to see her giving in like this. If she refused to play whatever game he'd just thought up, then he could make it worse, drag it out longer. Out of the corner of her eye, she saw Erin sliding her last piece of chicken into the napkin in her lap.

Anna took Al's plate all the way to the sink, turned around, and walked it back to him very slowly to give Erin as much time as she needed. She set it down with elaborate precision.

"Good," he said. "Good job."

She settled into her chair.

"I've got to do my homework, Mom," Erin said.

"Okay. Go on up."

"Wait a minute," Al said. "What about dessert?"

"Al, there isn't any. I didn't get around to it."

"Erin's got some. I promised to save it for her."

Both of them watched as he pulled a plate out of the refrigerator. It was the egg-covered pancake from breakfast. He undid the plastic wrap and put the whole plate in the microwave. Erin looked at her mother, her eyes wide with fear. She shook her head. Anna nodded to her to go upstairs, and Erin slipped out of the room while her father was still fussing with the buttons on the microwave.

"Erin, get back here," he called to her.

"No, Daddy, I don't want it. It will make me throw up again." Her door slammed.

"Al, for God's sake, leave her alone. We don't want to have to take her back down to that doctor again."

He took the plate out of the microwave and held it in front of her. "Why don't you eat it, then?" he asked.

"It isn't even fit for the dogs," she said.

"You and your dogs. This is perfectly good food. I happen to know because I cooked it. And I'm not going to see it wasted." He settled himself down at his place, drowned the sodden pancakes in syrup and set about eating them with a grin on his face. "Good stuff," he said. "Sure you don't want some?" He speared a forkful and held it an inch from her mouth. The syrup dripped off the side of his fork onto the table.

Anna thought she might throw up. She got up without a word and walked over to the sink.

"Why were you and that doctor all locked up in his office together today?"

"Erin was asleep in the other room," she said over the running water. "We were waiting for her to wake up."

"You should have just picked her up and brought her home. No reason to hang around down there. I don't know what kind of doctor that man can be. He looked like a damn fool trying to cast a line from the Point without any weight on it. Even the regulars didn't bother today with that heavy west wind. And they've got spinners on."

Maybe he really didn't care about catching a fish, Anna thought. Maybe he just liked being out by the water, listening to the gulls and watching the waves roll in one after another. She often did this, answered every one of Al's sentences. She just kept the words to herself.

"How's Randy?" she asked to divert him.

"Okay, I guess. Must be having a hell of a time with that girl wanting to jump his bones every five minutes. I said to him, Randy, you are getting too old for this and he said, oh yeah, just try me. Sure would like to know how that felt, a young thing like that in my bed. Anybody in my bed who was interested."

Anna moved her hands very quietly in the soapy water. She'd stepped on another mine. The field was full of them tonight. She wasn't paying enough attention. She really must be tired.

"So how long were you in that office?"

"I don't know, Al. I didn't look at my watch."

"Why was the door closed? What were you two doing in there?"

She took a breath and let it out quietly. Rolling around on the floor together. "Al, he's a doctor. We were talking about Erin. He wants to teach her a way to measure her own breathing rate. So she can have more control of the asthma."

"Does it cost anything?"

"No." She wasn't lying exactly. He hadn't mentioned any charge for the meter.

"That doctor on the mainland didn't say anything about this."

"We haven't been over there in a long time. They've got new treatments now. Things we don't know about out here." Al was always talking about how expensive the doctor was on the mainland, and how it was better to use the island clinic because they charged low rates to year-rounders.

"That's what we've got this doctor for. He just took care of it."

"But Al, she might not have even had that attack today if she were checked out more often on the mainland."

"Don't be ridiculous, Anna. You're not making any sense."

Let him have the last word, she told herself. Keep moving the sponge around the plate.

He stood up and walked over to the list on the bulletin board. He'd started this nonsense a year ago and she didn't pay much attention to it. Every so often, he changed something. Last week, he'd added two items. "IRON MY SHIRTS." That's so we don't have to pay Annie Slocum to do it anymore. "STOP WASTING FOOD." He put that down the time he found the moldy cottage cheese in the garbage can. He'd taken the container right out and leaned against the counter talking to her the whole time as if it were perfectly normal to be eating cottage cheese out of the garbage with a spoon from the dishwasher. "You just go around the green parts," he'd said when he was finished. Now she'd started hiding food that had gone bad under pieces of paper, taking the trash out before he got to it.

He wrote down some new entry. She dried the pots, pretending not to notice.

Chuck had seen that list a few months ago when she'd invited him in for coffee. When he'd said something about it, she told him to lay off. What he didn't understand was that the list actually helped her. If Al put things down on the list, he felt like he was really in charge. Things always went better around the house if Al felt in charge.

Erin was tucked under her covers reading when Anna walked in to say good-night. She sat down on the edge of the bed and started to drop her ear to Erin's chest. The girl pushed her away.

"Stop doing that, Mommy. It's fine. I used the inhaler already."

"Dr. Lacey seems to be a nice man."

"He's okay."

"How's that bruise on your arm? He was asking me about it. Can I see it?"

Erin pulled up the sleeve of her nightgown. "It's fine. It's almost gone."

Anna let it be. She studied her daughter for a minute. Erin kept on reading.

"Good book?"

"Yup. Katie gave it to me. We don't have it in the library here. There's nothing in this library I haven't read."

"Mrs. Malloy told me we can borrow books from other places now." Sally Malloy was the librarian.

"I know, but it takes two weeks to get them."

"How's school?"

"Fine. Can we go to the mall tomorrow?"

"Tomorrow'll be hard. I'm with the hunters again." By the time Murch got his nine birds, Anna thought, it'd be too late to take the boat over and back.

Erin sighed. "You've always got the hunters."

"Maybe Lauren would take you."

"I don't want to go with Lauren."

"How would you like to go up island with me and Chuck tomorrow, help us with the dogs?"

"And get up at six o'clock in the morning? Forget that, Mom."

A real teenager, Anna thought. Just a year ago, Erin loved going with her even if it meant she sat in the car and listened to books on tape.

"I wish I could live with Katie on the mainland. There's nothing to do on this stupid island."

Anna felt as if somebody had socked her. "I keep thinking I'll order that tent. So you and I could have a sleepover on the beach. Wake up and cook breakfast on a fire." The one time Anna had brought this idea up to Al, he'd hooted with laughter at the thought. She'd wanted to cross the kitchen to where he sat tilted back in his chair, and stuff the dishrag into his wide-open mouth. "You're going to camp out on a beach when you've got a perfectly good house to sleep in? You really have gone nuts."

"It's getting pretty cold for camping out," Erin said. "Not really my idea of a good time, Mom."

"But this island is so beautiful, Erin. You'd get tired of all those roads and stores and noise after a while."

"You and I are different, Mom. Nature's great, but I think I've had enough of it. I could use some noise and lights. Movies. Malls." She picked up her book and began to read again.

Anna couldn't think of anything more to say. Had this happened to her at thirteen? No, it never had. The outdoors had always been her refuge, the place she ran to when her father started yelling at her brothers and she couldn't block the noise no matter how hard she pressed her hands against her ears.

SHE STAYED UP as late as she could stand it, then slipped into bed in the dark. Al was turned away from her, snoring gently on his side of the mattress. The fishing must have worn him out. She lay each bone of her body down separately, as carefully as she'd put the dinner plate in front of him earlier. He didn't stir.

Some time later in the night, she felt his arm go around her, hunt under the nightgown, cup her breast, and she forced herself to breathe in and out regularly as if she were still sleeping. He moved his hand around her body and she could feel the rough calluses at the place where his fingers met the palm. He squeezed, tickled, poked, then with an elaborate groan, he rolled away from her. Done, she said. For another night. A little while later, he got out of bed and left the room. He often roamed the house in the dark.

She rolled over onto her back and spread her legs, claiming the whole width of the bed for this moment of freedom. Sometimes he'd be gone for only a little while, sometimes for hours. She didn't know what he was doing and she didn't care. She thrashed about, trying to release the muscles which had tightened over the hours of holding herself so still. Finally, she fell asleep.

ERIN DIDN'T KNOW what woke her. Her eyes were open, staring at the pattern of her wallpaper in the dim light from the window before her brain kicked in. Somebody was in her room. It was her father. He did this sometimes, came in while she was asleep. They didn't say anything about it then or later. They didn't speak. She pretended to be asleep. He just lay down next to her on the bed, curled up against her like a sick puppy. His knees bent into the crook of her knees. He rested his arm across the top of her and it felt so heavy. What if she started wheezing again? Then she would wake him up, and they would each know that the other knew he'd been in her bed, and something would have to be said or done about it by someone. She wanted him to think that she slept right through these times, that she never even knew he'd been there. She felt how warm his body was through the pyjamas. She hated how much space he took up. She felt sorry for him, but it wasn't her fault that he couldn't sleep, she wanted him please to go away. She never tried to go back to sleep when he was next to her. She just lay there in the dark and counted things in her head. How many boys were in her school, how many girls? How many windows on this side of the house? How many windows in the whole house? How many female dogs did her mother have in the kennels this year? How many male dogs? Her hand was always aching to slide up and start twisting her hair, but she was scared to move one muscle.

She was sure her mother didn't know he was in the bed with her. It'd only happened a couple of times, maybe five or six. Just this year. She didn't think it had happened before, but then she wondered if she had just forgotten it or she hadn't really woken up. She didn't know. She didn't want to think about that.

Sometime before the morning, he always snuck out again. That's when she fell asleep.

Nine

Miss Yola never did bother getting a driver's license, and now that her hip was better, she walked most places to keep herself limber. The car had started acting funny some time ago, and it didn't seem worth the money to fix it. Her neighbors were good to her, took her along when they were going to the post office or down to the hardware store. Sunday mornings in hunting season, Miss Yola knew that Anna wouldn't be attending church, so she prepared herself earlier than usual in time to make the trip. It wasn't a bad walk except when there was snow or ice on the ground. And besides that, the first car that passed her always picked her up. It was island etiquette. This morning it was Al Craven. He never went to church himself except for occasions like funerals.

"Hop in, Miss Yola," he said. "I'll get you to the church on time."

"I haven't hopped anywhere in a while, Al," she said as she slid her aluminum cane in under the seat. "But I will take the ride you're offering." Her diction was always precise. She reminded Al of an old-maid schoolteacher.

"Manner of speaking," he said.

These two didn't like each other, but on an island, you learned to act polite to the ones you didn't like because you were bound to rub up against them all the time.

"Nice morning," she said. "But that's a hard frost we got last night."

"Yes, it is. Anna'll be happy. Frost holds the scent for the dogs. She's out on the marshes with Ben Murch and some buddies of his."

"Your wife is a wonder," Miss Yola said, smoothing her skirts.

"All that work with the dogs and then the post office and taking care of her family too."

He wondered if he was getting a lecture. "Oh, I know how lucky I am with my Anna. Not another woman like her in the world."

"You're right about that. Will you be joining us at church this morning?" She stared straight ahead through the windshield.

"Not today," he said, as if he ever went any other time. "Work to catch up on down at the office."

"Wearing your sheriff hat today?"

"Both hats," he said. "Sheriff and construction."

"How's the work on the community center? That Catholic church has the moldiest basement. It's hard to feel joyous about Thanksgiving when the place smells like that. It puts you off your food."

"Well, it's coming along, Miss Yola, but we've got some problems we hadn't counted on. Not sure we're actually going to make Thanksgiving. It's only a couple of weeks off now." He took the next corner at high speed and saw that she had to grab for the door handle. Good. Nosy old bitch.

"I understand Erin had one of her attacks yesterday. Is she okay?"

"Just fine. Sam probably overreacted. Erin's growing out of it."

"You had asthma as a child, didn't you?"

He glanced over at her. "You don't forget anything do you, Miss Yola? Asthma and eczema. I got over them both myself. Just made up my mind to be done with them." Or had it made up for me, he thought.

He let her off on the sidewalk right outside the church. She took her time lowering herself from the high seat of the truck and he was forced to endure a certain amount of ribbing from the other churchgoers streaming past him.

"Hey, Al, going to break a record and join us?"

"The Lord is waiting for you, Al, and He doesn't plan to wait forever."

He set his face and waited for Miss Yola to slam the door and wave before he took off, making his way slowly through the crowd, then slamming his foot to the floor when he was clear of the people. He was tempted to flick on the blue flashing light on the top of the truck to make it look as if he were about the business of policing this community, but that would start a whole lot of useless radio chatter that he didn't want to be bothered with this morning.

SAM HAD MADE coffee and scrambled eggs by the time Maggie got downstairs. Her face looked sad, sucked in on itself.

"I'm not sure I can eat," she said.

"It's the Italian blood in me. Whenever there's trouble, I cook. How about coffee?"

"Yes, please. That I need." She took one sip and then another.

"The birds on Gull Beach woke me," he said.

"Funny. When I first came, their carrying on got me up every morning. Now I barely notice them anymore. Same thing with the fog horn."

"We may have to rename the place soon," he said. "It used to be a prime nesting site for the herring gull, but in the last few years, the cormorants have taken over and are driving them out."

His chatter wasn't working. Her eyes had a glazed look. They were trained on him, but her mind was far away. He remembered their first meeting on the porch over a month ago. Her rapid-fire talk, one question right on top of the last, the list at hand, the way her foot had bounced up and down under the wicker couch. That kind of nervous energy always produced a counter-reaction in him, and if anything, he talked more slowly, moved more deliberately, as if by sheer force of example he could get the other person to slow down. But today, around her, he was the one who felt speeded up. The loss of Kasha seemed to have knocked her into stillness.

"I'm ready to go out looking again," he said. "Whenever you are."

"If we don't find her, how can I ever leave? Not knowing if she's alive or dead. First Nan drags me back here and now Kasha takes off. I'll never get off this damn island."

They were sitting across from one another at the narrow kitchen table. He put down his coffee cup and gathered up one of her pale cold hands between his.

"I can't go out again," she said. "I will soon. But I can't do it just yet. I think I need to be here alone."

"I understand," he said. He squeezed her hand once and got up to put the dishes in the sink.

"You don't need to bother with those," she said. "I'll do them later."

"I'll keep looking," he said on his way out. "Call me if you need anything."

From the front hall, he glanced back at her one more time. She was still sitting at the table in the cluttered kitchen. Her hands were covering her face and her shoulders had begun to shake.

"Maggie, I'll stay if you want," he called softly.

She shook her head back and forth without lifting it. He unlocked the front door and let himself out.

WHEN PEOPLE HAVE lived alone for a long time, it's a disturbance to their natural rhythms to bump up against other people. They are clumsy, talk too much, give away secrets they don't mean to. They go home and lie down with all sorts of regrets. Mostly this was an island of loners, of people who preferred their own company. Too much sociableness drove them back into their shells like hermit crabs.

Chuck knew he'd drunk only three beers the night before, and he knew he didn't give away much, but he also knew he had broken the unspoken island rule that you never handed outsiders any information. He told himself that Sam and Maggie were hardly outsiders, but that argument didn't hold much water. Technically, he himself was an outsider because he hadn't been born here. You were dealing with all levels of society on this one little place. First you had the people whose families had been here for generations. Then you had the ones whose parents were born here, then the ones who were born here themselves, then the ones who'd lived here for a considerable amount of time, at least twenty years or over. That's where Chuck fell in the pecking order. He was treated like an insider most of the time, and when he wasn't, it was mainly because he didn't go fishing with the other men, didn't show up at the Wednesday poker games, didn't drag his stool up to the bar at the Harbor Lounge too often except in the dead of winter when everything began to weigh on him.

He didn't give a damn what he'd said, except if those kids decided to mess where they didn't belong and it hurt Anna. Then he remembered the talk about Erin's bruise and he wondered. He wouldn't put anything past Al.

"Chuck?"

"Yeah, what?"

"I called your name three times," Anna said.

"Sorry."

"Kennel the dogs, will you? Murch wants to move down to the marsh. I told him we'd spotted pheasant down there last week."

"They've bagged eight for Chrissake." Chuck checked his watch. "Guess he doesn't want to make the four o'clock boat."

"He had his boat brought over this morning from the marina and he has a car on the other side. He doesn't need to worry about the ferries."

Anna was talking in a calm, contained voice as if she didn't want to waste any extra energy. She looked exhausted. Whistler had been restless, and when he didn't hold point, the bird flushed early and Murch's buddy had missed his shot. Murch went for the dog with the back of his hand and Anna had stepped between them. The man looked like he wanted to hit her even more than the dog. It had been a tense moment for everybody.

All Chuck knew was that this was the last place on earth he wanted to be. He was sick to death of people. He wanted to be sitting at his kitchen table with a beer and the football game on the radio and no reason to talk to another human being for at least a week.

Sometime after Sam left, Maggie walked into the front room, intending to rework the drawer runners in the Pembroke table. Work would make the time pass. It always did. She put the piece up on the table and stared at it for a long time, but she could not make herself start. Beyond it, on the bottom level of the bookshelf, Nan's photograph albums were piled in a messy tower. Every summer, Nan would set up an extra card table in the corner of the living room to do her albums. Maggie would sit on the couch near the one good lamp and read aloud from the books on her required summer list while Nan cut and glued and wrote captions in white ink on the black pages.

Maggie crawled over to the shelf and picked three books at random. In tailor position on the rug, she opened the first. July 12, 1970, the date read. Beach picnic at Chincoteale with the Alstons. Maggie sun worshipping. Maggie teaching little Sandy Alston how to body surf. The whole group on the rocks. Boiling mussels on the fire. Maggie eating mussels. Gag, Nan had written in capital letters.

She stared at the pictures, page after page of them. These were just the physical record. Nan was her real archive, the one who carried her history. Nan was the one who knew about the boyfriends. Rick, who bagged groceries in Island Foods the summer she was thirteen. Dan, the love of her seventeenth year, who had his own motorboat and took her waterskiing in the inlet one night under a full moon. When she'd come in at two A.M., Nan's light was still on.

"As long as I could hear the engine, I figured you were all right," she'd said at breakfast the next morning.

And there were other men, the ones after college, the doctor during graduate school, the romantic affairs in European hotels. Nan knew about all of them right up to the last one, Jack Riley, the man Maggie had almost married three years ago.

"Darling, I don't think you should do this," Nan had said after his third weekend on the island.

"Why?"

"Because he's missing the eccentric edge that passion produces in a man. He doesn't care deeply about anything. In the end, he will bore you."

Once Nan had pointed it out, Maggie could see nothing else. She broke the engagement two months later.

SEPTEMBER 6, 1972. *Maggie's Last Day.*

Nan had handed the camera to someone else. The two of them stood up on a freight flat with the ferry boat behind them, the cars backing their way on. Nan tall, one hand anchoring her straw hat, the other draped loosely around Maggie's shoulders. Maggie was dressed defiantly in blue jeans for the train trip home because Nan disapproved of them. But even at the rebellious age of fifteen, she was leaning close to Nan's body.

That was the summer her father had taken off without waiting to say good-bye. Late in July and again in August, she'd received those two casual postcards from out west. He said he'd seen a grizzly bear and was climbing mountains. California looked like a nice place to live, he'd written in the second one, as if it had all been settled between them that he would be finding another home.

Nan was the one who knew that Maggie cried late at night, that she slept with the postcards under her pillow.

"He'll be back by Christmas, won't he?"

"Magster, I don't think he will."

"Then when?"

"Maybe he won't be coming back at all."

"But Mom said he would."

"There's a difference," Nan had said, "between what you hope for and what will be."

And because Nan had always told her the truth, Maggie began to imagine a future that did not include her father.

"He stuck around longer than I thought he ever would," Nan said to her years later when they were staying in Paris in that little hotel on the rue de Varennes. "He married your mother for the wrong reasons."

"You mean for the money?"

"Yes, and when he knew for sure your grandparents were never going to give them any, he didn't bolt. He actually tried to make a go of it. I credit him for that."

"I credit him for nothing," Maggie said. By then, he'd been gone for twelve years.

HOURS LATER, MAGGIE was still sitting on the floor, the albums piled around her. Whenever she thought the tears had finally spent themselves, they would start again without any warning. Her head ached and she felt deep-down tired, the way she used to feel as a child when Nan had let her spend hours playing in the waves at Chincoteale.

She walked around the house twice calling for Kasha. On her way back in, she heard the phone and snatched it up on the third ring.

"Did you find her?" Maggie asked as soon as she heard Sam's voice.

"I thought maybe you had," he said. "I walked through the sanctuary just now and there was no sign."

"Oh, God, I was hoping—" she said, and her voice broke. He waited in silence as the tears came up again. She wasn't able to speak for a minute or two. It felt like hours.

"Breathe," he said at last. "It helps."

"Thanks, Sam. I've got to go. Thanks," she said again and put the receiver down quickly before the next wave hit her.

WHEN DARKNESS BEGAN to press in against the house, she groped her way up the stairs to Nan's bedroom on the third floor. She turned on the light and stared for a moment at the ancient perfume bottles on the marble-topped bureau and the books with markers piled on the bedside table. Through the south-facing window she saw a cluster of lights across the inlet along the road that led to the ferry. Year-round people lived there. Downstairs, from her west-facing window, all Maggie could see was the sweep of the dark ocean, and on a particularly clear night, the faint twinkle of lights from the mainland.

She unhooked Nan's white terry-cloth robe that was hanging on the back of the closet door and put it on right over her sweater and jeans. It had soaked up the smells of the house, a strange combination of mildew and wood fires. With two pillows propped behind her, and Nan's old satin comforter tucked around her chin, she trained her eyes on the lighted rooms across the way. If Kasha came and scratched on a kitchen door at one of those houses, somebody would get up from the sofa and go to see what the noise was.

"Isn't this the husky Sam was telling us about?" one would say.

"Maggie Hammond's dog?"

"That's right. I'll go call her."

She fell asleep sitting up with the phone on the mattress next to her hand.

IN THE MIDDLE of the night, Anna heard a dog howling. She thought at first that it was one of hers, but hunting dogs barked. They didn't howl. This was the long, slow lament of a wolf or a coyote. She lay still in the darkness, listening for it to come again and finally it did, closer this time. It set her own dogs to barking.

"What is it?" Al said, struggling up from sleep.

"Nothing. Just the dogs. I'll check on them."

She slipped into her mud boots and Al's thick jacket, which was hanging by the kitchen door. With a flashlight, she lit her way to the kennels and once inside, ordered her dogs into silence. They settled down uneasily. The howling was not a sound they were used to, and it had stirred them up.

She stood outside the kennel door in the cold air. The moon was full tonight, and when she turned off the light, she could see all the way across their yard to the trees around the Blair property. She knew it was the husky howling. There had been no wolves on the island since the days of the Mohegan Indians.

"Are you sure you want to come in, girl?" she called to the air. "She'll put that leash back on you."

Out of the corner of her eye, Anna saw something move in the underbrush.

"Kasha," she called softly. "Where are you?"

The dog trotted out on to the grass and lifted her nose as if to howl again.

"Don't do that," Anna said in a matter-of-fact voice. "You'll wake the whole neighborhood and then you're sunk."

The dog hesitated at the change in her tone of voice. She came closer to investigate and when Anna dropped to her haunches, Kasha bounded across the last space between them, but stopped just short of her.

"Not sure are you, girl? Well now, you've had yourself a time, haven't you? Out there roaming in the woods with everybody looking for you." The dog was still trailing a tattered scrap of the red leash. Her coat was filled with burrs and briars, and she was careful with the front left paw, allowed it to dangle above the ground when she came to a stop. Anna reached her hand out to take a look, but the dog warned her away with a low growl.

"Hungry?" she asked. "Stay here, then."

She came back from the kennel with a bowl full of dog food and another bowl of water and led Kasha away to the small shed off the garage where she kept the sick dogs.

The dog was obviously hungry, but she hesitated at the door of the shed. "I don't blame you, blue eyes," Anna said as she set down the bowls. "After a lifetime on a leash, it seems too early to come in again. How long have you had out there? It's not even two days since you took off."

Finally hunger and thirst got the better of the husky and she warily approached the bowl that Anna had placed inside the wire pen. Anna closed the door on her and latched it. Kasha turned her head at the sound of metal scraping against metal and gave Anna a long, slow look. Anna stared back into the two ice-blue eyes, a sign of high breeding in a husky. These were old, wise female eyes she was looking into, and she lost herself for a moment in the pool of them. This dog felt ancient to her, steady, sad, possessed of some knowing in her bones. Anna remembered the famous story of the Siberian huskies who ran the diphtheria medicine up to the town of Nome across God knows how many miles of frozen Alaska tundra. It was a favorite story of dog lovers, no matter which breed they handled. This dog was a descendant of those, dogs who were bred to run. And she had spent her whole life reined in, trotting down city streets at the end of a lead. Anna closed her eyes and opened them again to break the spell. Her vizslas did not make her feel this way. She was training them to perform exactly the job they had been bred for centuries to do. Until this last day and night, Kasha had never been allowed to run. It was the middle of the night and Anna knew she was tired, but it felt to her like an unbearable betrayal.

Anna turned out the light and left her there. "Sleep, Kasha. We'll figure something out in the morning." The dog's metal tags clinked against the bowl as she dropped her head to eat.

THE NEXT MORNING, after Erin and Al had left for school, Anna let herself into the shed with a basket of supplies. Kasha was lying on her side on the sleeping shelf in the pen. She lifted her head and looked at Anna.

"Why don't you let me take a look at that paw. I've brought the muzzle, but I'd rather not use it. Last thing I want to do is tie you up anymore."

Kasha scrabbled up to a sitting position. It was painful to watch her trying to line her arthritic hips up under her back.

"I have something that might help you with that pain," Anna said as if she were Dr. Lacey, talking to a patient who could answer. Anna had a magic voice with dogs. She talked, they listened, they calmed down.

Kasha allowed Anna to approach, rub her behind the ears. She leaned her head into Anna's touch as if to say, more, give me more, and Anna took a long time massaging her all over, pulling out the burrs where they'd become tangled in her thick fur. She slid her hand down to the injured paw and by that time, Kasha had fallen into a kind of trance.

"This isn't bad," she said, inspecting the dog's pads. "Looks like a shell cut. You were probably down on Chincoteale. Down by those rocks where the gulls drop their mussels. Good smells down there, girl?" Her voice soothed Kasha and the dog allowed her to bandage the wound. She fed her again, set out a bowl of water, then opened the door to the pen.

"This is it. I'm not going to be the one to lock you up again. You can stay or you can go. It's not my business." Kasha did not move, but stared at Anna, taking in her voice. "I think you should be allowed to run free. And that's all I have to say about it." Anna turned away and walked quickly to the truck. It was her morning at the post office. She took the black hat out from under the front seat, set it on her head and drove away without looking in the rearview mirror. The dogs started up their usual good-bye commotion, but they had quieted by the time she turned on to the main road.

Erin was surprised to see her mother sitting in her car outside of school.

"Hi, Mom. Why are you picking me up?"

"Remember, we have to go back to Dr. Lacey. He wants to check you out one more time and then he's going to teach you how to use the breathing meter."

"I hope it doesn't taste as gross as the inhaler."

"I don't think it tastes at all. How was school?"

Erin shrugged. "It was okay."

"Did you tell Katie about all the excitement this weekend?"

"Yeah. But suddenly she's hanging out with Patty Thayer. I hate Patty Thayer. She wears dark-red nail polish all the time. She sat with us at lunch and Katie kept whispering things to her that I couldn't hear."

Anna stayed silent. Her daughter was so intense about her friends, demanded so much of them, and burned through them quickly. Maybe it was because Erin was an only child. Anna didn't know, but it broke her heart to watch. She was convinced Erin would do fine in a bigger class. The school lost a few kids every year. People just didn't want to bring their children up on such a barren place.

Even the summer people recognized how dependent they were on the year-rounders, so a couple of years ago they'd started a housing fund to try and convince the younger couples to stay. So far they'd built seven houses and provided the buyers with low-interest loans, and that had helped a little. But still, except for the unexpected drop-in like Maggie Hammond, the circle of people on the island grew smaller every year.

Anna glanced over at her daughter, whose hand had slipped up to twist her hair.

"Swordfish," Anna said. It was the secret code they'd worked out to help Erin break the habit. She tucked her hands under her knees.

Where did Erin get that bruise? Anna wondered. She knew what the doctor was insinuating. Mentioning the fight with Al over the food. People were so ready to meddle in your business. Nobody really knew what went on behind closed doors, and these days they jumped to big soap opera conclusions about everything. Al loved his daughter the way he loved his wife. Maybe too much. He always wanted to be with them, wanted to know where they were, what they were doing. He worried all the time about Erin's weight. Anna knew other men who went off to the mainland for days at a time, got drunk, whored around. Al never did that. He stayed close by.

And worse things went on on this island. Everybody knew that Jerry Slocum hit his wife and he was the school superintendent. And Dan Malloy was pretty heavy-handed himself, especially in the winter when people got cooped up and began to act a little crazy. This was a man's island, and a lot of them didn't know how to behave. Al had never laid a hand on her. On either of them. He knew if he ever did that, she would be finished with him. If Dr. Lacey wanted to find some battered children, he'd better look somewhere else. She decided to be very curt with him today.

"Mom, you missed the turn."

"Whoops." Anna did a U-turn by the library and headed back down the hill. "My mind was somewhere else."

"Do you think Kasha is dead?" Erin asked out of the blue. "Do you think I killed her?"

"No, honey. You didn't kill her. She's fine."

"How do you know?"

"Because I know dogs." Actually, I know because I fed her and bandaged her paw and she may still be sleeping out in our pen. "I'm sure she's roaming around the island having herself a great time. Huskies are strong dogs. They were born and bred to run."

"I don't think Maggie will ever speak to me again."

Maggie, Anna heard. She didn't know that Erin was on a first-name basis with the red-haired woman.

"Of course she will."

"Can I try on your cowboy hat?"

Kids do U-turns all the time, Anna thought. "Sure." It was too big for Erin, fell down over her eyes.

"You look like Annie Oakley."

Erin handed it back. "It smells like the dogs," she said.

"It does?" Anna pulled over in front of the doctor's office and set the brake. "I don't smell it."

"Mom, you can't tell anymore because you're with the dogs all the time. All your clothes smell that way. So does the car."

Anna pulled up her sweater and sniffed it, then the sleeve of her jacket. Erin was right. Why hadn't she ever noticed that before? She rifled through the glove compartment for an old perfume vial she used to keep in there, one of the free samples that came in the mail. There were all sorts of advantages to working in the post office. She doused herself in it and followed Erin up the sidewalk.

Lauren wrinkled her nose and sniffed the moment they closed the outer door.

"What blew in here?" she asked. "Is that you, Erin, smelling so nice?"

Erin shook her head. "It's my mom. I told her she smells like the dogs so she put on some perfume."

Erin, please be quiet, Anna thought. She rolled her eyes at Lauren.

"Better than going to the dogs, kid. The doctor's ready for you."

Anna started in after her, but Erin waved her away. "Mom, I'm old enough to do this by myself."

Dr. Lacey was standing at the door to his office. She wondered if he'd heard the whole conversation about how she smelled. He must have.

"This won't take long, Mrs. Craven," he said. "I'll see you afterwards."

Anna settled into the chair by Lauren's desk. "Don't ever have any kids, Lauren. They send you to an early grave."

Lauren laughed. "Don't worry, it's not part of my life plan." She leaned across the desk and started whispering to Anna about the departure of the French wife.

"How do you know she left for good?" Anna asked. She hated to admit it, but she was interested. She never would have imagined this man with a sophisticated Frenchwoman. He seemed very quiet, kind, down to earth.

"I know. She came with a little bag, left with one. I saw him taking her down to the ferry. They are over, believe you me. I know the signs when I see them." Lauren was always talking about her knowledge of men, lording it over Anna. She knew Anna's limited sexual experiences. Basically it had been Al and a couple of men when he was off in the navy, experiments because she was already engaged to Al then, and she didn't want to die having slept with only one man. God knew how many men Lauren had slept with. When Anna asked her once, she laughed and said she'd given up counting long ago.

"This is going to be one very lonely man, come winter. February. All that ice on the roads. When fishing season is over." Lauren's eyes were shining with excitement. "I'm on this new diet I read about in *Woman's Day* magazine. By that time, I'll have taken off another eight or ten pounds."

Anna was suddenly irrationally irritated. She'd listened to this a hundred times before, all Lauren's plans to snare the latest man, available or not. Anna even wondered sometimes if Al might have slept with her, gone down to see her when Anna refused him. Lauren took it on herself to "keep the island men happy" as she liked to say. And a lot of the island wives were grateful to her for it. But this time Anna didn't want to hear about it. Her mind flashed to Lauren rolling around in that narrow bed next door with the doctor and his lilting accent and his kind gray eyes, and she was revolted. He would never do that. He was a sophisticated New York doctor. She didn't know what in God's name brought him to this island, but she couldn't imagine he'd be desperate enough to sink to Lauren Root. But then she knew she was naive. According to Lauren, men had to "have it" no matter what. They weren't like women.

"Maybe you shouldn't get your hopes up, Lauren. He seems to have a taste for skinny foreign women. You're not exactly the type."

But Lauren was unfazed. "I'll bring him around. In the dead of winter, a man needs some nice warm flesh to hold on to, not just a bag of bones."

"Mrs. Craven."

Anna started up guiltily. God, she hoped he hadn't heard any of this conversation. "You can wait in the other room, Erin. I want to explain to your mother exactly what I told you."

"Why can't I stay too?"

"Erin," Anna said quickly. "That's enough."

Erin shrugged and slid into the seat at Lauren's desk. "Do you have some nail polish here?" Anna heard her asking Lauren as she closed the doctor's office door behind her.

"I'm sorry. Erin seems to have turned into a teenager in the last month. I'm finding it difficult to take."

The doctor flipped through her chart and did a quick calculation. "Thirteen and a half. Right on schedule. Does she have her period yet?"

It was a routine question, but it made the blood rush to Anna's neck. She was glad she was wearing a scarf. "Not yet."

"I expect it'll be any time soon. Sit down." She did and he did, and there they were again in the same places they were on Saturday. "How was the weekend?" he asked, and she couldn't think for a minute what he was asking about. Her problems with Ben Murch or finding Kasha?

"The weekend?"

"With Erin. Any more attacks?"

"No. She was fine. She's been using the inhaler four times a day."

"Good. I'm glad the Theophylline did the trick. Now here's what I'm suggesting." He leaned toward her and began talking about the Peak Flow Meter and the new inhaler he'd prescribed, but she found it hard to concentrate. She was remembering his stories about the graveyard and the sweet shop, and she wondered what he did all day Sunday with no patients and no emergencies. He'd barely finished his explanation when she asked.

"And how was your weekend, Doctor?"

"Mine? Fine. I didn't need the inhaler at all." He grinned. "I took my easel out to the eastern point. By the lighthouse."

"You're a painter?"

"A weekend painter, I guess you'd call it. Sometimes I wish I were a weekend doctor and a full-time painter. But 't'wasn't in the cards. How long has the lighthouse been shut down?"

"Since the twenties. A young couple bought it just two years ago. They're totally redoing the place." She was surprised to hear her voice jabbering on like this. She'd never been prone to small talk. Except for Chuck and the shorthand they'd developed over a dog's back, she couldn't remember when she'd had a regular conversation like this with a man. She kept it up. "You must find our island a little dull. After New York and all." After your sophisticated life and your well-dressed wife.

He considered her question. "I was ready for a little dullness, to be honest. It suits my temperament better than the constant hustle of the city. The western coast of Ireland can be very dull. Besides, I'm a beachwalker from way back."

"Me too," she said. "It's an easy way to run the dogs." She should stand up now. The doorbell had jangled some time ago, which meant someone was in the waiting room. Erin would be restless and Lauren would definitely be wondering what was going on in here. That thought made her grin. "I train hunting dogs," she said. "Vizslas and pointers."

"So I understand. A vizsla is a Hungarian dog, isn't it?"

She nodded.

"I met a man up in Millbrook, New York, who hunts them. Trains them too, I think."

"Jonathan Taylor," she said.

"Yes, that's it."

"He's good," she said. "I used to run into him at the field trials, but I don't do those anymore. Only the hunting tests."

"Isn't that amazing," he said, getting to his feet. "Well, I'd much rather sit here and talk to you, but I think another patient is waiting."

She was flustered now and remembered that she had intended to be curt with him. "I didn't mean to take so much time."

" 'T'was my pleasure. Perhaps we'll meet on a beach sometime," he said. "My favorite is Chincoteale."

She didn't say anything.

"I've phoned in the prescription for the Intal. It should be on the morning boat."

They stood across the desk from each other. In New York at the big hospital, he would shake hands with a patient's mother. That seemed ridiculous here. Here they would cross paths in the grocery store or at the post office. "Till soon, then," he said.

Erin was waiting in the car so Anna just waved at Lauren as she walked by. Lauren gave her a look that said, I'll call you later and what took so long and why is your face red?

Ten

KASHA WAS GONE when they got home. Anna put another bowl of food in the open pen and replenished the water. Good for you, she said to the air. She tried not to think about Maggie Hammond, who must be sick with worry about her dog, and her own daughter who thought she'd killed Kasha. She was just giving her a few more hours or days of freedom. Someone else was sure to pick her up along the road soon. Or down on Chincoteale. The doctor, for example. He walked all the time on Chincoteale.

She was glad Al was not home yet as she went about cooking dinner. She liked having the time alone to herself to mull over her conversation with the doctor. Al was uncanny the way he seemed to know when she was thinking about something she didn't want to tell him. Lately, there'd been less and less to say to him. She woke up in the morning and lay in bed running through the safe topics of conversation, the ones that wouldn't make him critical or suspicious or start him on some harangue about this person or that.

SHE WAS STANDING at the sink, rinsing off the carrots for dinner, when she heard Al's truck pull in the driveway. The dogs started up as usual when his door slammed, but then she heard him shouting, "What in God's name? Go. Get the hell away from me," and she ran out the door, a carrot still in her hand.

Kasha had him up against the side of the truck. She was baring her teeth and growling, a low careful growl that erupted every so often into a series of short, warning barks. Al didn't move. He was terrified of dogs, always had been.

"Get her away from me," he yelled at Anna. "Hurry up. The goddamned wolf is going to bite me."

"She won't, Al," Anna said, but she wasn't so sure. She tossed the carrot away and walked slowly up from behind. "Kasha," she warned in a low voice. "Come on, Kasha." The dog didn't move and didn't take her eyes off Al. From the kennels came the frenzied barking of the hunting dogs, and the noise seemed to egg Kasha on. She growled again and then darted at him, her teeth snapping. The movement was lightning fast. Anna was glad Al was wearing boots.

"Anna," Al screamed, his voice rising. She'd never heard him sound so scared.

"Kasha," she said again, this time sharper.

Up above, Erin pushed her window open. "Kasha," she cried. "You came back."

The dog paid no attention to Erin. Anna didn't look up or answer either. All her energy was focused on the husky. "Kasha. Come here. Right now." Anna's voice was firm, the one she used when she trained the one-year-olds. The dog backed off from Al, but the hair on her back was still standing up straight. Anna approached, put a hand on her collar and Kasha whipped her head around with another snap. She missed Anna's wrist. "Stop it, Kasha," Anna said. She knew the dog didn't mean to bite her. Now that she was restrained, she let loose with a series of short barks and growls, lunging at Al.

"What in God's name is wrong with that bitch?" he said as he edged away. "She's dangerous. She should be put down."

"There's nothing wrong with her," Anna shouted, louder than she meant to. "She's been out in the woods for two days. She's probably just hungry."

"Just get her the hell away from me. If I see her again, I'll shoot her."

"Al, stop it. Stop it right now." She had never spoken to him like this before. He gave her a bewildered look and went inside with a slam of the kitchen door.

"Mom, are you going to take her back to Maggie now?" Erin called from her window.

"Yes, I guess so." With Al out of sight, Kasha had settled down, but Anna didn't dare let go of her collar. She could take off again.

"Can I come?"

"Sure. Bring a jacket for me. And one of those leads from the front hall closet. It's cold out here and I don't want to let her loose."

"Well, old girl, guess you've got to give up your roaming ways. Bad timing. If that hadn't happened, I might have bought you a few more days." Anna lifted Kasha into the front seat of the station wagon. Erin looked nervously in the passenger's window.

"Will she bite me?"

"No, she's settled down. Open the door slowly and put your hand out for her to sniff."

Erin did as she was told. Kasha dropped her head, sniffed Erin's hand and then licked it once.

"Good dog," Erin said. "This is the way she's been with me before. Why was she so crazy with Dad?"

Anna started the motor. "I don't know. I expect she's had some bad experience. Maybe with someone who looks like your father. Dogs have memories."

Erin chattered happily on the ride to Maggie's house about how glad the woman was going to be to see Kasha. The dog lowered herself down and hung her head over the edge of the front seat. Anna drove with a hand lost in the thick ruff of her neck fur. Strands of gray and black dog hair floated upward on the air currents circulating from the heating vent.

"She sheds a lot," Erin said.

"Is it making you wheeze?"

"Not really," Erin said. Which meant it was. "Not really" was Erin's answer when she didn't want the asthma to stop her from doing something. "I used the inhaler three times already today."

"I'll vacuum the car tomorrow. We're almost there. Better not touch her."

MAGGIE WAS SITTING on the floor of the workroom when she heard the front door push open. She thought she'd locked it.

"Sam?" she called. "Chuck?"

With a warning bark, Kasha trotted into the room and dropped into a half pounce just out of Maggie's reach.

"Kasha." Without moving, she put her hands out to catch the dog. Kasha skittered out of reach and barked again. She always played this game when they first saw each other. "Come here, Kasha, please, don't play with me." When Kasha heard the tone in Maggie's voice, she crept forward and pushed her nose into Maggie's chest. Maggie dropped her head onto the dog's neck. "I thought I'd never see you again," she whispered and began to cry. Kasha whimpered and held still as the tears slid down into her thick black-and-white coat. The two of them stayed that way for a long time.

Finally Maggie looked up. "Who's there?" she called.

"It's me and my mom," Erin said, coming forward into the lighted room. "We brought her back."

"I don't know how to thank you. Where did you find her?"

"She found us," Anna said. "I expect the noise of my dogs brought her in. She's got a cut on her front left paw. From a shell. It's not too bad. I put something on it. Other than that, she seems fine."

"I've been desperate," Maggie said as she got to her feet. "I thought she was dead."

"There's one more thing," Anna said. "She really went after my husband tonight out in the yard. I expect he surprised her. She had him pinned up against the truck."

"She can be unpredictable around men. Particularly if they come at her suddenly. It's gotten worse with age. I'm so sorry."

"Be prepared for people's reactions," Anna said. "It won't take long for Al to alert the island. He thinks she's a wolf." She didn't tell Maggie the rest of what he said.

"My dad is scared of dogs," Erin explained. "He got bitten when he was little."

"That must be difficult," Maggie said, glancing up at Anna. "Since your mother trains them." Anna's eyes revealed nothing.

"I'd better feed her. Would you like some coffee?"

"No thanks, we have to get back," Anna said, but she trailed along behind Maggie into the kitchen. "I have some medicine that seems to work for arthritis. One of my older dogs has dysplasia and it's helped him. Come on by if you want some."

"Thanks, I will," Maggie said. She set the bowl down. Kasha sniffed and looked up at her. "Go on, silly dog. Nobody's looking at you. We'd better get out of here. She won't eat with people watching."

"After a few days, you might consider letting her run wild," Anna said. "I'm sure she'd come back."

"Mrs. Craven—"

"Anna."

"Anna, then. I couldn't possibly do that. She'll be thirteen years old this year and she's never been off the lead. She's not trained to voice commands. I don't want to lose her again." Maggie's voice broke and she covered her mouth with her hand. "Sorry. It's been a long couple of days."

"I don't mean to intrude. It's just that huskies are runners. Sled dogs. No matter how much exercise you give her—" Anna stopped. "If you would like me to try training her, I'd be happy to."

"Thanks," Maggie said. "I'll think about it."

ANNA WAS RELUCTANT to leave. Chuck had told her about this house, but she'd never been inside it before and she was stunned by the clutter of the place. She often struck up a conversation with old Mrs. Phipps when they crossed paths, usually at the thrift shop in the basement of the Catholic church. They'd talked about the dogs and the weather and the gardens, but one time, the old lady had looked at her sharply and said, "You don't need to dress that little girl out of these bins of moldy old clothes. Your husband is a very rich man. You get Al Craven to give you some of that money he gets from the summer owners on this island and you take her over to the mainland for a real shopping spree." It had been such a personal comment out of the blue that Anna never forgot it. The next time they met, the old lady seemed to have forgotten what she'd said. They went back to talking about the weather.

"Would you like a tour?" Maggie asked.

"We should be getting back," Anna said again weakly.

"It won't take long."

"Please, Mom, can we?" Erin cried, and she started up the stairs before her mother could stop her. "Jimmy Slade told me this house has ghosts."

"I never heard that," Maggie said.

"Old island rumors," Anna said. "But you're brave. I don't think I'd want to sleep here alone, ghosts or no ghosts."

"I didn't think I would either, but I've gotten used to it." In the last few days, the house had wrapped itself around Maggie like an old quilt. She'd found it hard to go outside.

"I understand you're fixing it up to sell it," Anna said.

"Well, yes, that was my intention," Maggie said slowly. "But it's all taking longer than I had expected. There's so much to do. Come on, I'll show you."

Maggie took them through all the rooms on the second floor, and Erin skipped around, touching the trinkets on the bureaus, opening closet doors, sliding on the loose rag rugs that lay scattered here and there. Anna let her be. She was fascinated herself. The house felt like some kind of museum. The hallways were dim, the tables draped with antique lace tablecloths, the flower prints spotted with damp. Some of the light switches turned like a dial on a stove instead of flicking up and down. At the bottom of the stairs, the portrait of a thin, dark-haired man dressed in the uniform of some foreign army stared out at them from a simple gold frame.

"Who's that?" Anna asked.

"Nan's younger brother. He died in South Africa under myste- rious circumstances. She adored him, but would never talk about what happened."

"Maybe he's haunting the place," Erin said.

"Erin, enough," Anna said.

"I am so sorry about your father," Maggie said suddenly. "I've been meaning to tell you."

Anna couldn't think what to say. She'd barely thought about her father at all except to remind herself of the absence of him, of the space she'd found in her life now that she no longer worried about his debts and his boat and the gambling. Funny too how quickly that space got filled up with other worries.

"I'm sorry you were the one who had to find him," Anna finally said in a low voice. Erin clattered up to the third floor. "It must have been a terrible shock."

"He looked peaceful."

"I'm glad," Anna said. "He needed some peace. We all did."

The phone rang and Maggie disappeared into a bedroom to an- swer it. "Come on, Erin," Anna called. "We've really got to go." As she waited for Maggie to come back, she imagined herself rattling around in this huge place all alone. Nobody to cook for, worry about, compromise with. Would she be lonely living this way? she won- dered. Or scared? Or just relieved? Probably all of the above.

"What's this chair on the stairs?" Erin called from up above.

"It's a riding chair," Maggie said as she came back out of the room. "It's your husband on the phone," she told Anna. "You can take it right in there."

"Do you have any idea what time it is, Anna? What in God's name are you doing?" She kept the receiver pressed tight against her ear, hoping that Maggie couldn't hear his booming voice all the way out in the hallway. "Yes, Al, I'm coming right now. I'll be there soon. I promise." She hung up. "I had no idea it was so late."

"It's only seven-thirty," Maggie said.

"Erin," Anna said sharply, "you've got to come down right now."

"How do I work it, Maggie?" Erin called.

"Push the black button on the side."

The old wooden chair began to rumble down its track from the third floor to the second.

"My godmother put that in a few years ago so she could go on sleeping on the third floor," Maggie said as they stood watching Erin's progress. "There's a beautiful view of the island from up there."

Anna wanted to snatch Erin off the chair and race to the car. Breathe, she told herself. So the man's dinner was late. What was the big deal? But she knew she'd have to pay, not for the late dinner so much as for the shouting in the yard. The shouting that Erin witnessed. Anna didn't remember ever speaking to Al that way.

Erin wanted to ride the chair from the second floor to the first so they walked slowly down behind her to where Kasha was waiting at the bottom of the stairs.

They said their good-byes and Anna hurried Erin out to the car. She drove faster than usual.

"Mom, what's the rush?" Erin said.

"I haven't even started dinner," Anna said. "I completely forgot the time."

"Big deal," Erin said and turned on the radio.

But Anna's heart was pounding as if she were rushing to a crisis, a burning building or a car accident. She wanted to believe that if she just got there in time, she'd be able to head Al off, talk him out of the ugly mood that she knew was brewing, like one of those summer storms that seemed to come without any warning.

HE STARTED YELLING out the kitchen door before Anna had even turned off the car engine. "What were you doing?"

"We took Kasha back to Maggie's," Erin said.

"I know that. You've been gone an hour at least."

"We got distracted," Anna said as she slipped past him into the kitchen. "Maggie gave us a tour of the house. What's this?" Papers were strewn all over the kitchen table.

"Latham called. He wants me to bid on the new house he's finally going to build on that land above Chincoteale."

Anna took a deep breath. That's all it was. Al and money again. He always got this riled up when money was involved, especially when there was the possibility of making some more.

"So that's good, Al," she said as she dropped the unpeeled carrots in a pot and turned the heat on under it.

"I'm bidding against an off-island contractor. You know what that's like. I'll never get my prices down as low as the other guy. And we really need this job."

"You'll get the job," she told him. "Latham likes the way you handled those burst pipes on his other house last winter." And he likes my work too, she thought. He's promised to give me another dog to train this year now that Cinnamon's gotten too old to hunt.

But Al went worrying on, shuffling papers here and there, muttering to himself about why he wasn't going to get the job, while she moved quietly around the kitchen fixing dinner.

"We are really going to be scraping the bottom of the barrel this winter, Anna."

"Al, don't be ridiculous. You're doing the community center on top of all the other work."

"The community center? What a joke. I came in so low on that job, I'll never make a dime on it. What other work? Some reshingling. A roofing. That wing for the Winslows."

"But, Al, that's more work than all the other contractors on the island put together." Be quiet, Anna. Butter the potatoes. Get out the silverware. Let him rant on. He didn't want to be convinced. He liked to worry about money, to act as if they were always on the edge of some financial crisis. It seemed to make him feel important.

"Goddammit, Anna"—this with a crash of his fist on the table— "stop arguing with me. I know what I'm doing here. Just shut up for once and let me talk without interrupting all the goddamn time."

Anna closed her eyes and leaned against the sink. Her whole life she had listened to men talking in kitchens while she got their dinner ready. The last few years her mother was alive, she had been confined to her bed. Anna was chopping carrots and peeling potatoes when she should have been playing with dolls.

He was still talking. Okay, Al. I won't say another word. I won't tell you you're completely crazy about money. I won't tell you what I'm hearing down in town about the community center, that your price wasn't all that low after all and why aren't you pushing full time on that job for a change? Isn't it time to put your neighbors ahead of those rich summer owners who don't even need their house till next spring?

"Dinner's ready," she called up the stairs to Erin, cutting right through one of Al's sentences.

THERE WERE SIX swimming beaches on the island. One of them, at the easternmost end, was private, taken over by the exclusive country club built at the turn of the century. It was referred to simply as the club beach, and only members were allowed. Everybody who went there had to sign in at the office. The three beaches at the western end in walking distance of the ferry were available to day-trippers in the summer, but since there were no bicycle rentals, no real restaurants, and no published map of the island, day-trippers were rare. If some adventurous group should happen to stop at the ferry office on the mainland side to ask for information about the island, the boat crew was notoriously unhelpful and suggested they try the ferry to Robin Island. A longer ride, but more to see at the other end.

The beach that faced the yacht club used to be called Poor Man's Beach. At some point the name began to sound embarassing even to the old-timers who were used to it, so it was changed by informal decree to Murray's Beach after the family who owned the land around it. At low tide you had to walk for miles to get your knees wet. The sand felt more like mud and you were just as likely to put your foot down on the jagged edge of an oil can tossed over the side of a boat as on a crab. The water had never been tested, but it looked murky even to children, and you thought twice before you put your face in it. Around the corner, Periwinkle Beach had a float and a net to keep out the jellyfish and was used mainly by the year-rounders, who arranged for their children to have swimming lessons there in the summers. Further up island, Starfish Beach was spurned by the teenagers and frequented by the elderly members of the community, summer and winter, because the surf there was never as high as on Chincoteale.

Of all the island's beaches, Chincoteale was the most dramatic, dominated by high white cliffs that looked straight out across the Atlantic. On a clear day, you could see Portugal if your binoculars were strong enough. Chincoteale was the beach that got the best surf on the island, but over the years the winter storms had sucked away all but a thin strip of sand. In the summer, the beach was often lined with grumpy vacationers huddled on their towels in the six feet of sand the sea allotted them at high tide. They couldn't afford to lie down soaking up the sun, but had to crouch like watchdogs, one eye on the approaching waves, their books and suntan lotion and bags safely tossed out of reach onto the rocks behind them.

In the late afternoons, Anna had always run her dogs, two at a time, on Starfish because it was the closest to the field where she took them for their evening training sessions, and she could park the car right next to the boardwalk. Soon after her conversation with the doctor, she began taking them down to Chincoteale instead, and they were wild with excitement at this new development, tumbling over each other down the long sandy path to the beach. She didn't make any pretenses about it to herself. She hoped to run into the doctor, talk to him some more. She liked talking to a man who listened. Even a year ago, she might not have done this. But she was changing. Perhaps she actually felt no lonelier than she did last year at this time, when the dwindling light and the coming cold and the company of people she had known her whole life were closing in on her. But this year, with her father gone and Erin turning into a silent teenager, she could no longer push away the feeling of a dark hole in the center of her life.

On the third afternoon, the doctor hailed her with a shout as he loped down the path.

The wind was biting, and she had pulled her hat low over the tops of her ears. The dogs, Shooter and Paprika, were racing each other to the far end of the beach. She had her whistle in her mouth, but dropped it when she called hello.

"Now this is real Irish weather," he said, rubbing his hands together as he strode up to her. His cheeks were two red spots and he was wearing a tweed cap.

"This cold?"

"Ah yes, when the wind blows off the ocean like this. Very little snow of course, but we get this wind and the dampness."

"We'll probably have snow sometime before Christmas," she said. "But the ocean tempers it. We don't get the huge drifts they have on the mainland."

"Were you just leaving?" he asked.

"No," she lied. "The dogs are taking their run up ahead."

They fell into step next to each other. She blew two toots on the whistle, and the dogs came tearing back, circled around them, and at a nod from her, tore off again.

"Oh, to be able to run like that," he said.

"These are two of the younger ones. Paprika is not yet steady to wing and shot so I take her out with Shooter who can teach her some manners. Sometimes it backfires and he starts breaking point so I have to take him out with Polly to pull him back into line. Polly's a pointer. She's my star."

"I knew a man who had pointers in England. He said they were pure hunting dogs. Nothing else on their minds but the birds."

"True. That's why I like the vizslas. They're more of an all-around dog, good pets if you're willing to run them as often as they need it."

"How long have you been doing this?"

She told him all about it, how she had gotten bored with teaching fourth grade in the island school and had always been good with animals, and when Dick Monroe finally grew too old to keep it up, his son had already moved over to the mainland so Dick agreed to train her. "At first, the men in the hunting club weren't happy with the idea of a woman trainer and handler, but most of them have gotten used to it. They don't have much choice." She wanted to tell him how good she was, how she trained dogs for breeders up and down the coast, how well her dogs performed in their hunting tests. But she didn't. She felt she'd been talking too much already. They had walked the length of the beach once and were headed back.

"You must be good," he said.

"You have to be or you don't get the business. So now, how about you? How'd you get into the doctoring business?"

He seemed as eager to talk as she. He had never wanted to be a doctor, but it was his mother's wish. He won a scholarship to Trinity College, Dublin, and then to medical school.

"What kind of doctor are you?"

"Pediatric cardiologist."

"Heart," she said.

"Kid's hearts."

She winced. "That must be hard."

"Actually it's not. Kids are fixable. There's so much you can do with these problems if you catch them young enough."

"So why are you stuck out here for a year? You might end up with a heart attack, but it's most likely to be one of the old-timers."

"It's a long story," he said.

"You don't have to tell me." She whistled for the dogs again to cover her embarassment. She hated to be thought of as nosy.

"I don't mind. It's just a dull medical story. There was a boy, is a boy, I should say, a patient of mine who needed a very complicated heart operation. The best specialist for his kind of problem was a surgeon in Texas. The insurance company refused to pay for the boy to have the operation done out of state. I went on the line and told them it was necessary and the boy would die if this surgeon did not do the work. They were forced to pay."

"What was wrong with that?"

"Nothing," he said. "It was absolutely the right thing to do. But the hospital administration was furious with me because they had just signed a special deal with this insurance company. The insurance company wanted me fired."

"What happened?"

"I took a year off, came here." He shrugged. "It was fine, actually. I needed some time to think. About all sorts of things. I may not want the life I have anymore."

"All of it?"

"Most of it. New York, medicine, my marriage. Actually, that's over. My wife just told me officially when she came to visit this weekend. This place would never suit her. But it's been over for a while."

She thought of telling him she was sorry, but she wasn't. Maybe if I can't tell the truth, she thought, I'll try not saying anything at all.

They had arrived back at the foot of the path. She only had an hour of daylight left to work with the dogs. She whistled again, but this time ordered the dogs to stay. They lowered their haunches, eyes on her, tongues hanging out and dripping.

"Impressive," he said. "I'm going to take one more turn. Hope I didn't bore you."

"Not at all."

She released the dogs with one blast and they scrambled up the hill ahead of her. She was not aware that he was standing and watching her until she turned around to get a last look at him. He waved first and she waved back. The look of a man taking the time to watch her, to watch Anna Craven walk up a hill and then to wave at her, she carried that picture in her head like a secret treasure through the rest of the day and into the night. Later on, lying under Al, she conjured it up again, kept her mind fixed on that one picture while Al did what he wanted with her body, took what he felt had been due him for weeks.

———

THE NEXT TIME Maggie saw Sam, she was backing her car onto the ferry under Chuck's direction. Kasha was curled up in her usual circle on the second seat. Sam walked along beside her open window. She'd phoned him to tell him Kasha was back, but they hadn't seen each other.

"This feels strange," Maggie said. "Whenever I did this before it meant I was going for a while."

"And this time?"

"Only a few days. I need to pick up some warmer clothes and my veneering tools. I'm up to my eyeballs in Nan's furniture. Every time I go up to the attic I find more." She was trying to look at him and keep her eye on Chuck's upraised right hand at the same time.

"Left a little more," Chuck called. "Sam, stop distracting her."

"He's not distracting me," Maggie called back. "I'm doing fine. By the way, I called Woodworth this morning."

"Are you going to do the survey?" he asked.

She nodded.

"And you'll be staying the winter?"

"Well, I'll be staying as long as it takes. All of it. The house, the furniture, the survey. Two or three months at least."

"Yes!" he shouted, as if he'd been waiting for just this piece of news. He pounded once on the side of the car. "That's great. Drive safely," he called when he made room for Chuck.

"Back it up real slow," Chuck said. "What's the good news?"

Maggie grinned. "I'm sticking around a while longer."

"Now that is good news," he said. "Stop it right there and set your brake," he added as he went off to pick up the next car.

THE NEXT NIGHT Sam left for a weekend off island. Every so often, he did this, took himself away to a place where nobody knew him. This time he fixed on Providence, and on the way there, he left one new specimen with McGiffin, the taxidermist. It was a lesser yellow-legs that he'd found washed up at the edge of Barley Marsh. The museum already had a stuffed version, but it must have been done some time ago. One glass eye had slipped, and the tail feathers had begun to disintegrate. At the same time he picked up the gadwall he'd left there at the beginning of the summer. He had some other specimens at home, but he was careful not to overwhelm McGiffin. The man was good, but he was well past seventy now and got fussed if you tried to rush him.

He dropped by to see the archaeologist who was making arrangements for a new dig to start on the island in May, but the man had forgotten their appointment and was out somewhere in the field. Sam didn't mind. They could do their business on the phone. He reached Providence at dusk and to his delight, found a market in the Italian section of town with the kind of food he could never get on the island. Sun-dried tomatoes, peasant bread that he could freeze, a hunk of Parmesan that would last the winter, flageolet beans, anchovies, his favorite brand of risotto rice, and two pounds of red peppers that he would roast and store in oil and garlic. In the afternoon, he took in an old Bogey movie and spent the rest of his evening shooting pool. He had a good time, but as usual, he began to miss the island sooner than he wanted to admit. On Sunday, he took off in time to catch the afternoon ferry, happy to leave behind the noise and the grime and the tacky malls. On the mainland, as far as he could see, nobody knew your business and nobody much cared. That was the best and the worst part about it. That's what he was looking for when island living got to him and that was also what he was glad to leave behind.

"Good weekend, Sam?" Dan Chester asked him when he backed him on the boat. There were only two cars going over. Typical Sunday afternoon traffic off-season.

"Fine," said Sam. "How about you?"

"About the same as usual. Not much traffic over and back this weekend and next weekend I'm off. Listen, I've been meaning to tell you. I saw a seal on those rocks off Stony Point."

"I'll walk out there this afternoon and take a look."

"I see you brought a friend," Dan said, nodding at the passenger seat. "Who's that?"

"A gadwall. Randy found him up at the eastern end last spring. He was in good shape. He turned out well, didn't he?" Sam lifted the box so Dan could get the full effect.

"Looks fine to me. Set your brake. Time to get this boat moving."

Like it or not, I'm home, Sam thought as he made his way up to the deck for the ride over.

Eleven

DURING THE HOLIDAY stretch from Thanksgiving to New Year's, the people on the island reached out to each other. It was a long-standing tradition that Thanksgiving dinner was served at the community center, and there was considerable grumbling when the notice went up on the bulletin board in the post office from Craven Construction that the event would be held yet again in the basement of the Catholic church "due to unforeseen weather delays."

Diane Thayer, the full-time postmistress, was treated to a steady stream of disgruntled remarks from the local citizenry. Luckily the notice was posted on a Tuesday, not one of Anna's regular days at the post office. Al Craven kept out of people's way most of that week.

"What in hell does this mean? Driest weather we've had in years."

"It means that Al is putting in all his time on that Davidson house up island. More money in that. Have you seen the kitchen that man is installing? Solid granite floor."

"Al better remember who hired him for the community center."

"Yeah"—this with a snort—"the community."

DIANE REMINDED EVERYBODY to sign up on that same bulletin board the week before Thanksgiving for their contributions to the meal. Anything was welcome, a dish as big as a cooked turkey or as small as the roasted chestnuts Chuck was known for. There were other traditions they had come to count on year after year. Annie Slocum always brought her famous creamed carrots mixed with sweet potatoes, Sam provided a good number of the pies, and Miss Yola usually could be prevailed upon to sing "Amazing Grace." The whole room got real quiet for that, even the little kids chasing around in the back. The oldest member of the community stood up and read off the names of the people who had died in the preceding year. For the last four years, it had been Wilfred Hines who read the list. He was ninety-four years old, and his daughter Louise, who took care of him (she was seventy-one and not in such great shape herself), helped him to his feet and stood behind him propping him up. The list was short this year. Katherine Lawrence, the former librarian who'd been living in a nursing home over on the mainland for the last ten years, John Burling, and Nan Phipps. Maggie was sitting next to Dennis Lacey, and he took her arm as they got to their feet with the rest of the crowd. The entire assemblage raised their glasses and drank in silence. Chuck Montclair caught Maggie's eye, and they both raised their glasses a second time in honor of Nan. There was a general scraping of chairs and shuffling of feet as the group found their seats again, which opened the room back up to general conversation. Dennis and Maggie were clearly welcome at this occasion, but they were also glad to be elbow-to-elbow as the two outsiders. The only other rank newcomer was Randy Baker's girlfriend, Ellie, who was shunning her parents' annual family get-together to come here. She knew she would have to visit with them at least once over the weekend. It would be the first time since a nasty shouting match on the ferry dock over Labor Day and she was nervous. She and Randy left early.

Many of the summer owners had come back for their last long stretch of time until spring house cleaning. Extra ferries were sched-uled, and Al issued a certain number of tickets for speeding just to remind everybody that someone was definitely in charge, even though he was the only winter replacement for the two state troopers stationed on the island from June through September. Saturday night, he had to take two of the kids in for drunken driving, but as usual the parents slipped him some money to be sure the names were kept off the record. Luckily nobody had been killed since that Murray boy hit a telephone pole six, seven years ago.

The summer and the winter people mingled more this time of year. They met over drinks at Lila's and shot a friendly game of pool. The teenagers raised hell together although, because of the cold, they were forced to do it inside, not around the bonfires on Chincoteale the way they did in the summer. The year-round kids actually got invited to some of the bigger houses for parties down in the basement. Unless they got drunk and loose-tongued, they never did let on that they partied in these places all winter long, especially the houses where the owners left the heat on instead of draining the pipes. By the time you got through ninth grade in the island school, the older kids had taught you how to get into every summer house on the place—which windows were left unlocked, or whose father was the caretaker and where he kept the keys.

For a few days, the island felt almost as crowded as it did on an August weekend, but when Monday came around the summer owners were all gone again. In the grocery store, the year-rounders congratulated themselves on surviving the onslaught, but truth was, most of them hated the way the silence settled back down on them like a shroud. The darkness was rolling in earlier every day, like waves on an incoming tide.

ANNA KNEW SHE was being reckless. She and Dennis Lacey managed to run into each other on the beach two or three afternoons a week, earlier and earlier as the light failed. Nothing happened between them except conversation, but she was a good judge of the gossip barometer on the island. The doctor had been late responding to a couple of calls because he liked to leave his radio in the car, and Lauren was already curious and had wondered out loud where he went in the afternoons. The fact that Anna pretended not to know meant that she was telling a kind of lie. Every so often she walked the dogs over from her house because she knew people would take notice if her station wagon and his Mercedes were parked near each other at the top of the Chincoteale hill too often.

Dennis himself was aware that he was being foolish. For all her confidence and experience with the dogs, Anna Craven was an innocent woman who had spent very little time off this island. She didn't talk about her marriage, but he'd heard that she and Al were high school sweethearts, and he wondered whether she'd ever slept with another man. She was hungry for his stories of life as a student in Dublin, of trips to Europe, of New York dinner parties. Nobody had ever listened to him before with such complete absorption and he'd come to rely on it almost like a drug. It was the perfect antidote to mornings in the clinic when he was the listener, and the long dark evenings alone with a book or his sketch pad. Her steady uncomplicated interest was such a relief after the twists and turns of life with Isabelle. But he didn't plan to do anything more about this, and probably soon, Anna would tire of him. The weather would make it impossible for them to continue to meet on the beach, and he knew it was just as well. Al Craven was the sheriff on the island, and clearly he was a jealous and controlling man. The few times Dennis had dropped into the Harbor Lounge for a beer, he had found Craven presiding, eager to make sure the doctor knew the position of power he held on the island. He had never again mentioned to Anna the bruise on her daughter's arm, and when he checked Erin recently as a follow-up on the new medicine, he saw nothing more. He could have been mistaken about that bruise. He simply had a feeling in his bones that Craven was the kind of man who was capable of such an act.

AL WAS DISTRACTED. He had a meeting with Latham in less than two weeks and he'd refigured the job three different ways, but he always worried that he wasn't going to get his prices as low as the competition. He planned to let Latham know that the off-island construction companies always came in lower in the beginning because they didn't understand the problems of building on an island first-hand the way Al Craven did. What Latham didn't know either was that there was an unspoken agreement to make life miserable for any off-island contractors. Supply trucks didn't make it on the ferry even though they'd called ahead and scheduled. Brakes got unset, loads slipped and got damaged. If the owner went off island for the work, the cost overruns would kill him in the end.

Paul Thayer, who served as town councilman, told the summer owners straight out at a civic association meeting last August that if they wanted their island to stay the way it was, they sure as hell better patronize the year-rounders. Paul was a big burly man, well over six-four, and when he opened his mouth, people listened.

"That means the grocery store and the lobstermen and the landscape businesses and the construction people. All of us. It burns me up to see those bags of fruits and vegetables coming over from the mainland on the afternoon boat."

"The fruit here is perfectly terrible," said a loud female voice from the back row. Her tone was imperious and the room rustled. "If you want us to buy your products, you're going to have to make sure they're top quality."

"Mrs. Harrison, it's a tough thing to run a year-round business on a resort island. A lot of us are pretty fed up with it. And frankly, if you didn't have us to supply your groceries and fix your over-flowing toilets, you'd be in a hell of a lot of trouble."

People on both sides of the issue had managed to smooth over the talk before it got out of hand, but these ideas were always rumbling just below the surface. The summer people claimed they were charged too much and the work was shoddy. The year-rounders said they didn't appreciate how lucky they were to have anybody willing to do this kind of work. The summer owners were all perceived as rich and the year-rounders as poor. As with most generalizations, neither one was true.

THE WEEK AFTER Thanksgiving, Maggie drove Kasha over to Anna's. They had made this date on the phone and Anna was waiting. She greeted Kasha warmly and the dog seemed to remember her.

"I have no idea whether this will work," she warned Maggie. "But I'll start her on the check cord the way I do my young dogs. That's really the only way with an older dog like this. Did you ever try training her when she was young?"

Maggie shrugged. "A few sessions in a dog training school, but with my traveling schedule it became impossible. And then I heard from other people that huskies are hopeless to train and you have to keep them on a leash. I believed it."

"No promises. But I'll try. Why don't you drop her off here every day around two. That's really the only time for me." That way Al wasn't likely to run into the husky, she thought. She'd told him about the training lessons and he'd agreed to let her do it only because Maggie was paying. Al was crazier than usual about money these days.

Kasha was a smart dog, and she understood the lessons of the check cord very quickly even though Anna was mindful of her aching hips and gentler with her than the younger dogs. When Anna called and Kasha did not come, she let her roam a little longer, then called again. If Kasha did not come the second time, she stepped immediately on the cord and brought the dog up short. She then took her back to the exact place where she did not respond to the first command and warned her in a strong voice. It only took a week of this kind of reminder for Kasha to trot back when called.

Anna brought Maggie in then and started her working with the dog.

"Never drag her back with the cord when she doesn't obey," she warned. "That gives her the wrong message, tells her you're going to do the work for her. Call her a second time and if she ignores you, simply step on the cord to stop her in her tracks."

"The big problem will come when she scents something and there's no check cord."

Anna agreed. "There are some handlers who put electronic collars on their pointing dogs because they can't stop them from chasing deer. Every time they run off, the owner gives them a zap."

"I don't want to do that," Maggie said. "There are so many rabbits here I'd be zapping her every five minutes."

"Good," Anna said. "Thought you should know about them, but I don't ever use one. Of course, I don't have the problem because we don't have deer on the island. My dogs ignore the smell of rabbit. They've been trained since they were ten weeks old to go for the birds."

"Too bad Kasha isn't in love with the smell of deer," Maggie said with a grin. "She'd never go anywhere." With the focus on Kasha, the two women had come to like each other's company. Maggie admired the way Anna worked with the dogs. She was calm and practical. She liked to say that dog training was common sense. "A dog loves praise and it can only relate punishment to the last thing it did," she told Maggie. "Just remember that."

Now Maggie took Kasha out walking with the thirty-foot cord, but she only reined Kasha in when the dog did not respond to a voice command. The island was amused by the training program, and the ones who passed the two of them on the road inevitably stopped to comment.

"Watch that line, it can get really tangled up," they said, or their favorite "You can't teach an old dog new tricks." Maggie smiled and waved. They meant well.

ONE EVENING SHE walked Kasha over to Sam's. They had seen very little of each other in the last few weeks. She had been closeted in the front room, moving back and forth between a pedestal table and a pair of lyre-back chairs, and Sam was teaching school most of the day. Whenever he wasn't in the classroom, she figured he was out roaming the island or keeping up on his records at the museum or working on the nature column he wrote for the monthly newspaper.

She knocked twice and was turning away when the porch light went on and he appeared. His hair was all standing on end, and when he pushed open the storm door, she saw that his shirt was untucked. He had the rumpled look of someone who'd just woken up.

"Hi," she said, suddenly shy, thinking she should have called first.

"What time is it?" He looked at his wrist, but his watch wasn't there.

"Eight o'clock. Kasha and I were taking our evening walk. Thought we'd drop by. Sorry. It looks like a bad time."

"No, it's okay. Come in. I fell asleep in front of the television. I was out late last night on an owl prowl. Full moon. I couldn't resist."

"I read your column in the November issue of the *News*," she said.

He stretched and ran his hands through his hair. "What's that?" He was still coming to.

"Bats."

"Oh, that," he said with a grin. "I meant to thank you for the research material. The kids loved it. Much better than a stuffed beaver."

Once inside the narrow front hall, she rolled up the cord and unhooked it from Kasha's collar.

"Now that's a serious leash," he said.

"It's actually called a check cord. Anna is training me and Kasha at the same time."

"Anna's good. Is it working?"

"We think so. But I'm not quite ready to let her run wild."

He scratched his head. "Do you want something to drink? A beer? Or juice? Or what about dinner? I don't think I've eaten yet. If I did I don't remember it."

"What have you got? I do remember eating and it was terrible. Me and food," she said with a shrug.

He shook his head in disbelief and set about making them a meal. Kasha prowled around the house sniffing in corners.

Maggie slipped onto a stool and planted both elbows on the kitchen counter. He gave her a cold beer and started to boil water. Then he washed lettuce, chopped up a cucumber and some red onion, and took a hunk of bread out of the freezer. He moved around the kitchen easily.

"Did you see any owls?" she asked.

"Yup. Two barred owls live in the sanctuary behind the museum. I've been hearing them call to each other at dusk so I went out looking for them. Found them too. And a surprise. A great gray owl just before midnight. It floated over my head so I saw it before I heard it. It was quite a sight."

He'd heard that the great gray owls might be migrating far south of their usual wintering range this year, but it was too early in the season to tell if this was a major irruption. It would be February before the real counts were in. The last invasion was ten years ago when four hundred seven great grays spent the winter along this coast. Nobody knew why the birds moved this way, although there was talk of severe winters and scarcity of prey further north.

The risotto was beginning to stick to the bottom of the pan. He poured in some more chicken stock and stirred vigorously. Maggie was staring at him.

"Earth to Sam."

"Sorry, I checked out there for a minute. What did I miss?"

"I was asking if I could go with you sometime. To look for owls."

"Sure. Have you ever been birding?"

"A couple of times with Nan when I was young. But I got restless and made too much noise. She gave up on me."

"She was a good birder. She came out with me a couple of times a summer on the Wednesday afternoon nature walks." He pulled some plates from the cupboard above the sink. "I'll let you know when I go owling again."

"How did you get started with all this?" she asked.

"Birding?"

"All of it. What made you become a naturalist?"

"I grew up on the coast of Maine. My father was a lobsterman so we were out on the water all the time. He taught me about the birds. I feel sorry for people who have to work inside in an office." He shuddered. "Trapped in those airless buildings with their feet planted all day long under a desk. I don't know how they stand it."

"I feel the same way."

He pushed the salad bowl and a jar of homemade dressing over to her. "You toss while I dish up the food."

He set a plate in front of her and put out roasted red peppers, the salad, goat cheese, and some bread. She stuck her nose down close to her plate and breathed deeply. "I love risotto."

"You've had it before?"

"Oh, yes." Last time in Rome, but she didn't say it.

"Parmesan?" he asked and when she nodded, he grated it for her, then a scattering for himself. "My mother wasn't Italian, but she loved risotto. My father taught her how to make it." He took the stool beside her, then jumped up again. "Forgot something," he said as he started rifling through the cabinets. He came back with a fat, half-burned evergreen candle and a box of matches. "It's not Christmas yet, but it will do." He lit it and flicked off the overhead light.

They ate for a while in silence. Kasha got to her feet at the smell of food and settled again near Maggie's feet.

"Now I owe you two dinners and a breakfast," Maggie said as she mopped up the last of her sauce with a piece of bread.

"I'm not counting. How's the survey going?"

"It's a perfect job for me because I'm an unrepentant snoop. Conserving furniture gives you a lot of chance to snoop, but this is even better. My grandparents' house is on the list."

"Which one's that?"

Maggie was struck again by Sam's total lack of interest in island gossip. Everybody else seemed to know she was the Whartons' grandchild. "The Whartons. My mother's parents."

"Do you remember it from when you were little?"

"I was never there. My mother was disowned when she married my father. My grandparents never met me or my two brothers."

"That seems harsh," he said.

She shrugged. "Funny when you're a kid, you just accept things. I didn't think much about it. By the time I started coming up to visit Nan, they had sold the house. She drove me around it once. It was the first time I realized how much my mother had given up when she married my father."

"Have you been inside it this time?"

"No," she said. "I'm putting it off."

He got up to clear the plates.

"That was delicious," she said. "Where did you find the red peppers?"

"Off island. You never get produce like that here after Labor Day."

"I noticed," she said. "Do your parents still live in Maine?"

"My mother does. Near Portland. My father's dead."

There was a moment of silence between them. "How old were you when he died?" she asked.

"Twelve. He was killed by a drunk driver." His back was turned to her.

"How awful, Sam."

"Something like that changes you." He turned the water on in the sink.

"Yes, it does."

She thought of getting up to help him with the washing, but she liked watching his back, the rhythmic way he soaped the dishes, turning the water on only to rinse and then off again. He was a precise man, as conserving of his movements as he was of the natural resources. And strong. She remembered his arms pulling the dead weight of her up out of the cold water, away from John Burling's body.

"Want some ice cream?" He opened the freezer door and went back to the dishes. "Not a bad selection. You can choose. I like them all."

She got two dishes from the draining board. "Vanilla chocolate chunk, raspberry ice." She stopped and looked more closely. "Or if you prefer, there's frozen bluebird, cardinal sorbet, and warbler ice."

"Whoops." He grinned at her over his shoulder. "Forgot to warn you about that. One of those is actually a Chuckwill's widow. Sort of like a whippoorwill. Rare species."

"I bet. Just please tell me why they're there."

"I pick up any dead birds I find and keep them for the taxidermist."

"For the bird display in the museum?"

"Exactly. In the old days they used to shoot the birds and stuff them, but now we just take what nature leaves for us."

"Can anybody do that?"

"No, you have to have a license. The museum has one."

"So you pick up road kill too?"

"Only the salvageable ones."

"It's possible then that a person could open your freezer and find a dead fox or a porcupine."

"Not this freezer," he said amiably. "The larger one down in the basement."

"Remind me not to go downstairs," she said as she slid the vanilla chocolate chunk out past the stiff bodies in freezer bags.

"I have one more project for you," he said over dessert.

"You don't think I have enough to do?"

"Well, a body needs to keep busy, especially on the island in the winter. It can get to you. For example, who was the last person you talked to?"

"Besides Kasha?" She thought for a minute. "Gloria in the grocery store. Yesterday morning."

"That's what I mean. Now this job I'm thinking of will get you involved with people. I want you to teach a class in furniture repair at the school. Only a day or two a week in the afternoon."

She studied him.

"Nothing complicated," he said. "I bet you've found some furniture around your place that could use some repair, but isn't fancy enough for you to sell at any auction. Last year, Billy Slade brought in a beat-up old bicycle. The kids completely refurbished it and they raffled it off to raise money for a school trip. That kind of project."

"Do you lie around at night thinking up projects for everybody to do or is it just me?"

"Just you," he said. "I lie around at night thinking up ways to keep you on this island."

"Well," she said, "it seems to be working."

"Will you think about it?"

"When would it start?"

"After Christmas."

Kasha stretched and let out a high-pitched musical whine.

"Good God," he said. "What was that?"

"That was a yawn. And she's letting me know she needs to go out."

"I'll run you home in the truck."

"That's all right. I'd really rather walk. I love the night sky." She hooked Kasha to the cord and he followed her out onto the front porch.

The house was a simple white clapboard with gray trim and a big wide porch running the width of it. "I remember this house," she said. "Nan took me to a birthday party here when I was seven. We played pin-the-tail-on-the-donkey on that porch and I was dressed in shorts and everybody else had on frilly pink dresses and black patent leather shoes. It was a disaster. I never did fit in with the fancy crowd."

They were standing close together, his eyes fixed on her. "Are you going to be warm enough?" he asked suddenly.

"Yes. I'm fine."

Suddenly he wrapped his arms around her. "I'm glad you're staying a while," he whispered into her ear.

It felt safe inside this circle made by the two of them. Her cheek was pressed against the soft wool of his plaid shirt. "Me too," she said, but her voice was muffled and she wasn't sure he heard her.

He let her go at last and stood on the porch, his hands on his hips.

"You didn't give me an answer," he called out when she was halfway down his hill, Kasha far out in front on the cord. "About the furniture project?"

She turned around. "Does it mean I get to see you more?"

"Yes."

"All right, all right," she said as she half skipped, half slid down the hill after Kasha. "Then I'll do it."

He stood watching until she turned the corner.

As LATE AS December, schools of stripers and bluefish, migrating south, swam close in to the beaches down the east coast, stocking up on food, chasing the smaller herring. This phenomenon did not occur every year, but the island fishermen knew to be on the watch for it, particularly this fall, which had stretched long and languorous like a cat sunbathing on hot cement.

Randy Baker was the first to see it. On an overcast Saturday morning, he stopped his truck on the little bluff above the golf course and looked through his binoculars down to White Beach. The birds were clustered just above the surface of the water, wheeling and diving for what looked like bait fish. To an untutored eye, it might be whitecaps, but there was not enough wind to raise the water like that. He raced the truck down to the beach and with the door hanging open, ran out onto the wet sand. He didn't need the binoculars to see what this was. It was a school of fish in a feeding frenzy, probably blues and stripers mixed.

"Hallelujah," he shouted, and got on the radio with a single call. He knew he was breaking the cardinal rule of the island. The radio was to be used only for emergencies. But the fishermen had come up with a simple code.

"Port Six to all EMTs. White Beach. High Tide." That gave everybody the location and the news that it was both blues and stripers. Within twenty minutes, there were twelve fishermen lining the beach, calling news of lures and catches to one other. The blues had chased the smaller fish into ten inches of water and were swimming sideways, swallowing up herring whole.

Lauren Root picked up the news on her radio and jumped into her car. The doctor told her he would be working in his office, but there were no scheduled patients on the weekends and he didn't know the code. She burst into his office and told him the news. He was half out of his white coat before she had finished her sentence.

"Where again?" he asked, throwing papers into drawers.

"White Beach. Get your gear. I'll show you. I'm going down there myself. I always do." There was nothing she liked better than seeing those big men lined up to fish. And she'd learned over the years how to unhook the fish without harming them. The men used to keep everything they caught and sell the smaller ones off to the lobstermen to chop up as bait fish. But now, there was a twenty-eight-inch legal limit on striped bass, and many even larger than that were released voluntarily. The fishermen, who had seen species dwindle up and down the coast, had become conservationists themselves.

The men turned at the sound of slamming car doors and welcomed the doctor. The walls that separated summer from winter people, off islanders from regulars, fly-fishermen from spin-fishermen, came tumbling down on a day like this. Every fisherman on the island would hit the beach by noon. Today and possibly tomorrow would be their last real chance until early April.

"What are you using?" Paul Thayer asked as the doctor waded into water up to his thighs between Thayer and Al Craven.

"Flies. Good thing there's no wind. What's the tide doing?"

"Coming in," Thayer said. "Pushing the fish in front of it."

"You barely need a rod, man," Al called from down the way. "The goddamned fish are bumping into my feet."

Dennis was pleased with himself. He'd made all the right choices for these conditions, his ten-foot graphite rod, the intermediate line that sank slowly, and yellow foam poppers for the blues. He had some slab flies that imitated herring and Lefty's Deceivers if he wanted to go after the stripers. This was the day he'd been waiting for all fall.

His first fish hit on the second cast, and he remembered to keep his rod tip low, parallel to the surface of the water, and tug on the line with his hand to get the hook to set. The fish wanted to run, so he let it go for a while until the line tightened and he could reel up the extra from the stripping basket at his waist. By that time, he had set the drag strong enough to let the fish know its time was up. The blue was big, about fifteen pounds, and when he lay it on its side on the beach, four herring tails were hanging out of its mouth.

"Greedy bugger," he said to Lauren, who came over with a bucket.

"Are you keeping it?" Lauren asked.

"This one."

She used a cloth rag to hold the fish down and a pair of long-handled forceps to remove the hook, then popped the fish in a bucket. He was impressed.

"I see your nursing prepares you for all sorts of things." She gave him a warm smile and moved down the line to Al, who had pulled in a striper.

"How do you like our island fishing now, Doctor?" Al called.

"It's great," Dennis replied as he checked his fly and cast again.

MOST OF THE island stopped by to watch. Lauren was keeping count and by one in the afternoon, the fishermen had landed sixty-eight blues and thirty stripers. A lot of them called it quits after that and stood around over a fire someone had built on the beach, drinking beer and marveling with each other over the catch, trading stories about the biggest one they'd brought in that day. The women were complaining that they had no room in their freezers for that much fish. Maggie, who was standing next to Sam, elbowed him and asked if they knew what was in his freezer, and he smiled and rolled his eyes. Lauren said they should have a cleaning party. Al and Paul Thayer asked Dennis to show them how to cast, and a circle of people gathered to watch the lesson. Anna was there, standing next to Annie Slocum.

"He certainly is different from the type of doctor we usually get," Annie said.

"Yes, he is," said Anna, and she wanted to tell Annie all she knew about the man, about the little tidal island and the drowned father. But she held her tongue and edged close enough to hear what he was saying.

" 'Tis a different kind of casting than you do with a spinning rod. A lighter touch if you know what I mean," and as he said this, he lifted his right arm so that the line floated backward in a graceful arc behind him, sailed between his ear and Al's, and uncurled itself delicately along the surface of the water.

Al was the first to try, but he couldn't get the hang of the thing. "Try using your wrist more," Dennis said. "You don't need the whole arm the way you do when you have the weight of a spinner on the end of the line."

Al tried again, but he handed the rod to Paul after two more casts that landed in the shallow water a few feet from the shore. He was aware that people were watching. He swaggered back up to where the crowd was standing and draped his arm heavily around Anna's shoulders.

"So you couldn't handle it, Al," Randy called out.

"Sissy fishing, if you ask me," Al shouted back, and the crowd laughed. Anna knew that the doctor had heard. Any minute now he would turn around and see Al's arm on her, and she wanted him to forget that Al Craven was her husband. She wanted to forget herself. She slipped away, muttering some excuse about the dogs.

"This school will be feeding off Chincoteale tomorrow," Al shouted. "See you all there at six A.M."

The crowd laughed and began to collect itself, to wind its way to the cars.

"So Dr. Dennis Lacey," Al said, clapping the man on the back. "Do you get fishing like this in New York City?"

"No, I certainly do not," the doctor said good-naturedly. "You don't get fishing like this many places in the world."

"Well, I wouldn't know about many other places because it's well known I don't travel much. Who needs to travel the world when you can live right here on the best island in the Atlantic Ocean?"

Anna wanted to put her fingers in her ears. Al was talking so loud, his voice sounded so stupid and raucous to her, like the crows that call back and forth between one tree and another in the mornings. Dennis Lacey was a quiet, cultured man who'd left the island he was born on, who had traveled all over the world. He must think her husband was a dolt. He must wonder how she could bear to put up with him. She always felt that when people heard Al going on about something or making a fool of himself, they must think immediately of her and wonder why that wife of his didn't do a better job of controlling him, of making him behave himself. She used to feel the same way with her father. When did she first appoint herself keeper of all the foolish, drunken, gambling men in her family? she wondered as she climbed into her car. She knew what Miss Yola would say. "You were a little grown-up from the day your mother passed on. Everybody's mother and nobody's child."

Anna was blocked in and sat there waiting as the people slowly streamed by her.

"Mayor Craven is going on again," she heard someone say as they passed. They obviously didn't notice her sitting there, the windows rolled almost all the way up. She felt so trapped suddenly, by the cars parked in front of her, by the people, by Al, by the island itself. Don't start this now, she told herself. It will drive you mad to think this way so early in the season.

In a week she was going off island for Whistler's hunting test. One week. She couldn't wait.

Twelve

THE SECOND WEEK of December, colored lights were strung on the big evergreen that stood outside the post office. The fire department launched its annual toy collection for the party that was thrown for all the children of the island the Saturday before Christmas. As usual, Santa Claus was selected by picking a name out of a hat, and the costume came down out of the Thayers' attic, where it had been stored in mothballs since the year before. The island school began practicing its Christmas program. Mr. Slocum announced at assembly that they would be presenting a special island rendition of Scrooge and Tiny Tim.

"Not again," Erin groaned.

"I think it will be fun," Katie said.

"You haven't done it three times already."

"At my old school they just stood around and lighted menorahs and sang carols. It was really boring."

"What's a menorah?"

Katie gave her a look that Erin was getting very used to. A sort of, oh my God, you don't know anything look. "A menorah has got a lot of candles on it. Jewish people light the candles for Hanukah."

"Right," Erin said as if she actually did know but had just forgotten. She had no idea what Hanukah was either, but she certainly wasn't going to let on.

"I'm trying out for the play," Katie said.

"You'll never get anything," Erin said. "They give all the parts to the high school kids. We get to walk around the stage pretending we're on the beach singing songs while somebody carries Tiny Tim on his shoulders. Scrooge is a rich lobsterman and the ghost drags in a lot of nets and buoys behind him."

"It sounds great," said Katie.

"It was okay the first time," Erin said. "But it's getting a little old." She'd heard Katie use that phrase before and she liked how it sounded. "Besides, there are no parts for girls. Just Tiny Tim's mother."

"Who gets to be Tiny Tim?"

"They'll pick one of the little kids."

"I still think it sounds like fun," Katie said and later at gym, she paired off with Patty Thayer for basketball practice. Erin was stuck with fat old Annie Malloy who could't even hit the rim and wheezed all the time.

ERIN HAD TAKEN to dropping by Maggie's house after school. She came so often that Maggie had given her a key.

"Nobody on the island locks their doors," Erin had said.

"I'm still a city person at heart," Maggie had replied. She was amused to have been adopted by this secretive, intense child who, without knowing it, could be so transparent. She reminded Maggie of herself at the same age. Except for her summer trips up to the island to see Nan, she had nowhere to go to get away from the drab daily life with a family, rubbing up against other people all the time who had known you since you were born and acted as if that gave them some power over you. Maggie had reinvented herself with Nan. She liked the idea that she was giving Erin a chance to do the same thing. Many afternoons when she came in from a house survey, Maggie opened the front door to the sound of typewriter keys slamming down, one and then another, and she found it a companionable, comforting noise. She never asked what Erin was writing and Erin never showed her.

"What's Hanukah?" Erin asked Maggie when she stopped by her house that afternoon. They were standing out in the yard with Kasha off the check cord. The dog lifted her head when Maggie called and trotted back to her side every time, although it was clear she couldn't see the point of the exercise.

"It's a Jewish holiday," Maggie said. "They celebrate right around now. Kids get presents for eight nights in a row and they light candles. Why?"

"I just wondered."

Maggie didn't question further. She was getting used to these questions that came out of the blue.

"You call her now," Maggie said. "She's sick of coming back to me."

Erin called, and Kasha lifted her head from some smell she was investigating in the corner of the yard.

"Come on, Kasha, come on, girl."

Kasha obliged and got a neck massage from Erin. She pushed her head against Erin's hand, urging her on.

"She likes you," Maggie said. "All right, time for tea. It's cold out here. Tomorrow I'll take her out without the check cord."

In the kitchen over smoky Chinese tea with spoonfuls of honey, Erin talked about her problems at school. Maggie listened without saying much. She used to hate it when her mother gave advice. Once when she was eight years old, she screamed at her, "I don't want you to fix it. I just want you to listen." Her mother couldn't understand that concept at all. After all, mothers were supposed to fix things like dirty diapers and ear infections. Maybe they never got out of the fixing habit. The other day when her mother phoned, she'd told Maggie to put the house on the market right away. And Maggie hadn't even asked her opinion.

"Katie acts as if she knows everything," Erin was saying. "It's getting boring."

"Sounds that way."

"I'm going to figure out something I know about that she doesn't."

"Sex," Maggie said with a grin. Erin looked horrified. "My brother told me all about sex and I made the other kids in my class beg me to tell them. The power only lasted a little while, but it was worth it."

"Maybe Katie already knows everything about sex," Erin said. More than I know, she thought.

"Probably you're right. Okay, what else? Dog training."

"She doesn't want to know about that."

Maggie went on making outrageous suggestions, all of which Erin rejected, but Maggie's first idea reminded her of something. A couple of days before, she'd found a book on the third floor that showed naked Japanese people all tangled around each other in different positions. The women had chopsticks stuck through the shiny black hair piled on their heads and the men were kissing them down there.

When Maggie had called to her from downstairs, she'd slammed the book closed and shoved it back into the bookshelf. She remembered exactly where it was. She was going to look at it again, first chance she got. There had to be something in there Katie didn't know.

THAT NIGHT WHEN Erin woke to her father's furtive movements in her room, the way he slid into the bed making almost no sound and spooned his body up against her, she couldn't stop thinking about the book. She shivered.

"Erin?" he whispered softly, like a secret in her ear. She didn't answer, willed her body to be still.

When she felt his breathing drop into that regular pattern, she started her rhythmic counting, but it didn't work. All she could think about was the way those people had looked all tangled up with each other, like that nest of snakes Mr. M. found two years ago behind the museum. It took her a long time to fall asleep.

THE FIRST SNOWSTORM of the season dusted the island with only a couple of inches, but the layer of white glittered in the afternoon sun and lifted everyone's spirits. The kids managed to scrape together just enough snow to make dry snowballs that flew apart in the air. Jimmy Slade put a handful down Erin's shirt and she screamed at him.

"You owe me one already, Jimmy, from when you pushed me off the monkey bars. The doctor said that was a really bad bruise. This time I'm going to tell."

"Go ahead," he said. "I don't care." But he did. His father had yelled at him yesterday because of his bad report card. He was planning to run away and live in the old naval fort. He and his best friend, Brian, were exploring the place, choosing the best room for a hideout. Last week they'd found a whole pile of *Playboy* magazines in one of the run-down gun emplacements. They took the stack and hid them in a new place and most days, they went down after school and stared at the pictures of the naked women.

"Yes, you do," she said. "I heard my father telling my mother that you're in big trouble." This wasn't true, but it was a good guess. Jimmy's mother left the island when he was three and she had never come back once, not even to visit. Jimmy's father worked for her father and Mr. Slade was always talking about what a lousy student

Jimmy was, that he didn't know what to do with him. Erin saw the fear in Jimmy's eyes.

"I've got something I can show you," he said.

"What?"

"After school. Meet me down behind the bowling alley. Don't tell anybody."

That afternoon she waited for him right where he'd said, but he wasn't there. Cheater Jimmy Slade. She should have known.

KASHA ALWAYS WENT nuts the first snow of the season. She rolled in it, dug ferociously, covered her snout in the fine white powder, crouched in her pouncing position.

"Snow witch," Maggie called her. This was her third day off the check cord, and even though she went exploring, she eventually came trotting back at Maggie's call. "Come on girl, let's go to Chincoteale. See what the surf looks like." They ran into Erin walking up the road and Maggie stopped the car. "Come to the beach with us. I'm going to let Kasha run. The snow's made her wild."

Erin got in. She really wanted to go back to Maggie's house and look at the book again, but Maggie seemed so eager for her company that she was flattered.

"Someone else had the same idea," Maggie said as she pulled her car into place next to the Mercedes. "Looks like Dr. Lacey."

Kasha took off like a rocket down the path and by the time Maggie and Erin reached the rocks, the husky had disappeared. Two figures were walking towards them, heads bent, arms folded against the cold. In Maggie's mind, the tiniest warning bell went off as Erin said, "Those are Mom's dogs." Two of Anna's copper-colored hunting dogs were racing with Kasha, all three of them tearing in circles up and down the beach. Anna and the doctor hadn't yet noticed the company. There was no harm in what they were doing; after all, they must have run into each other down here, but my, Maggie thought, they seem very intent on their conversation.

"Hey," she shouted to give them a warning. They looked up, stepped apart, and before Anna waved, she put the whistle to her mouth and blew as if to say, the dogs are why I'm here, of course.

"That's funny. Mom usually walks the dogs on Starfish," Erin said. "She's taking Whistler off island for his hunting test on Friday."

By this time, the four people were close enough to call greetings to one another. The dogs came racing back at the whistle and Kasha followed them, but she was beginning to lag.

"Not bad for an old lady," Maggie said nodding at Kasha.

"She must love the snow," Anna said.

"Mom, why didn't you go to Starfish?"

"We were bored," she said. "I've been giving them the run down here instead. Even dogs like the change. How was school, honey?"

Erin shrugged. "School was school. Mr. M. is taking us on a nature walk tomorrow afternoon. Up by Mink Pond. We're looking for animal tracks."

Maggie remembered another nature walk and hoped nobody else did. "So how do you like our winter weather, Doctor?" she asked. And what are you doing out here on the beach with Mrs. Craven with those two spots of color in your cheeks?

" 'Tis lovely. I like a little snow with my cold. Seems right for the season. I'd better be getting back. Paperwork to be done. Goodbye then. Nice to run into you, Mrs. Craven."

"Yes," she said, but did not look at him.

Erin and Maggie and Anna fell into step and walked for a while in silence.

"Kasha's behaving herself, then," Anna said.

"Very well," said Maggie. "I never would have believed it."

"I'd keep giving her reminders," Anna warned. "Dogs need them just like humans."

"Erin said something about a hunting test," Maggie said. "What's Whistler going for?"

"The junior class. I'll show you." She blew the whistle twice and the dogs raced back. "Sit," she said and both dogs lowered their haunches. "Stay." With her hand down, palm spread, she walked away from them. Their wiry bodies were trembling, begging to be released. She kept walking, the whistle in her mouth. They waited. At last, she blew, just one toot and they were off again. "Of course in the junior class, they have to find the bird and move in to point," Anna explained as she came back. "But they're still allowed to chase the bird. By senior class, they have to hold point. It's not the best thing to run them on the beach because sometimes they take off after the shorebirds, but I always work with them up in the field after this, remind them that their first love is the scent of pheasant." All the time Anna was talking, she was thinking, did Maggie know, did Erin see anything, could they tell that this wasn't simply a chance meeting, could they hear her heart still banging away under the thin wall of her chest? She had done nothing wrong, she'd been telling herself over and over again in the last few weeks when her thoughts drifted to Dennis as she stirred a pot on the stove with her back to Al, or when she made change for a stamp purchase in the post office. To walk on a beach and talk to a man, this was not a sin. She had kept the secrets of her marriage, of the island. Anna was not a gossip, never had been. But now it would have to stop. Once was a chance meeting, twice was an appointment. He knew that too. The way he lied, pretended he and Mrs. Craven had just happened to run into each other.

"He's a nice man, Dennis Lacey," Maggie said, looking straight ahead. "We're lucky to get him through the winter. Not many city people could put up with this kind of assignment."

"He's been very helpful about Erin's asthma."

"He's an island man from way back. We rode the same ferry over the day I arrived."

Anna wanted to say, oh I know that and so much more, but she kept quiet.

"Shall I give Erin a ride home?" Maggie asked. Erin was already ahead of them, winding her way toward the path.

"Yes, thanks. I'll take the dogs across the street to that field behind the old red barn. There's only another thirty minutes of light."

AL WAS STANDING in the driveway when Maggie turned the car in.

"Uh oh," Erin said almost to herself. Kasha's growl began low in her chest, a warning noise. "Hold on to her collar," Erin said. "She goes crazy around Dad."

Al strolled up to the side of the car, but as soon as he saw the dog, he hesitated.

"Down, Kasha!" Maggie shouted, but the dog planted a leg right in the middle of Maggie's thigh and began a wild barking and snarling at the man on the other side of the window. Her wet snout left trails of mucus on the glass.

Erin slipped out her side and slammed the door quickly. It was impossible for Maggie to carry on any kind of conversation, so she pushed Kasha down in the seat and rammed the gearshift into reverse. By the time she had turned the car around, Erin had already gone inside the house. Al was standing in the same place, staring at her.

"Geez, Kash, I don't like him either but what is your problem? That man is the law on this island. Not a good idea to get on the wrong side of the law, if you know what I mean."

THE NEXT AFTERNOON Erin watched Jimmy Slade very carefully. He didn't get on the school bus and neither did she. She followed him down the road behind the bowling alley, creeping from bush to bush. He was intent on where he was going and didn't turn around once. He took the small paved road off to the left, the one with a single railroad track that led into the old fort. She'd been down here lots of times before. It was a creepy place with stone rooms built underground where they stored ammunition during the war. Some of the rooms had iron doors with rusted metal bars at the top and people said they kept prisoners here too. If you called out your name it echoed back to you. The weeds had grown up through the cracks in the cement and down over the top from the hillside. In the summertime, the rich kids threw pit parties down here. They brought in a keg and a band from the mainland and built a huge bonfire and people danced along the walls. Everybody snuck in to the parties, even the ones who weren't invited.

Jimmy stopped once and turned around as if he'd heard something, but she ducked behind a half-opened door just in time. He went on and she waited, listening until his footsteps stopped. A door was pulled open and then some scuffling noises and then silence. She put each foot down carefully, avoided the loose rocks lying about on the cement, took her time. From inside one of the windowless rooms, she saw the glow of a light. He had a candle or a flashlight. She took a deep breath, peeked around the door, and boo. He screamed and dropped the flashlight.

"What are you doing here?" he shouted.

She was pleased with her scouting. "I came to see what you had to show me. "

"You followed me," he said, all the while trying to kick something under a cardboard box.

"What's that?" she asked, and when he put it behind his back, she pulled it out. They both yanked at it and the moldy magazine parted in the middle, cutting a naked lady in half. Erin got the bottom half. "Is this what you were going to show me?" She knew they sold these magazines in the back of the grocery store and there was a calendar with a lady like this over the desk in her father's office.

"Yup," Jimmy said. "Brian and I found them in one of the bunkers. You better not tell him."

Erin settled down on the floor with her back against the wall. "These are gross," she said as she turned the pages of her half. The damp magazines were covered with green spots and some of the pages were stuck together. Jimmy sat down beside her. Without a word, he handed her another one and they both went on looking.

Erin had never seen her mother naked, but she couldn't believe she looked like this. Those mounds of flesh with the dark nipples and the way the woman smiled with her back arched like she was proud of how big her breasts were. And the man with the camera must be looking right back at her while he was taking all these pictures. She turned more pages. The women lay down on their backs and smiled and in some of them, they were touching themselves down there between their legs. Erin got a fluttering feeling in her stomach. She felt sick and excited at the same time. She didn't dare look at Jimmy. She could hear him turning the pages slowly next to her.

"You got boobs yet?" he asked.

"Maybe." She did, she had bumps that were getting bigger, and last year at the mall, her mother bought her three bras made out of T-shirt material. "Annie Malloy has the biggest ones in our class."

"I'll say." Jimmy giggled. "She has knockers."

"Give me another one," Erin said, and they looked again for a while in silence. She got an idea. "I'll take my shirt off if you take your pants off," she said.

"That's gross," he said.

"Baby."

"I am not a baby," he said, and she could see that he was curious. He wanted to see. She did too. Katie Morrison had probably never done anything like this.

He went out the door and looked around. When he came back in, they both agreed to stand in the light. Then neither one had to fool with the flashlight. It was easy for him. He didn't have to take his jacket off or anything.

"Hurry up," he said with his belt undone. "I'm ready."

"It's cold," she said and dropped her jacket and sweater in a pile on the floor. She reached up in the back under her shirt and unhooked her bra. He was watching and she felt like one of the women in the magazine except he hadn't seen anything yet.

"How long are we going to do it for?" she said.

"Count of ten."

But neither one of them trusted the other so she inched her shirt up and he slid his pants down at the same rate. She saw the white of his underpants behind the open zipper even though he was holding both layers together. Finally there was no room left to maneuver.

"On the count of three," she said in an irritated voice as if she'd done this before. "Hurry up, I'm cold. One, two, three," and they both lived up to the bargain.

She saw his thing pop straight out of his pants as stiff as a stick with what looked like a cap of darker flesh at the end of it. She felt her own nipples hardening in the cold and counted, one, two, three, as fast as she could to ten and pulled her shirt down. He yanked his pants up just as quickly. She thought that stiff thing would break off if he didn't watch out.

They didn't look at each other while they put their clothes on. "Yours aren't very big," he said, and she felt like smacking him.

"Yours isn't either."

"How do you know?"

"I've seen bigger."

"Sure. Where've you been? In the boy's locker room."

"I've seen my father's," she said. "I bet you haven't seen your mother's." He started for her then, but she was ready for him and bent over so he couldn't hit her in the stomach. Then she shot up again and landed a blow on his ear that made him howl. He backed off.

"You'd better not tell Brian about this."

"I know how to keep a secret," she said. "If you do."

And each one had something on the other, which was the only way they could both go out feeling safe. They left by different routes. When Jimmy was sure she was gone, he doubled back and moved the stash of magazines to a new hiding place. All he'd tell Brian tomorrow was that he thought someone had been snooping around.

FROM HIS PLACE on the upper deck, the doctor watched Mrs. Craven backing her station wagon onto the Friday afternoon boat. He was not surprised to see her. He remembered her talk of taking one of the dogs to the mainland for a hunting test, and he could make out the wire cage in the back of the wagon. He wouldn't speak to her, of course. After their chance meeting with Maggie, he knew that their beach walks were over. The weather was going to end them soon anyway. In the winter on an island, the wind at the water's edge bit into a body. He remembered that from his childhood. He would miss her, he thought. The island would feel like a lonelier place without a chance to talk things over with a sympathetic woman. The men were fine, perfectly agreeable when he joined them at the Harbor Lounge for a beer, but he had not grown up here. He did not understand the jokes about this local person or that, hated American football, which seemed to be on the television every night. He could only join in when fishing became the topic of conversation. Chuck Montclair was different, had warmed up to him a bit. The other night, with three beers under his belt, he'd actually offered to show the doctor his collection of island photographs.

He watched her get out of the car, turn around to say something to the dog, then glance up at the deck. Their eyes met and held for a minute. He took it as a warning from her to stay away. Of course he would. She should know by now that he was not the kind of man who would put her at any risk. She didn't talk much about her marriage. It was as if there was some part of her that was walled off, not only from the rest of the world, but from herself as well. It saddened him. Al Craven seemed to be one of those insecure people who constantly needed to bring the attention in the room back to himself. You wouldn't want to be trapped in a house day after day with a man like that.

By the time she came upstairs, he had retired to a bench in one corner and was reading the latest issue of *Fly Fisherman*. Without looking up, he could track her movements about the cabin of the boat. She greeted one person after another. It was a larger crowd than usual, but of course it was Friday afternoon. The mainland kids were headed home, Miss Yola was going over with her little white dog to see friends up the coast, and a couple of the schoolteachers had some conference to attend on the mainland. Anna moved through the crowd easily and to his amazement, she took the seat across from him.

"Hello, Dr. Lacey," she said. "How are you?" Her voice was pitched a notch higher than usual.

"Fine, Mrs. Craven."

"I wanted to ask you about Erin's medicine. If she has a string of good days, can she cut back on the inhaler?"

This was a completely fabricated question, but he answered it as if she were serious. She lowered her voice for a follow-up about the Peak Flow Meter, and soon everybody had turned back to their business. The teenagers were making a lot of noise in the opposite corner and their raucous shouting commanded attention, each adult waiting edgily for another to control them. Finally one of the teachers walked over to quiet them down. It seemed perfectly natural for Mrs. Craven to have a little free consultation with the doctor. After all, this was the worst season for Erin's asthma, poor skinny little thing, you know she had a very bad attack a couple of weeks ago.

"Hunting test?" he asked.

"Yes. For Whistler. I left him in the car. He's riled up enough as it is."

"Do you have a long drive?"

"No," she said. "Just up the coast a bit. And you?"

"I'm going to the city for the weekend. Some business to clear up." His wife, she thought. She'd been listening to his talk about papers, how eager the woman was to divorce him. Four-year marriage, four-week divorce, he'd said the last time they had walked on the beach.

"—and some pleasure, I hope," he was saying.

She felt reckless, glanced around. The other passengers seemed occupied, although you could never tell who was pretending to read a newspaper and all the while was listening to every word you said. She dug through her purse and with her hands deep inside the leather folds, she wrote the name of her motel on a deposit slip torn out of her checkbook. He had gone back to his magazine, but she knew he wasn't really reading it. She tucked the slip of paper under the bench cushion and then got up and said her good-byes. From across the room where she settled herself with Miss Yola, she saw his hand slide down to retrieve the note.

Chuck had left the ticket window open longer than usual. The boat was full, and although he was pretending to wait for late stragglers, he was pretty sure everybody had paid. People forgot him when he stood behind that window. He might as well be invisible. He saw Anna talking to the doctor. Lately she'd been acting funny. Not exactly distant, but distracted, and when they talked, she kept it all business. The dogs, the hunters who had reserved for the weekend, when she needed him. He'd go to the house and check the dogs tonight, then again early in the morning. She'd be back with Whistler tomorrow on the last boat, a five P.M. run on a winter Saturday afternoon. She wouldn't have much company on that boat.

The doctor was hiding behind his magazine. Not a bad man really, Chuck had decided. Seemed to be satisfied with his own company, which was a rare thing for a city person. Apparently he was a landscape painter, but he only got serious about it when the fishing season was over. Or so he'd told Chuck the other night over a beer at the Lounge.

DENNIS'S CAR WAS the first on the boat, so the rest of the cars had long since dispersed by the time he made his way off the ramp. Anna was nowhere in sight. He had her note in the pocket of his shirt. "The Roadside Inn, Madison" was all it said. He wondered whether Mrs. Craven had ever slipped a man a note like this before. And for all that she thought he was a sophisticated New York doctor, he had old-fashioned scruples about affairs with married women. Deep down, he was still the Irish Catholic boy who worried that someone was watching, someone would catch him. But he liked Anna. He liked the way her body moved, the straightforward way she talked to him, the look in her wide-set eyes, both kind and frightened at the same time. He had forty miles to decide. Her station wagon pulled out from the shoulder of the road under the bridge and moved into line in front of his just before the entrance ramp onto the interstate. He expected that she glanced at him in the rearview mirror from time to time, but the wire netting of the dog cage obscured his view. Whistler was prowling back and forth. At some point, she must have spoken to him in that calm, certain voice of hers because suddenly, the dog settled down out of view.

On the left a car honked as it passed. The two schoolteachers headed to their conference waved at him and he waved back. They saw Anna too. A small fleet of islanders making their way out into the big wide world, like fishermen setting out in their boats to net the day's catch. Fog and wind and tide would come between them, separate them one from another, and even though he told himself that he had no real connection with these people, he was reminded of the homesick feeling he used to get when he raced the tide off Omey Island to make the bus to Dublin after the Christmas holidays. In those days, he couldn't wait to get away, but at the same time, he hated to leave it behind. He was reminded too that this divided feeling about islands and the people you tangle with on them was exactly why he left Omey in the first place and hadn't returned in years. He shifted into the middle lane and pushed the pedal to the floor. He did not look over at her when he passed. For once, New York and its big noisy anonymity was exactly what he needed.

ALWAYS BEFORE ON these solo trips to the mainland, Anna had reveled in each hour off island, each hour she could spend by herself with nobody demanding attention from her, nobody knowing who she was. She often bought a pack of cigarettes, dressed in a skirt and lingered over her dinner in a strange restaurant, a woman alone, untethered. And back in her room, she would lie spread-eagled in the king-sized bed, stark naked, loose and easy, taking every inch of the space for herself.

But this night was different. After a quick dinner, she curled up at the very edge of the bed with the extra pillow lined up along her back. Her eyes were closed against the sight of Dennis Lacey's unmoving profile as he shot past her in his fancy car. What a fool she'd made of herself. The little naive island girl thinking the good doctor wanted anything more of her than a sympathetic ear. All the daydreaming she'd done over the dinner dishes in the last few weeks seemed pathetic to her now. She didn't want to see Dennis Lacey ever again and yet for this year at least, they lived on the same island twelve miles long and three miles wide. She envied him his exotic life in New York, and at the same time, she envied all the women she was sure he'd slept with. The world had passed her by while she was married to Al, trying to have babies, bringing up Erin. Her life with Al stretched behind her and before her like an endless rope.

She remembered the time that Lauren had persuaded her to henna her hair. She liked the way it looked all smooth and shiny with this surprising red tinge to it. But Al said her head smelled funny and he didn't like it and it wasn't worth getting him all steamed up, so she never did it again. He could get crazy about one little thing and just work it into the ground until you didn't know if you could stand to hear about it one minute longer. That's why she kept the cowboy hat in the cupboard in the kennel or under the seat in her car and wore it only when she knew he wasn't around. He had staying power, Al, the power to wear you down. He was patient too. He stalked along the edge of the shore like the blue heron, one careful foot at a time, guarding his life. Change terrified Al. He was a man who was always waiting for something to go wrong, something bad to happen, someone to screw him out of money or steal something that was his, his new tractor, his truck, his workers, his wife.

One night in a mainland motel with Dennis Lacey wouldn't have been enough anyway. But the idea of it, the fact that she would have gone through with it, meant that she had changed. She couldn't go back to being the girl who thought that being married to Al Craven, to your childhood sweetheart from the Island High School, was the best she would ever do, would ever get.

Lying here in the big empty bed, she wished for a moment that she could have stayed in the numbness. Then she might barely have noticed the doctor. She would never have gone walking on the beach with him. And this one night alone in the motel, the eyes of strangers on her at dinner, people who had no idea who she was or where she was from, the smoke from her cigarette blowing away in the wind, it all would have been enough to carry her through the long days ahead in the kitchen with Al's eyes boring through her back.

The summer people said they loved the island because it never changed, it looked the same to them every June when they came back for their vacations. But things did change. New houses went up, the sea sucked away some of the beach, the osprey population decreased, more pheasants escaped the hunters this year than last. She had changed too. Her father had died and she'd spent time walking along the beach with a man who leaned his head toward her voice and it had made her unsatisfied with her life. She wanted more now than she ever had before.

Thirteen

O<small>N THE RETURN</small> ferry Saturday afternoon, Chuck closed down the purser's window as soon as he took Anna's ticket and slid onto the seat next to her. They were each grateful for the company and the warmth of another human body. She was the only passenger over on this bitter Saturday evening. The wind leaked in and around the metal-edged windows, which were crusted over with months of salt spray, one layer dried on top of another. The boat got a good cleaning only once a year, in the spring.

"How did Whistler do?" Chuck asked.

"Passed with flying colors," Anna said. "I picked up two more dogs to train. The owner has a bitch in heat."

"Anyone we know?"

"Walter Perkins. I've heard of him. John Taylor introduced us at the hunting tests over in Millbrook last winter. The guy lives in Maryland. He's inherited a lot of money and he's suddenly gone crazy for vizslas."

You look sad, Anna Craven, Chuck thought. You're keeping something locked up inside. "The rest of your brood is fine," he said. "I took two of the dogs out for a run on Starfish. Cinnamon seems pretty droopy these days."

"She's getting old. I'm wondering whether she'll last the winter. It's rough out there, isn't it?"

Dan Chester was steering the boat way upwind, so they didn't take the swells on the beam. Anna didn't mind. The longer the trip took, the better. I don't want to go home, Anna thought. What's happened to me? How am I going to keep on this way?

"You okay?" Chuck asked. Their eyes met. She was the first to look away.

"Why didn't you ever get married, Chuck?"

He felt the tips of his ears getting red. "Never found a woman as nice as you," he said.

She had a sudden urge to rest her head on his shoulder, close her eyes, and fall asleep. Maybe then she would wake up in the middle of some other life. There was nobody in the cabin with them, but she restrained herself. She knew that Chuck had always had a crush on her, and she didn't want to do anything to upset the delicate relationship they'd forged over the years. She thought of Dennis Lacey's broad shoulder, the brown wax coat he was wearing on the boat. Was it only yesterday that she'd slipped him that foolish note? It seemed like a million years ago.

"Al didn't get the Latham job," Chuck said quietly. Better she be warned.

She snapped to attention. "How do you know?"

"He was down at the Lounge last night, ranting and raving about the summer people. Billy Slade told me he got a call yesterday afternoon."

"Shit," Anna said. She didn't swear often.

Chuck didn't tell her what the whole island must know by now, that Al went home from the Lounge with Lauren. Hell, the asshole hadn't even tried to make a secret of it. But he must not have spent the night with her because when Chuck drove up at seven to let the dogs out, Al's truck was back in his driveway. Lauren was probably the one who shoved him out of bed, reminded him that his daughter was home alone last night. You deserve better, he wanted to say to Anna.

"It's going to be a long night," she said staring straight ahead of her. He wondered if she even knew she'd said the words out loud.

It was times like these that Chuck hated this small circle of land they lived on. You knew everybody's business, and with some you didn't give a damn, and with others you were forced to watch and pretend you didn't notice anything. He had to look at Anna every day, watch her shoulders slump at the sound of Al's name, the dark circles deepen under her eyes. If only she would ask him for help, he thought for the thousandth time. But she never asked. And what could he do really? A marriage between two people contained all sorts of secrets and bargains and compromises that nobody else understood. It wasn't a place where you meddled.

AL INSISTED ON cooking dinner that night. He'd actually remembered to get the hamburger out of the freezer ahead of time and he was making his mother's recipe for meat loaf, the only dinner he really knew how to cook, but Anna didn't care. She would eat meat loaf three times a week if he felt like cooking it. She was surprised by the candles on the table and the country western music on the radio. She wondered when he would tell her about the Latham job.

"Where's Erin?" she asked.

"She's gone down to the Malloys' to watch a movie on their VCR. Dan got a new thirty-five-inch set the other day. He's building a cabinet for it. Says he's gonna have himself a whole theater in his den."

"That's nice," Anna said.

"We could have something like that if we had some extra money."

She didn't say anything.

"I'm going to have big cost overruns on that community center job," he said. "Everybody on this island acts like they did me a favor when they gave me that job, but it's no picnic, let me tell you. It's nothing but trouble." He looked at her as if he was expecting some argument, but she still didn't speak. "And now they're all at me because we're not going to get in there until the spring probably."

"The spring?"

"I told them February at the earliest, more likely March."

"For the St. Patrick's Day party?" It was an island tradition, a celebration of winter's end. This year they'd have a real Irishman on hand. The thought of him still made her face go red.

"We'll see."

"Did you hear from Latham?" she asked. Might as well get it over with.

"Bastard took an off islander. Some construction company in Massachusetts. He'll find out."

"That's terrible, Al."

"That's terrible, Al," he mimicked with his back to her. He always said she didn't care about his business. Maybe he was right. No matter how hard she tried now, she couldn't sound sympathetic enough. Too many years, too much water under the bridge, too many slights piled up, one on top of the other. She thought how carefully she'd listened to Dennis Lacey as he told her his childhood stories, the frustrations of the doctor's life. She hadn't heard them all a hundred times before, she didn't know intimately every dip in his voice, every intonation, and what it signified. But he had never made fun of her, imitated her, laughed at her. She wondered if it was possible to sustain kindness like that when you lived day in and day out with another human being. If she had married the doctor fifteen years ago, would he still be acting kindly toward her today? She thought he would, but she didn't trust her girlish romantic notions anymore.

"Stop it, Al," she warned.

"Stop what?"

"Stop imitating me," she said.

They had a moment of silence. Each waited to see what the other would do. Al stirred the gravy so vigorously that some of it splashed up on the wall. She was happy Erin was out of the house. She put up with so much from Al so that Erin wouldn't hear them fighting, but Anna was beginning to realize how absurd that was. Erin knew exactly what was going on. No wonder she spent so much time locked in her bedroom. The silence drew on, and Anna resisted her usual urge to say something to fill it, to make nice. On the radio a woman was singing about a man leaving her. If only, Anna thought.

"Your dog pass the test?"

"Yes," she said, and let out her breath. She hadn't been aware she'd stopped breathing. She stayed silent again. She would not tell him about the new dogs. She would no longer toss him bits of herself just so that he could spit them back at her.

He set the plates down on the table and she pulled in her chair. He popped the tab off two cans of Miller and shoved one in front of her. She hated beer, never drank it, and he knew that.

"No thanks, Al, not for me." This was fun, she thought, just being herself every single minute, not doing what he wanted her to do, doing what she wanted.

"Nothing else to drink," he said.

"I'll have water."

When she started to get up, he caught her by the wrist and held on.

"Al?" she said. "I'm just getting the water."

"You're acting strange tonight," he said. "What's going on?"

You mean I'm not acting like a scared rabbit, she thought. "I'm getting myself some water to drink," she said, pronouncing every word carefully as if she were talking to a child. "Once you let go of my wrist."

They ate in silence, the forks clinking against the china plates, the radio chattering in the background. Usually, she chattered herself because she'd always been frightened of silence. Silent men in her childhood meant secrets, someone drinking, something about to erupt. Tonight, she forced herself to keep quiet. He stared at her once or twice as if willing her to speak, but she pretended not to notice. She chewed slowly, swallowed purposefully. She remembered she'd read somewhere that it took thirty-two muscles to swallow. Think of that. She tried to count the muscles as the food went down, but it didn't seem to be more than three or four. Maybe it wasn't thirty-two. Maybe she'd got that wrong.

"You don't have anything to say?"

"About what, Al?"

"Anything, dammit. Thanks for the meat loaf, Al. Thanks for taking care of that leaky pipe in the upstairs bathroom. Let's go to bed right now while Erin's away. Your gorgeous body turns me on. I can't wait to get my hands on it."

Her throat closed up. "It doesn't," she said.

"What did you say?"

"Your body doesn't turn me on. You can't be at me all day long and expect me to want you at night, Al. It doesn't work that way."

"And how would you know how it works?" he asked, his voice rising. He threw his fork down on the plate and she winced at the noise. She'd never pushed him this far. "How would you know? Have you been out there testing?"

"Don't be ridiculous."

"How do I know what you do when you go to the mainland? How do I know who you're hanging around with, sleeping with?"

She stared at him for a moment without answering because she knew suddenly what this was all about.

"You spent last night with Lauren," she said.

There was a flicker, a tiny moment when his face froze, and he looked like a little boy who'd been caught. Then he started shouting about her goddamn nerve. "I might as well go to another woman for all I get from you." He was standing up now, pointing his finger at her. "Who in God's name do you think you are, Anna Craven? You are my wife, that's who. Nobody else's. I tell you what to do, where to go, how to think, how to spend money. Look at that list," he raged on, pointing at the bulletin board. "Those are your orders. That's so you know what you are expected to do."

While he was yelling, he leaned over until his face was level with hers and she saw the veins in his eyes and the way his skin stretched over his high cheekbones and how thin his blond hair had become. These were things she hadn't noticed in the last few months because she had tried so hard not to look at him. But here, in the kitchen light, she studied him while he yelled and swaggered and dipped in front of her, and she could not understand why, but for the first time ever, she was not scared. She was not scared of Al Craven, her husband, and what he might say or do. And he knew it. And it made him crazy.

"Do you hear me? Do you?"

When she still didn't answer, he grabbed her by the upper arms and pulled her out of her seat.

"Stop it, Al," she said in the calm voice a mother might use with a child who was having a tantrum.

He began to shake her back and forth, ever so slowly, and she tightened her neck muscles against the movement. "Don't you get it?" For a moment, he sounded perplexed. "You need me. You would be nowhere without me. Nothing. Do you get that, Anna?"

His grip was bruising her upper arms. "Al," she said and her voice remained eerily calm. "You're hurting me. Let go."

"Tell me you would be nobody without me," he ordered. "Tell me that. Tell me you're not going anywhere, you're not going to leave me."

She knew he would let her go if she did as he asked, but she could not start lying, not now, not after being one hundred percent herself for at least the last hour. She wouldn't go backward.

"Al, let me go right now, you're not making any sense."

And he did. His hands slid off her and she could see that he had started to cry. This was where he went when nothing else worked because he knew that it always got to her, pulled her back in.

"You're not going to leave me, are you, Anna?" he blubbered as he sank back into his chair and put his head down on the table. "What would I do?" She'd read in magazines about women who wanted their men to cry and show their emotions, but she didn't think this was what they meant. His crying felt forced and melodramatic, just another of his tricks, another way to get her to do what he wanted.

"Were you with Lauren last night?" she asked.

He put his hands over his ears without answering. From the driveway, they heard the slamming of a car door.

"Erin is home," she said in a low voice. "Get up, Al," she said louder, but he shook his head back and forth. Fine. Another moment of truth. If he wanted his daughter to see him this way, then that was his decision. Always before, Anna had tried to stand between them, kept their secrets, protected each from the truth of the other. Not tonight. She picked up the plates and went over to the sink to start washing up.

"Hi," Erin called.

"Hi, sweetie," Anna called back from the sink without turning around.

"What's wrong with Daddy?"

"I don't know," Anna said. There was a moment of silence in the kitchen. One plate slipped out of Anna's hand and clattered against another.

"What's wrong, Daddy?" Erin asked. Her voice had already dropped to its normal wary level.

"Ask your mother." He lifted his head. "If you want to know what's wrong with me, you go and ask your mother."

"I don't want to know," Erin said suddenly, and rushed up the stairs to her room. Her bedroom door closed quietly.

"You are ruining that little girl's life," Al said.

Anna whipped around. "Don't you ever try that with me," she said in a steely voice that surprised both of them. "Ever. Go wash your face. You look ridiculous."

She picked up a jacket and slammed out the door to the kennels.

The dogs jumped up at her unexpected late-night entrance. She leaned her face against the cage and let Cinnamon lick the skin of her cheek through the wire netting.

"Hello, old girl," she whispered. "Want to go for a drive?"

The dog whimpered and the others barked excitedly when they heard the scrape of the metal padlock on Cinnamon's cage.

"No hunting tonight, guys. Just a little fresh air and exercise for Cinnamon and me."

She lifted Cinnamon onto the front seat of the station wagon and slammed the door while the old dog turned and turned before she lowered herself.

AN ISLAND IS a body of land surrounded by water. It is a simple and obvious fact and one you never forget. After living on an island for a while, you begin to internalize the ferry schedules, so your daily rhythm may feel askew if you miss the four o'clock whistle of the incoming boat. You are hemmed in, reminded constantly of edges, of the line drawn between two elements, earth and water. You cannot get in a car and simply keep on driving forever, which is what Anna would have liked so much to do now.

She drove up to the eastern end of the island and back down again. Her driving was reckless; she put the pedal down and smiled at the screech of the tires as they took the corners. A screech around the town green that would bring Annie Slocum to her front picture window, another fast turn at the old duck pond, another at the corner of White Beach. She was headed back home again when she saw the lights of the Harbor Lounge and at the last minute, took that turn on two wheels. Cinnamon lifted her head when the car pulled to a stop, but didn't try to get up.

Saturday night and the bar was full. The place went silent whenever a newcomer showed up, but when the faces saw Anna at the door, it stayed silent longer than usual. Anna was not a frequent visitor at the Harbor Lounge. She nodded at Lila, Jim, Billy Slade, Randy, and some of the others. She was pretty sure that everybody in this little crowd knew where her husband had spent last night. For a fleeting moment, she wished she hadn't come, but it was too late to turn back. She walked the entire length of the bar, past a couple of empty places and slid onto a stool next to Lauren. That actually gave her some pleasure. Lauren's smile of greeting was a little too wide, her voice pitched a bit high.

"What'll it be, Anna?" Lila asked.

"Rum and coke, please."

"How was your trip, Anna?" Billy called from the other end. Everybody in this room was now going to try to keep the two women from talking to each other. Anna liked that she knew what they thought she didn't know. The first sip of her drink filled her throat with a thick sweet taste. She took another. It helped her hold on to the reckless feeling.

"It was good, Billy. Whistler did his stuff. Passed his class."

"Good dog."

"Good trainer," Anna replied as she took off her black hat and laid it on the bar.

"I saw that fellow Murch getting on his boat a while ago. He must be a hell of a guy to take out. Wouldn't want to be around him with a loaded gun."

"It's harder on the dogs than it is on me," Anna said. She'd raised her voice so it reached Billy and all the conversations in between were suspended for the moment. "So what happened around here last night?"

People shifted on their stools and murmured and harumphed. "Somebody vandalized that old BMW Mrs. Oliver leaves down at the dock," Lila said. "Painted slogans all over the doors and the hood."

"Who was it?" Anna asked.

"Probably the Tremayne boys. They could have gotten the paint out of their father's garage."

"They could have gotten the paint out of anybody's garage," Jim said.

"Randy thinks they're hitting the pot pretty hard," Lila said.

"How come?" Anna asked. You'd think she'd been away for a month instead of a night.

Randy leaned forward. His girlfriend, Ellie, was twined so tightly around his arm that she leaned with him. "I caught them hanging around down at the pits two weekends in a row. All the paraphernalia was there."

"Better get the sheriff on it," Anna said. "Unless he's too busy with other matters." She lifted her glass again and enjoyed the silence. It seemed suddenly that nobody could think of any topic to discuss. "So, Lauren, what did you do last night?"

Lauren stared straight ahead at the mirror behind the bar. She shrugged. "Nothing much. Got a movie. *Racing with the Moon*. Same old one, but I love that Sean Penn."

Anna took a chance. "Funny. Al said he saw you down here last night."

"Well, I was here too. What's the deal? Who made you the big detective all of a sudden?"

Now the crowd was shifting, talking about the weather, the new dump schedule, anything to derail these two.

Anna didn't drink often. The rum had given her a quick buzz and she savored the feeling. She put her hand on Lauren's bare arm, was surprised by the silky plumpness of it. All that moisturizer did make a difference, then. How rough and callused her own palms must feel to Lauren. "So, how was he?" Anna asked, her voice turned down only one notch. Lila could still hear them. So could Jim and Randy and a few others.

"You're drunk, Anna."

"Not yet," Anna said. "But it sounds like a good idea to me. Everybody here knows where Al went last night. Why shouldn't I? Lila, I'll have another drink, please. One more for the road as they say."

"Sure thing," Lila said. She was enjoying this exchange.

"I find that he does a lot of talking and swaggering around, but when it comes right down to things, he's a little clumsy, don't you think?"

Lauren had decided to stonewall. She rolled her eyes at Lila, who simply stared back at her. Once again the crowd had given up their feeble attempts at conversation. None of them had ever seen Anna Craven like this. What had happened to her?

Anna rubbed Lauren's arm again. "You think I've got calluses," she said. "Have you ever tried to get him to use some of your lotions?"

"Anna, you're crazy," Lauren said as she shook off the other woman's hand.

Anna turned back to her audience. "First I'm drunk, now I'm crazy."

A few of them chuckled.

Lauren got to her feet and pulled on her jacket. "Your husband is a lonely man, Anna. If you gave him what he wanted, then he wouldn't have to come to me."

Anna picked up her glass and threw the drink in Lauren's face. She savored the look of surprise and then horror as the sticky liquid hit the other woman's wide soft cheekbones. "Hope that doesn't mess up the dye in your hair," Anna said. "Here, I'll help you dry you off." She picked up a fistful of napkins from the bar and moved toward her.

"Don't you get near me," Lauren screamed. "You've gone nuts. The hell with all of you." She dropped her keys, retrieved them, and flounced out of the room. All of this took some time, but nobody tried to stop her.

"Did she pay her bill, Lila?" Randy sang out as the front door of the bar slammed in their ears.

"She'll be back another day," Lila said. "You can count on it. How about you, Anna? Looks like you lost your drink."

All the energy had drained out of Anna's body. She didn't want to stay here and listen to them gossip about Lauren. They'd be on her side while she was sitting here, but the moment she left, Anna knew the talk would go against her. Gossip on this island turned and turned again as regular as the tides.

"No thanks, Lila. I'd better pay my bill because I may not be back anytime soon."

"It's true, we don't see you in here much. Three dollars. The second one's on the house."

"Actually, it's on the floor," Anna said with a grin. "But thanks."

"And I didn't even offer to mop it up," she reported to Cinnamon on the way home. "Now that is something."

THE LIGHTS WERE on in the kitchen. For the first time that she could remember, she walked right past the dirty dishes still on the table, the meat loaf pan out on the counter. Let it go bad. Let someone else deal, she thought.

On the way home, she had made up her mind that she would sleep on the couch in the study, but she tiptoed up the stairs first, as she always did, to look in on Erin. She slipped through a narrow crack in the door so the light from the hallway didn't wake her daughter. When did she first notice that something was wrong? Halfway to the bed? Standing over the body that should be one and was actually two? Or was it simply another symptom of her peculiar illness, the one that must have started when she was small, the sickness that would not allow what her eyes were seeing to register on the brain or what her ears were hearing to connect with her heart. Maybe it started all the way back when she was ten years old, the day her mother went to bed and refused to get up again. Your mother is okay, she is not sick, she will get well, she will not leave, she will stay, after all she is your mother. Her father used to repeat those words over and over to Anna. It always sounded more like a prayer than a promise. Maybe the day the prayers started was the day she started going deaf, dumb, and blind.

She pushed the door wide open and flipped on the overhead light. Erin did not move, her face toward the flowered wallpaper, her eyes squeezed shut. Al rolled over from where he had curled up against his daughter's body, stretched his arm, put a hand up to shield his eyes from the light.

"What in God's name—"

"Al, get out," Anna snarled. "Right now." She did not raise her voice, she allowed Erin the pretense of continued sleep.

Al was already moving. When he stood up, she saw that he had on a pair of pajamas. He had not worn pajamas in bed with her since their honeymoon, and she wondered where he'd been keeping these. She didn't remember ever seeing them before. He looked like a little boy in them, the white cotton drawstring dangling down in front.

She pointed to the hallway and flattened herself against the wall to let him pass. Then she followed him out and shut the door behind them.

"I don't know what's gotten into you, Anna. You've gone crazy."

"What were you doing in my daughter's bed?" she asked. "Did you touch her?"

"Don't you dare say that to me. I'm not a goddamned pervert," he roared.

"How would I know?" she said.

This time he reached out and took her face between his two hands. She felt the calluses on his palms, the tips of his fingers pressed against her cheekbones.

"Listen, you bitch, if you're not going to take care of me, then—" he stopped. Even he stopped there, Anna thought. Maybe for a moment, he actually heard what he was saying.

"Your thirteen-year-old daughter is supposed to take care of you, Al?" she asked, and he was holding her face so tightly that his fingers moved up and down with the muscles of her jaw as she talked. "Isn't Lauren Root enough?"

"And why the hell not?" he spat as he pushed her away from him. "You lock yourself in the bathroom."

He roared then, but she paid no attention. She kept walking away from him down the narrow upstairs hallway, expecting each second to feel his hands on her from behind. His words were almost meaningless, a jumble of incoherent curses strung together, one tumbling over another like little animals scrambling to get out of his mouth. At the top of the stairs, she reached for the banister, but she misjudged the distance, missed it, and went down. Her cheekbone slapped against the edge of a step and the pain shot up past her eye. Another step caught her in the small of the back and she rolled over one more time before she managed to stop herself a foot from the bottom. Erin must have been listening with her ear pressed against her bedroom door because suddenly she was scuttling along the hall past her father. She slipped and slid down the stairs to her mother.

"Mommy, are you okay?" she cried. "Are you okay?"

"Just bruised, sweetie," she whispered.

"Your mother tripped, Erin," Al said from the top of the stairs.

They ignored him. Anna's back was aching badly. She was not ready to move yet.

"Are you sure you're okay?" Erin whispered.

"Yup. How about you?"

"I'm fine. I was sleeping, but the noise woke me up."

Poor baby, Anna thought. How long ago did she start playing deaf, dumb, and blind too?

"You two stop whispering," Al said, still at the top of the stairs. He made no move toward them. "Everybody should get back to bed."

He sounded so strange, his large voice booming in the hallway. This is not a civic association meeting, Anna thought. You are talking to your wife who just fell down the stairs, and your daughter, who you've been sleeping with. She shuddered.

"Are you cold, Mom?"

"A little. Come on, I'll take you back to bed."

I will be much stiffer tomorrow, Anna thought as she hauled herself, hand over hand, up the banister. Al walked ahead of them down the hall and into Erin's room. He started rearranging the sheets on her bed.

"Daddy," Erin said. "I want to go to sleep. I'm tired." She crawled in, and her father sat on the edge of the bed. He put up his hand to smooth the hair off her forehead. A shiver ran through Anna's body. She wanted to get him up off the bed, out of there, away from Erin, but she knew if she tried to hurry him, he would refuse to go.

"My turn, Al," she said.

He leaned over and kissed Erin good night. Anna couldn't remember the last time he'd done this. The gap in his pajama bottoms fell open and she looked away. Finally, he got to his feet, but he didn't leave the room. Anna had expected this. He never left them alone together. He stood at the door with his arms folded across his chest, watching.

"Good night, sweetie," Anna whispered in her ear. "We'll talk tomorrow."

"I don't want to talk," Erin said.

"Talk about what?" Al asked.

"Nothing, Al," Anna said as she started out of the room.

This was why she often stayed away from Erin when Al was in the house. She hated for her daughter to feel like a bone they fought over.

Anna put a cold washcloth on her swelling cheekbone and a hot water bottle under her tailbone, and fell into a restless sleep on the couch in the living room. Toward morning, she opened her eyes and stared at the unfamiliar ceiling. People were used to the ceilings in their bedrooms, but who bothered to look at the ceiling in a living room? She was sore all over, but it was not the pain that had woken her. It was a presence in the room. Al was sitting in his easy chair, the place where he normally settled down to watch television and shout questions at her about dinner. He was sitting up absolutely still, his eyes on her.

"What are you doing?"

"I'm watching you," he said.

"Why?"

"You can't be trusted anymore."

"Me?" She stared at him. "What a joke. What if I had decided to get on your radio and put out an emergency call. Port Five to all stations. Situation at the Cravens' house. Or maybe I should have phoned the Harbor Lounge and asked Lila to send everybody up here. What's the problem? she'd ask. I need some help getting Al Craven out of his daughter's bed, I'd say. What would they think of that?"

He didn't speak for a while. "You know, Anna," he said sometime later, and his voice floated over her in the dark, "when one of your dogs starts to lose its training, you have to put them back on the check cord, pull 'em in. I have never laid a hand on you. Other men would do that, Anna, would snap on that cord hard for the kinds of things you say to me. You don't have any idea how lucky you are."

"And I should be grateful to you for this? I should be happy because you don't hit me? Is that your idea of a marriage, Al?"

For once, he seemed to have nothing more to say.

She rolled over, turned her back to him, and pulled her knees up until they brushed the thick cushions of the couch. Fine. If he wanted to watch her sleep, then let him. At least he wasn't in Erin's room.

Fourteen

ANNA COULD NOT hide the bruise on her cheek. The ugly red lump splayed upward, where by morning, it had turned the well socket of her eye a deep blue and purple. When she looked closely in the mirror, she could see tiny strands of red woven in. Her skin was puffy and tender.

When Miss Yola called to ask about a ride to church, Anna pretended to be coming down with a cold. The same excuse got her out of her morning job at the post office the next day, and she put Chuck off for two days by telling him the dogs needed a rest. He didn't believe her, but he stayed away.

There was nothing she could do when he showed up with no warning the third day. He must have waited until he saw Al in town before he drove up. He caught her in the kitchen, cleaning up after breakfast and the look on his face convinced her that the bruise must not have faded as much as she had hoped.

"Stop staring, Chuck. It rattles me."

By the way she lowered herself into one of the straightbacked chairs, he saw that other parts of her body must have been bruised too. He had brought her coffee from the Rocky Point.

"Sorry, it's pretty cooled off already."

"It doesn't matter," she said. Her voice was thick. A man had brought her a cup of coffee. Such a small thing really and yet so huge.

"What happened?"

"I fell down the stairs," she said.

"Saturday night?" he asked.

"Yes. Why?"

"I heard about your run-in with Lauren down at the Lounge."

She allowed herself a grin. "And what did you hear?"

"That you threw a drink in her face. People said you were pretty looped."

"On one rum and coke?" She snorted. "I may not be a regular customer at Lila's, but I can hold my liquor a little better than that. I knew exactly what I was doing." But never mind, she thought. Let people think she was drunk and fell down the stairs.

"Are you going to tell me what happened?"

"I don't think so."

"Why?"

"Because I know you," she said. "You will feel that you have to do something about it. I want to work my way through this on my own."

"Have you got any ideas?"

"I'm thinking," she said, lifting her head with a brave smile. "It's more complicated than it looks."

"Humph," he said. "Things that seem complicated are usually very simple. Is this the first time he hit you?"

"He didn't hit me," she said. "I missed the banister."

"Are you sure?"

"Yes. You knew about him and Lauren, didn't you? When you saw me on the boat?"

"I didn't know for sure, but they left the bar together Friday night. I saw no reason to tell you. He was wild enough about losing the Latham job. I thought you should be warned about that."

"Thanks," she said. It had allowed her that one reckless night.

"I don't think he spent the whole night at Lauren's. He must have realized he was leaving Erin alone, because his truck was back here when I came to do the dogs early Saturday morning."

"No. He doesn't like to leave Erin alone." She spoke so slowly that her words almost sounded slurred.

WHEN DENNIS LACEY got back from New York, he was struck by the silence on the island. He had never realized before how much he hated the noise of the city, the car alarms, the horns, the fuck you's echoing up from the street at three in the morning. He didn't think about the island over the weekend, but he was perfectly happy to find himself leaving the city behind on Sunday afternoon. A play, a pleasant dinner with an old friend, a brief meeting with Isabelle over divorce details. It had all gone off perfectly well, but he had felt distanced from it, as if he were dropping in on his old life the way you revisit a childhood house.

All week, Lauren flirted with him. By Thursday, she had taken to brushing up against him whenever they happened to meet in the narrow hallway outside his offices. He didn't mind particularly, even let down his professional guard a bit to joke with her about a movie they had both seen.

"I hope you're not going to hole yourself up on Christmas Day," she said with a wide smile. "You're certainly welcome to join me if you'd like."

"Thanks," he said. "But I do have plans."

He planned to take a long walk on the beach, cook himself a chicken, and get some painting done if he could. Christmas had always felt oppressive to him. "Who's in the waiting room?" he asked, happy to change the subject.

"Chuck Montclair. He's got a bad knee. That's probably what he's here for. It acts up every once in a while."

"Well, Chuck, what's the problem?" Dennis said once the man was settled on the table.

Chuck went on about his knee for a bit, and Dennis asked the requisite questions and twisted the leg about, but all along he had the feeling Chuck was there for some other reason. Finally the man got around to it.

"Mrs. Craven come in today?" Chuck asked once Dennis had written out a prescription for some anti-inflammatory pills.

Dennis hesitated a minute before he answered.

"No. Should she?"

"I think so."

"Why, what's happened to her?"

"She's got a nasty bruise on her cheek, just below the eye."

Dennis turned to his desk and pretended to search for something. He had a feeling this conversation would be easier for both of them if their eyes didn't meet.

"I saw her going over on the boat to the mainland on Friday and she looked fine then. What happened?"

"She *says* she fell down the stairs." Another pause.

"But you don't think she fell."

"No sir, I don't."

"And what do you want me to do about it?"

"I think she should have that eye looked at."

Finally Dennis turned around. "Chuck, I can't go out looking for patients. She's got to come in here to see me."

"She says she's going to figure things out herself. She's a stubborn woman, Doctor."

And you're in love with her, Dennis thought. "I expect she is. If you train dogs, you've got to be tougher than they are."

Chuck pulled the leg of his khakis back down over his bony knee.

"Do you think her husband hit her?" Dennis asked.

"I think he did something. Maybe he pushed her down the stairs."

"What is your opinion of Al Craven? Is he a dangerous man?"

Chuck considered his answer for a long time. Dangerous in a subtle way, he thought. Just yesterday some of the materials came in for the community center. The wiring was Billy Slade's department, but Chuck had a look at some of the other stuff. Al had ordered half-inch plywood, that lower-grade C/D stuff to go in under the roof shingles. No roofing paper. The exterior cedar shingles were arriving on today's boat, and Chuck was pretty sure he knew already what grade they would be. Al was up to all his old tricks.

"Chuck?" the doctor said. "If you think there's a real problem at the Cravens, you can call it in to the office of social services over on the mainland. Report it anonymously."

That idea horrified Chuck. He wished he had never opened his mouth. It was seeing Anna's face like that the day before. It made him forget that this doctor didn't belong here, didn't understand their ways.

"Nah, it's not that bad," Chuck said quickly. "Forget I brought it up."

Island mentality, Dennis thought as he watched Chuck tying his shoe. He remembered it from Omey, all those years ago. We take care of our own. We don't want any meddling from mainlanders. Dennis couldn't blame him. When he thought back to his own experiences in the city hospitals with social service agencies, he was pretty sure his patients would have been better off taking care of their own business. After all, these were crimes without witnesses, one person's word against another. What could the police and the courts and the social workers presume to know about what happened on a staircase between a husband and wife?

"Chuck, I'll see what I can do," the doctor said as the other man struggled into his jacket.

"You're not going to call anybody from the outside," Chuck said.

"No, I wouldn't do that."

"Don't forget. Al Craven is the sheriff."

"I know that. I know what you're saying. I grew up on an island myself."

They shook hands. "I'd still like to see your photographs sometime if you feel like showing me."

"Sure thing," Chuck said, although the doctor was sure he wouldn't be hearing from the older man any time soon. Chuck stumped off down the hall to Lauren's desk to give her his insurance card. Lauren tried to chat him up, but Chuck gave her monosyllabic answers and got out of there as soon as he could.

"What's wrong with him?" Lauren asked.

"He's worried about Anna Craven," the doctor said from the door of his office. "Have you seen her? Apparently she's got a bad bruise on her cheek."

There was a look on Lauren's face that slowed the doctor down. He thought the two women were friends. "Anna got drunk on Saturday night. Made a real fool of herself. I wouldn't show my face in town this week either if I'd behaved the way she did."

The doctor went back into his office and closed the door. He'd broken the cardinal island rule. Get your information sideways. Never ask a direct question. Everything in him was warning him not to get involved in this. He was only here until Memorial Day. Just keep your head low and do your job. Don't stick your neck out. Last time you did that, you got booted out of the hospital.

THAT AFTERNOON HE drove up the island to Starfish Beach. Sure enough, her station wagon was parked in the lot with a dog crate in the back. He sat in his car for a while, fighting with himself. Back up and turn around, one voice said. Go see for yourself, said the other. He sat in the middle doing nothing until the decision was made for him. The dogs came first, padding along the narrow boardwalk from the beach. He got out and waited for her by her car, his hands down for the dogs to lick. She approached slowly, her eyes on the ground in front of her. She was wearing the cowboy hat and a scarf pulled up high around her face. She didn't see him until the last minute.

"You look like a desperado," he said lightly. When at last she lifted her face, he saw that she had been crying.

"Good afternoon, Dr. Lacey," she said. Her voice was firm, matter of fact, as disconnected from the tears in her eyes as she could make it. "Did you have a good trip?"

He put his hand up to pull the scarf down and to his surprise, she allowed him to look and even to press gently with his fingertips. She winced.

"Still hurts?"

"Yes," she said. "Who told you to come looking for me?"

"Nobody," he said.

"You're a lousy liar."

He nodded. "Always have been. Not a good trait for a doctor."

"So, is anything broken?"

"Not as far as I can tell. It would be better if I could take a look at you in the office."

"No way," she said. "I'm staying away from town a little while. I expect you've heard already that I can't hold my liquor." He didn't answer. She put up the whistle and blew for the dogs, then lowered the tailgate and kenneled them.

"Did Whistler pass the test?" he asked.

"With flying colors. It seems like a million years ago."

"Anna, there are things you can do. People you can call."

She shook her head. "No, Dr. Lacey, you're wrong this time. There is nobody I can call. This is a personal matter. It looks easy to figure out on the surface of things, but it's not."

He listened to her, and he knew she wanted to get away from him, but he didn't make room for her. "I'm sorry," he said.

"About what?" Her voice was sharp, and when he didn't answer right away, she laughed. "About my foolishness the other day? I'm just a naive island girl, Doctor. I'm not one of your sophisticated city ladies. I let my mind run away with me. You were smart to pass on by. Best not to get involved."

Of course that was exactly what he'd been thinking himself, so he didn't mean to do what he did next. It simply happened. He put his arms around her and pulled her close against him. Her hair smelled of leather, and he thought maybe it was the hat, which had fallen off onto the ground. When she started to cry again, he swayed back and forth, tipping all his weight first onto one foot and then onto the other, and he felt her body sink against his, soothed by the rocking motion. How long did they stay this way? Long enough that he thought her ears must be getting cold so he put his hand up and cupped the exposed one. The other was still pressed against his chest. She continued to cry quietly, whimpering. When the sobs got trapped in her chest, her whole body shook with the force of them and he loosened his arms a bit to be sure she had room to breathe. Finally, she grew still.

She slid a hand into her pocket and pulled out a Kleenex. "Now I'm the one who's sorry," she muttered, her head still pressed against his jacket. She would have to move away soon, any minute now. It was getting dark, Erin was waiting for her at home, the dogs were restless in their cage. But she wanted simply to rest against the wall of this man for a few minutes more.

"Better?" he asked, and she nodded.

"Has anything like this happened before?" he asked. Now he had broken the spell, and she pulled away. She wanted no more talking. The voices in her own head were so loud and clamorous and insistent that she didn't think she could bear to hear one more word.

"Thank you," she said. "I need to get home now." He stepped away from the door. His look on her was steady and accepting.

"If you need help, please call me."

"I will. Thank you." She took his hand and squeezed it, grateful that he was not wearing gloves. She wanted the touch of his skin. He squeezed back. And then she got out of there as fast as she could.

THE BLIZZARD WAS supposed to start sometime during Christmas Eve night. Everybody had been watching the television and by noon, the store shelves were stripped. Maggie stocked up on food in the morning. She was pulling an extra load of firewood in off the porch when Chuck came by to check on her in the afternoon.

"How's Kasha like the new door?"

Even though he hadn't managed to get the roof fixed before the cold weather socked in, Chuck had built Kasha a dog door off the kitchen two days after Maggie had called him about it.

"She loves it," she said. "She's acting like a puppy again. But she's always back for dinner. I guess her rabbit hunting hasn't produced much results."

"And you're letting her roam off by herself? Good for you."

"The first couple of days were hard for me, but I think Kasha knew that," Maggie said. "She checks back in. She never stays away more than a couple of hours."

"The hot water heater is fine and the furnace seems to be holding up," he said as he stomped up the stairs from the basement. "I added an extra layer of insulation around that corner pipe last summer. Should keep it from freezing."

"Do you think it's going to be as bad as they say? I've heard predictions of three feet of snow."

He shrugged. "These weathermen turn every snowflake into a crisis. I probably would too if I had nothing else to talk about all day. But this time it looks like a big one. Fifty-mile-an-hour winds and drifting snow. That's like a hurricane with snow instead of rain. Whatever boats aren't already in dry dock are going to have a hard time of it. Even Dan Malloy's got a crew down there hauling in his boat and I don't remember the last time he took it out of the water."

"I guess we'll have a white Christmas," she said.

"There's a community carol service tonight in the Catholic church. An island tradition that started a while ago. Only time most of the people here ever darken the door of that church. "

"Sam told me. I'll be there. Singing carols is my favorite part of Christmas."

She didn't tell him that afterward Sam had invited her to go on an owl walk. She called him after Chuck left to see if he wanted to cancel.

"No reason. They're saying the snow isn't due to start until midnight anyway. But no Kasha."

"I figured."

THE CATHOLICS ON the island were a small but hardy group, many of them descended from the French who came at the end of the last century to work as fishermen. In July and August, the overall church population on the island tripled with the influx of summer people, mostly Episcopalians, who attended the ten o'clock service in the quaint white clapboard church with a different minister imported every Sunday from like-minded resorts up and down the coast. These thin, reedy men knew to preach gentle sermons taken from the Bible lesson of the day, and always to use the old form of the liturgy, which meant Communion was only offered the first week of every month, and there was none of that nonsense about hand-shaking and giving the peace in the middle of the service. It was well known that Episcopalians did not go in much for pressing the flesh, particularly if the fellow was your next-door neighbor and a member of your golf foursome from the day before. Afterward the minister could expect a lavish lunch at the club with well-meaning members of the vestry and a pleasant trip home on the afternoon ferry.

The Catholic priest came every Saturday for the late-afternoon

Mass and stayed over to say the two Masses the next day. For a while, some years ago, the local Catholics actually found a priest who was willing to live on the island. He bought some property with money he had inherited and built a modern wooden house with a second-story deck, where he could be seen early in the morning doing aerobic exercises in aged sweatpants. He had long since moved on, and despite the neighbors' efforts to screen it with plantings, the house was still considered the island eyesore.

Maggie looked for Sam when she first arrived but when she couldn't find him, she sat with Dan Chester who moved over to make room for her. They shared a hymnal, and she slid down the Glorias in her strong alto voice right along with him. She was glad to be sitting next to a man. Women with high sopranos like Lauren and Miss Yola made Maggie feel clumsy. Two pews ahead, Erin was sitting between her parents. Erin turned around and waved a couple of times. Anna had a scarf pulled right up to her ears.

"What was she fighting with Lauren over?" Maggie had asked Sam when he told her the story. "I thought they were friends."

"Over where her husband spent last Friday night."

"Al Craven spent the night with Lauren?" Maggie said. "You mean when Anna took the dog off island?"

"Right. Probably not the first time either."

"What about Erin? Was she all alone up there?"

Sam shrugged. "For most of the night at least."

"Al Craven's a creep," Maggie said.

"My sentiments precisely."

SHE AND SAM found each other during the general greetings out in the vestibule. Talk was all of the approaching snow and they managed to slip away easily. They drove in his truck to the wilderness area halfway up island. He didn't speak much and she was happy to ride along next to him in silence. Over on the mainland, this season had become too bright, too tinseled, too packaged for Maggie. Christmas on the island felt low-key and quiet in comparison. The enormous pine on the town green had been festooned with multi-colored lights, and a week ago everybody had trooped dutifully into the school gym for the Christmas program.

Sam had met her at the door and led her to a seat near the front. He was wearing blue jeans, a button-down shirt, and a wild red-and-green tie.

"I've never seen you dressed up before. I love it."

"I was hoping you would," he'd said before he disappeared behind the curtain to help with some last-minute set repair.

"We may not see any owls after all," Sam said, cocking his head to peer up through the windshield at the sky. "The moon is up, but it's already begun to cloud over."

She nodded without speaking. She'd love to see an owl, but she was happy to be out in the brisk air, a million miles away from lights and people and her old life.

He pulled the car into the parking area for the driving range and led her back down the road, searching for the entrance. "Here we go," he said, as he dipped left down a scrabbly path. "Careful here, it's slippery."

She followed him up and down the little hills. Above, the trees stood stripped of leaves, black lines against a clouding sky. The three-quarter moon was high enough to wash the land with a pale silver light. In the distance, the waves crashed on Chincoteale, and she imagined the water sluicing between the rocks, scooping up some sand, and racing back to the sea with its prize. It was as if the sea and the land were always arguing over their borders, not unlike human beings with their endless territorial disputes.

Up ahead, Sam raised his right hand to warn her that he was stopping. They stood that way in complete silence for some minutes as he listened. Then he called and his voice sounded just like an owl's, a deep repetitive hoo, hoo, hoo. "Eight notes," he whispered in her ear. "The barred owl's call."

The breath from his voice tickled the hair on her cheek. He smelled of garlic, and she wondered what he'd been cooking this time. He called again, waited, then walked on. She hunched her shoulders against the cold and wished she'd taken that extra few minutes to find her scarf before she ran out the door.

"Hoo, hoo, hoo," he called again. From somewhere out in front of them, she heard a loud screaming *shree, shree*. He caught her hand and squeezed it.

"What was that?" she whispered.

"Barn owl. Watch the sky."

They waited and they watched. She was aware of a million different tiny sounds in the woods, branches creaking in the wind, snuffling in the underbrush, the tiny mouse scurrying for cover because maybe it knew what was waiting for it, circling, searching. Sam was still holding her hand and he squeezed again once and pointed, and up above, a dark shape floated. She could not make out where it came from, what branch served as its launching pad. It circled, a big, wide, slow, leisurely circle, flapped once, circled again, then dropped like a stone out of sight. She imagined the squeal of a small animal caught in the clearing. What must that be like to feel a shadow that large drop on you from nowhere? The first hint you have is the rushing of the wind, then out of the corner of your eye, the shape, then the sharp claws in your neck. She didn't realize how hard she'd been squeezing Sam's hand until he gently undid her fingers one at a time.

"I'm losing circulation," he whispered and shifted her hand to his other one.

"Sorry. Male or female?"

"Probably the male. Bringing home offerings for the little woman."

"Do you think we'll see him again?"

"Depends on whether he caught something, how much of a meal the something was, whether he's still hungry."

"Poor something," she said. "Did you hear it scream?"

"No. Did you?"

"I imagined I did."

"You can imagine all sorts of things in the woods at night."

She knew what he meant. They waited a few minutes longer, then he started off along another path, one that climbed steadily upward until they broke out of the woods into a clearing over a sandy bluff. Down below lay the grassy meadow beyond the driving range and the wetlands that bordered the easternmost edge of Chincoteale. In the bad autumn storms, the waves often sent the sea water spilling over the rocks and the wetlands would become a pond for a while. From this high up, the greenish-white line of the foamy water at the edge of the distant beach was barely visible as the waves attacked and retreated, attacked and retreated.

"I love the sea," she said.

He let go of her hand and swept the shoreline with his binoculars. The owl called again and they turned around just in time to see him float out of a thick set of branches and make his patient, ghostly circle, head down, scanning the landscape.

"If he doesn't see the mouse, he hears it," Sam said. "They have the most incredible hearing, as good as their sight. And because they fly so silently, they never seem to be in a rush."

"Don't tell me that," Maggie said. "You mean the mouse has no chance."

"Very little if he's out in the open. The hunter and the hunted."

The owl floated back into the woods. A bank of clouds was moving across the face of the moon.

"We'd better head back. The wind is coming up." He was disappointed. He had wanted to show her a great gray. It would have served as a kind of Christmas present from the island, but he had learned over the years that nature rarely adjusted itself to his desires.

Even with his flashlight, it took them a while to find their way down the narrow paths. By the time they reached the truck, it had started to snow, big sloppy flakes that melted the instant they hit the windshield. Ten minutes later, he had slowed to a crawl. The wind was rocking the truck and the rear wheels were starting to slide on the curves. Now the snow was sticking.

"I can't see anything," he said in that low voice of his. "Except the snowflakes two inches in front of the lights. Lucky I know every twist and turn in this damn road."

She rested her hand lightly on his right shoulder. Maybe he didn't even feel it through his thick plaid jacket. He kept his eyes on the road.

"There's the platform for the osprey nest," she said. "We must be next to the water filtration plant."

"Thought we were farther down. Watch for the barn across the road from the entrance to Chincoteale. I don't want to land in that ditch."

They both hunched forward and stared out the windshield. The only sound was the motor gunning whenever he dropped down a gear and the slap of the wipers back and forth.

"Merry Christmas Eve," she said, and he chuckled.

"Hope we don't spend it out in the elements." He didn't take his eyes off the road, and she stared out at the falling snow, but she was imagining herself waking up on Christmas morning with this still, thoughtful man under her down comforter. She didn't believe she'd ever spent this much time with a man in almost total silence. Silent night, holy night.

"There's the barn," she called out as the ghostly shape slid by her window.

"I see it, thanks. I'm kicking myself. I went off without my radio. Of all the times."

She saw now that it was not on the front seat, not hooked to his belt. Funny how used she'd grown to the sight of those radios sticking out of the men's back pockets, slung on the dashboard of trucks parked at the post office. When you were in the grocery store next to a volunteer fireman, you could always hear the low crackle of static with a voice breaking through from time to time.

The truck slid off the road when he made the turn by the golf course.

"Here we go," he sang out as he tried to pull it around, like a sailboat in a high wind. But the wheels did not respond, and the truck finally came to rest facing the wrong way in the opposite lane, half in a ditch. He turned off the engine and they sat for a minute in silence.

"Sorry about that," he said.

"Nothing you could do. I'm glad I wore my good boots."

"I should leave the flashers on, but it will drain the battery."

"I doubt anybody will run into it," she said. "We're the only ones crazy enough to be out in this."

The wind was fierce. It picked the snowflakes up and drove them horizontally into the cracks of space between their hats and scarves. They held hands and leaned into the wind, slipping and sliding down the hill above the Catholic church. The lights from the houses they passed shed a hazy glow on the swirling snow. Down the hill to the town green, right at the big pine tree with its trails of colored bulbs, past the row of summer stores, shuttered up since Labor Day. Now there were no lights to follow because Nan's house lay at the end of the road of mansion cottages. Only summer people lived here. Maggie imagined them tossing back eggnog in their Beacon Street houses or their Park Avenue apartments. She wondered if they ever thought about their island homes, buried under a winter blizzard. Sam's voice in her ear startled her. They hadn't spoken for a while.

"Can you see anything?" he shouted. "We've got to take a left here soon."

"I know. I'm watching for the big yellow house, but it's too far off the road, I think. And there are no lights."

"Summer houses," he said, and they trudged on. The radio said that morning that the snow could come down at the rate of two to three inches an hour. Maggie figured there were three on the ground, but she couldn't really tell because in some places they had come across bare patches of ground, and in others the wind had blown the dry snow into a drift that seemed to crawl right up the side of a tree. She was aware of every leak in her armor, every tiny crack where the snow managed to blow in and melt against her skin. She was cold and wet and tired, and they seemed to have lost their way. He was holding her under the arm now the way you hold an old lady you are helping across the street. She leaned against his body, trying to close all the gaps between them.

"Can you make it?" he called to her, and she nodded. She didn't have the energy to yell back. The wind snatched their words away.

"Left here," he said, and steered her in that direction. She was sure he was wrong, it was too early to make the left, but it turned out they were both wrong. It was too late. They found themselves blundering around in somebody's backyard.

"The Hales," he called, and she knew where they were now. More summer people, this was one of the oldest houses on the island. It stood across from the ballfield, and in good weather you could see the reflection of the sun off its white clapboard siding all the way from the harbor. She was beginning to feel panicky now. Kasha could go in and out of the house with the new dog door, but she hadn't eaten since last night. Maggie thought of stories she'd read about people lost in the deep Northern woods who lay down in the snow and simply went to sleep because they couldn't bother to make the effort anymore. It was a dramatic thought when she knew they were only a mile from home, and in her mind, she could see every house, every twist and turn in Nan's road. Once they found the road. If they found the road.

"We're headed in the right direction at least," he called as he pushed them through another snow-covered hedge. "We must be on the upper road above the club."

"I left the porch light on," she said. "We can look for that."

He didn't answer, and she was not sure whether he heard her. She was too tired to repeat herself.

She didn't remember the last part. Her eyes were closed almost all the time to keep the snow out. His arm circled her waist and she simply let him lead her along like a blind person. Sometimes he steered her left, sometimes right, sometimes they bushwhacked around houses or followed the line of somebody's garage until it ended and he started looking for the next landmark. She knew she was of no help to him, but she simply tried to stay in rhythm with his gait, to pick one booted foot up and put it down. It was all she knew how to do.

Then she heard him fumbling with the doorknob and she managed to slide the key out of her pocket with two frozen fingers. As soon as he pushed the door open, Kasha shot past them.

"Kasha," he called. "Kasha."

"It's all right," Maggie said. "She'll come back."

She caught sight of the two of them in the front hall mirror and pulled him over so he could see. They looked like big overgrown children stuffed into snowsuits, children who had been out sledding all afternoon and could not move. Even their eyebrows were crusted over with white.

"We should go back out and shake this off," he said.

"Too late now." At their feet, the snow was already melting into the ancient metal heating grate, dripping down into the dirt-floored cellar below. "Just stand there while you take things off."

She threw both their wet coats into the tub in the downstairs bathroom.

"I brought in wood this afternoon," she said. "If you light a fire, I'll find us some dry socks."

He built a fire, put on the socks she'd found, rolled up his pants, rubbed his hands. She led the way into the kitchen where she put on the pot of soup she had made that morning. In case he wanted dinner.

"Homemade," she said proudly. "Potato."

"I'm impressed. What inspired you?"

"Boredom with what I could get at the store. When you live in a city, and can order anything in, it seems foolish to cook. But this island has driven me to it. My mother sent me a cookbook for Christmas." She put her hands up to her cheeks, which were chapped from the wind.

He covered them with his palms. "You're still cold."

She closed her eyes for a minute. "You're warm," she said.

Kasha burst in the dog door, tore around the kitchen table, shook the snow off, sniffed at them, and rushed out again.

"My God," he said. "What was that?"

"A husky in snow. She makes tunnels in the stuff, rolls in it, eats it. I bet this is more snow than she's ever seen. Sit down while I heat this up. Tell me about owls."

"What would you like to know?"

"Interesting facts. For example, do barn owls only nest in barns?"

"Nope. Church steeples, bridges, sometimes birdhouses. Owls often mate for life. They keep very messy nests. Down at the bottom you'll find bones and fur and pellets. One species of owl actually catches blind snakes and drops them into their nests to clean up."

"Maid service," she said as she set out their soup bowls and three candles. She handed him the matches.

"Exactly. Owls can turn their heads completely around to look at things. They have acute hearing. They doze all day long and hunt at night. People think they are part of the raptor family like hawks, but they're closer cousins to the nighthawk and the whippoorwill." He lowered his nose. "This soup smells great."

"I hope it tastes as good as it smells. It's a bit intimidating to cook for a master chef. Here's salad, wine, bread, and the big surprise. Smoked salmon."

"With lemon and capers. I'm truly impressed. Where did you get this?"

"A friend in New York shipped the salmon up to me." She took her seat across from him and they clinked glasses.

"Here's to your Nan," he said. "For dragging you up here—"

"Kicking and screaming."

"And here's to you for staying." He had a way of looking at her with that steady accepting gaze of his that made a shiver go through her.

"Still cold?" he asked.

"No. Happy."

"Mmm," he said, and with his eyes still on her, he took a sip of soup. "It's good."

"Really?" She tried some. "It is."

"You sound surprised." The second mouthful he savored. "Delicious. Leeks, potatoes, cream, chicken stock, dill. Good hearty winter soup. Just what the doctor ordered."

He had a second helping of soup and together, they finished the salmon. Kasha came in, shook herself and collapsed on the floor, her tongue hanging out. Snow dripped off her coat and melted in a circle around her.

"I've picked out the furniture project for the kids," Maggie said when he got up to clear the dishes. "Leave those. Come on, I'll show you."

She'd found the Windsor chair two days ago, right under her nose in a corner of the living room. He turned it upside down so she could show him what it needed.

"It's loose in all the usual places. Where the stretchers meet the legs, where the legs meet the seat and the back. Plus that, in one of her artistic moments, Nan or one of her ancestors seem to have taken it into their minds to paint it green so we'll have to strip it down. I'll probably find she hammered some nails into it as well. Nan was always too cheap to have her furniture properly repaired. I once found her touching up an antique picture frame with radiator paint."

"Not good," he said.

"Not good at all," she replied. "In fact, totally unacceptable. Nothing like old-line WASPs to ruin things."

"The kids will have a ball with this."

"Sam, the only teaching I've done is four-week courses to curators on collection care. I have no experience with kids. Don't expect too much."

"You'll be fine. You're straight with kids. They appreciate that more than anything else."

The wind picked up suddenly. Maggie walked over to the window. She cupped her hands around her eyes and stared out through the cold black glass. Snow was blowing horizontally along the porch.

"No sign of it stopping," she said.

"Through tomorrow."

"Merry Christmas," she said when the clock upstairs began to toll.

Without turning around, she sensed him crossing the room to her, felt his arms slide around her from behind and hold her tight. It was exactly what she had wanted from him some hours before when they stood above the shoreline. She leaned back into his warmth, into the solid feeling of his arms lined up along hers, his cheek against her ear.

"Mmm," she said. "You feel cozy."

"I am," he murmured, his lips on her neck.

"I feel as if we're inside one of those glass domes that you turn upside down and shake to make the snow fall."

"We are," he said. "I call it blizzard time. The world stops. Are you ready for bed?"

"Yes," she said, and he led her up the stairs and into the dark blue bedroom on the right. She was happy to go with him, happy to have him undress her, each button of the plaid shirt twisted through its buttonhole, each thick sock slid off each foot. He took his time, and she felt languid and easy as if the snow outside had truly slowed the world down. She gave her body over to him and to the storm that wrapped itself around the house. They had the rest of the night and all tomorrow, nowhere to go, nobody on this gossipy island to see that they had burrowed down together under her feather quilt.

She loved the way his skin smelled, she loved the strong wall of muscle in his arms and his back, she loved the way he closed his eyes as he explored each dip and crevice of her naked body. He was a lover who lingered over details, who kissed and licked and stroked each tiny acre of her skin into such a charged frenzy that she both longed for the release and delighted in its excruciating delay. He looked like a blind man who used all of his other senses to take her in. Once when he opened his eyes and found her watching him, he grinned, but said nothing, simply lowered his face to her skin again, like a thirsty animal drinking deep.

They made love, they slept, they woke, they talked, they slid along each other's skin, they kissed, they held each other, they rolled away, and then back together, spooned up against each other's warmth. The blizzard went on. Night ended and day began, but it was hard to tell one from the other. At some point, they finally admitted to normal, everyday hunger. He went down to the kitchen and rattled around for quite a while before he appeared at the bedside with a tray. A pile of scrambled eggs, a plate of toast, a pot of coffee, and two apples.

"Yummy," she said. "I'm starving."

"It's actually closer to lunchtime, but I felt like breakfast. It's my favorite meal."

"Is Kasha down there?"

"Curled up under the table," he said. "Sleeping like a baby."

"Tired herself out in the snow. How deep do you think it is?"

"With the wind blowing so hard, you can't tell. Two feet in places."

"I should get up and look," she said. "But I don't feel like it."

"Hurry up and finish your breakfast. It's getting in my way."

It was late in the afternoon when they finally crawled out of the bed and showered and made their way downstairs. They moved slowly and stiffly.

"Would you like to try the riding chair?" she teased.

"It's been a long time since I've spent that many hours in bed," he said.

"Not exactly sleeping the whole time either."

"Not exactly." He took her hand and they helped each other down the stairs.

Outside the world had gone white, top to bottom. It was hard to tell whether the snow had stopped or not because the wind was still blowing so hard that the flakes moved left to right across the windowpane.

"Do you believe that stuff about each snowflake being absolutely unique and different from every other one?"

"Yes," he said. He was sitting cross-legged in front of the fire. For a thick-muscled man, she had discovered that he was surprisingly flexible. "It's a scientific fact."

She hunched down behind him and slid her arms around his neck. "I believe you," she said. "Anything you tell me about the natural world, I believe."

He was grinning. She felt the muscles of his cheek moving next to hers. She loved the way his smile opened up his face, crinkled the skin around his eyes.

"For a man prone to despair, you at least seem equally inclined to happiness," she whispered in his ear.

"In my current position, who wouldn't be?" He turned her hands over and kissed the palms, first one and then the other.

The phone rang, a harsh jangle in the stillness of the house.

"I don't want to answer it," she said.

"If it's somebody on island, they'll come over to check on you if you don't."

She let him go reluctantly and made her way to the phone in the corner.

"You okay?" Chuck asked without any preamble.

"Fine," she said. "The house is warm. Kasha's had herself a great time. This blizzard is her own personal Christmas present."

"We've got close to three feet of snow in some places," Chuck said. "Dan Chester hasn't run the ferry for twenty-four hours. That's a record."

"Any other problems?"

"The Slocums' heat went off, but they've moved in with Lauren. Some trees are down, the power went off for about an hour over on the peninsula. Louise Grimes, that's old Wilfred's daughter, called in to say that her father's heartbeat is very erratic, but she's always worrying about that. She wears that stethoscope around her neck like a badge or a medal or something. The doctor actually managed to get over there in his Mercedes. Nothing else I've heard of except that nobody can raise Sam. He's not answering his radio or his phone."

"Hold on a minute." She covered the receiver. "They're looking for you. No answer on the radio or the phone."

He pulled himself to his feet and took the receiver from her. He tilted it so they both could listen. "I'm right here, Chuck. We're fine. I forgot my radio."

Just the slightest pause. "Glad we found you," Chuck said. "Tell Maggie I'll be over to help dig her out eventually."

"No rush. Merry Christmas, Chuck."

He grinned at some comment of Chuck's before he rang off.

"What did he say at the end?" Maggie asked.

"He said to tell you that this is one Christmas he's sure you won't forget."

"I wonder what he meant by that," she said as she slipped back into Sam's arms. "The blizzard or something else."

Fifteen

THE DAY AFTER the blizzard, Al went out before breakfast to hook the yellow snowplow up to the front of his truck so he could help Paul Thayer clear the secondary roads. Anybody in town who had a snowplow would be out. Besides serving as town councilman, Paul had the contract for all the road maintenance on the island. Normally it was a pretty easy job and in the summer, he would hire a crew of teenagers to patch the roads, cut back the overgrowth, and repair the mirrors on the tight corners. But this was the kind of blizzard that didn't hit the island very often. Paul had managed to plow the main road from the ferry dock up to the guardhouse. Only summer people lived out east of the guardhouse, so the roads out there could wait for a thaw. But the call had come over the radio that Paul needed help with the side roads in case of emergencies. People on the island liked Paul. He was a hard worker and a community man, and when he asked for help, you knew he really needed it.

"Can I go into town with you, Daddy?" Erin asked over breakfast.

Everybody froze. Her mother turned the water off, her father stopped scraping his fork along the plate. This was the way they lived now. When one of them spoke, everybody else stopped what they were doing to listen. It gave Erin the creeps.

"What are you going to do in there?"

"Hang out with the other kids." She was really going to Maggie's, but she didn't want to say that. Any mention of Maggie would get her father going again. Kasha was off the check cord all the time now, and you'd see her trotting along the side of the road. She came over to visit sometimes. Her father kept talking about how that goddamn woman should leash her dog.

"Al, Maggie paid me to train the dog so she could let her roam," her mother had said. "Don't you remember?"

"That doesn't mean she's got license to hang around here, getting our dogs all riled up."

The pointers weren't riled up, Erin thought. Daddy was riled up because for some reason Kasha loved Mom. Maybe we should switch places for a while, Erin said to Kasha when nobody else was around. You live over here with them. I'll move in with Maggie.

"Sure," her father said to Erin. "You can come with me. Be ready in ten minutes. The men are all meeting down at the firehouse at nine." Erin saw her mother's shoulders drop as if she needed to hold them up like that to listen. She turned the water back on.

"Why do you need your backpack?" Anna asked as she was heading out the door.

"I'll probably go see Maggie. She's lending me a book."

"All right, sweetie. Be careful." Her mother gave her a fierce hug and Erin endured it although it made her uncomfortable. She wasn't a baby anymore. Ever since that fight between her parents, her mother tried to touch her and talk to her whenever her father was out of the room. Everybody in this house was watching everybody else and pretending they weren't. Erin couldn't wait to get away from it.

"I can still go to Katie's tomorrow night, can't I, Mom?"

"I'm sure you can. The ferry's running again and they plow much quicker over on the mainland."

The bruise on her mother's cheek had almost completely faded away. It went from blue and purple to green to yellow. Erin had heard people talking about it in town. When they saw Erin, they'd look self-conscious and begin discussing the weather in loud voices.

ERIN LIKED THE sound of the metal plow scraping along the road, the satisfying waterfall of snow that spewed over the side. She rolled the window down to watch until her father told her to put it up again, that it was making a draft on his neck. They slowed to a stop at the corner where Mr. M. was digging out his truck.

"Need help, Sam?" her father called.

"Hey, thanks. Billy said he'd come by and pull me out in an hour. I've got some more digging to do first. Hi, Erin."

"Hi, Mr. M."

"We've got some plowing over on the peninsula," her father said. "We tried to raise you on the radio all yesterday."

"I heard. Sorry about that. First time in ages I left it behind." He turned back to his shoveling, which signaled that he thought it was time the conversation ended. Al put his truck in gear. Erin wondered what her father was grinning about.

He dropped Erin off at the town green, where the Malloy kids were building a huge snow fort. They yelled at her to join them, but as soon as her father's truck had turned the corner, she set off down the road past the grocery store to Maggie's house.

She unlocked the front door with her key.

"Maggie?" she called. "Where are you?"

"Here. In the workroom. I'm setting a clamp. Come on in."

Erin stood in the doorway and stamped her feet. The snow fell off in two neat little circles around her boots. She followed Maggie's eyes.

"Oops," Erin said. "Sorry."

"It's all right. I have to redo the floors anyway."

Kasha was curled in her usual circle under Maggie's feet. She raised her head to look at Erin, then tucked it back down.

"Why don't you leave your boots by the front door and put on the kettle for tea. How was Christmas?"

"It was okay. I got some tapes and books and stuff. Katie asked me over to her house for tomorrow night."

"Lucky you," Maggie said. "Go get the tea ready. I'll be there in a minute. I just want to make sure this clamp is holding."

Erin liked the way Maggie let her mess around in the kitchen. Her own mother wanted everything done a certain way, so she always said it was easier to do it herself. Maggie didn't seem to care which mug she used or whether she put the tea bags back in exactly the same spot on the shelf. Erin set everything out on the beat-up old wooden table.

"Now this is nice," Maggie said when she walked in. "How's your mother?"

"She's fine," Erin said. She stirred her tea with the spoon, round and round until it set up a miniature whirlpool that sloshed creamy liquid over the top.

"That was a nasty bruise she got on her cheek."

"She slipped on the stairs," Erin said quickly.

"I heard," said Maggie.

"You look pretty," she said suddenly, and Maggie smiled.

"So do you."

Erin didn't mean to exactly say that. It just blurted out of her mouth, but it was true. Maggie had this nice grin on her face. She looked happy.

"I'm going to be starting that furniture repair project at the school next week. "

"Which grades?"

"Sam thinks sixth through eighth. We're going to strip and repair a chair. It sounds boring, but it actually can be a lot of fun."

Sam, Erin heard. Well, that's different. Another tidbit to tell Katie. Erin was really here because she wanted to borrow that book from the third-floor bookcase so she could show it to Katie. She was not going to ask Maggie. She was just going to take it for a while and bring it back. She figured there was nothing wrong with that. And she was sure it would make Katie come back to being her best friend and leave Patty Thayer and her stupid nail polish behind.

When Erin clattered up the steps to the third floor, Maggie stayed at the kitchen table stirring her cold tea. She and Sam had spoken twice on the phone since he'd left yesterday evening, but she felt as if he'd been gone for weeks.

They had taken a long time shoveling out her front walk. He threw snowballs at her and made a snow angel and chased Kasha until it was too dark to see much.

"Don't go," she said catching him around the waist. "It's too late to dig out the truck tonight. "

"I don't want to, but I'd better check on my house." He squeezed her hard. "I'll deal with the truck tomorrow." He kissed her once on each cheek, where the wind had left patches of chapped skin. "Don't worry. I'll be back."

"You'd better."

"Merry Christmas. Best present I ever found under my tree." And he stood absolutely still for a moment and looked so intensely into her eyes that she got worried.

"What is it?" she asked.

"I'm just imprinting you on my brain."

She stood behind the front door watching his padded body lumber away from her and felt an irrational desire to rush after him. This was a new and novel feeling for her. She had always been easy with her body and her sexuality, had slipped into bed with men before she really knew them and had then played emotional catch-up. When the man would kiss her good-bye at the door and walk away after that first night together, always before there had been this little sense of relief. Good. She could take her bath, reclaim her body, her space, figure out in the peace and quiet of her own life what this all meant. Whether, in fact, it meant anything at all.

But it was different with Sam. She wasn't ready for him to leave. She fought down the urge to call him back. There were things she wanted to say to him, stories she meant to tell him. She and Sam had become friends before they ever became lovers. They'd found a dead body together. They'd spent a whole day searching for Kasha together. She'd discovered that he kept dead birds in his freezer, that he was crazy about salamanders, that he made great pasta. Now their bodies had met and made friends too.

When she was much younger, after the first few lovers, she had learned an important fact: that a man could walk into your apartment, into your shower, into your bed, that you could share the minutiae of your daily life with him, that he could come to know the most ridiculously intimate details of your personal habits—that your hips stiffened up after you made love, that you liked a wet spoon dipped into the sugar bowl then into your coffee. And then one day he could go—completely and utterly disappear—taking that little piece of your history with him and leaving his with you. A month or two later, she would look up from the newspaper at breakfast and wonder if her last lover had ever actually bought that new car he kept talking about or fired his incompetent secretary or put his cat to sleep. None of these questions seemed important enough to disturb the silence between them. It was just that the leap from the knowing of his daily life to the not knowing seemed so sudden, so irreversible, so incomprehensible.

She stared at the kitchen wall now, at the jumble of pots and colanders and potato mashers and wondered how long it had taken Sam to get home and whether he'd found his radio and was getting any help digging out his truck. Suddenly it seemed imperative that she know the answers to these questions.

"Maggie, are you okay?"

Erin was standing in the doorway staring at her.

"Hmm. Just thinking about something. What did you say?"

"Can I use the typewriter?"

"Sure. I moved it into the front living room, over in the corner by the dollhouse. I'd better check that clamp." She pushed her chair back and got stiffly to her feet. "Did you walk over?"

"No, my father drove me to the town green."

"Did you take the road along the golf course?"

"Yup. We saw Mr. M. digging out his truck."

"You did?" Maggie had found out if she just waited long enough, Erin would give her details.

"It was really buried. He said Mr. Slade was going to come help him."

"Good."

She felt Erin's eyes on her. Kids. They didn't miss anything. Particularly if they'd been brought up on this island.

Erin disappeared into the front room and they spent a couple of hours separated by a wall, working comfortably on their own projects with nothing in the air between them but the erratic clack of Erin's typing and a scratchy symphony on Nan's old radio in the bookshelf.

After lunch, Maggie decided to walk into town with Erin. They slid along, with Kasha rushing ahead, rolling in the snow, then looking back to see if they'd noticed.

"Yes, Kasha," Maggie called. "We think you are one fabulous dog."

The sound of her encouraging voice riled Kasha up, so that the dog strived to execute even more exciting and unique snow tricks. She twisted, she turned, she planted her front feet and barked, then tunneled down and came back out with a face full of snow. This made Erin and Maggie hoot with laughter, and the sound of their own merriment echoed back at them from the still white landscape.

They took the turn into town where Erin was pulled into a snowball fight on the green. Maggie stopped to exchange blizzard stories with Sally Malloy, who had been helping her track down records on some of the old houses Maggie was researching for the survey. When they parted, she felt Sally's eyes watching her as she headed up the hill to Sam's house. He wasn't home, of course. If he'd managed to dig the truck out by now, he was probably helping someone else or checking on the museum.

She let herself in the kitchen door and prowled around the kitchen until she found some paper and a pen.

"I miss you," the note read. She didn't believe she'd ever said that to a man before. "Call me when you get back. Maggie."

Kasha had disappeared around the corner into the living room. Maggie followed.

The room was simply and sparsely furnished. A futon couch and comfortable reading chair were separated by a plain cherry table with walnut detailing. Handmade, Maggie could see, by an excellent craftsman. A navy blue dhurrie rug covered the wide planking of the floor. The bookshelf held some surpises. In among the natural history guides and the ornithological encyclopedias, she found well-thumbed poetry collections—Auden, John Ashbery, and Emily Dickinson, along with others she didn't recognize. On the top shelf, clustered together, there was a collection of fiction, some modern, along with a few of those left-over college paperbacks.

The mantelpiece over the woodstove was decorated with a line of shells, bleached white by the sun. She went down the row, touching and naming each one. Limpet, moon snail, whelk, sea urchin, oyster, mussel, scallop, periwinkle. Nothing extraordinary, but each was flawless. She imagined that the collection had taken him some time to assemble, that he had picked up and considered many others before he settled on these. Above the mantelpiece, instead of a sea-scape, hung a painting of a western landscape, a snow-covered mountain range at dusk. Wyoming or Montana, she thought.

Propped up on a side table she found two framed photographs. In one, Sam at the age of eleven or twelve was standing on the deck of a small wooden sailboat with one arm wrapped around the mast. A man, his father probably, was seated with a hand on the tiller. The boat was tied up to the dock. It looked as if they had just come in from a sail, and whoever was waiting for them took the picture when all was stowed and shipshape. Sam looked proud and happy, his father stiff and formal, as if he was not used to having his picture taken.

In the second photograph, Sam was dressed in cap and gown. He had his arms around two women, his mother, probably, and the younger sister he had told Maggie about, and they both leaned in against him as if they were used to his position as the man of the family. His mother looked directly out at the camera with her chin lifted proudly, while half the sister's face was hidden against Sam's black-robed chest. He was whispering something to her and she was grinning shyly.

Now that Maggie knew how safe it felt to be sheltered in those arms herself, she was briefly and irrationally jealous of these two. Nan and her mother were the only family who attended her college graduation. Maggie had sent an invitation to the last address they had for her father, but it was returned months later with the stamp "addressee unknown."

Kasha whined from the kitchen. The noise startled her and she put the picture back in its place.

"I think I started missing him a long time ago," she told Kasha on their way down the hill. "Before I even knew him."

LAUREN LIVED IN a small house behind the Slocums, and she was not exactly happy about sheltering the whole family in the middle of the blizzard on Christmas Day. But of course, there was nothing she could do. When a person needed help on this island, you gave it, no matter what history you had with the people. Lauren had nothing against the Slocums. The little girl was a pitiful thing, still sucking her thumb in sixth grade, and Annie liked to complain about her bad knee, but she liked to gossip too, almost as much as Lauren did. They settled down to it at the kitchen table once Lauren set Jerry and the kids up in front of her television.

Annie had a sly grin on her face. "So, Lauren, you would know. Did Anna take herself to the doctor last week so he could have a look at that bruise on her cheek?"

"She didn't come in during clinic hours," Lauren said. " And she didn't come in after hours either because Dennis keeps very good records." Dennis. She liked saying that in front of Annie. To show her what terms they were on.

"Do you think Al smacked her?" Annie whispered.

"If he didn't, he should have. Anna Craven has gotten way out of line if you ask me. One thing everybody knows now, she sure can't hold her liquor. But then she never could."

The island was still buzzing about the fight in the bar, but nobody was taking sides. They knew that Al spent time with Lauren, that he'd done it before, that lots of the husbands had when they felt like it. It was a man's island in the winter. Everybody knew that. Maybe it helped make up for all the ass-kissing the men had to do with the rich women in the summertime. The men made the rules. They broke them if they wanted to. And Lauren kept the men happy.

"You look pretty pleased with yourself about something, Mrs.

Slocum," Lauren teased. And what do you have to grin about, she wondered. You've shown up in town with a bruise here or there yourself.

"You know I'm still washing the doctor's shirts."

"I guess so."

"So look what I found in his pocket last week," Annie said, holding up a piece of paper. She unfolded it and spread it out on the table. Before Lauren could even read the writing on it, Annie said, "It's one of Anna Craven's deposit slips from her bank. And look on the back."

"The Roadside Inn, Madison," Lauren read out loud.

"Ma, tell Danny to stop leaning on me," Liz called from the other room.

"Oh, hush, Lizzie," her mother yelled back. She lowered her voice again. "So, what do you think?"

"That must be where Anna stays when she takes the dogs off for the hunting tests."

"Right."

"And you found this in Doctor Lacey's pocket?"

Annie sat back with both hands folded across her aproned belly. She watched with amusement as the whole thing began to come clear for her friend.

"So," Lauren said slowly, "the night she's marching into that bar and making a scene with me, she spent the night before with Dennis Lacey. Miss High and Mighty herself. A married woman. And he's married too. At least he's not divorced yet."

Al Craven's married too, Annie thought, but she didn't say it. She was getting a rush and tingle in her belly, the one that came whenever she told somebody a secret she alone knew. This was a big one. This may have been the biggest morsel of gossip she'd ever had. It was why she'd sat on it ever since last Tuesday when she did her usual check on the doctor's shirts. Men were always leaving things in their pockets. The only cure for that bad habit was doing enough laundry yourself so you got sick of drying dollar bills on the top of the stove or picking off the lint from a shredded Kleenex. The doctor left scraps of paper and pens in his shirts. Once she'd even found a photograph of some beach grasses that he probably intended to paint. She had returned it the next week on top of his pile of shirts and he had thanked her. But this piece of paper, she'd read and pocketed and savored for almost a week. When Jerry came upstairs from the basement that morning in the middle of the kids opening their presents to say that the furnace had gone on the blink, she got on the phone right away to Lauren to ask if they could come over. This was the moment she'd been waiting for.

"I never would have expected this of Anna," Lauren said out loud, but inside she was thinking worse than that. He was mine. Dennis Lacey was mine. How dare she go under my nose and start fooling around with him. And how dare he? Lauren thought back now to the times in the last week when she'd been teasing him about his lonely Christmas and how maybe he would like to spend it with some company and her face flushed, just thinking about it. All along, he'd been crawling in bed with Anna Craven and Lauren didn't know it. Just went on making a fool of herself with him. She used to think she could count Anna as one of her friends. What a joke. She was the worst kind of snake in the grass, the kind of woman who kept secrets from other women.

"Can I have the paper back?" Annie said.

"I'll just keep it a little while," Lauren said and buried it deep in her own jeans pocket. "It might prove useful."

Annie got nervous at this. "You're not going to do anything with it, are you, Lauren? Don't stir up any trouble. That doctor will know where it came from."

Lauren picked up the other woman's hand. "Don't you worry. I'm not going to say a word to that doctor. Not a word. You look like you could use a manicure, honey. It's on the house." She took her tray down from a shelf above the washing machine, and prattled on about the new colors that had come in the week before. The light talk calmed Annie. She liked to gossip, but she didn't like anybody to know where it came from. And deep down, there was a little itchy feeling of guilt. She knew what it felt like to be slapped around by a man. Jerry'd been better lately, but last year she made sure she had the kettle on the boil whenever he was in the house. Just in case she needed it to protect herself when he went into one of his moods. She wouldn't want to spend much time on the wrong side of Al Craven, she thought. And it looked like that was exactly where Anna had ended up last week.

ERIN WAS PLEASED to see that Katie Morrison's house wasn't as fancy as Patty Thayer had made it out to be. It was just a plain old house on a plain old street, and whenever Katie wanted to go somewhere, she had to ask her mother or father to drive her. Because of the blizzard, the mall parking lot hadn't been plowed out yet, so they ended up watching movies on the VCR all afternoon and her television wasn't even that big. When the Morrisons went out for dinner that night, they got stuck with Katie's little sister. Erin didn't mind. Erin colored with her and read her a story for a while, because Katie was talking on the phone with one of her friends from her old school. The kid wasn't so bad. It was better than being an only child where your parents were always watching you and you felt like a Ping-Pong ball bouncing back and forth between them.

She told Katie this later when they had gone to bed.

"What do you mean they're always watching you?"

"They don't have anybody else to look at so they stare at you. And if they have a fight, they stare at you more because they don't want to look at each other."

"Your parents fight?" Katie asked.

"Sure. Everybody's parents fight," Erin said.

"Not mine."

"Not ever?"

"Nope."

Probably not, Erin thought. Mrs. Morrison looked like someone who would jump if a dog barked at her. And Mr. Morrison was tall and lurchy. He lumbered around and talked in a low serious voice all the time. He said he was going to get the car the same way you would say that your mother had just been murdered. Suddenly, Erin couldn't understand what she ever saw in Katie Morrison with her boring old suburban house and her boring perfect parents. If Erin weren't stuck on an island with nobody else to choose from, she wouldn't have paid any attention to Katie.

"I brought a surprise," Erin said. She pulled the book out of her backpack.

"What?"

"Dirty pictures," Erin said with a giggle.

"Erin," Katie said in a prim little voice. She sounded like her mother.

"Oh, maybe you don't want to see them. I'll take them home again." She made a great show of putting the book away.

Katie folded her arms across her chest and pouted for a while. "My parents would kill me if they caught me doing something like that."

"They're not even home yet," Erin said.

"All right. Bring it over here and we'll use the flashlight."

They sat under the covers with their knees hitched up and stared.

Every time Erin was ready to turn a page, Katie stopped her and stared some more. Erin had already looked through it once by herself.

"They certainly have thought of a million different ways of doing it," Erin said.

"They sure have."

"Have you ever seen a man's thing?"

"No," Katie said. "Have you?"

"Sure."

"Where?"

"I'm not telling. I just have. It's pretty gross if you ask me."

"What's it look like?"

She thought about Jimmy Slade's silly-looking boner sticking straight out of his pants like it was pointing at something. "Big and hairy. It's got hair on it."

Katie shuddered. "Where did you see it?"

"I told you. I'm not telling."

"Do you know anybody who's done it?"

"Sure." She liked the tone of awe in Katie's voice. She didn't really know anybody personally. She'd just heard the ninth-grade girls talking about someone they knew. The kids in the high school went down to the wildlife sanctuary in the summer to do it.

"Who?" Katie asked.

"Nobody you'd know," Erin said airily. "Some of my friends in the high school."

"Girls."

"It's my mother," Katie squeaked. They pushed the book down to the bottom of the bed and turned off the flashlight.

Mrs. Morrison opened the door. "I could hear you whispering up here. It's way past your bedtime, Katherine. What are you two doing in the same bed? Come on Erin, up you get."

She tucked Erin into the other bed as if she were a baby. Then she smoothed down the covers on Katie's bed. "What's this?"

Erin squeezed her eyes shut and wished she could melt away. Stupid dumb Katie Morrison. Why didn't she lie right on top of the book? That way her mother would never have found it.

"It's Erin's," Katie said.

Traitor.

Her mother slid the book out from between the sheets. "Why are you hiding it down here?"

Neither one of them could think of a thing to say. She took it over to the hall light to have a look.

"I'll give it back to her," Katie said. But it was too late.

"Erin," said Mrs. Morrison. "Where did you get this?"

"One of the kids at school gave it to me." She was surprised at how smoothly the lie came out.

"This is not something either of you should be looking at. Ever."

"Sorry, Mommy," Katie said. She sounded like she was about to cry.

"I'm going to be talking to your father about this, Katie. And Erin will go home first thing in the morning. Do you understand?"

"Yes, Mommy."

WHEN ERIN GOT off the boat, nobody was there to meet her. Her parents weren't expecting her until the afternoon. She'd only pretended to call them from the Morrisons. When Mrs. Morrison asked to speak to her mother, Erin said she had hung up quickly because she was rushing out. "I'll speak to her later, then," she had said. I bet you will, Mrs. Snootytootface, Erin had thought. And she did keep the book. She probably wanted to lock herself in the bathroom and look at those pictures herself. She probably had never done anything like that with her husband.

Erin tramped along, climbing up and down the banks of plowed snow. She felt strangely free and easy. She no longer wanted to be Katie Morrison's friend. She didn't need her or any of the rest of the kids her age. They were too young for her. They didn't know the things she knew.

A truck pulled up beside her. It was the Tremayne boys. "Hey kid, want a ride?" Bo Tremayne yelled.

"Sure."

"Hop in back," he called, pointing with his thumb. She hesitated. "You don't want a ride after all?"

"No," she said. "I'll take it." She flung her backpack over the tailgate and scrambled up herself. The Tremaynes' golden retriever was standing with his feet splayed apart. He barked at her. "Oh, shut up," she muttered. Derry, the younger brother, leaned out on the other side. "Hang on, kid," he yelled.

She grabbed on just in time as Bo put his foot to the floor and the truck spun its wheels in the packed snow, then shot forward when the tires found some bare road. They didn't bother with the stop sign at the top of the hill, but took the corner at high speed so the rear end of the truck fishtailed out to the side. The cold wind was coming at Erin so fast that she had to duck her head every now and again just to get a breath.

"Hey, kid, you all right?" Derry called back to her. She nodded her head. He wasn't even looking. The dog slipped and fell twice, but he scrambled back to his feet on the straightaways. Erin felt giddy and sick and scared and crazy with excitement all at the same time. When they finally pulled over behind the post office to let her out, she took her time getting down from the truck. Her legs were still shaking as she walked up to where Bo was watching her approach in his sideview mirror.

"You okay, kid?"

"Sure," she said, and was proud of her strong voice.

"You're tough. You should hit the rodeo circuit when you grow up. Go into bronco busting. Hang in there," he said, and took off again. She jumped out of the way as the truck slid sideways, the wheels spitting snow and gravel.

She stood there for the longest time, waiting for her heartbeat to slow back down to normal. She sucked in a long draw from her inhaler to stave off the wheeze that was starting up in the bottom of her chest. Bo Tremayne called her tough. She liked that. She was through with Katie Morrison and Patty Thayer and Liz Slocum. Those kids were pathetic. They didn't know what Erin knew about life and people. She was different, and it was useless for her to pretend she had anything at all to say to them.

Sixteen

SAM HAD A hard time concentrating, particularly on the days that Maggie was due in school in the afternoon. His mind wandered off to the memory of her pale naked hip upturned in the light or the tangled thicket of her hair on the pillow, and when one of the kids shouted his name and he'd come back to the seventh-grade science class, he'd worry that he'd said something out loud.

"You're weird, Mr. M.," the kids told him, and he agreed.

They were acting like drunks, thirsty for each other's skin all the time. He merely thought the unthinkable, but Maggie slid her hand down the back of his jeans in the pasta aisle in the grocery store or teased him with a French kiss around the corner from his classroom. He had never been a modest man in private, but in public he was a conservative country boy. He acted horrified, and at the same time he had to admit, it turned him on.

"This is worse than the chaperones at my high school dances," she told him, her eyes scanning the halls. "A million eyes watching us all the time."

"Wait till I get you home," he said in a low voice while flipping through a pile of papers from his eighth-graders.

"Promise?" she whispered as she headed back to the classroom, where the kids were calling out to her that they were bored with sanding.

As he had expected, she was good with the kids. She talked to them in a direct, matter-of-fact way, and she expected a lot of them.

"Am I pushing them too hard?" she asked one night, curled up on his couch.

"Have you gotten any complaints?"

"Not really. Except for Erin, who seems to be avoiding me."

"What are you staring at?" he asked.

"Your eyebrows. I love the way they move up and down when you talk. Separately." She tried to show him with her own and ended up looking cockeyed. "Mine won't do it."

"I've never had anybody compliment me on my eyebrows before. Other parts of me, but not my eyebrows. As for you, I love the freckles between your toes."

She rolled her eyes. "That's no big deal. Red-haired people have freckles everywhere. In the summer, they melt together in big blotches. That's why I stay out of the sun."

"I hope I get to see that," he said. "You on Chincoteale in one of those big straw hats from your front hall."

She was silent for a minute. "The real estate agent left me a message last week. He has someone who wants to look at the house."

"A buyer?"

"Supposedly."

"When are they coming?" He lifted his arm off her shoulders and turned to get a better look at her face.

"I didn't call him back. I'm not ready to show it. There's still too much to be done."

"Mmm." He tucked one of her curls behind her ear.

"I may not sell it this spring after all," she went on. "It might be more sensible to rent it out for the summer. I hear I could make as much as ten thousand for the season. That would cover the taxes and some of the upkeep."

"Sounds smart," he said, keeping his voice even. As if they were simply talking about a good business decision and nothing else.

There were times when he approached her the way he did a migrating bird. He had to be sure to make no sudden movements or sounds for fear that splash of yellow would burst out of the branches and be gone before he could get the binoculars on it for a positive identification. Maggie was the same, always poised for flight.

Late one night, after they'd made love and gone deeper together than either of them had ever thought possible, she'd told him about her father. It enraged him to think a man would do that to his own children, and especially to the woman he held in his arms. It helped him understand better why she could be fiercely independent and at other times so fragile. Sam had wished so often for his own father that he couldn't imagine what it would feel like to know that the man was choosing to stay away from you, day after day, Christmas after Christmas. One missed opportunity after another. She started to cry so quietly that he felt the tears on her cheeks before he heard anything. He pulled her as close as he could and stayed awake through the night. No harm would come to her on his watch.

THEY SPENT MOST of the weekend in bed together. She made feeble protestations about the new corner chair she was restoring, and he'd talk about the animal tracks he was missing with all that snow on the ground, but neither one was very serious. All he had to do was run the soft palm of his hand down her upper arm and she was butter, melting, sliding off the plate of the day.

He whispered in her ear when they made love, teased her, called her names, told her his fantasies, and she played. It turned her on as much as his hands sliding up and down her body. Afterward they talked, lying side by side under the comforter, her leg thrown casually over his, his arm under her shoulders. The sex seemed to energize him. Even at night after a full day of teaching, he liked to talk. He remembered stories that he had saved up to tell her, he asked her questions, she answered and asked back. The hours slipped away, and when he wanted to know the time, she lied just a little because she couldn't believe that it was three in the morning and they hadn't slept yet.

"Is everybody talking about us?" she asked one morning as they parted at his door.

"I expect so. Lot of men grinning at me in the Rocky Point when I pick up my coffee in the mornings."

"Do you say anything?" she asked.

"No. Just go about my business. It's better than the old days when they felt sorry for me and Lauren kept letting me know she was available."

"Did she do that?"

"In her own way. She thinks it's her job to keep the men on this island happy."

"So Al Craven isn't the only one."

"God, no. Anybody who's willing. Where are you going today?"

"The Blairs' house. I know it's the second turn past the gatehouse."

"They share a driveway with the Cravens. You'll have to walk in when it forks right. They're summer people so they won't be plowed out."

"How long until I get to see you again?" she asked.

He checked his watch. "Seven hours. You're due in school at two for class."

"What happens if I'm late?"

"I tie you to the bed tonight and do unmentionable things to your body."

"I'll be late."

ANNA CAME OUT of the kennel at the sound of a car in the driveway at that time of the morning. She saw Maggie hesitate at the turnoff to the Blairs', then roll down her window.

"Hi," she called.

Anna waved. She was about to work Paprika on the check cord. "Kasha isn't here. I haven't seen her since yesterday."

Maggie shook her head. She drove up and got out of the car.

"I actually wasn't looking for Kasha. I'm here to fill out the survey questionnaire on the Blairs' house."

"Want some coffee?" Anna asked.

"That's exactly what I'd like," Maggie said.

"Let me put Paprika back."

Maggie followed her into the kennel and the dogs all started up at the sound of their approach. Anna unlatched Paprika's door; the dog took her time walking through. "She's confused," she explained. "We were headed out."

"Sam says you have quite a reputation," Maggie said when she took a seat at the kitchen table.

Anna looked pleased. "That's nice of him. I never thought of Sam as one of my biggest fans," she added. "Considering his feelings about hunting."

"He seems to have that ability to separate one thing from another. He admires your work with the dogs and hates the hunting," Maggie said happily. This was exactly what she wanted. To get to talk about this man as if she had known him forever.

"I feel the same way sometimes," Anna said as she busied herself with the coffee. She'd heard the talk of Maggie and Sam in town. Just the other day Annie Slocum had gone on and on about it when she was buying stamps from Anna. Anna recognized that in some strange way, Annie was trying to make up for gossiping about the Cravens the week before, which Anna knew everybody on the island was doing. And of course, Annie Slocum would never have believed the story of Anna falling down the stairs. She'd turned up with too many funny bruises on her body over the years herself.

"Milk?" Anna asked.

Maggie shook her head.

"So how's the historical survey going?"

"Fine. It's not a bad project, getting into everybody's house to snoop around and take pictures."

"Sam's the one who thought that up, wasn't he?" Anna asked as she set the mugs down. She knew Maggie wanted to talk about him. She understood.

Between sips of coffee, Maggie talked about Sam's conservation ideas and how alike they were. He preserved nature, she preserved furniture. Anna listened, but her thoughts floated in and out. She wondered if she'd ever felt this way about Al Craven. Perhaps early on when she was in high school. So young. How was she to know? She would have loved to talk about Dennis Lacey right now, about the kindness of the man, how he came up island to find her, to put his arms around her.

When Maggie stopped for a minute to draw breath, Anna asked, "Have you ever been in love like this before?"

Maggie grinned. "I've got it bad, don't I?"

Anna nodded. "Pretty bad. I don't think it would be possible to say the name Sam more often than you have."

"To answer your question, no, I've never fallen this hard before. I broke up with a man three years ago. There hasn't really been anybody since then."

"And you weren't that crazy about him?"

"I guess not," Maggie said. "I liked the package, the exteriors. He had money, a good job. He was a lawyer. But things always seemed to be an effort. What to talk about? Where to go for dinner? Vacation? Nan said he had no passions. She was right."

Anna smiled. Dinner? Vacation? What did she and Al talk about? How much to spend on Erin's new shoes and where's the cheapest source of shingles and why don't I wait and buy the tomato sauce from the Pathmark when I go over with one of the dogs? The last time she and Al had dinner out was in the summer when a bunch of people got together and rode in Randy's boat to that lobster place on the mainland. Randy'd asked them all to chip in for gas, which made Al furious. Then he went on and on about how much the lobsters cost and how he certainly couldn't afford to throw his money away like that. He ate a hamburger, but she ordered a lobster and paid for it out of her own wallet. She took her time with it, picking out each little morsel of pink meat until Al got so mad, he went and sat in the boat while the rest of them finished their meal. She didn't hear about anything else for the next week.

Maggie was watching her. "How about you?" she asked. "Have you ever been in love like this?"

"Yes," Anna lied. "It was in my twenties. I took a trip to Ireland with my grandmother. Met him there. I loved Ireland. That's why I gave Erin an Irish name. Al thought it was a crazy idea, but I insisted on it." She went on telling Maggie all about this man who grew up on the western coast in a little thatched cottage and how she'd met him on a bus and fell very hard for him. She loved the sound of her own voice telling the story, the extravagant details, the lies mixed with the truth and all of it giving her membership in the club of women who fell madly in love and had affairs and survived them.

"What was his name?" Maggie asked.

Anna almost let the name Dennis drop out of her mouth by accident. "Ian," she said after a pause.

"That's actually a Scottish name," Maggie said.

Anna didn't try to explain. She was a lousy liar and anything she said now would make it worse. "So, do you think Sam's crazy about you?" she asked.

"I hope so."

"Think you'll get married and move to the island?"

"Oh, God, it's crazy to even talk about that. I've only known the man three months."

"Time doesn't necessarily mean anything. I'd known Al Craven my whole life when I married him. It doesn't mean I knew what I needed to know."

"What do you need to know?"

"Is he good to you?" Anna said immediately as if the words had been sitting on the end of her tongue waiting to spill out. "Do you feel safe with him?"

Maggie closed her eyes for a moment. "Yes to both," she said. "But it could change so easily. People change. You think you can trust them and then you find out you can't. Or you can't trust yourself to pick the right person. With Nan gone, I'm not sure of anything."

"I married when I was just a kid," Anna said. "I always thought people our age knew themselves better."

"I know this about myself," Maggie said. "I travel light. It's what my work demands. I've stayed here longer than I've stayed anywhere for years."

"Maybe you're changing," Anna said.

She stood up to take the coffee cups to the sink. Maggie's chair scraped as if she intended to join her there, but Anna steered her toward the door. She didn't want Maggie to catch sight of Al's stupid list on the bulletin board.

"I'd better get back to Paprika," Anna said.

"Sorry I went on and on."

"No problem. " She stood at the kitchen door and watched Maggie trudge down the Blairs' driveway through the high-packed snow. Anna hadn't meant to be so abrupt. In some other place or time, the two of us might have been good friends, she thought. I would have liked that. But right now I'm keeping too many secrets. And the gulf that lies between us seems too wide.

It wasn't Maggie's inherited house or her trips to Europe or even her talk of dinners out and vacations that got to Anna. It was her freedom. She could leave on the afternoon boat with no real consequences. Sam's heart might break a little, but the two of them would have only known each other for a few months. Broken hearts heal. Maggie had no children, no husband, nothing to keep her in place, nothing to keep her standing in this kitchen waiting for things to get better.

Lauren went looking for Al one afternoon after she closed the clinic. His truck was parked at the airport behind the garage where he kept all his heavy equipment. The parking lot was slowly filling up with an assortment of wrecked and rusting vehicles, old heaps in various stages of disintegration.

Lauren heard raised voices in Al's office and hesitated outside the door.

"Goddammit, Al, they're not up to code."

Lauren couldn't hear what Al said, but she retreated to her car and pretended to have just arrived when Billy Slade slammed out of the office. He barely nodded at Lauren before he got in his truck and took the hill at full speed.

"Jesus, what was his problem?" Lauren said.

"What are you doing here?"

"That's not exactly the warmest of greetings, Al baby," she said. She walked around the metal desk, which was strewn with papers, and lowered herself on to the arm of his chair.

"Cut it out, Lauren," he said. "I've got work to do. Did Billy see you coming in here?"

"He sure did," she said. "You worried?" She ran one finger up and down his neck. Lauren prided herself on knowing how to push a man's buttons and on connecting the right button with the right man. Al was a fool for a woman's touch on his neck and in that little place in the hollow of his throat. She slipped her hand down there now and rubbed ever so lightly.

"Damn you," he grunted, but the anger had gone out of his voice. There was an ache in it that she recognized. "Lock the door."

She took her time walking over there, let him watch her move her hips from side to side, twirl around after the bolt was slid. "I've got a present for you," she said.

"What's that?" he asked as he undid his belt.

"Two presents actually, now that I think about it."

He was scrabbling at his fly now.

"My, aren't we in a hurry?" she said, but she knelt down between his legs and rolled the chair back a little. "Always did like these office chairs. They've got wheels, which makes things so much easier. Adjustable, you know what I mean?" This she said as he eased his cock out and she took a moment to lick her lips and survey it.

"Come on, Lauren. You make me crazy."

"That's the point, lover boy."

He reached over to undo her buttons. "Careful," she said. "You'll get grease on my uniform. I wouldn't want the doctor to get any ideas. I'll do it." She unhooked her bra in the front and let her breasts out. She was proud of them, ran her hands over them herself while he watched. "Go ahead," she said. "You can touch. I don't mind a little grease on my bare skin."

Then she took him in her mouth and at the same time, slipped her hand up under her skirt. Lauren always made sure to take care of herself, and she knew it turned a man on even more to know she was doing it.

Al didn't last long. Pity he's stuck with Anna, Lauren thought, as she washed herself off at his sink. Such a prudish woman. At least we all thought she was.

"So that was the first present," Al said, grabbing her ass as she came up beside him again. "What's the second?"

"This," she said, sliding the deposit slip out of the pocket of her sweater. "Thought you might like to see this."

Al studied it for a minute. "Where did you find this?" He flipped it over and read the handwriting on the back.

"Annie Slocum found it in the doctor's shirt. She does his laundry, you know."

It took a moment for this information to register on Al's brain. Lauren pulled on her sweater. She didn't relish hanging around too long once he'd figured out what this meant.

"Bitch," he said, a low word, uttered perfectly clearly.

"See you, Al," Lauren said as she backed out the door. "Happy New Year."

As she drove back to the clinic, Lauren passed Anna's station wagon headed toward the school. Island etiquette dictated that you waved at everybody you passed, but ever since that night in the bar, Lauren and Anna had avoided one another even on the roads. Anna pretended to be concentrating on making her turn, but Lauren stared straight at her. "Watch yourself, Mrs. Craven," she said over the sound of the country song blaring from her radio. Maybe you need to carry a gun to go with that stupid cowboy hat of yours.

AL SAT FOR a long time in the desk chair at his office. When it got dark, he did not move to turn on a lamp. In the distance, a plane buzzed the airport and flew away. Some joker, he thought. They didn't have much traffic in the winter. The pilots from the mainland had Sally Malloy's phone number at home and up at the library. If they wanted to land in the winter, they had to call her first so she could come down to the airport office to read them the wind conditions and turn on the runway lights.

Sitting in the darkening room, his mind skittered around. He remembered all the way back to those dark days after his little sister died when his mother gave up on life. She'd gone into that bedroom and it seemed to him now that she didn't speak for months. She would just stick her fingers in her ears and let his father drink and rage and slap Al around when it moved him to do so. Al had been only six when it started, eight when it began to get really bad. His father had a dog then, a German shepherd, who seemed to pick up the old man's bitterness, and one day when Al had gotten too close, the dog bit him on the hand. His father had blamed him for it, said he was tormenting the animal.

Al hated his mother for those times, hated her for just giving up on him, hated her even more than his father. Hell, his father probably had had a reason, must have knocked the shit out of him to make him strong, to make sure he didn't die too, like the baby. After all, his father's beatings gave him something. They made him strong and wily, they taught him how to fight, how to watch the other fellow, keep an eye out. What did his mother do for him? Nothing. She'd given up on the only kid she had left. Didn't Al Craven count for anything? Apparently not. All she'd wanted from the beginning was that little baby girl.

Ever since then, Al had known for a fact that people were out to get him, to take things away from him. He'd trained himself to watch out, keep an eye open. He never let down his guard. That was one of the reasons he made such a good sheriff. Nothing escaped his notice. Nothing. So where had he been? he wondered now. How long had this been going on? How many people knew his wife had been dicking around with that prissy, wise-ass, mainland doctor? He thought about Anna that night she came back from the hunting tests, how she stood there making her high and mighty moral pronouncements about him and Lauren, then Erin. And she'd walked into her kitchen, back to her family, straight from a night in a motel fucking that doctor.

There was a voice in his head that he couldn't seem to shut down. It had been whispering to him all his life, but now it was getting louder. It was a little boy's voice. He argued with it. It said things like this:

She's getting ready to leave us.

Anna? Leave us? Al said. Are you kidding? She'd never dare. We're all she's got. Those brothers of hers don't do her any good and the father's dead and gone at last.

But now she had the doctor. Ever since her father had died, she'd been acting strange. Out every afternoon with the dogs. Supposedly. How did we know where she went? Maybe it didn't just happen on the mainland. Maybe it's happening right here too. We know women can't ever be trusted. You have to watch them all the time, find out what they're up to, make sure you aren't ever left. What would we do if she left us on our own?

I'm in charge here. Nobody is leaving me. Ever. Got that? Now shut up. He said this last out loud and the sound of his own voice bounced back at him from the concrete walls of the office.

Some men like Jimmy Slocum would just go home and beat the shit out of their wives, but Al didn't operate that way. Al had never hit Anna. Never. He prided himself on that. Didn't mean he didn't believe that people needed to be punished, but there were much better ways to get the point across. He knew how to keep his mouth shut and think on a situation for a while, come up with a plan. That's what he was doing now. He planned to sit here until he figured something out. When he was through, that doctor would be sorry he ever set foot on that ferry boat. And Anna. Well, Anna would be back on a tight check cord where she belonged.

ERIN HAD BEEN hanging out with the Tremaynes. They took her for rides in their truck after school. Bo called her the bronco rider. Derry the younger one didn't seem particularly happy to have her squeezed in the front seat between them. They let her light their cigarettes.

"So how's your dad?" Bo asked her one day.

She shrugged. "Okay, I guess."

"He's one hell of a sheriff, your father."

Erin didn't say anything. With all the cigarette smoke trapped in the cab of the truck, she could feel her wheezing starting. She was trying to hold it down.

"You know he's on my case about that BMW down by the dock. Thinks Derry and me sprayed all that red paint on it. He's full of shit, you know that?"

Erin nodded.

"Yeah," Derry said. "Got his head up his ass."

"Now careful, bro. You're talking about the bronco rider's father. Show some respect."

Erin couldn't figure out where to put herself in this conversation so she kept silent. She liked Bo better. She knew Derry didn't like that his brother always let her ride around in the truck with them. Once they had driven over to the marina, climbed up into some of the boats in dry dock, and rummaged around. Another time Bo had gone into the grocery store and come out with a couple of packages of cookies and two beers stuffed under his coat. She was pretty sure he didn't pay for them, but she ate the cookies anyway and took a sip of the beer.

Another day Bo started talking about their weekend plans. "Going to pick up a few things here and there," he said. "You know what we mean, bronco rider?"

"Sure," she said. But she didn't have any idea what they were talking about.

"Want to be in on it?"

"Okay," she said, although deep down in the very bottom of her stomach, she wasn't sure she did.

"Hey, Bo, what are you doing?" Derry asked over her head. He talked about her as if she weren't there.

Bo shrugged. "The bronco rider could prove useful. She is, after all, related to the big man. And we owe him one."

"You can let me off here," Erin said suddenly. "I have to go to the doctor's office."

"Sure, kid. Don't call us. We'll call you."

Erin pretended to be going up the walk to the clinic, but once their truck turned the corner, she crossed the street and took the hill past the library. Mr. Montclair pulled over when he saw her.

"Want a ride?" he called, and she hopped in.

"Are you going up to work with my mom?"

"Yup. Now that the snow's finally melted, we're going to take Daisy out with Polly. Some hunters coming up this weekend."

"There are always hunters coming."

"Not since Christmas. Dogs can't get the scent with all that snow."

"I know," Erin said. I know everything there is to know about dogs.

"How're you doing, Erin? I haven't seen you in a while."

"I'm fine." She looked at Mr. Montclair and saw the wispy strands of gray hair plastered across his shiny bald spot. Funny how everything seemed different to her than it used to be. She used to love Mr. Montclair and now she couldn't think why. He was just a skinny old man with baggy pants and a beat-up truck.

"How's school?"

"Stupid and boring."

"Sounds about right. That's what I thought of school myself. But I wished I'd stuck to it a little longer than I did. I might have gotten farther in life."

She turned away and stared out the window at all the familiar sights rolling by. How many times had she ridden past this rich summer person's white house, this golf course, Miss Yola's little brown house, the funny log cabin that nobody lived in right now, the big tree hit by lightning the year she turned seven. Back and forth from home to town to school to the beach to home to town again.

"This island is so boring," she said. Her breath made a cloud circle on the cold glass. "Same old boring places, same old people."

"Probably wherever you live feels boring after a while."

"Living on an island feels boringer," Erin said even though she knew it wasn't a word.

When they turned into the driveway, Anna was standing in the fenced yard by the kennels. Polly was curled in a cage in the back of the station wagon and Anna had Daisy, one of the younger dogs, on a check cord. Kasha was standing by the back door watching.

"Hi," Anna called as she walked the dog over to the car. Kasha trotted along behind, but at a certain distance. Anna had been firm with her about disturbing the training.

"Hi, Mom."

"Have either of you seen my hat? I can't find it anywhere."

"You had it yesterday morning when we went out," Chuck said. "I remember that."

She shrugged. "There are cookies in the oven, Erin. Can you take them out? The timer is set. Chuck, I've got my gun too. This dog is really skittish with shots. We're going to have to get her used to the noise early on." She leaned over to kiss Erin on the top of her head, then stepped back. "You smell of smoke. You haven't been smoking have you, Erin?"

"No, Mom. Some of the kids were after school."

"With your asthma—"

"I was not smoking," Erin shouted. "Don't you ever believe me about anything?" She stuck her fingers in her ears and ran for the house.

Chuck took the check cord from Anna and kenneled Daisy. "Hop in," he said. "I'll drive."

"Go on home, Kasha," she called from the car as Chuck started it up. "Go on." This time her voice was sharp, edgy. Kasha tilted her head and whined, but she knew enough not to follow.

"Kids," Anna said on the way up island.

"I know."

"How would you know? You've never had one."

"Nope, but I was one."

"It's different," Anna said. "Completely different."

"Whatever you say."

They drove the next mile in silence. Anna was thinking about

Erin. After an uncomfortable phone call from Mrs. Morrison ten days ago, Anna had confronted Erin about the book of dirty pictures. The girl had tossed her head and pretended she didn't know what her mother was talking about.

"Look at me, Erin," Anna had demanded. "Did you bring a book to Katie's house?"

"Sure, I brought a book. I always take a book places."

"Mrs. Morrison said it was a book about sex."

"Mrs. Morrison is full of it," Erin had shouted. "I'm not ever going back there again. I hate Katie Morrison and her stupid house and her baby sister. Her parents are total nerds. I can't believe you care about what they say."

"I care about you, Erin. And I'm worried about you."

"Mom, it's time for you to get out of my life. I need my privacy."

"SALLY MALLOY TELLS me she saw Erin down at the marina hanging out with the Tremayne boys," Anna said to Chuck.

"Those boys are trouble," Chuck said. His eyes were on the road. The melted snow had frozen to icy patches here and there.

"She's only thirteen, for God's sake. Why would they even bother with her?"

"Boredom. Erin was just telling me how bored she is with this island."

"There are worse things than boredom," Anna said.

EVER SINCE THE night she fell down the stairs, she had said almost nothing to Al. They still lay side by side in the bed together. She watched him. He watched her. If he got up in the middle of the night, she got up a little while later, padding down the hall looking for him. He'd wander through the house and she'd shadow him. As far as she knew, he had not gone back to Erin's room. She'd bought a slide bolt for Erin's door and installed it one afternoon.

When she showed it to Erin, the girl shrugged and said nothing.

"You deserve privacy," Anna had said by way of explanation. "Everybody in a family deserves privacy."

"Whatever, Mom," Erin had said wearily.

Two days later, Anna found that Al had removed the lock. The four fresh screw holes were still there in the door. A new item appeared on the list on the kitchen wall: "NO ROOMS IN THE HOUSE SHALL BE LOCKED AT ANYTIME," it read in Al's big block handwriting. He took the lock off the bathroom door too, and one evening, he yanked it open and stared at her in the tub.

"Get out," she had said in a cold voice.

"This is my house," he said. "I can go anywhere I want in my house. I've seen your body before. As far as I know, you're still my wife."

"Get out," she cried, and he'd put his finger up to his lips as if she were the one making a disturbance.

"Calm down, Anna," he said. "You're getting hysterical."

She wanted so much to scream, to open up and scream the lifelong scream that had been locked inside of her ever since her mother died. But there was Erin to think of. Always there was the threat that if somehow she managed to get out safely, Erin would be left behind. That thought was not thinkable.

She was taking certain precautions. When she first started working with the dogs, Al had told her it was stupid to waste money on a training pistol, so he'd given her one of his extras, a thirty-two caliber Smith & Wesson. Taught her how to clean it, and ever since then, she'd used it with blanks as a training pistol. A week ago, she'd bought a box of live ammunition, and she now kept three or four bullets in the left-hand pocket of her jeans. It had become a ritual with her at night before bed to move those bullets from one pair of pants to the next. Blanks in the right pocket, live shells in the left. L. L. Live left. She used little tricks like that to keep from making too many mistakes. It seemed to require all her concentration now to perform the simplest tasks.

"Anna, did you hear me?" Chuck asked as he pulled the car up on to the side of the road. "You're a million miles away."

She looked at him blankly.

"I said next thing you'll be ordering boots and a horse. You've got the hat and the gun."

"I've always had the gun."

"But you never kept it so close by your side before," he said.

"Please, Chuck, let it be."

Seventeen

WINTER HAD TAKEN hold of the island. The shallow ponds and marshes were frozen. Sam took a class up to Mink Pond, where he had the kids shovel off a clear spot and make a detailed list of everything they could see through the fuzzy pock-marked window of ice. The snow from the blizzard had melted, thawed, and crusted over, and another eight inches of powder had fallen since then. Pipes had frozen, and a couple of roofs had given way under the heavy weight of the accumulated snow. The pushier summer owners called once a week to be sure someone was checking their houses. The caretakers on the island made nice on the phone, but they had their own problems. There was a certain amount of the usual winter grumbling down at the Rocky Point about people with too many houses and too little sense. Ellie, Randy Baker's young girlfriend, decided she needed a break from the winter and agreed to go to Florida with her family to try and patch things up. On the side, people were making bets about whether she'd ever come back. Randy was taking it hard. He'd shown up earlier than usual at the Harbor Lounge. The first time Lila tried to comfort him, he gave her a look she understood. Now she just tried to make sure he ate something between drinks.

Maggie had to walk down long unplowed driveways to reach the houses she was surveying. She'd cut the tips off her gloves so she could take notes and work the camera shutter in houses where the heat was down at fifty, just enough to keep the pipes from freezing. She brought a small portable heater with her, and when she couldn't stand the cold anymore, she'd huddle down next to it to take notes and drink coffee out of her thermos. Sam tried to persuade her to put off some of the houses until the spring, but for some reason, she liked the harshness of her winter forays. When she pushed open each new front door, the still, trapped air would greet her as if the house had been holding its breath since summer. She imagined that behind the musty odor of mouse, she smelled newly mown grass and perfume and southern sea wind that carried a hint of kelp. In most of the houses, the furniture had been pushed together and covered with sheets. While Kasha made her steady way around the oddly shaped obstacles, her nose to the cold floors, quivering at the fresh scent of mouse, Maggie stopped to lift the cloths and run her fingers along the curved wooden edge of a settee, across the top of an antique lap desk. After years of advising museums on the contents of their storage, she was happy to be back in houses where people actually sat on a Queen Anne chair, instead of reading the label on the wall above it and staring at it from behind a red silk guard rope. These houses held some good furniture. She made a mental list of the pieces in each house that were of particular interest to her.

Maggie's love of fine furniture had started on her trips with Nan to museums up and down the east coast, then later on in Europe. The two of them gravitated to the period rooms filled with beautifully maintained objects, where they could spend endless time together marveling over the detailed marquetry of a French commode. By the time she got to graduate school for fine arts training, she had fallen hopelessly in love with wood, the way she imagined an artist might get high on the endless variety of color and texture and shape that could be sucked out of paint. Now that she was not spending her time on airplanes, rushing from one place to another, she had come back to it. For this survey, she was being paid to record the beauty of what human beings could craft out of trees, whether it was the ribbed and paneled ceiling of a dining room, the cherry wainscoting of a library, or the sumptuous carving of a Victorian card table. When Sam looked through the photographs she'd taken of the interiors, even he agreed that to create something that beautiful, it might be worth cutting down a tree.

Now THAT SHE and Erin didn't speak, Katie Morrison was finding herself the center of attention in the seventh grade, and she was enjoying it. She'd never been popular at school before, but the other girls were telling her that they liked her clothes and the new scrungies she was wearing in her hair.

One day at lunch, Patty Thayer started talking about Erin.

"She's gotten very snooty hasn't she, hanging out at the high school tables. She looks stupid over there."

All eyes swung to Erin who had her back to them and was talking to Raymond Grimes, a pimply-faced boy in the tenth grade.

"Erin is trouble," Katie said. "That's what my mother says. She won't let me have her over to my house again."

"Why?"

"Because of something she did."

The girls at the table all hitched closer and put their heads together.

"What?" Patty asked.

"Remember when Erin came to my house after the blizzard? Well, she brought this book with her that had dirty pictures in it."

"What kind of dirty pictures?"

Katie whispered to them what was in the pictures. The circle of heads pulled back.

"She's sicko," said Patty Thayer. "Jimmy Slade told me that she said she'd seen her father's thing."

"She told me too," Katie said quickly. "I don't remember whether it was her father's, but she told me she'd seen someone's." She blushed. "You know, a man's thing."

"That whole family is sick, if you ask me," Patty said, and the circle of heads nodded. Then she caught Katie up on all the island gossip about the Cravens, at least what she had heard around her own dinner table. Behind closed doors, people were always grumbling about Al Craven, how cheap he was, how full of himself. Mr. Sheriff strutting around, sucking up to the summer people and charging them a hundred dollars to fix a leaky sink, then when it came time for the annual church drive, he was nothing but a lot of big talk and empty pockets. Everybody on the island knew he was rich, but he acted really poor. Annie Malloy chimed in with a story she'd heard about Anna Craven and the time she had a big row with one of the hunters who mistreated his dog. Liz Slocum had been included in the circle for a change. She'd finally stopped sucking her thumb so Patty had let her join.

"My mother and Lauren were talking about Mrs. Craven on Christmas Day. Remember we had to go to Lauren's because our heat went off?"

All heads turned to look at Liz.

"Who's Lauren?" Katie asked.

"Lauren Root, the nurse," Patty explained. "So tell us, Liz, what did they say?"

Liz wasn't used to having the spotlight on her. She couldn't remember what they had said exactly. Something over the manicure table that afternoon.

"About the doctor," she blurted out. "My mother does the doctor's shirts."

Patty rolled her eyes. "What does the doctor have to do with this, Liz? We're talking about the Cravens."

"I know," Liz said a little too loudly, and the lunch room quieted for a minute.

"Keep your voice down," Patty whispered. "What?"

"Lauren said that Mrs. Craven acted so high and mighty and the doctor was a sly one."

This was an odd piece of information which the girls tried to absorb and weave into the other stories.

"Maybe Mrs. Craven has a crush on the doctor," Annie said.

They were still mulling over this possibility when they were interrupted by Mr. M.

"What's going on here?" he asked, clapping Katie on the shoulder. "Looks like a secret club meeting."

"It is," Patty said in a loud nervous voice. The others were glancing guiltily at each other from under hooded eyes.

"Where's Erin?"

"Over there," Annie said. "With Raymond Grimes, her new best friend." This unleashed a flood of giggles.

"She's not in the club?" Sam asked.

"We were just kidding about the club, Mr. M. You believe anything, don't you?" Patty said. She stood up to take her tray back and this got everybody stirring.

ANNA WAS so sure of where she'd left her hat that she was down on her knees with her head under the steering wheel of the car looking for it, when she smelled something odd. She felt around under the seat and pulled out a charred piece of black felt. She turned it over in her fingers, again and again, staring at it. Al had been burning trash out in the back yesterday, she remembered. Leaves and old newspapers. The smoke brought a call over the radio from Dan Malloy, the fire chief, but Al had told him not to worry. Just some old junk, things he'd been meaning to get rid of for a while now.

Good time with the ground frozen and no wind, Anna had heard him bark into his radio.

She drove the short distance to Miss Yola's house, the hat fragment still in her hand.

When they were both settled at the kitchen table, Anna handed the other woman the piece of black felt.

"He burned it?"

"Like a piece of old trash. He must have. There's no other explanation."

"What are you going to do?" Miss Yola asked, her eyes steady.

"I'll have to leave, I guess. Take Erin sometime when he isn't watching and go."

"You can always come here."

"For a night or two," Anna said. "But I'm not safe on the island for longer than that. I figure I can work as a waitress over on the mainland. I've got the car. I've got some money hidden away. I haven't been handing it all over to Al. I've got more sense than that."

"He'll come after you."

Anna slumped in her chair.

"The law says you can't take a child away from her father like that."

"I've caught him in bed with her," Anna said, and Miss Yola's eyes widened. "What would the law say about that?"

"Bastard," Miss Yola said in a quiet, thoughtful voice.

Anna shrugged. "It doesn't make any difference what he's done. After all, we both know who is the law on this island. At least until the summer when the state trooper arrives."

"He's the sheriff, but he's not the judge and jury," Miss Yola said.

"What do you mean by that?"

"The island takes care of its own problems. We always have."

"And it's a man's island."

"True," Miss Yola said. "And your husband can be a problem to the men too. There's a lot of grumblings from Billy Slade and Chuck that Al's been ordering cheap materials, and at the same time cutting back on their share of the profits."

"Chuck hasn't mentioned anything about that to me."

"Maybe he thinks you're too busy with other concerns."

"What do you mean by that?"

Miss Yola rearranged the salt and pepper shakers on her kitchen table.

"What are you saying?"

"The rumors have been flying around. Lauren started them, I expect. Something about you and the doctor."

"What about me and the doctor?"

"That you've been seeing him on the side, on the mainland."

Anna pounded her fists on the table and screamed. It made the dog lift his little white head from the kitchen linoleum and howl in reply.

Miss Yola said nothing. She wiped some crumbs off the table into her other hand and dusted them off into her pocket.

Anna put up her head and screamed again, a long, throat-burning cry of frustration and rage. When she was done, she put her head down on her arms. "To tell you the truth, I let the doctor know I was available, but he refused me," she said at last, her voice muffled. "What a joke. I'm being accused of something I didn't even do."

Miss Yola reached over and massaged her neck. "Feel better?" she asked.

"A little," Anna mumbled. "So that's what Al thinks now. Lauren told him, of course."

Miss Yola stayed silent.

"I must have twenty years of screams bottled up inside me."

"At least that many."

"I feel trapped by everything. By Al, by this island, by the dogs, by Erin. If it weren't for Erin, I'd take off today. I can get out safely, but how do I get her out too?"

Miss Yola didn't speak. She didn't have any answers for Anna. She had run away a long time ago, had left behind a husband and a baby, but hers had been buried. Died in her crib at the age of two. Doctors said they thought it was heart failure, but they didn't really know.

"Sometimes I think of shooting him," Anna mumbled into her folded arms.

"You're not the first woman who's thought of that. Trouble is the ones who do it usually end up in jail. And they're not the people who should be there."

Anna dragged herself to her feet.

"Where are you going now?"

"Down to the post office. I'm going to order another hat. The new catalog came in yesterday."

Miss Yola looked at her. "It seems to me you need to figure out different ways to scream."

"I'm not sure what you mean, but I think you're right," Anna said.

ON SATURDAY NIGHT, Erin met the Tremayne boys at ten o'clock behind the post office.

"Are you sure nobody heard you leave?" Bo asked.

"Absolutely sure." The dogs had barked when her foot knocked against a bucket by the side door, but the dogs were always starting up about something. Nobody paid attention to their noise anymore. Her mother had been out with hunters all day and had gone to bed early.

"Where's your dad?"

She shrugged. "Out somewhere. He goes out a lot. I don't know." She hated these questions about her father. Bo and Derry talked about him all the time. They were obsessed with him.

Derry had picked two houses. He had done the planning work. Bo didn't like to be bothered with details. The first one was up island, a big old white clapboard summer house. Erin had never even been down the driveway before. Apparently, some older retired couple had bought it five years ago and had remodeled the whole place. Derry lifted the keys to the front door from his father's collection, but he was having a hard time getting in. Bo got pissed off.

"You were supposed to figure all this out ahead of time, asshole," Bo muttered.

"Shut up," Derry said. With an exaggerated shrug of his shoulders, Bo went off to the edge of the lawn near where the truck was parked. "Don't look, bronco rider," he called out to Erin. He unzipped his fly. Erin could hear the spattering of drops on the bushes, but she pretended not to notice. She'd been hanging out by the truck watching for anybody who might decide to drive down the half-mile driveway at midnight on a Saturday in February. It was an unlikely possibility, but the job made her feel useful and took some of the edge off her fear. When she had agreed to meet the boys at night, she knew they would be doing something bad, but she hadn't thought it would be this.

Derry finally got one of the keys to work and he and Bo went inside. From her post by the truck, Erin saw the flashlight working its way through the rooms. They came out carrying a television set and a stereo.

"No silver and a lousy VCR," Bo said to Erin as he lowered the set into the back of the truck. "Not even worth picking up. Lock up, Derry and let's get going. The summer owners are getting too stingy and suspicious."

"You can't really blame them with people like us loose on this place all winter," Derry said with a chuckle.

On the way to the next place, Bo lit up a thin cigarette that smelled sweet almost. It was pot. Erin knew that. When he passed it to her to hand on to Derry, she put it to her lips.

"Well, will you look at this?" Bo said, and she liked the sound of admiration in his voice. "The bronco rider is going to suck on a little weed. Take it slow, kid, and hold it down in there. It'll make you feel real good."

It burned in her chest, and try as she might, she couldn't hold it in her lungs for long. She burst out coughing and Derry grabbed her hand and slipped the thin cigarette from between her fingers just before she dropped it.

Bo clapped her on the back. "That's okay. You'll learn. It takes time."

She slid her inhaler out of her pocket and sprayed as she sucked in air. This nasty taste she did hold down for as long as she could.

"Oh, great, now she's going to have an asthma attack," Derry said.

She shook her head and exhaled. "No, I'm not." The new medicine was working. She hadn't had an attack since the day Kasha ran away.

The second house went as smoothly as the first, and Erin was feeling great as she sat up in the seat between them, rolling down the dark island road. She liked the warm bulk of each of them surrounding her. She was a part of the team. She belonged to something. The three musketeers.

"What do you do with all the stuff?" she asked.

"That's none of your business," Derry said quickly. "We take care of things."

"You don't think I can keep a secret," she said.

"You're a new recruit," Bo said. He was smoking pot again. "Got to prove to us that you can be trusted."

He turned the wheel of the truck with one finger and it spun left, off the road from the town green. "Now you're going to get your chance."

"What do you mean?" She was suddenly scared. She liked guarding the truck, watching for headlights. What did they want her to do now? Her hand slid up to her hair and she began to twist it back and forth, but Derry gave her a punch in the side.

"Move over, kid, you're crowding me."

"You're going to give us a tour," Bo said. "Of your friend's house."

"What friend?"

"Miss Hammond. The red-haired lady," Derry said. "She's a friend of yours, isn't she?"

"We'd better not go there," Erin said quickly. "Kasha will come after us."

"Who's Kasha?"

"The wolf," Bo said.

She's a husky, Erin thought, but for once she didn't say it. Let them think she was a wolf. "Kasha can be really nasty. She's gone after my father a couple of times."

"Sounds like my kind of dog," Derry said. "Well, you're going to calm her down."

"Maggie's probably there," Erin said.

"Maybe, maybe not," Bo said. "From what we hear, Miss Hammond spends a lot of nights over with Mr. M."

Erin was amazed at this piece of information and forgot her fear for a moment. With all the other stuff that had been going on, she'd forgotten to watch Maggie and Sam. She hadn't been to Maggie's since that day she had taken the book from the third floor.

"Looks like we're in luck," Derry said as the truck slid by the quiet house. "Her car's not here."

"Sometimes she leaves Kasha," Erin said. Please, let's not do this. Please.

"Let's find out," Bo said as he swung the truck into the driveway next door and parked it up against some high bushes. That place was owned by summer people. The lights burning in their house were run by timers that they set back in November when they left after Thanksgiving. Nobody on the island was fooled by those things, but summer owners did it anyway. It made them feel safer.

They knocked on Maggie's front door, once and then twice more. They hallooed up at the windows. Silence.

"No people, no dog," Derry said, elbowing Erin in the ribs. "We're in luck, kid."

"She doesn't have anything here worth stealing," Erin said. "Honestly, she doesn't."

"We'll see."

When Bo found the door locked, he gave it a swift kick with his boot. "That's great," he said.

Thank you, Maggie, for still locking up, Erin thought.

"We'd better go someplace else," she said. But they were talking over her head.

"So, Derry, what's your plan?" Bo asked.

"Christ, I never thought she'd lock the place."

"She's a city person," Erin said. "She always locks up."

"Shut up, kid," Bo said in an absent-minded voice. "My brother needs to think."

Derry led them around the side of the house where they tried a couple of windows. "No luck," he said. "They're swollen shut."

"Let's break one," Bo said. He was acting pretty cocky after the two joints he'd had in the truck.

"Not one of the big ones," Derry said. "But I bet there's one leading down to the basement. This is where we'll use the bronco rider."

"Buster," Bo said. "Get it? Bronco buster?" He was so amused by his own joke that he stumbled along after them, giggling in a high-pitched voice.

"You're wasted," Derry said amiably. He had a firm hand on Erin's shoulder to make sure she didn't run off.

"I sure am, brother."

Derry knelt down by a narrow basement window. With one swift movement, he smashed the pane of glass with the butt end of the flashlight. Erin flinched at the loud noise of breaking glass. Bo had wandered off and was pissing in the bushes again. He had begun to sing and Derry called to him to shut up. They were much closer to town here and the housing complex for year-round people was just around the next corner on this back road.

Derry reached past the jagged glass to untwist the lock.

"I'm going to drop you down," he said to Erin. "You come up through the house and let us in the front door."

"It's dark."

"No kidding. You can take the flashlight."

She still didn't move.

"You're not going to wimp out on us, are you? Why do you think we dragged you along like this?"

"She's a friend of mine," Erin started, but the words were barely out of her mouth before she wished she could suck them back. Derry never had wanted her along.

"Big deal, kid." He grabbed her by the upper arms and spun her around. "Now you climb down through there or I'll drop you in myself."

He held the window open as she scrambled through the narrow space. She was still hanging on to the windowsill with her head poking out when he barked at her.

"What's the problem?"

"I can't feel the floor. I don't know how far I'll drop."

He grabbed her hands and pulled so that her arms straightened out with a snap. She screamed as the rough surface of the sill scraped her skin.

"I'll lower you," he said.

Even with her arms stretched out full length above her, her feet didn't find the floor. She felt as if she were being dropped down a long well.

"All right, I'm going to let you go now," he said.

"Don't drop me," she cried. "I don't know how far down it is."

"Come on, kid, it's just a frigging basement. It can't be that far." He undid her hands from his and with her fingernails scrabbling for a hold, she slid a short distance down a rough rock wall till her feet slammed into the floor. She huddled there for a minute.

"You okay?" he called.

She didn't answer. Served him right.

"Kid, are you all right?"

He poked his head and one arm in through the narrow window and shined the light on her. "Wake up, Erin. Time to get moving."

She stood up and dusted herself off.

"Here's the flashlight," he said as he tossed it down to her. "Meet you by the front door."

The stairs that led up into the hall next to the kitchen were rotting, and she climbed slowly, one shoulder against the cool stone wall.

She took her time getting to the front door. From inside the house, she heard Bo, who had started up singing again. Derry was trying to keep his brother quiet while he watched for her, his nose pressed up against the glass, his hands cupped around his face. When he caught sight of her, he beckoned at her impatiently.

"What took you so damn long?" he asked as the two boys stumbled into the front hall.

"It's dark. There's nothing here to take. She just has a lot of old broken-down furniture."

The boys paid no more attention to her but spread out through the house. She could hear them banging around. Upstairs, the lights went on and off as they made their way through the rooms. Erin stood in the front hall, staring stupidly at the hatrack and hating herself. Maggie had been her friend, the only one she'd had on this island in a long time, and here she was, helping the Tremayne boys rob her house. She wished Maggie would come home now and find them. She wanted to be caught, wanted to get into public trouble, wanted to be locked up somewhere away from everybody and everything.

"Why are you just standing there?" Derry said as he started back down the stairs. "Grab something." He was carrying a VCR that he must have found in one of the bedrooms.

"I don't think that works," Erin said. "Maggie hates television. She never watches it."

"It's not a television. It works," he said, but he looked at it uncertainly for a moment. "Come on, Bo," he yelled. "We've got to get out of here."

"This place is a dump. What'd you get, bronco rider?" Bo asked. He'd taken some jewelry and the portable radio from the living room bookshelf.

"I don't want anything," Erin said.

"Yes, you do, kid," Derry said. "You don't leave here without something. Go on."

"I won't," she said.

He put down the VCR and started toward her. "You are pissing me off." He placed his face right next to hers and she could smell the smoke still on his breath and the beer behind that. His hand closed around her upper arm and squeezed until it hurt. She whimpered. The lights went off suddenly.

"What's going on?" Derry said.

"I turned them off," Bo whispered. "Headlights on the road." They froze as a car rolled by.

"Is it gone?" Derry asked.

"I think so. We'd better get out of here."

"Not till she takes something too," Derry said. He squeezed her upper arm one more time and shoved her toward the living room. "Pick something."

In the end, she took the typewriter. Maggie probably wouldn't miss it, Erin thought. I'm the only one who ever uses it. She's practically given it to me anyway.

They let themselves out the back door, the one that locked behind them. Once they were safely away from the house, the boys were eager to be rid of her. Derry wanted to dump her in the middle of town, but Bo said she'd be too obvious walking up the road carrying that typewriter so they drove her all the way to the end of her driveway.

"Remember, kid, we're in this together," Bo said as he shifted the truck back into gear.

She nodded wearily. She knew what he was saying. She hid the typewriter in the very back of one of the sheds. Nobody went out there much. They wouldn't find it.

The house was still. She tiptoed down the long upstairs hallway and hesitated for a moment outside her parents' door. No sound. She could not ever remember a time that she'd heard her parents talking together in bed. It seemed as if they'd never had much to say to each other. She wondered what it would be like to have a mother and father who laughed over a joke together or teased each other or held hands. She couldn't think of anybody she knew who had parents like that. Maybe Maggie and Mr. M. held hands now. Maybe they would get married and have children and still laugh together.

Her arm hurt. She had always bruised easily, so tomorrow there would be a purple mark. She felt very old and used up and tired.

Eighteen

THE WHARTON HOUSE was situated halfway up the island with a view west over the sound. It had been built in 1879 by the firm of Arthur Little and "is considered one of the prime examples of an early nineteenth-century clapboard house, which also contains several features specific to Georgian Colonial houses," Maggie read to Sam on their way up island. It was a warm Sunday afternoon late in January. She'd asked him to go through this one house with her.

"That sounds impressive," he said as he took the first left after the gatehouse and slowed the truck to a crawl. The driveway was rutted and rocky. "Where'd you learn all this?"

"From a book I got on American country houses through inter-library loan. Sally Malloy's been very helpful. This house was built for a wealthy Boston couple who went belly up soon after they finished. My great-grandfather bought it in the late 1890s. He made most of his money in real estate. Have you ever been down here?"

"Many times."

"That back wing was for the servants," she said, peering up through the windshield. "Look how he gave them no dormer windows and no balustrade. It was the architect's way of saying this isn't important, don't look here."

"Have you got a key?"

"No, I called Randy yesterday. He said he'd leave the door open for us. We'll do the outside first."

She handed him the clipboard so he could take notes as she talked. With the camera up to her eye, she rattled off details. "Two-story

corner pilasters, hipped roof with evenly spaced dormers and bal-
ustrades, a classical cornice under the eaves, fan windows—"

"Hold up," he said. "I can't write that fast."

"Sorry. I'll slow down."

But she didn't. They made their way around the veranda, then
let themselves into the front hall.

"Centrally placed double-height hall with two rooms on either
side," she went on, snapping all the while. "Library and parlor connected. An unusual projection of the parlor alcove onto the front
veranda. Atypical of this style and era."

Sam trailed along behind her, scribbling as fast as he could. She
lifted the sheets on the furniture as she went. "Most of this is re-
production," she said. "Here's a good piece. Can you pull out a
separate sheet of paper and take this down? Parlor, eighteenth-
century chest on chest, Chippendale, note dentiling along cornice.
Needs stripping and refinishing, new handles." She held aside the
white sheet in order to pull out the drawers. "They look fine," she
muttered to herself.

They moved from room to room and all through the second floor
as she snapped pictures, assessed the quality of the furniture, noted
the architectural details. Whenever Sam had to ask her to repeat
something, she would glance over at him with a disconnected look
in her eye as if the sound of his voice had jarred her out of a trance.

"We're all done," she said when she pulled the front door closed
behind them. He handed her the clipboard.

"You didn't give the ghosts much time."

"What do you mean?"

"We went through there at breakneck speed."

"Did we? That's the way I like to work. Very concentrated."

"So it felt like just another job?"

She considered his question. "Most of the time. When we were
in the corner bedroom upstairs, it did occur to me that my mother
had probably slept there. But by the time I was born, she had left
all that so far behind. It doesn't feel connected to me." She hopped
up into the front seat of the truck. He had pulled a pair of binoculars
out of the glove compartment and strung them around his neck.

"That makes sense," he said. "After all, Nan's house was your
home."

"Not exactly. Nan was my home. She's the one who carried my
history."

"You mean the other one. You carry your own history, don't you? We all do."

"Yes, I guess you're right. I hadn't thought of it that way."

He walked back around to her side of the truck and opened the door.

"Where are we going?" she asked.

"Come and see." He took her hand. "I have a surprise for you."

He led her down the sloping front lawn of the house and helped her up onto a stone wall that looked over the water. "Now sit right in front of me." He checked once through the binoculars, then handed them to her. "Train them on those rocks over there."

She took some time focusing. "I see. A bunch of rocks in the middle of Shell Harbor. Am I looking for birds?"

"No. Just keep your eye on those rocks."

"Oh, my God," she said. "One of them moved."

He slipped his arms around her from behind and whispered "seals" in her ear. "The wind is in the right direction," he said. "If we listen, we might be able to hear them."

"There are so many of them. At least twenty. One just slid into the water."

"Listen," he whispered again. They held still for a minute, then another. A seal lifted its head and an awkward croaking call wafted back to them across the water. Another echoed the message, then another, until four or five sleek gray heads were lifted to the sky. Two more slid off into the water and dived. In a short time, they resurfaced, barked, and dived again. Another hunched forward using its flippers to reposition itself on the rock.

"Oh, Sam, they're beautiful. Do you want to look?"

"When you're done. I've been watching them for years. From your grandparents' front lawn, it turns out." He slipped his hands under her elbows to support her arms. "You haven't developed your binocular muscles yet."

"Do they live here?"

"It's their winter home. They breed here in April and then go up to Maine for the summer. I've seen single harbor seals in our waters as early as October, but we get the real influx in December."

"They look as if they like the sun."

"Mmm. The weather cooperated. During the January thaw, they get a little more active."

"Do they always come back here?"

"Always. The numbers go up and down a little depending on the breeding season."

"I mean to this clump of rocks. How do they know to swim to this exact place?"

"Instinct. The pull of home, their breeding ground. These seals have to travel down the coast from Maine. Not that far when you compare them to the osprey."

"How far do they travel?"

"We have some that come from the Caribbean every spring to build their nest on the same platform next to the same telephone pole."

"Imagine that," she said, and her voice was quiet. "To look down from that high up and to know exactly which platform is yours." She leaned back against him. "Is this all right?"

"Make yourself comfortable." He lifted the thick tangle of her hair and kissed her neck. "We're in no rush."

They went back to bed in the middle of the afternoon and made gentle love with their eyes open, each drinking in the other. Every movement seemed to flow naturally from the one before as if they were dancing together in a wide slow circle of flesh and bone. Afterward, he pulled her close in and they held each other for a long time without speaking.

"This is home," he said at last in the quiet of the darkening room.

ONE WEDNESDAY EVENING, when Al had gone off to his regular poker game at Paul Thayer's house, Anna drove herself down to the doctor's. In customary island fashion, she parked her car half on and half off the narrow sidewalk. From where she sat, she could see the silhouette of Lacey's head leaning over some work on a table in his living room. A car drove down the hill behind her to the post office. Somebody would see her sitting there and would tell Al. Well, let them. For a woman to sit in her car, was that a sin? On this island, everything was a sin. Everything was suspect. Everybody was watching.

She slammed the car door. The doctor glanced up from what he was doing and peered out into the dark night. When she rang the doorbell, it did not take him long to answer it.

"Anna?" His expression showed concern. "Is everything all right?"

She didn't answer.

"Erin?"

"She's fine. Nothing medical anyway. Can I come in?"

He hesitated for a fraction of a second before he stepped aside.

"Of course," he said.

He made her a cup of tea, and they settled down at the dining room table away from the light. Maybe they'd get lucky, she thought. Maybe at this hour, nobody would drive down the little road past the doctor's office. It was a small road after all, just a shortcut between the post office and the marina. Her courage came and went like waves on the beach. The hell with them all, she thought in one moment, and please God, don't let them catch me in the next. She hated herself for the waxing and waning of her strength.

In the background, she heard the static from the two-way radio on low volume. A noise unique to the island. It made her feel as if she were sitting in her own kitchen.

"I saw you by the window working on something," she said.

"Pencil sketches. Fooling around."

"Would you rather be an artist than a doctor?"

"Much. But it's hard to make a living that way."

"Are you good?"

"I'm probably the wrong person to ask," he said.

"I'm not modest about the dogs. If someone asks me if I'm good, I tell them yes."

He studied her for a minute as if he were seeing something new and different. "I'm good enough to have sold some work, had some shows. I have one coming up in Ireland. But that's not why you're here."

"I don't know why I'm here."

"Why don't you start at the beginning," he said. "Tell me what's going on."

She burst out laughing at the thought of that. The beginning? Where did it start? The day she was born. The day her mother died. That first day in kindergarten when Al shoved his way ahead of her in line?

She told him about the hat. That seemed as good a place as any.

"From all I've heard, your husband is a bully."

She didn't ask him what he'd heard or who from. It didn't matter.

"You've got that one right," she said. "And he thinks you and I got together that day back in December over on the mainland. That's the latest rumor flying around the island."

"Who started that?" he asked. His voice was calm and to his credit, he didn't take his eyes from her face.

"Your nurse, probably."

He clearly was not surprised.

"Want me to leave right now?" she asked. She was feeling reckless, nutty, full of piss and vinegar, as her father used to say. "Or at least move my car around to the post office?"

"What are you going to do, Anna?"

"Shoot him." She shrugged. "It seems the simplest solution. Put us all out of our misery." He was studying her again. He must look at his patients this way when he was trying to decide how much bad news they could take. She didn't like it. It made her feel like a bug under a microscope. "People who get in bed with their thirteen-year-old daughters should not be allowed to live."

"He's done that?"

"I found him there."

"More than once?"

"I'm pretty sure of it."

"Did Erin ever tell you?"

"No." Her bravado was washing out to sea again. A picture of her daughter curled up next to the wall, frozen, waiting for her father to go away came up in front of Anna like a scene on a movie screen. "Erin isn't telling me much these days."

"Do you think he molested her?"

"How the hell do I know, Doctor?" she asked in a soft voice. "I wasn't lying in the bed with them at the time. Knowing him, he was just curled up like a puppy dog, sleeping next to her. He's a pathetic man. Sometimes he throws himself on the floor and begs me not to leave him, says he'll die if I ever do. He makes me sick."

"So why don't you leave him?"

"Because he'll kill me before he'll let me do that. Humiliate him in front of this whole island. Walk out, take his daughter. And where would I go? They'd find me and make me come back. Nobody will believe what he's done. Annie Slocum tried once. She went off island to one of those places for battered women. She got all the way to a judge who dismissed the case because she didn't have photographable bruises. She just came back with her head hanging. That one time Jerry didn't beat her up. Said she'd learned her lesson. How do you like that?"

He shook his head. "The school superintendent," he said.

"You don't believe me."

"Just the opposite. I worked in the emergency rooms long

enough to have seen worse." He shuddered. "But a man who gets in bed with his own child. That I find repellent. Inexplicable. What kind of sickness makes a man look there—"

"You're an island man yourself," she broke in to stop his train of thought. She couldn't bear to listen anymore to what he was saying. "You know island people are different. They solve their own problems."

"Shooting him isn't going to solve anything."

"Got any other ideas?"

"I could talk to him. Or maybe some of the other men. Chuck, for example."

What a funny idea, she thought. Talk to Al? Chuck talk to Al?

"You haven't been paying much attention or else you'd know that Al has nothing but contempt for Chuck. He implies all the time that Chuck is queer because he lives alone and loves photography and doesn't swagger around boasting about the women he's screwed."

The lights of a car traveled across the wall of the dining room above their heads. Dennis shifted his head to the side.

"It's Henry Willard," he said.

She nodded. The man lived across the street, kept to himself. Purser on the ferry in the mornings. Not one of the gossips.

"I should go," she said, but did not move.

"Is there anybody else who can talk to your husband?" Dennis asked even though he knew he wasn't making much sense. All he needed to do was catapult himself back to Omey Island. Did any of them ever speak to Patrick McClaren to make him stop beating on Bridget? Some nights it was so bad that you'd stick cotton in your ears if you lived next door or across the street the way the Laceys did. What must she have thought, that poor woman, screaming so loudly and nobody saying a word, picking up the paper from her shop on Sunday mornings as if they'd heard nothing, and the days that the bruises on her face were particularly bad, staring down at their scuffed shoes as she counted out their change? In the end, she ran away. It was all the news one weekend when he was home from Dublin.

Anna was staring at him.

"I'm sorry, did you say something?" he asked.

"Nothing important. Where did you go?"

"Back to the past. Island living," he said with an apologetic shrug. "I don't have any solutions."

"It's a relief to hear a man say that," she said. "They always think they have to solve the problem."

"Do you want another cup of tea?"

She didn't, but she still couldn't bear to get in the car, drive herself home, lie down next to Al Craven, and listen to him snore while she stared at the ceiling and waited for another morning to come.

He took her cup and refilled it.

"Tell me about Ireland," she said when he set the tea back down in front of her.

"What?"

"Anything. Just tell me a story."

He told her about Galway and the fields above the beaches on the little island of Inishbofin. "That word means 'island of the cow' in Gaelic. I used to put in there with my father and we'd walk all around the place in a day and end up in the village pub in the afternoon and my father would give me a sip of his shandy and I'd sit up on a high stool next to him."

She was lulled by his voice and put her head down on her arms. I don't want to do anything else, she thought. I don't even want him to take me into his bed. I just want to stay here, safe and quiet, and listen to him talking. She thought she felt his hand stroking her hair, but she couldn't be sure. She didn't even know anymore whether she was awake or asleep.

AROUND EIGHT-THIRTY ON a Wednesday night, Maggie discovered she'd been robbed. She liked to listen to music while she was in the bath, and this particular night, she wasted a good half hour looking for the portable radio. It wasn't anywhere in the house, and she knew for certain she'd seen it in the living room on the bookshelf some time recently. When she looked around upstairs, she discovered the VCR was gone together with some pieces of Nan's jewelry that Maggie had left in the top of a closet. Such small stupid things that she kept second-guessing herself. Finally, she called Sam, but there was no answer. Next she dialed Al Craven's number. Erin answered.

"Erin," she said. "It's Maggie. How are you?"

She heard the girl take a deep breath. "Fine."

"You never come visit me anymore. I miss you."

"I've been busy."

"Drop by anytime. Kasha misses you too."

"I see her. She comes over here sometimes to hang out with Mom and the dogs."

"She's gotten very independent," Maggie said. "Listen, is your father there?"

"Why do you need him?" Erin asked quickly. "Is something wrong?"

"Nothing serious, but I think I've been robbed."

Erin didn't answer for quite a long time. "Well, he's not here. His truck is gone. My mother's gone somewhere too. It's just me and the dogs."

"Okay. No big deal. Sorry to wake you."

"That's okay. You didn't." The phone went dead almost immediately, as if Erin's finger had been hovering over the receiver button.

Maggie called Chuck next.

"I'll be right over."

"You don't need to—" Maggie started to say, but he had already hung up.

She wasn't scared for some reason. It felt like an old robbery, something that could have happened weeks, even months ago, although she knew she'd used the radio more recently than that.

Chuck knocked on the front door and she unlocked it to let him in.

"I guess all your locking up didn't do much good," he said. "What did they take?"

"That old VCR Nan had in her bedroom, my portable radio, and some bits and pieces of jewelry. That's all I've found so far."

"How did they get in?"

"I hadn't thought about that," she said.

He'd brought a flashlight and together they walked through the first floor of the house, checking the windows.

"Nothing," he said. "You stay here. I'll look downstairs."

She walked into the kitchen, opened the refrigerator door, and stared at the shelves for a long time before she closed it again. She couldn't figure out what she was looking for.

"They got in down here," he called, his voice echoing up through the floorboards. He must have been standing right under the kitchen. He sounded like a ghost.

"How?" she yelled back.

"Broke one of the small windows."

She sat down abruptly in a straightbacked kitchen chair. It was real then. Somebody had broken into her house and stolen things from her. Could they have done it while she was sleeping, taking care not to step on a creaky floorboard, moving about in the darkness, lifting up little pieces of her life, and carrying them away? It made her shiver, and suddenly, she longed for the townhouse in Philadelphia, the familiar wail of a police siren. She wanted to be in a place where there were laws and courts and numbers to call when you were in trouble.

"Must have been a pretty small person to get in through that window," Chuck said when he came back up the stairs.

"Al Craven wasn't home. I called him already," she said. "What happens if I dial nine-one-one?"

"The call goes to the mainland and then they'll put it out over the radio. Al will be here in no time."

"Sam will pick it up too, won't he?"

"Sure." Chuck grinned. "If he remembered his radio."

She wanted them all here. She wanted sirens and lights going on so that whoever robbed her would know that the alarm had been raised. She wanted Sam's arms around her. She didn't want to sleep here alone.

"It's got to be someone on the island, right Chuck?" she asked before she picked up the heavy black receiver and started to dial.

"I expect so. Not too many visitors this time of year. The occasional delivery truck comes over on the ferry, but that's all."

"Someone I see in the grocery store," she said slowly.

"Dial," he said. "Don't make yourself crazy. Let Al do that. It's his job after all."

"I just wish he weren't the sheriff."

"You're not the only one."

"Really?"

He shrugged. Island business, he was saying.

Damn this island with all its intrigues and secrets, she thought as she dialed.

AT THE SOUND of sirens, Anna sat bolt upright, startled out of a thick, drugged sleep. She was lying on his living room couch and didn't remember getting there.

"What's that?"

The doctor was standing by the window with the lights out. Two trucks raced down his road with their blue lights flashing. The men in the fire department kept those lights under the front seats of their vehicles and slapped them on the roof or the dashboard when a call came.

"Robbery," he said. "I heard it over the radio. Maggie Hammond's house."

"Oh, God."

"Sounds like it happened a while ago. Don't think it's too serious. I heard your husband's voice. He was calling in from Paul's."

"They play poker on Wednesday nights." She was feeling around in the dark for her coat. "I've got to get out of here, get home before Al does."

He turned on the light as another car took the corner on two wheels. "You'd think it was a nuclear bomb, the way everybody is driving."

"They love an emergency," she said wryly. " You should have seen the crowd when I went into early labor with Erin. Billy Slade came right from the Harbor Lounge and piled into a tree by the Catholic church. All the women were fighting over who got to go with me to the mainland." She found her coat hung over the back of a chair and pulled it on. "I guess everybody's seen my car out there by now."

"I doubt it. They're all driving too fast to see much of anything."

"Don't count on it." Her voice sounded tired and he crossed the room toward her. He was going to hold her again, the way he did up at the beach. She couldn't stand that.

She backed away. "Please don't touch me," she said, and she knew her voice sounded hysterical. "They'll all be over at Maggie's house for a few minutes. The roads won't be too busy if I go right away."

"Call me if you need me. I mean it, Anna."

"Thanks. But what can you do?" she asked with a short laugh. "Shoot him for me?"

He didn't answer.

Al's truck wasn't there when she got home, but Erin was waiting for her at the top of the stairs.

"Where did you go, Mom?"

"I just went out for a drive."

"I was scared. I heard sirens."

"Maggie's house was robbed. Some time ago, apparently. It's nothing serious."

For once, Erin looked at her directly. There was such an expression of fear and alarm in her face that Anna dared to put her arms around the girl's skinny body and hold her. Erin did not pull away so Anna rocked her back and forth from side to side.

"When you were little, I used to rock you like this in your cradle. Do you remember that old cradle we had?"

"No." Her voice was muffled.

"Of course you don't. We gave it to the Slocums when you grew out of it. Lord knows where it's gone by now." It felt so good to have Erin accept this hug that she went on babbling to keep her there, safe in her arms. "Shall we go shopping on Friday? Go to the mall together?"

"Maybe," Erin said, and finally pulled away. "I'm tired."

The whole time Anna followed her daughter into the room and tucked her in, a plan was taking shape in her mind. They would run away together. She wouldn't tell Erin, of course. Just pretend they were going shopping, the two of them, a mother-daughter outing. And then she could keep driving. She'd need cash, but she could get that with her credit card. And she had quite a bit stashed away herself. She would leave the dogs for Chuck. It would take some planning, but they could do it. Move to a small town, change their names. Her heart lifted suddenly at the thought of action. What would it be like to wake up alone every morning, to have an uncomplicated connection with her daughter without Al always listening in, ready to interfere, invade, attack. She leaned over and kissed Erin on the cheek.

"Let's wait and go in two weeks when you're on vacation and I have more time," she said. "We could drive up the coast, go to the movies, have dinner, maybe even stay over in a motel. We haven't done that in ages."

"Okay, Mom." The weary, bored teenager tone had crept back into Erin's voice.

"Don't tell your father. It will be our trip. The two girls."

Erin didn't answer. She rolled over toward the wall and shrugged off Anna's hand. Anna let her be. She wondered if Al told Erin to keep secrets from her. But Anna would get her away from all that soon. At last she had a plan. She was no longer sitting around waiting.

AL CRAVEN SPENT his time going over the whole house and Maggie began to wonder whether he was investigating the crime or simply snooping. Most of the other men raised by the radio call had already headed home, but Sam and Chuck were standing with her downstairs when Al reappeared.

He was fiddling with a notebook and Maggie couldn't get out of her mind some bumbling detective from a TV show she used to watch as a kid.

"So this is all that's missing?" he asked for the third time and read off the list. It sounded pathetic.

"That's all."

"It's those kids again." He snapped his notebook shut. "They rob just for the pleasure of it, even where there isn't a damn thing worth taking."

Now hold on just a minute, Maggie thought.

"Which kids?" Chuck asked.

"The Tremaynes. I'm sure of it. This time I'm going to nail them."

"They must have had someone with them," Chuck pointed out.

"Why?"

"There's no way one of those Tremayne boys could have gotten in through that basement window. They're too big."

Al absorbed this information. "I already figured that," he said lamely, and everybody held very still for a minute. Maggie could feel the men trying hard not to make Al look foolish.

"When do you think it happened?" Sam asked.

"Sometime in the last week or so," Al said. But Maggie had told him that when he'd first arrived. "I'll look into it tomorrow. Be sure to lock up from now on."

"I always lock up," Maggie said, and she could barely contain her fury. "In fact, people make fun of me because I'm the only one on this island who does. And it seems to me these robbers got in anyway."

Al paid no attention. "And be sure to let me know if you find anything else missing. They like to work in houses like this, you know, the ones that are too cluttered to tell what's gone."

The door shut behind him.

"There you have it," Chuck said. "Our noble sheriff."

Maggie had begun to shiver from fury or fear, she wasn't sure which. Sam slid an arm around her shoulder.

"You two all right?" Chuck asked.

"I'll take her over to my place."

They heard Al shouting and swearing outside.

"Christ," Chuck said. "Now what?'

In the light from the porch they saw that Kasha had backed Al up against the side of his truck. Maggie had never seen the dog like this, her teeth bared and a low rumble issuing from deep in her belly. Al had his gun drawn.

"Put the gun away, Al," Chuck said.

"You get that goddamned wolf off me now or I'll shoot the bitch."

Maggie came up behind the dog, talking in the quiet rolling voice she used with her when she was a puppy. She got herself around to the front so that Kasha could see her. Then she walked directly toward her, which distracted Kasha from Al long enough. Al yanked open his truck door just as Maggie dropped her hand onto the dog's collar and braced her feet. With a snarl, Kasha lunged and was snapped back by Maggie's shout and her hand.

"Kasha, stop it."

The dog subsided. Al rolled his window down a little way and lifted his mouth to speak through the crack. "I'm reporting her," he warned, then whipped his truck into a U-turn on the narrow road.

Maggie dragged Kasha into the house and locked her in the room behind the kitchen.

"I think it's time for me to leave," she said. "Before Al makes good on his threat."

"Who the hell is Al going to report her to?" Chuck asked.

"The county commissioner," Sam said. "He might get him to come over one of these days although I doubt it. He's pretty lazy."

"What does Kasha have against Al?" Maggie asked. "She's never singled someone out like that. It's only people who creep up behind and pounce on her."

"If you ask me, she's got good taste," Chuck said. "I'm leaving. See you kids."

"I like the way Chuck calls us kids," Maggie said later that night. Kasha was sleeping on the hooked rug at the end of Sam's bed. When she curled up in her usual circle, it looked as if the rug were made for her.

"Chuck's an old romantic from way back," Sam said. Maggie was turned away from him and he was running his fingernails lazily up and down her spine. The light was still on. It looked as if someone had picked up a bucket of freckles and sprinkled them all over her back. He'd never seen anything like it before. Once he tried to count them, but she got restless and mischievous before he'd even finished with one shoulder.

"How dare some stranger walk through Nan's house and touch her things?" She shivered. "What do they want with her old jewelry? It wasn't even worth anything."

"Yours," Sam said.

She looked at him, not understanding.

"Your house. Not Nan's."

"My house," she said.

"Were you serious about leaving?"

She sat up in bed. "I've been meaning to ask you something. I have to drive some furniture down to New York in late March for the auctions. Why don't you come with me?"

"New York City?" he asked.

She nodded.

"Not my favorite place in the world."

"Have you ever been there?"

"Nope," he said with a grin. "But I've been to Providence and that's close enough."

"I'll show you the town."

"We'll see. It all depends on the salamander walk."

"Right. Tell me, Sam, the salamander man. Why do the salamanders cross the road?"

"To get to the other side so they can make babies."

"Bet you've never heard that before."

"Only a hundred times."

"When do they go?"

"Last year they started crossing the end of March, but you never know. They get their signals from the weather, the temperature, the earth. When's your auction?"

"First week of April."

"Bad timing," he said. She looked sad. "I'm not really your big city type. Never have felt comfortable with all those people shoved into small places. Reminds me of a rat experiment I read about in college. On overpopulation. You put too many rats into too small a place and they start acting really strange. The male rats lose interest in sex—"

"Now that is strange," she said.

"—and the females eat their babies."

"Well, my friends in the city seem to be enjoying their sex lives and of the two couples with babies, I don't know of any mothers chewing on their kids' legs for breakfast."

"You ever want children?" he asked.

Maggie took a deep breath. "I never have before," she said. "I didn't see any way that I could put it all together. My work isn't exactly conducive to child rearing. And you?"

"Two sides of me war over this question. The greatest threat to the environment is overpopulation so as a naturalist, it's hard to justify bringing one more human being into the world."

"Unless it's the child of a naturalist who could help save the world," she said. "Sorry, didn't mean to interrupt. That's one side. What's the other?"

"I had a good father so I think I'd make a good one myself."

"Is that a prerequisite for parenthood?" she asked later when they were lying down. "A good father?"

He could have kicked himself. "No, I don't think so. Nan counts."

"I wonder," she said. "Nan once told me that I was like my father in some ways. I make sure I know where the exits are."

"Meaning?"

"I leave before I can get left."

Her body felt rigid and still. He took her hand and squeezed it. "I'm not going anywhere," he said.

"Today. But who can count on tomorrow?"

He didn't let go of her hand, but he said nothing more. It had been a rough night. Let her be for now, he thought.

Nineteen

THREE NIGHTS AFTER his visit from Anna Craven, the doctor woke to the sound of glass breaking and the thud of a heavy object hitting the thick shag carpeting on the living room floor. He stayed in the warm bed and listened to the squeal of tires at the corner. Something was starting and he was not eager to find out what shape it would take.

When at last he dragged himself from the bed and went to inspect, he found a brick. He picked it up and turned it over. "Island Yards" was stamped into the center of it. In his wanderings through the historical section of the little museum, Dennis had read that a brickyard operated quite successfully on the island in the late nineteenth century, until it had been no longer feasible to ship the product to the mainland. Whoever tossed this brick through his front window had kindly decided to provide him with a sample from the old yard. A souvenir, he thought.

He dressed quickly in a couple of extra layers. Cold air was pouring through the shattered window, and if he didn't do something about it soon, some pipes would freeze. In any case, he figured he'd have to spend the rest of the night on his examining table in the clinic.

At nine o'clock the next morning, Dennis closed himself in his office and called Morris Woodworth at his bank in Boston. Besides serving as head of the museum board, Mr. Woodworth also ran the Island Medical Services Committee and was the man responsible for interviewing all applicants for the position of winter doctor. In a small community, it always turned out that the people who volunteered their time were the ones who ended up with all the headaches and all the control. Woodworth liked the power, but he clearly didn't want to hear about any problems.

"This is the first incident?" he asked.

"And I hope the last," Dennis said. "But I don't expect it will be."

"What is this all about?"

Dennis feigned ignorance. He remembered that Anna Craven lay down in bed with her husband every night, alone in that house except for a thirteen-year-old child and some dogs locked up in a nearby kennel. "Somebody seems to have taken a dislike to me," he said at long last. "They were willing to damage your property to let me know it."

"Well, that island is peculiar in the winter, Dr. Lacey. Too few people, too much drinking and inbreeding."

Dennis bristled at the condescension in the man's voice. It reminded him of his readings in Irish history. The English used to speak of the Irish peasants this way. Easy for you to say, Mr. Woodworth, up there in your glass office in Boston. Without these people keeping this place going, your precious, private island would not be here waiting for you every Memorial Day.

"Odd you didn't mention that during our interview last year, Mr. Woodworth."

"You told me you'd been brought up on an island, Dr. Lacey. I figured you knew how to handle these things."

Me and my big mouth, Dennis thought.

"Listen, I'll call Al Craven and get him over there to fix your window. He's also the sheriff so I'll have him look into it."

"I don't think that will do any good," Dennis said.

"Why not? Craven's a perfectly good man."

"Look, I'm sorry I bothered you. I'll handle it at this end for a while. I'll let you know if I need any help."

"What are you saying about Craven?"

"Nothing in particular. He's just full of himself." Dennis was backpedaling fast. He wished he had never called, but suddenly Woodworth was like a dog with a bone.

"We've had some complaints about Craven overstepping his job in the past. He likes to throw his weight around, settle old scores. What's his beef with you?"

"Who knows? I'm a fly-fisherman and he's a man dedicated to

the spin rod," Dennis said and got a chuckle in return. Woodworth relaxed.

"Well, you go on and take care of it, then. We don't want to lose you, Dr. Lacey."

I bet you don't, Dennis thought as he hung up. What other fool would volunteer to come out here in the dead of winter so people could toss bricks at them?

Chuck dropped by later that morning to measure for a new pane. Dennis met him out front away from Lauren, who had not asked any questions, but was finding lots of excuses to disturb him in the office.

"When did this happen?" Chuck asked.

"About two in the morning. I found the plywood in the garage. That held the temperature at about fifty-five."

"Enough to keep the pipes from freezing at least. Who does Craven Construction send the bill to?"

"Island Medical Services Committee," Dennis said. "I spoke to Woodworth this morning."

"What did you tell him?"

"Nothing for now. But I'm not just going to sit here for another one of these things. God knows what Craven will take in his mind to do next."

"You sure it's Craven?"

Dennis looked at Chuck. "Either he did it or he got someone else to do it. You know he burned Anna's hat last week."

Dennis could tell from Chuck's face that he didn't know. He wondered what bothered Chuck the most. The information itself or the fact that Anna had told him and not Chuck. "Someone needs to confront the bully. Stand up to him."

"You need evidence."

"Of what, for God's sake? Nobody bothered to get any evidence from me or Mrs. Craven about the ridiculous rumor going around this island about us. That's what this is all about, isn't it?"

Chuck didn't answer. February, he thought. Right on schedule. This time of the winter someone always went over the edge and this year it looked like Al. Chuck knew it wasn't just Anna. It was all the pressure Al was under to get the community center done in time for the St. Patrick's Day party. He'd been pushing Billy Slade until Slade looked ready to kill. Al had put Chuck back on the job and warned him to keep his damn mouth shut about what materials Al was using. "When you're sitting at this desk, you can be the boss," Al had said to him last week. "I'm the one running this show and I'm sick of you and Slade beefing at me." Chuck hated Al Craven, but he'd come to hate himself and his worrying little ways even more. He'd gone directly to the Harbor Lounge that afternoon even though he had a self-imposed rule never to drink before six. This time he'd broken it. By the middle of February, when the black cold had settled down around them, he broke his rule more often than not.

"I've lost you, Mr. Montclair," Dennis said.

"Mind wandered. Sorry. I'll have this window in by late afternoon."

"You might tell Craven that this is a pretty shoddy way of making a little extra money. Woodworth was none too pleased about it."

Chuck shrugged and said nothing more.

ONE DAY AFTER SCHOOL, Sam called Erin into his office. "You haven't been coming to the museum on Saturdays," he said. "Anything wrong?"

"Nope," she said. "I've got other stuff to do now."

"And what might that be?"

She gave him a look that said *None of your business,* and found something about the thumbnail of her left hand that needed to be closely studied.

"How are you and Katie?"

"Katie was never really my friend. I just pretended to like her to make her feel better. You know, 'cuz she was in a new school."

"Well, that was nice of you." Sam realized he'd run straight up against a teenager stonewalling him. He hated the moment when the hormones kicked in. It seemed that in some indefinable way, you lost a kid forever after this. Suddenly they'd slouch around pretending to care about nothing because they were so terrified of being humiliated by some other kid who was slouching around pretending to care about nothing.

"Erin, I really could use your help on Saturdays. I have a mountain of stuff to catalog and send in to the herp atlas. And you know me. I'm no good at all that paperwork."

She smiled. "I know. You always want to be out in the field." Defiance in teenagers could come and go at the drop of a hat. Right now, it was gone. She was sitting in the chair across from his desk, swinging her feet back and forth like a little girl.

"Exactly. How about if I could pay you?"

"Are you in love with Maggie?" she asked.

Normally, he would brush off a question like that from a student, but Sam felt all the longing behind it.

"Yes," he said.

"Is she in love with you?" Erin asked.

"I hope so," Sam said.

"Are you going to get married?"

"We haven't talked about it. She's used to traveling all around the world for her work."

"She loves that house," Erin said. "So she could go on her trips and come back here."

"Good idea," Sam said, as if that same thought had never occurred to him. "Why don't you tell her that?"

Erin went silent.

"She's been asking about you. She says you haven't been by to see her in a while. Kasha misses you."

The girl looked at him with such a sad expression in her face that he wished he could lift her up and shake the troubles out of her like loose coins out of a pocket.

"I'm too busy," she said and stood up. "See you, Mr. M. I've got to go."

"SHE LOOKS so old suddenly," Sam reported to Maggie that night. "Old and tired and wise beyond her years."

"I definitely feel her avoiding me. I don't see her as much now that I'm working on the Windsor chair with the high school kids, but even in the hallways she ducks out of the way if she sees me coming. Almost as if she's scared of me. Did I do something wrong?"

"No. At this age kids change their minds all the time. One minute they have a crush on you, the next you're the enemy."

CHUCK AND BILLY had begun to install the wiring in the walls of the community center. They were at it every morning. Al came by to check on them, but he never stopped to chat. The work was dull and cold.

They took care to stay pretty far apart from each other, which made it easier to avoid the subject both of them were reluctant to raise. One day, Billy let fly.

"This stuff is bullshit," he said. "Sixteen-gauge wire and he's running ten outlets and four switches off each circuit."

Chuck didn't move. They'd installed Sheetrock that was under spec, and the studs were two feet apart instead of sixteen inches. They were using half-inch plywood under the C-quality roof shingles that had come from God knows where. Al even had them toenail the floor joists instead of using metal hangers. Christ, what was he saving? Six bucks a joist hanger? Ten bucks per bundle of shingles? Thirty dollars a roll for roof paper? It was nickel and dime stuff, but ever since he'd lost that Latham job, Al had been on a tear. He was cutting every damn corner there was to cut.

"Wonder how much it's going to cost him to pay off the building inspector?" Chuck said.

"Not much," Billy said. "Tony and Al have been working things out between them for years."

The two men had not moved from their positions some feet apart and neither one of them was looking at the other. That way they could both pretend later that this conversation had never happened.

"I don't give a shit what he does with the summer people," Chuck said to the wall. "They've got the money to burn. But this is all ours."

They both knew what would happen if they blew the whistle. They'd be out of a job. And jobs were hard to come by on this island. For Chuck, it wasn't so bad. But Billy had a kid to raise. With no wife. Just him. He slapped the boy around a bit, but what could you expect? It was times like this Chuck was glad he had managed to sidestep every time a woman came after him with the idea of marriage in her head.

Erin heard her father yelling her name as soon as he pulled into the driveway. From her upstairs window, she saw him slam the truck into gear and kick the door open.

"Erin." His voice had a growl to it that she hadn't heard before.

She grabbed her jacket, ran down the stairs, and bolted for the front door, the one out of the living room that nobody ever used.

"Goddammit, Erin, where are you? I want to talk to you."

He knew. He must have known by now that she had stolen the typewriter. The Tremayne boys had told her. How could he arrest them when his own daughter was with them? That's why they'd wanted her along, that's why Derry had made her take something. She knew that now, she knew it even then somewhere in the back of her mind, but the idea kept slipping away from her the night she'd stood in Maggie's front hall and watched them coming down the stairs.

She took the path behind Miss Yola's, keeping the bushes between her and her own house. Miss Yola must have been out with the little dog because there was no sound from the other side of the kitchen door. Erin thought for a minute of letting herself in and hiding there, but decided against it. She wanted to put more distance between her and her father.

From a lifetime of scouring the island, Erin knew all the back ways from one end of the place to the other. For hundreds of years, people had cut their own paths through the wooded areas, on their own land and on others'. The boundaries between properties were registered in the county office on the mainland, but nobody cared much where one lot ended and another began. They had cut paths through the tangled undergrowth for different reasons, sometimes to tame the land for a garden, or to carve a secret way down to the shore, or as teenagers to make a hidden trail to one of the abandoned navy bunkers that, for a summer, they would turn into a hangout. Erin knew them all. The walk took longer than if she had used the roads, so by the time she made her way out of the brush just below Maggie's porch, the scratches on her cheeks stung in the cold air. If her father knew where she had gotten the typewriter, then he would never suspect that she'd come right back to the scene of the crime. Maggie's car was gone and the front door was locked as usual. Good, they were out. Erin let herself in with her key and slipped up the stairs to the third floor. Much later in the night, she heard two car doors slam and voices on the floor below, but nobody came near her. She was safe.

ANNA CAME HOME to an empty house. She put the dogs to bed and made herself a bowl of soup. It was late for Erin to be out. Where could she be this time?

Al's truck slammed to a stop close to the back door.

He walked into the kitchen and lifted Anna up by her right arm. Her left hand went immediately to her pants pocket. The gun wasn't there. She'd gotten sloppy and left it in the kennel. But would she ever have the nerve to pull a gun on Al? She couldn't imagine it, even now as he stuck his face into hers. His breath stank.

"Where's Erin?" he growled.

"I don't know. I haven't seen her. What's wrong?"

"That daughter of yours has turned into a goddamned petty thief." He was propelling her up the stairs, his thick hand clamped around her upper arm like a choke collar.

"Al, stop it. Let me go. What are you doing?"

"I'm locking you up until I find her. I can't trust either of you anymore."

"Al, don't act crazy." She kept her voice low and even, the way she did with an edgy vizsla. "I'll help you look for her. What do you mean she's a thief? What are you talking about?"

"You know," he said, and those were the last words he spoke to her before he shoved her into the storage closet and locked the door. He must have planned this ahead of time because he'd thought far enough ahead to take the key from the rack on the kitchen wall. She screamed and beat on the door, calling him names she'd been storing up and swallowing for years, but he'd already walked away. In the distance, she heard the engine of the truck start up again, the dogs barking, then silence.

She curled up in one corner of the closet, hugged her knees, and forced herself to concentrate. All the planning she had done was still in place. There was no way he could know about the new credit card. She always got to the mail first. And the extra cash she'd been saving was hidden away in the jar behind the big sacks of dog food in the kennel. She was sure of that. She'd checked it just this morning.

Two of Dennis Lacey's tires had been slashed yesterday morning. Everybody on the island knew now that Al had hit some kind of wall. Each year, it happened to one of them, like a plague or the measles or something. Last winter, Randy Baker had tangled with a couple of guys off a Coast Guard boat. Islanders called it the winter woolies. Standing in the post office line, they'd laugh nervously about who was going to catch it this year. And nobody ever did anything about it. If someone fell down and broke a leg, the EMTs would be careening around with their blue lights flashing, rushing the patient to the ambulance boat. But a person could go stark raving mad, dance through the aisles of the grocery store spouting gibberish, or worse still, slap his woman or kids around in public, and nobody would say a word. They'd just edge away like they didn't see anything, mumble stuff about the long winter, and flee. She knew. She'd done it herself.

Anna would not let herself think about where Erin was and what he might be doing to her. That thought would drive her mad. To make the hours go by, she ran through what to pack, how to keep it light. She made plans to put some stuff over on the mainland in the luggage checkroom at the train station. A couple of suitcases ahead of time. Clothes Erin would want when they settled in a new place. She made lists over and over again in her head, recited the items like poetry. From time to time, she held herself absolutely still and listened for any sound. None came. She waited.

"I THINK I heard a ghost last night," Maggie said to Sam in the morning.

"What do you mean?"

"It sounded like someone tiptoeing around in the room above our heads." She licked the back of her spoon. He'd gotten her into the habit of breakfast. Oatmeal with brown sugar and sliced apples was her current favorite.

"Why didn't you wake me?"

"When I listened again, it seemed to have stopped. Kasha went up to investigate. I figured if she found anything interesting, she'd let us know."

"Where is she now?"

"She hasn't come down yet. Let sleeping dogs lie."

"Did you hear the phone?" he asked.

"Yes. I just couldn't be bothered to answer it. Who would be calling me at midnight?"

"Only some kind of trouble," he said. "Island business would have come over the radio. But there was nothing."

He rinsed his dishes and put them in the dishwasher.

"You're leaving early," she said.

"A science experiment with the seventh grade. I haven't set it up yet."

He slid his arms around her and buried his nose in her neck. "I can think of a lot of things I'd rather do."

She held on to him. She'd never felt this comfortable with a man before. She wanted so badly to trust this, but how could she let herself? After so many years of not trusting.

In the silence, something crashed. It sounded like a chair tipping over. They both froze.

"That's coming from the third floor," she whispered in his ear. "Same as last night. I didn't think ghosts walked after dawn."

"Let's go see who's up there."

Sam led the way, with one of Nan's thick walking canes in his right hand and Maggie close behind.

Nan's bedroom was empty, but the door to the other third floor room was closed, which was odd. Maggie liked the rooms up here to stay open because even a little air circulating cut down on the musty smell. Sam pushed the door with his foot. The bed was rumpled.

"Now who's been sleeping in my bed, asked the baby bear?" Sam said quietly.

Kasha was lying in the middle of the floor. She lifted her head to look at them.

"Some watch dog you are," Maggie said.

Sam put a hand on her arm to silence her and pointed at the closet door. He walked over and opened it carefully. When nothing jumped out, he poked through the old dresses with the cane.

"Good morning, Erin," he said in a loud voice.

She crawled out on all fours.

Nobody knew what to say. Erin picked herself up and sneezed once and then again.

"Bless you," Maggie said. "Sorry about the dust."

"How did you know it was me?" Erin asked.

"I recognized your boots," Sam said.

"How remarkable," Maggie said.

"A naturalist is trained to notice things."

"Maybe you should be a detective," Maggie said. She was glad to see their banter had brought a smile to Erin's face.

"Want some breakfast?" Maggie asked.

Erin nodded.

"I'm off to school," Sam said when they got downstairs and Maggie had poured Erin a glass of juice and a bowl of cornflakes. "See you later, Erin."

Maggie followed him out to the front hall. "Shouldn't you drive her to school?" she whispered.

"I think she'll tell you what's going on," he said. "Remember I'm her teacher. You're not."

"What should I say to her?"

"Just listen. You'll do fine," he said and gave her a quick kiss before he slipped out the door.

Erin munched her way through two bowls of cereal and a piece of toast. Maggie waited.

"Did my father come looking for me last night?" Erin finally asked.

"No. The phone rang late, but I didn't answer it."

"He's really mad at me this time."

"What did you do?"

"You know."

Maggie shook her head.

"He didn't tell you yet?"

"No, your father hasn't told me anything. I haven't talked to him since the night my house was robbed."

Erin was silent again. Wrong tack, Maggie thought. I should have pretended I knew what she was talking about.

"Why don't I call your parents?" Maggie said, stirring in her seat. "They must be worried about you."

"No, don't. Don't do that."

Maggie poured herself another cup of coffee. Erin pushed a piece of soggy cereal around the rim of the bowl with her spoon.

"You look a girl with a pile of secrets," Maggie said.

Erin turned the spoon over and mashed the cornflake against the bottom of the bowl.

"I remember a time in seventh grade when I cheated on my math test and I didn't tell anybody. I walked around with that secret for the longest time. It made me sick. I had stomachaches about it. You know, I was good at math. I didn't even need to cheat."

"Why'd you do it?"

Maggie thought for a minute. "It had something to do with a girl named Valerie and beating her out for the math prize that year."

"Did you beat her?"

"No. They changed the rules on us without ever saying anything. That year they decided to give the prize for most improved instead of high marks so Angela Benton won it. She was terrible at math. Goes to show you. Crime doesn't pay."

"You never told anybody?"

Uh oh, Maggie thought. This was going the wrong way. "I'm telling you. Besides, Erin, it sounds as if your father already knows your secret. And I can't keep you hidden over here forever."

"I stole your typewriter," Erin blurted out. "And a book from the third floor."

"What book?"

Erin's face turned red. "A book with naked pictures."

"Oh, my," Maggie said. "I remember that book. I used to look at it when Nan went out for dinner. I think she put it on the bottom shelf just so I'd find it. Where is it?"

"Katie Morrison's mother has it."

"Now why does she need a book with pictures of naked people?" Maggie asked.

Erin giggled.

There was another silence while Maggie sorted through these revelations. "When did you take the typewriter? I must admit I haven't even missed it."

"That night. With the Tremayne boys."

Now Maggie understood. "So you were one of the robbers. Of course. The one small enough to get through the window. What a lot of secrets you've been keeping. Why didn't you just let yourself in the front door with your key?"

"I wouldn't do that," Erin said, and she sounded indignant.

The phone rang, a harsh jangling noise from the hall that made them both jump. Maggie looked at Erin. "It might be your parents."

Erin nodded.

"You'll have to see them sometime."

Maggie picked up the phone. It was a prospective client calling from London. She kept her eye on Erin who looked as if she might bolt. The connection was bad and Maggie hung up, promising to call back in an hour or two.

"Business," she said as she came back to the table.

"Are you going to leave the island?" Erin asked.

"I'm not sure yet. And we'd better stick to the subject at hand. I don't think we have much more time, Erin. Why did you help the Tremaynes rob my house? I thought we were friends."

"I never knew we were going to rob your house. I didn't even know what we were doing until we went to that big house up island. Then I thought we were just doing summer people."

"So there were others?"

"Yes," Erin said and she got that defiant look on her face again. It was an expression that Maggie found more poignant than the apologetic one. Such a little girl, trying to be so big.

"Does your father know about the other places?"

"I don't know. "

"You'll have to tell him."

"Maybe Bo and Derry told him. "

"Doesn't matter. You'll have to tell him yourself."

"Can I live here with you?" Erin asked.

The little girl back in her face again. Can you make me safe? Maggie took a deep breath. "I don't think your mother would be happy with that."

"My father wouldn't either," Erin said. "He likes me to be where he can see me."

A chilling concept, Maggie thought. To be where Al Craven could always see you. Could families keep going like this forever, with the walls closing in on them and nobody stopping it? Of course they could. People kept their own secrets. They always had. You were taught not to interfere. You saw a woman in a mall screaming at her kid and slapping him and you looked away and you prayed that she'd stop. You ordered french fries. The kid cried, maybe stared at you with the tears coming down his cheeks. And you tried not to catch his eye.

There was a pounding on the front door.

"It's Daddy," Erin said in a tiny voice. She didn't move, but Kasha, stiff from sleep, struggled to her feet. Maggie caught her by the collar and locked her in the back room.

Then she went to open the door.

"Al."

"Is my daughter here?"

"Come on in," Maggie said.

She led him back to the kitchen. Erin was out of the chair now, standing over by the stove.

"Would you like some coffee?" Maggie asked.

"Where have you been all night?" At the sound of the man's voice, Kasha began to bark from the back room. Al glanced over his shoulder for a moment. "That dog locked up?"

Maggie nodded. He looked back at his daughter. "So?"

"I was here," Erin said. "Maggie didn't know. I hid upstairs."

"Is it true what the Tremayne boys tell me?"

"What did they tell you?"

"That you stole a typewriter from Miss Hammond's house."

"No," Maggie said quickly. "It is not true. I lent Erin that type-writer." His eyes narrowed and he looked back and forth from one to the other. "I never listed a typewriter as missing," Maggie added. "Look back over your notes from the night I reported the robbery."

Al was still talking to Erin. "Those boys said you came over here and helped them rob this house. They said you're the one who broke in through that basement window."

"What else did they say?" Erin asked. Her back was pressed

against the stove, but her voice was tough. "Did they tell you about the other houses they robbed?"

"What other houses?"

"Summer ones. Up at the eastern end. I don't know the names of the people."

"What did they take?"

"Stereos, VCR, things like that."

"You come with me right now and show me which houses. You and I are going to have a little talk, Miss Erin Craven. There are going to be some new rules around our house."

"I'll go too," Maggie said.

He walked over to Erin and put an arm around her shoulder. "No, thank you, Miss Hammond. I appreciate you putting up my daughter for the night. We'll be getting out of your way now."

He propelled Erin out the door and Maggie trailed after them, hating herself. She had no idea how to stop this and she felt like a fool. At the last minute, Erin twisted around and waved.

"See you soon," Maggie called, but the words sounded ridiculous. After all she wasn't waving good-bye to dinner guests.

As soon as the door closed, she went to the phone and called Chuck.

"I'm headed up there anyway," Chuck said. "Anna's supposed to be at the post office this morning and she hasn't shown up."

"We've got to do something," Maggie said. "I'm going to call somebody over in the county office. The child welfare bureau. Somebody like that."

"Maggie, calm down. I told you I'll take care of it."

"This whole island always thinks they can take care of their own business. That child could be killed before we get around to doing something." She knew she sounded hysterical.

"Maggie, stop it," Chuck said. "You're going off the deep end. You sit tight and I'll go up there now."

"But what if—"

"Maggie, for God's sake, will you let me go?" For the first time, she heard the panic in his voice too.

"Yes, sorry. Go."

Twenty

ANNA HAD STRETCHED out on the floor on her back. She dozed for a little while and woke up cramped, her cheek creased from where it had come to rest on the seam of a sneaker. She sat up in tailor position, bent over one knee and then the other. Her spine cracked in response. She was fighting down the panic now. Al might have decided to leave her here forever. He might have taken Erin and run. No, she told herself. He would never do that. He was just punishing her. She had to be cagey from now on. Pretend to Al that she was back in line, play the role until she could get away. A week from Friday. She had a hunting test that day. She'd tell Al she was taking the afternoon boat, but then she'd pull Erin out of school and go at noon.

A truck door slammed. Chuck, she thought. The dogs were barking. Please Chuck, come in the house first. Please let the dogs alone this once. And miraculously, she heard him down in the kitchen calling her name.

She pounded on the door. "I'm up here," she screamed. "Here, here." And she was crying for the first time since she'd been locked in. "Please come get me. Please God, don't leave me here."

"Anna." It was Chuck's voice again this time right outside the closet. "Are you okay?"

"Al locked me in. Go down to the kitchen. There should be another key on the rack behind the door. The same place we keep the kennel keys. It will say storage closet. Please hurry."

He went away, and now, after a whole night of willing herself to be calm, she felt as if she were going to jump out of her skin, that each minute of waiting for him to return was taking longer than all the hours that had come before. When the door finally opened, she was leaning so hard against it that she fell right onto him. He put his arms on her shoulders to prop her up.

"Are you okay?"

She blinked in the light.

"Did he hurt you?"

"No. He locked me in there last night." Her voice sounded odd to her own ears, too slow. "Is Erin here?"

"No, but she's all right. She spent the night at Maggie's. Al found her there this morning. Come on, I'll make you coffee."

Downstairs, Chuck explained all that Maggie had told him.

"I don't believe that. Those Tremaynes made it up."

"Maggie says Erin admits to being with them."

I'm losing her, Anna thought. I'm living in the same house with my own daughter and she's slipping away from me. She remembered the stories she'd read in the papers about runaway children. Some of them lived in packs in cities where the gang would become their family. The child would look out at you from some snapshot of an earlier, happier time, often with a shy grin and a tooth missing or hair in braids. And lots of those kids had hit the road, struck out on their own because anything was better than living at home. She had to get Erin away from here soon.

"Drink some coffee," Chuck said.

She took a sip and swallowed, but tasted nothing. "You'd better go deal with the dogs," she said.

"Don't you want me here when they come back?"

"No. Absolutely not. This is a family matter, Chuck."

"Maggie Hammond is threatening to call child welfare over on the mainland."

"She mustn't do that, Chuck. She can't. You have to stop her."

Chuck heard the panic in her voice.

"Nothing has happened to Erin. I can take care of my own child."

"I told her that. I told her not to call."

"You make sure she doesn't, Chuck. Summer people meddle. They always have, they always will."

"It's because she's worried, Anna."

"I told you I'm taking care of this. If she gets somebody over here, it will make things worse. Much worse. Don't you see?"

He pressed once more. "Are you sure you can handle it, Anna? I've never seen Al like this. You heard about Lacey's tires."

"I just need a little more time. Then it won't matter what Al Craven does. And don't say a word to Al either. Do you hear me? It will only hurt me and Erin if you do." She reached out and touched his hand. "Please Chuck, please trust me."

"What else can I do?" he said. "I sure hope I don't regret it."

HE HAD FINISHED cleaning the kennels and was heading out of the driveway in his pickup when Al pulled in with Erin in the front seat. At the sound of engines, Anna came outside and waited with her arms folded. The two vehicles passed within inches of each other. Chuck looked directly at Al, who stared straight ahead. I just let your wife out of the storage closet, Chuck said out loud knowing the other man couldn't hear him. He stopped at the main road and watched in his rearview mirror as the family convened in the yard. From a distance like this, it looked so normal. A father bringing his daughter home from an overnight. The mother waiting to give them some breakfast. The two-bedroom house with the mortgage all paid off by now. The dogs barking from the kennel. He suddenly remembered John Burling and the body washing up on Maggie's beach. So much had happened since then. Something must have snapped in Anna when that old man finally died. Something had pushed her to mess with Al. Chuck could have told her, you don't mess with a man like Al Craven. If Chuck had learned one thing in his miserable, cowardly life it was that you stay away from bullies. No matter what you do, they always win.

"ERIN," ANNA SAID, looking at Al all the while. "Go get your books and I'll take you down to school."

Erin slipped past her and they could hear her feet pounding upstairs.

"She was out that night with the Tremayne boys. Your daughter's turning into a juvenile delinquent right under your nose."

"So I hear," Anna said evenly. "Where have you been?"

"Up at the scene of two of the crimes. The Watkins and another one. Can't remember the name. The Tremaynes didn't bother to tell me that they hit two of the summer houses that night."

"So Erin told you?"

"That's right."

"Doesn't sound like a juvenile delinquent to me. Sounds like a kid who knows how to tell the truth. Maybe you should give her a badge, make her a deputy sheriff. She's going to need some protection."

"What are you talking about?"

"She's turned state's witness, Al. You'd better make sure you have those Tremayne boys locked up before you let them know she told on them."

"I already thought of that," he said. She knew he hadn't.

There was always a time right after Al behaved in some particularly outrageous way that he felt sheepish. He knew perfectly well that he'd dragged his wife upstairs last night and locked her in the storage closet. If anybody'd asked him now why he did that, he would come up with a million reasons that might sound perfectly valid to him. But if you didn't bring it up, if you ignored it, the voices would start up in his own head, and one of them must have been telling him that he looked like a damned fool. He must have known now that Chuck had found her there and let her out. Anna counted on the one voice in Al's head that might still be getting through to him.

LATE THAT MORNING, Anna knocked on the window of the science lab, and Sam came out to the hall to talk to her.

"I want you to keep an eye on Erin, Sam. Don't let the Tremayne boys anywhere near her. I've told the other teachers the same thing. I'm going to pick her up after school every day."

"Listen, Anna—"

She put up her hand. "And please tell Maggie Hammond to stay out of my business."

"Maggie's worried about Erin. We both are."

"I know that, Sam, but she can't go calling in someone from the outside."

"What are you talking about?"

"She told Chuck she's going to call child welfare. If she does something like that, she will make things much worse. I know Al better than anybody. I know how to handle this."

"Some things you can't do all by yourself, Anna."

"You agree with her then?"

"Not necessarily. I didn't even know she was talking that way. But maybe you need help with this one."

Anna ignored this last comment. "If you let her do that, I'll hold you responsible for what happens, Sam." Her voice was low, controlled, even. He had never heard her use that tone before. Perhaps this was the way she talked to the dogs.

"Anna, I am not in charge of Maggie. She's her own woman." And so it seems are you, he thought.

"You sleep with her, don't you? Doesn't that give you a certain influence?"

The bitter sarcasm in her voice stopped him. Not like Anna at all. She looked as if she hadn't slept in weeks. "Not outside of the bed," he said at last, his hand on the doorknob of the classroom. "I have to get back in there before they blow something up. I'll keep an eye on Erin as best I can."

On the way home Anna stopped at the post office to pick up the mail just off the noon boat.

"Al already came by," Diane Thayer said, leaning out from the window. "You two must be expecting something important. He checks twice a day."

"Anything in our box today?" Anna asked as casually as possible.

"Now how am I going to remember that?" Diane said, which Anna knew was a lie. When they were sorting the mail in the mornings, Diane had a comment about each piece of mail she passed out. Well, she'd say, I see the Malloys still haven't paid the bill for that television. A collection agency's onto them now. After fifteen years as postmistress, she didn't even need to hold an envelope up to the light to know what was in it.

"Come on, Diane," Anna said.

"A couple of bills," she said. "That's all."

Anna's heart slowed down. Diane called out to her as she was heading out the door. "And a credit card company, I think. One of those envelopes with just a post office box number for return address. Who do they think they're fooling with that? All you need to do is feel around a bit for the plastic card."

Anna found the credit card cut into ten pieces and pieced back together on her bureau. No comment, no note. She took the money from behind the dog food and hid it in the Blair's garage next door. They never came up until the beginning of April at the earliest and she'd be long gone by then. And she still had that credit card she'd ordered last year and hid from Al. Luckily, there'd been no bills since she'd charged nothing on it. And a five-thousand-dollar credit limit. That should get them pretty far. She put in a call to the company and changed the address to her brother's place in Rhode Island so that when the bills started coming in, Al wouldn't be able to trace her movements.

That afternoon, working the dogs in the field near Mink Pond, Anna was aware that fear had taken up residence in her head. It was a background noise not unlike a ringing in the ears. To drown it out, she began to talk to herself all the time without speaking out loud. She listed the departure times of the weekend boats or the phone numbers of everybody she could remember in the island book or the registration numbers on the dog tags. This constant inane counting seemed to turn down the volume on the fear sometimes for as much as an hour and she was grateful that for some odd reason, numbers had always lodged easily in her brain. But if she rested for a moment, got distracted by a sharp noise on the road or the unexpected flush of a wild bird, then the fear blared up louder than ever and it seemed to take her longer each time to beat it back down.

THE TOWN MEETING was held twice a year, once in August in deference to the summer owners, and once on the first of March. The island people had picked that date twenty years ago because they were pretty sure they would have the place to themselves. Not too many summer owners were willing to brave the bad weather and the rough passage on the boat just to listen to a lot of talk about school business and new sites for the metal dump and plans for potluck suppers.

A couple of the men went over to the church basement early to clear away the thrift-shop clothing racks and the cardboard boxes stuffed with old books and toys that nobody wanted. Every June, when things began to smell too moldy from a full damp year in the basement, the thrift-shop ladies would throw out a good portion of the stock to make room for the summer owners' spring cleaning. Summer people cleared out their houses when they first arrived, and they got rid of amazing things. Miss Yola and Annie Slocum, the most regular customers of the thrift shop, had learned to check the stock early and often in June. Last year, Miss Yola had bought an entire set of Depression glass for twenty dollars.

It wasn't often that the community gathered together like this. Some of the elderly members hadn't emerged from their houses since the Christmas pageant at the school. People leaned down rows to wave and acknowledge one another. Randy Baker walked in with Ellie, who had come back on the island the week before, but the word had already gone around that she was packing up. Her father had offered her a job in his office in New York, and she'd decided to try it. Randy kept an arm around her shoulders the whole time and she looked uncomfortable under the weight of it. The women tended to sit in the front and the men, still in their work clothes, held up the wall in the back, their arms folded, shifting their weight from one foot to the other. The room smelled of mildew, but the acoustics were good and there was no real need for a microphone as Paul Thayer had a booming voice that carried well. When the men in the back had something to say, they just lifted their chins and shouted.

Anna arrived separately from Al and sat with Miss Yola. She had thought of not coming at all, but she knew Al cared about the way things looked to the community. And for now, it was to her advantage to keep Al quiet, let him think he was winning. Maggie ended up sitting between Lauren Root and Annie Slocum, which made her uncomfortable. She knew they'd much rather be sitting together, but when she offered to move over, they pretended it didn't matter.

Paul Thayer called the meeting to order promptly at 5:30 P.M., and latecomers were made to stand in the back. The dishes brought in for the potluck supper were tightly wrapped in foil, but the warm inviting smells would soon become distracting, and there was business to be done. People liked Paul, and they gave him their attention.

The first hour of the meeting droned on with a report from the ferry district officers and a long wrangle about guidelines for the new recycling station. Just as the crowd was beginning to get restless, Thayer asked Craven for an update on the renovation of the community center.

"It's coming along," Al said. "You know the weather this winter has held things up, but the boys and I are on it pretty regular now."

The boys, Chuck thought. Al was never there at all.

"It will be ready for the St. Patrick's Day party, won't it?" Lauren called out. "We want Dr. Lacey to feel at home this year."

The crowd laughed, but the sound was uneasy. A couple of people turned around to locate Lacey, who was standing in the corner near the door. He lifted his head when he heard his name, but said nothing.

"I don't know about that," Al started, but his voice was drowned out by a couple of exaggerated groans.

"Al, you've been dragging your feet on this thing all winter," someone shouted from the back room. It was Gus Tremayne. He'd come directly to the meeting from the Harbor Lounge.

"Dammit, Tremayne, you stick to your business and I'll watch mine. Chasing your boys around is taking up a lot of my precious time."

"What are you saying about my boys?" Tremayne shouted back and started to work his way around the room, but some of the men held him where he was.

Paul Thayer pounded on his lectern. "You two settle down. So, Al, the women can start making plans for the St. Patrick's Day party, right?"

Al threw up his hands. "If you say so, boss."

"We all say so. You remember we were supposed to be in there for Thanksgiving originally. "

"And you seem to get all the work done that's needed on the summer houses," someone shouted from the side.

"This is our hard-earned money, Al. Don't forget that." This remark came from Lila Keller, who was never one to mince her words.

Al kept silent.

Paul called on Sam, who got to his feet. "I want to remind everyone about the salamander walk. We need volunteers as soon as the ground begins to thaw to dig holes for the buckets and then the usual volunteers for the first major crossing. Watch the bulletin boards around town for sign-up sheets. The salamanders will probably start stirring the last week of March if the weather keeps up this way."

"Any other business?" Paul called. "Yes, Dr. Lacey. You have your hand up."

Dennis took a step forward and waited for the room to settle into stillness. "As I'm sure many of you know, I've had a number of unpleasant incidents recently. A brick through my window, some slashed tires and yesterday, somebody broke into my house and snapped a couple of my brand-new graphite fishing rods." The room was dead silent. People were staring straight ahead or looking at their hands twisting in their laps.

"This really isn't the place, Dr. Lacey—" Thayer started, but to everybody's surprise, Chuck interrupted.

"Why don't you let him finish, Paul?"

"I have been in touch with Mr. Woodworth about this," Dennis went on.

Thayer tried again. "You know these incidents should be reported to the proper authorities. There's nothing we can do in a meeting of this size."

"And who, Mr. Thayer, might you suggest as the proper authorities?"

The room stirred and there was a scraping of metal chair legs against the pocked linoleum floor.

"Well, the sheriff of course and—" Thayer was mumbling now.

All eyes found Al who was leaning against the wall with one shoulder. "Dr. Lacey hasn't come in to write up a report," Al said, staring forward.

"I wonder why I haven't bothered to do that," Dennis said, his voice notched up an extra decibel. " 'Tis a mystery." After another short silence, he spoke again. "I am letting the community know that if one more incident like this occurs, I will be packing my bags and leaving. And I have already used my considerable influence with the hospital to assure that any other doctor contemplating this position will get a full report on the activities here. Naturally that will make an already low-priority position even less desirable. I'm sure that the members here who sit on the Island Medical Services Committee can attest to the difficulty of filling this job every year. To put it simply, I'm not sure when or if you can ever expect to have a full-time doctor on the island again."

Al did not move as the rumblings went around the room. People leaned over and muttered to their neighbors. Paul Thayer brought the meeting to a close with a bang of his fist on the lectern. After that speech, he had no intention of asking whether there was any further business. God knows what other worms might crawl out of the can.

As SOME OF the women made for the kitchen and the rest of the group began to pull the chairs aside to set up the folding tables, Maggie found Dennis. People gave the two of them a wide berth.

"Good speech," Maggie said.

"I didn't plan it ahead of time. It just came out that way. Exposure seems to be the only weapon that works on places like this. As long as everybody keeps the secrets, nothing happens."

"Apparently I really ruffled some feathers because I threatened to call the child welfare office about Erin Craven. Sam says Anna is angry with me."

Dennis nodded. "I can see why."

"What do you mean?"

"Don't be a fool, Maggie." The vehemence in his own voice surprised both of them. "You're implying she is not taking good enough care of her own child."

"She's not the one I'm worried about. It's Al."

"And knowing the bureaucracy of your typical child welfare office, they wouldn't distinguish between one and the other. They'd march in, ask a lot of questions and write up a useless report which would get lost in the system. That means Anna would be left to deal with her husband and his rage over the incident. And Al knows full well that the best way to torment Anna is by messing with her daughter." He shrugged. "But Anna doesn't have anything to worry about. First of all, it would take a lot more than one call from an interested citizen to bring out a caseworker. And I doubt you'd find anybody else on this island willing to back you up."

"So you're saying I'd make a bigger mess."

"Absolutely convinced of it."

"And you have no faith in the system to protect people?"

"None. Government has no business messing about in the private lives of people. I watched it over and over again in the emergency rooms of too many hospitals. These problems started much farther back with the Craven family. With all these people. With me and you too. How can you expect a government agency to step in at the last minute and rescue someone whose father beats him because *his* father was an alcoholic and beat him because *his* mother was consigned to a mental institution and so on and so forth all the way back?"

"Well, then, dammit, who is going to do something?"

"You and me. "

"How?"

He lifted his eyebrows. "Tell the truth. Shout it from the rooftops. 'Tis all I can think to do. Have you got any better ideas?"

They were parted by a parade of island women carrying various dishes for the supper.

"I wish this island had a restaurant," Maggie said. "Tonight is one night I'd like to sit down and eat in peace without people watching me."

"Yes, we do seem to be the outsiders once again. My little speech didn't help one bit either."

Even Sam seemed to be avoiding them. Across the room, she caught sight of him laughing with Lauren Root. Dennis followed her eyes.

"How are you and Sam doing?"

"It works on the island, but I doubt it would anywhere else. He's never even been to New York City. I've spent the last ten years winging from one European capital to another. I've got a house in Philadelphia."

Dennis handed her a plate and the two of them concentrated on dishing up the food. They found seats in the corner.

"You could move," he said after some minutes of thoughtful chewing. "Sell the house in Philadelphia."

"It's a rental. I don't own it."

"There you go."

"But I can be away on business for as much as a month at a time, sometimes longer. No man would put up with that."

"Have you asked Sam if he's willing to put up with that?"

She kept her eyes on her plate. No, she hadn't asked him because she wasn't ready to hear the answer. What if he said yes? It would mean she'd have to change all her assumptions about her life. She'd have to give up the freedom of knowing that nobody was waiting for her to come home, nobody was expecting her.

"I came to New York with grand ideas about the life I wanted," Dennis said. "A private practice, a fancy apartment, membership in clubs. Everything my childhood had not been. And I got it all. Even the beautiful, sophisticated wife. That's what I thought I wanted and now I'm not so sure." He put the plate down on the floor and wiped his mouth with the paper napkin. "I'm going back to Omey Island this summer for a visit." He shrugged. "Or maybe longer. Islands get into your blood, Maggie."

She pushed her helping of salad around the plate. "When were you last there?"

"Ten years ago. I have a little show of my artwork going up nearby in Clifden. And my job here is up at the end of May. If I last that long."

She dropped her voice. "You're sure it's Al Craven who's harassing you?"

"Positive. Who else would bother?"

"Because of you and Anna?"

He sat back and shook his head. "Because of the rumors about me and his wife. There's no truth to them, Maggie. There could have been, but there isn't."

"She's an attractive woman," Maggie said. Suddenly the room

seemed to grow quieter as if people sitting nearby had caught enough of what they were saying to listen in.

"And brave," Dennis said. "And a professional like yourself." He didn't bother to lower his voice because he could have been talking about anyone. The noise level around them rose again.

"You and I should have gotten together," Maggie said impulsively. "It would have made things easier on everybody. The two outsiders. Very convenient."

He looked at her and laughed. "It crossed my mind."

"It did?"

"Sure it did. You're a good-looking woman yourself, but I hardly need tell you that."

"I don't mind hearing it, Dr. Lacey."

"But by the time I thought to do something about it, Sam had made his move. A younger man who can introduce you to the natural treasures of the island and who doesn't have a gray hair on his head. Too much competition. I retired from the field without even trying."

"What were you and Dr. Lacey laughing about?" Sam asked later on their way home.

"Love and Ireland and the future."

"Sounds interesting," he said.

"It was. He's a nice man. This island doesn't appreciate him."

Sam didn't answer and for the first time, she felt a space between them. Sam hadn't lived here that long, but he was counted as a year-rounder. And much as they'd both like to pretend otherwise, she was from the summer people, the opposing tribe.

"That speech he gave isn't going to help him any with the people here," Sam said.

"He was telling the truth. Calling a spade a spade in public."

Sam was quiet. He didn't fight, he retreated. It made her edgy. Sometimes she wished for the fights.

"I'm sick of all the secrets this island keeps."

"It's true we don't air our troubles in public," he said. She heard the *we* louder than any other word in the sentence.

"Oh, no, but you also allow people to get slapped around and harassed and tormented and nobody says a damn word. Everybody here is great at looking the other way when somebody's in trouble."

"And what about you, Maggie? You're the one with your eye on the exit sign."

"I actually considered calling child welfare about Erin."

"I heard."

"Don't worry, I'm not going to call. Dennis Lacey convinced me that they would create more problems than they would solve. Maybe I should kidnap her."

He pulled the truck up behind her car. "Do you mean that?" he asked.

"Of course not," she said. "What would I do with a thirteen-year-old girl? It's enough to be worrying about a thirteen-year-old dog. It's just that I hate sitting around and doing nothing."

"And do you think any of the rest of us likes it?"

"I think you've gotten used to it. You're in the habit of closing your eyes to things. You have to be if you live on this island in the winter."

"And you, Miss Hammond, the girl from Philadelphia, do you stop and take every homeless person you pass into your home and cook them a good meal? Somehow I don't think so. I think you're just as used to closing your eyes." His voice was cold, the words clipped. It was a voice she hadn't heard from him before. This must be the anger Chuck had told her about.

Neither one got out of the truck. It had been their plan to spend the night at her place.

"Why are we fighting about this?" she asked.

"Maybe it's because we are different," he said. "We don't want to think about it. On the island, for the most part, we can pretend it doesn't change anything. But it does."

This must happen to people all the time, she thought. You find the person of your dreams, that rare combination of friend and lover and companion. You roll into bed, you laugh together, you discover you have the same politics, the same values, the same rhythm between the sheets. But time passes and the cracks begin to appear. Here was a crack and it felt like a big one.

She reached out and touched the top of his hand. "It's because I showed you my grandparents' house," she said. "Is that what you mean by different?"

He shook his head. "It has nothing to do with that. It has to do with this," he said as he put his hand on her jiggling knee and pressed it firmly into stillness.

"Good night, then," she said, turning away.

He slid his fingers around her other wrist and pulled her toward him, took her face in his hands and kissed her. It was a rough kiss, his tongue greedy in her mouth. His hands slid the jacket off her shoulders and she thought for a moment to suggest that they move inside, but she didn't because she liked what was happening to her, the way he was taking her here, outside the front door of her house, in full view of anybody who decided to drive home on the back road. The front seat of a truck on a cold night in early March was not the most comfortable place to make love, but she let him tear at her clothes, arrange her body to suit him and slide up inside of her like a teenager in heat. He came first and halfway through his ride, she found the rhythm and let herself open up to it. Under his body, she screamed the way she rarely did in bed and thought later how grateful she was that her neighbors were all away in the winter months.

"You slut," he whispered lovingly in her ear.

"Mmm. I consider that a compliment. How long have you been keeping condoms in your glove compartment, I wonder."

"Not long," he said. "In case of emergencies. Like this."

"Right next to the flares and the Band-Aids and the matches. Were you ever a Boy Scout?"

"No. Why?"

"Be prepared. Isn't that the Boy Scout motto?"

He gave her neck a friendly nibble. Above them, the rearview mirror picked up a set of headlights.

"Shit," he said.

"Don't move," she whispered in his ear. "They can't see anything as long as we stay down."

They held their breath as the car passed slowly by and disappeared around the curve.

He lifted himself off her and helped her up. "They took a good long look," he said.

"Lucky for them. It'll give the morning crowd in the post office something to talk about."

He spent the night after all. In the morning, she woke up to his arms around her.

"I'm hopelessly addicted to your skin," he said.

"Even though we're different?" she asked.

"Even though," he said. "Or maybe because."

Twenty-one

ONE MUDDY AFTERNOON in early March, Erin knocked on Maggie's door. She was carrying the typewriter.

"Did you haul that all the way from your house?" Maggie held out her arms to take it back.

"No. Mom gave me a ride."

"I was just going to call you about it. I'm ready to type up my notes for the house survey. You can have it back when I'm done."

Erin didn't answer. She looked uncertain.

"Come in. Shut the door. I'm cleaning a table and I could use a hand. I see you've signed up for my Tech Ed class," Maggie called over her shoulder as she lowered the typewriter onto the front hall table and headed into the workroom. She was babbling away, hoping that Erin wouldn't bolt.

"Mr. M. made me."

"He's a pushy fellow, that Matera, isn't he?"

Erin smiled. At least she'd edged into the room, Maggie thought.

"What are you doing? I didn't know you smoked."

Maggie laughed. "I don't. It's an old home remedy I learned from one of my teachers. Come here, I'll show you. See this white ring? It means someone put a wet glass down on the table."

Erin traced it with her finger.

"My godmother was very sloppy with her furniture. She never bothered with coasters, just put her glasses down wherever she pleased. See, there are two more spots. I've already tried to wax these out, but it didn't work. So what I do now is mix a little mineral oil with cigarette ash. It makes a paste. " She put a gray lump of it on Erin's finger. "Rub the ring with that for a little while. Good. Now do the other ones and I'll follow along behind you with a cloth."

"It's working," Erin said after a while. "It's fun."

"Furniture conservation is always fun when you can see the difference right away. Unfortunately, most problems don't get solved this easily."

Maggie lit up another cigarette and puffed away on it to produce some ash.

"I can tell you don't smoke," Erin said. "You look a little kid."

"A lot of the kids in school smoke," Maggie said. "I can smell it on their clothes. You ever tried it?"

Erin shrugged. "A couple of times."

"How was it?"

"I started wheezing."

"Does this bother your asthma?" Maggie asked, waving at the smoke that was drifting across the room.

"No, it's okay. Dr. Lacey gave me this new meter so I can test my own breathing. Where's the next one?"

"You can start on that sideboard in the corner. I'm not going to do a full restoration on it because it's not really good enough to sell at auction, but there are some dealers down in Philadelphia that might want it."

They worked along side by side in silence for a while. Once Erin had finished the sideboard, Maggie got her to write out shipping labels with a big black magic marker. She took her time with the letters, trying to make the address come out evenly.

"I made this one crooked," Erin said.

Maggie came over to inspect. "Don't worry, I can read it."

"You're not going to sell this house are you?"

"I don't know, Erin, I haven't made up my mind. I do a lot of traveling in my work."

"You could marry Mr. M. and come back here in between trips. But you don't have to change your name. I don't think Maggie Matera is a good name. I like Maggie Hammond better."

Maggie laughed. "You've been doing a lot of thinking, haven't you?"

Kasha padded into the room, greeted Erin with a sniff, then lowered herself slowly.

"Mom's taking me with her this Friday. For the hunting test. She says we can go to a mall and maybe stay in a motel for the night.

It's a secret. I'm not supposed to tell my father." Erin's voice sounded mechanical as if she were reciting some passage she'd memorized.

"It sounds like Anna's planning to bolt," Sam said that night when Maggie told him about Erin's visit.

"What other choice does she have?"

He didn't answer.

"I hope she makes it," Maggie said.

Anna was counting the days. Five, four, three. Last week, she had stowed two suitcases in the train station when she was over taking Shooter to the vet and now she was worried about that. Two days ago, Erin had been looking for a skirt that Anna had packed in one of those suitcases.

"That's a summer skirt, Erin. It's too cold to wear it now."

"I don't care. I'm sick of my winter clothes."

Al was standing in the corner of the kitchen, turning the dial on the radio and half listening to the two of them.

"Where is it, Mom? I looked in the storage closet and it's not there."

"I don't know, sweetie. I haven't seen it." She kept her eyes on the cutting board, concentrating on each separate slice of apple. The knife was sharp and her hands were trembling.

"I know I put it in the bag of summer clothes last fall," Erin said. "Remember when we were putting everything away that day and I had to stop because the mothballs made me wheeze?"

"We'll buy you another skirt," Anna said. She was keeping her voice light, praying that Al wasn't really listening. Any conversation felt dangerous when you were planning a getaway. "Just pick out something else to wear today or you'll be late for school."

"We're not going to buy you another skirt," Al said as he turned down the volume. "You've got to stop losing things, Erin. Clothes cost money."

"But I don't lose things, Dad," Erin said. "I put that skirt in the storage closet last fall. I remember."

Anna was glad to hear Erin standing up to him, but not now, she thought. It wasn't the time. Just let me get you away from here. "Al, what was all that talk on the radio?" she asked.

Al shrugged. "Engine gave out on a lobster boat. The Coast Guard is hauling them in. Two- to three-foot swells out there." Erin pounded her way up the stairs. "You keep letting that kid get away with murder. If she loses her clothes, too damn bad for her. She can go to school in something else. She can go to school in a plastic bag if she has to. Teach her a lesson."

"I know," she said. And then, "You're right." Those words were very hard to spit out. She couldn't remember the last time she'd told him he was right about anything.

It seemed to satisfy him. He poured another cup of coffee. "I'm going off island on Friday to pick up supplies for the community center. Last load of stuff from that guy up the coast. He's got the best prices."

Anna kept herself turned away from him. Friday, she thought. It couldn't just be luck. She was meant to go. Everything was falling into place. "That's the day I'm taking Daisy over for the hunting test."

"What boat?"

"The afternoon," she lied. "When are you coming back?"

"The six o'clock, probably. Depends. I've got some other business to take care of over there."

EARLY THE MORNING before she was to leave, Anna went up island with Chuck. They took Polly out to work her with Daisy one last time before the hunting test. Although she was still a little gun-shy, the dog had been better trained than Anna had expected and they'd decided she was ready for the master class. Anna had to keep reminding herself that they were never going to get to the hunting test at all, but nobody else knew that.

She whistled Daisy in early. Clouds were building in the west. "Can you imagine doing this job for a living?" she asked Chuck.

"What, training dogs?" He shook his head. "Nope. I don't have your patience. I'd probably shoot the dog instead of the bird if they got on my nerves too much."

"Chuck, don't say that." He looked up at the note of alarm in her voice.

"Just kidding. I couldn't shoot you, could I, girl?" he said as Daisy trotted up to them, tongue hanging out of her mouth.

Anna pulled down the tailgate of the station wagon. "Kennel," she said to the dog, who circled once on the ground to gauge the distance, then bounded up. She curled quickly into the cage.

"That's a real good dog," Chuck said. "Responsive, smart. Even better than Whistler."

Anna was studying his face as he settled himself in the front seat of her car. Will I see you again, she wondered. "How many years have we been working together?"

"Six or seven. Don't really remember. Why?"

"I don't know. Just thinking."

Suddenly his face seemed very dear to her. She knew it so well. The age spots, the thinning gray eyebrows, the lopsided grin. He said he couldn't be bothered to go over to the barber shop on the mainland in the winter, so by this time of year, his hair had gotten long and stringy. He kept a hat smashed down on it as much to cut the wind as for vanity.

"What are you staring at? Something wrong? Did I grow a wart on my nose?"

She couldn't afford to say good-bye. Chuck had been hanging out most nights at the Harbor Lounge and beer made him sloppy.

"Just appreciating you," she said. "People don't appreciate each other enough when they're thrown together every day."

"How are things with you?" he asked.

"Fine." That light voice again, the one she practiced when she was alone in the bathroom. I'm fine. You're right, Al. Whatever you say, Al. I agree with you, Al. "Al told me he's going off island tomorrow to pick up the last supplies for the community center."

"He doesn't need to tramp around buying more cheap crap. He needs to stay down there and do some of the work, dammit. We'd probably make better time if he hadn't dumped those Tremayne boys on us. Did you hear he found their stash?"

"He told me he'd followed them to one of those abandoned navy bunkers."

"That's right. He found just about everything they'd stolen in the last two years."

"He's put them on the community center job?" Anna asked.

"The deal is the boys work for Al through next summer and he won't file a report on them over in the county sheriff's office. That means Billy and I are stuck with them. They'll steal the paint faster than they'll slap it on the walls. Sooner those kids leave this island, the better off we'll all be."

"Sounds like you and Billy are the ones being punished."

"Well, out here, as you know, we have our own unique form of justice."

"Al will do anything to avoid taking island troubles to the mainland."

"That's why your husband's been sheriff for so long, Anna. He keeps island business on the island."

"But Al *is* going to the mainland tomorrow, isn't he?"

"Don't ask me," Chuck said with a shrug. "I don't know where he goes or what he does."

"Of course he is," she said mostly to herself, and he gave her a look. But he didn't say anything more about it.

"I'll be up tomorrow afternoon to cover the dogs," he said as he left her. "When will you be back?"

"Afternoon boat on Saturday," she said. "The usual."

THE NEXT MORNING she took her time with the dogs. Inside each cage, she hunkered down to say her good-byes. They were surprised and pleased by this extra attention. The vizslas rolled over for their stomachs to be stroked, acting for all the world like house pets. The pointers were alert to her every move, hoping this attention meant she'd be taking them out any minute to hunt birds.

How long would it take Chuck to figure out that she wasn't coming back? Not long. The word would be around the island as soon as she didn't show up for that Saturday boat. Most of the dogs could be shipped back to their owners. But he'd have to keep Polly himself. He'd never wanted dogs of his own, but he'd do it. For her. He wouldn't leave Polly to Al.

Polly shoved her pink-brown nose into Anna's hand, sniffed, licked, shoved deeper. What if Chuck didn't get it until it was too late. Until Al had taken out his rage the way he always did. On something that couldn't strike back. She sank to her knees in Polly's cage, staring deep into the dog's brown eyes with her hand cupped around the bones of her jaw. The dog was stilled, stared back. Al could—she stopped the thought. The other ones Al wouldn't touch. They belonged to rich owners. He wouldn't dare. But Polly was hers. And Al had always gone after what she loved if it meant he could get to her. That's why she had to take Erin with her. And this one. She had to take Polly, too.

She dragged another cage out to the station wagon and loaded Daisy and Polly in the back. She knew all the motels up and down the coast that would take dogs, and there weren't many of them. Never mind. They could always sleep in the back of the car if necessary. She'd figure out a way. She shut the kennel door after one last look, and the rest of the pack howled in protest as if they knew somehow that she wasn't coming back.

Methodically, she collected her small bag, the money from the Blair's garage, and walked one last time through the house. She left the kitchen neat as always, the dish towel poked through the handle of the refrigerator door, the dishwasher run and emptied. When Al read the note she'd left for him, the one saying she took Erin with her on the spur of the moment, he'd probably go down to the Harbor Lounge, spend Friday night with Lauren, come back home. Sit here waiting for her. He'd get in his truck and drive around when she didn't show up Saturday afternoon. How long would it take him to figure out that she wasn't coming back? What would it be like for him, rattling around this place by himself? How would it feel driving into town, the sheriff, the man whose wife ran off and left? Took the kid too. Better than Billy Slade's wife. She left that little three-year-old Jimmy behind and never came back once to see the boy. No, nobody had any idea where Anna was. She'd covered her tracks pretty well. How long do you think she'd been planning this?

She even felt sorry for him. What a lonely, angry man he was. If only it could have been different between them, if only she could have traced back to the moment when things had started to go bad. In the beginning, you are so loose and easy with each other. You tease, you make fun a little, and it doesn't hurt. But then somebody says something and it does hurt. And you don't mention it then or even the next time when it hurts more. You begin to keep secrets from each other. Then the day comes when you start to keep secrets from yourself. What a lot of unraveling it would take to set this right, she thought, her hand still curled around the brass knob of the kitchen door. And he would have to admit he had done things that hurt her and he would have to say that he was sorry for all of it. She took a breath. Hell would freeze over first, she thought. How many times had she run over this scenario in her mind and how many years had that kept her here, the hope that things could be different.

One more thing. She ripped Al's list of rules off the bulletin board, tore the sheet of paper into a pile of small strips and buried them in the trash can out by the garage. By the time he noticed that list was gone, she'd be far away from here.

Kasha was trotting down the driveway toward her, tail curled, head up.

"Hello, girl," she called, and knelt to bury her head in the shiny thick fur. "You'd better not come around anymore. I won't be here to protect you."

Kasha whined in reply.

"I mean it." She'd better warn Maggie somehow to keep Kasha on a check cord for a while. In a lifetime in one place, you got tangled up with so many hearts, even when you weren't looking, when you were intending to mind your own business. Anna was trying to slip out of their lives, tiptoeing backward, one careful foot after another.

SHE DROVE SLOWLY down island in plenty of time for the noon boat. There wouldn't be many people going over because it wasn't a round-trip day. Anybody who had serious business on the other side would have gone off like Al on the eight o'clock.

Margaret, the secretary in the school office, looked surprised to see her.

"I've come to take Erin out early," Anna said. "We've got a doctor's appointment on the mainland. They just called me because they've had a cancellation."

"So Dr. Lacey isn't seeing patients this morning?" Margaret said.

"It's a specialist for Erin's asthma. Somebody Dr. Lacey recommended, actually." And it's none of your business, Anna thought. But she was pleased with how easily the lies rolled off her tongue. She'd have to get used to this, she thought. Lying at the drop of a hat. Inventing stories, identities.

Erin looked confused herself.

"What doctor's appointment?" she said. Sam was holding the door of his classroom open for her.

"That specialist we've been trying to see. Remember, I told you about it a couple of weeks ago."

"Are we still going to the mall?"

"Sure. We're just taking off a little early."

The color was creeping up her neck. Sam was standing there. In the distance, they heard the long blow of the noon boat as it approached the dock.

"Ferry's coming in already. Hop in the car, Erin."

" 'Bye, Mr. M. See you later."

"Have fun, Erin," Sam said, then when the girl was out of earshot, he said to Anna, "Take care of yourself."

Their eyes met. He knows, she thought.

"Tell Maggie to keep Kasha on a check cord for a while," she said. "You know, Al and that dog."

"I'll tell her."

"Make sure," Anna said, then turned abruptly away.

DAN CHESTER BACKED her onto the boat. He walked along, his left hand resting on the hood of the station wagon, giving her the directions with his right. She turned the steering wheel in response, willing herself not to look over her shoulder. She'd thrown a blanket across the suitcases in the second seat, but she wished she had a car with a trunk. Some people were lined up on the upper deck watching the cars load, and she knew from experience that they could look right through her back windows.

"Taking two dogs over today," Dan said. "That's more than usual." He rarely stopped to chat, but one of the younger guys from the mainland was bringing on the next car.

"Hunting test," Anna said.

"You usually take the afternoon boat, don't you?"

"Yes. Erin's got a doctor's appointment."

"Too bad you couldn't go on Wednesday, get the round-trip rate."

She pulled out her purse and dug around in it as if she were searching for something. He watched for an extra minute, then patted the car twice on the open window frame.

"Al went off this morning," he said.

"I know. He needed some supplies."

"You have a good trip," he said. "I mean it, Anna."

"We will. We'll be back tomorrow, Dan," she said in that new light voice of hers.

"Sure. Of course." He leaned down. "See you, Erin," he said.

" 'Bye, Mr. Chester." On his way around the back of the car, he paused a moment to look in. Anna watched him in the rearview mirror. He pretended to be making a fuss over the dogs, but she knew better. He was trying to get a look at what was under the blanket. Polly barked at him.

"Down," Anna ordered from the front seat, and the dog settled.

"What was that all about?" Erin said. "Mr. Chester doesn't usually hang around like that."

Because he's guessed what I'm doing, Anna thought. The way Sam did. Would he tell Al? Maybe not. Maybe the island all knew now that she couldn't go on like this. Maybe they were cheering her on. If she left, they would not have to bear witness any longer. She and Erin would be safe, but nobody would have had to intercede, stand up and stop something. Go up against Al. People didn't talk in front of Anna, but Chuck had told her that the whole business with Dr. Lacey had made trouble. Some of the older islanders remembered the days before a full-time doctor. They'd lost some—Phil Dodge's wife to septicemia, Al's own baby sister to meningitis. Maybe a doctor couldn't have saved them, but people always wondered. Randy's name had been put forward for sheriff. With that girl Ellie packed up and gone for good, he could use some distraction.

As a topic of gossip, Anna and Erin might last until Memorial Day when the summer owners came back in droves. Their antics kept the island talkers occupied right through till the fall.

"Winter blues," Anna said to Erin. "People have been shut inside their houses for too long. I'll have to get out on your side. There's no room for my door to open."

"What about the dogs?"

"I'll leave them in the car. They're calmer that way."

EVERYBODY KNEW. ANNA was sure of it by the time they reached the other side. Henry, the purser, closed her fingers over her change and squeezed. She had bought a round-trip ticket that she would toss in the trash somewhere up the highway when she crossed the border into Pennsylvania. Or maybe she'd save it and give it to Erin one day, years from now. As a souvenir.

"Miss Yola went over today," Henry said. "A check-up I think."

"Funny, she usually goes on Wednesdays," Anna said to make conversation. Miss Yola was the one person she'd wanted to say good-bye to, but even that hadn't seemed wise. In the last few days, nothing had felt safe. She would write her in a couple of weeks. When they were far enough away. No return address. A postmark from a place they'd left behind.

"I'll tell her I saw you," Henry said.

Anna slid onto the bench next to Erin, who was staring out the window. "Did you bring something to read?"

"Mmm. But I don't want to read right now."

Anna wished she could have warned Erin, given her the time to say good-bye. What would this do to her daughter, to be spirited away like this from the island she'd lived on her whole life? Maybe one day, she would come back, when she was old enough. Try to pick up the pieces of memories. This is where I went to school, she'd tell her own daughter. This is the house we lived in. Grandma trained dogs back then.

And what did Grandma do after that? Anna wondered. How odd that she could feel all the sadness for Erin and even Al, but not for herself. After all, she'd spent her whole life on this flat piece of land too. She knew all the trails through the woods, how far the tide brought the water up on Chincoteale in the different seasons, the way the air smelled before the big fall storms that blew up the coast. They would live somewhere inland, Anna had been thinking. Drive west through New York and Pennsylania. Maybe settle on the shores of one of those lakes. She'd read that the wind could whip up a surf on one of the bigger ones that reminded you of the ocean. Al would never think to look there. Al would assume she'd want to stay by the sea because that's all she'd ever known. Al would assume as he always did that he knew how she thought. But he had no idea.

WHILE THE BOAT was docking, Anna scanned the parked cars in the lot. If he had been lying about his supply trip, this is where he would be waiting for her, standing over to the side while Henry retrieved the tickets from each passing car before he took her back into custody. But she saw no sign of him. She breathed once deeply and her heartbeat slowed. This was going to work. She was going to make it.

The train station was not as far from the ferry dock as Anna would have liked, so she drove the car around to the front where nobody from the island was likely to see her.

"What are we doing here, Mom?" Erin asked.

"I'm just picking up some things to take to your Uncle Dave."

"What things?"

"Extra clothes I've cleared out. Aunt Marian gives them to a charity and we get a tax deduction." This lie she'd thought up before. She wanted to get Erin as far away as possible before she told her what they were doing.

"What about the thrift shop on the island?"

"They don't give a tax deduction."

Erin was fiddling with the radio when Anna came back out and piled the two extra suitcases into the second seat. She hadn't counted on the whole back section being taken up with the dogs. She got each of them out and gave them a quick walk and some water.

"Can we go to the mall now?" Erin asked.

Anna didn't want to stop. She wanted to get away from here as fast as possible, but she'd promised Erin. Maybe it wouldn't hurt.

The mall was a few miles down the interstate in the right direction. They'd stop quickly and she'd buy Erin whatever she wanted. A send-off. What a relief it would be, not to have to go back and justify every purchase to Al. Or else hide a dress somewhere upstairs and slip it on some morning for church, thinking he wouldn't notice. He always did.

"Where did you get that dress?" he would ask her.

"At the thrift shop."

"It looks brand-new."

"Summer people are always turning in brand-new things. They get tired of them, they throw things away."

"What do you need a new dress for?"

"I didn't need it. I wanted it."

And then the lecture on money. The one she knew by heart.

Life is complicated enough, Al, she'd said to him once. Every minute is precious. You are wasting them. Mine and yours.

He had no idea what she was talking about and his voice had flowed on around her objections, like water around a rock.

ERIN WAS IN one of her drifting moods. She stopped and tried on perfume, scanned the jewelry counter, and wandered through the shoe department. She picked up one pair of boots after another. Anna felt like a caged animal. She kept looking over her shoulder.

"Sweetie, we do have to keep moving. I can't leave the dogs in the car very long."

"What time is the doctor's appointment?"

Anna went blank for a minute and then remembered. She must learn to keep her lies straight. "Not long," she said, checking her watch. "If you want some clothes, we'd better hurry."

"All right." They headed for the escalator, but still Erin trailed her fingers across the glass-topped scarf counter, glanced in every mirror, picked up things and put them down.

Upstairs, she took two pairs of jeans from a sale shelf and added two sweaters. Then, to Anna's surprise, she wandered over to a rack of dresses. Erin had refused to wear a dress for years.

"I like this one," she said, holding it up defiantly.

"It's a pretty purple," Anna said. "But it looks short for you."

"It's my size. Everybody's wearing short dresses now, Mom."

"Okay. Try it on, then."

"I will. In a minute. I'm still looking. Stop rushing me."

Erin picked out two more and disappeared at last into the dressing room. Anna knew better than to follow her so she leaned against one of the mirrors to wait. She turned and looked at her own face, saw the dark-brown wideset eyes, the sun spots that showed more each year from her childhood years on the beach, the strong jaw, the thick dark eyebrows. She liked what she saw. And then in the reflection, in the distance, just as Erin said, "Here I am, Mom," she saw Al. And he knew she had seen him because he stepped up from behind a rack of clothes and said "Surprise" in a hearty voice, too loud for the teenage department of the store. She knew that voice. He was embarrassed and even defensive. There was always this little moment when Al realized that normal people didn't do the things he did. They didn't burn hats and break fishing rods and follow their wife and daughter into department stores. They let people go on and live their lives. They didn't constantly put themselves in places where they were not wanted. Anna knew that he had these inklings, but he defended himself against them with a hearty voice and the pretense that he was where he was supposed to be and he had only done his duty after all. He'd suspected his wife was on the run and he was right. So it was his duty to follow her and bring her back. Anna thought of making a break for it the way they did in movies, pulling all the dresses off the racks as she went, pushing chairs in front of Al and bolting down the escalator.

And then Erin said again, "Mom, do you like it?"

Anna turned her head. The sight of Erin's knobby knees made her want to cry. "Yes, sweetie, it's pretty. You look great in purple."

"Hello, pumpkin," her father said. It was a baby nickname for her, one he hadn't used in years.

"What are you doing here, Daddy?" Erin asked, because up until this moment she and her mother had been ignoring him, hoping that if they just paid him no attention, he would disappear like a mirage.

"That dress is too short, Erin," he said. "You go take that off."

A normal teenager would have objected, stamped her foot, said everybody is wearing their dresses this short, my friend has two of these. But Erin turned without speaking and disappeared into the dressing room.

As they waited for her to return, Anna didn't say a word to Al. She looked at him, but she did not speak.

It must have made him nervous because he shifted from one foot to another. "Got an awful lot of stuff in the car, I see. For one night, I mean. Looks like you were packing for a month."

Or a year. Or a lifetime, she thought.

"Thought you were only taking Daisy over."

She was silent.

"I got back early with the supplies," he said. "Earlier than I expected."

The hell you did, Anna thought. You probably never went at all. You've been watching me ever since I drove off the boat. You were the eyes boring into my back, the ones I was sure I felt but could not locate.

"Excuse me," said a woman leading her teenage daughter into the dressing room. Al was blocking the way.

He stepped aside and when this woman gave him a look, Anna saw her husband through someone else's eyes. He looked out of place here. Any man would. Other men would know that you don't belong in the teenage department. They'd have the sense to wait out by the escalator. Or they'd have other things to do. They'd wait down in the truck with the radio on.

Then Anna looked further and saw his stained khaki pants, the mud-spattered boots, the old jacket he'd bought at the thrift shop ten years ago, the one he wore every single day from November to May. His thin blond hair hugged the bony scalp and his hands were shoved deep in his pockets, or else that woman would have seen the rough fingers, the calluses. He is an island man, Anna thought. There's not much reason out there to get cleaned up. Weeks slipped into weekends and you stayed in the same clothes. You didn't soak your hands in a hot soapy sink to get that black oily dirt out because down in the Harbor Lounge on a Saturday night, nobody was going to give a damn about the dirt under your fingernails.

THEY SPENT THE night in a motel. Al got a separate room for Erin, which surprised Anna. She had thought he would object to the extra money, but when he closed the door behind them and gave her a certain look, she knew why. He made her lie down crossways on the bed so he could watch the dirty movie he'd ordered and screw her at the same time. She closed her eyes and concentrated on breathing because she felt so dead inside that she was scared she would forget how.

When he was done and had rolled off her, she picked her body up from the bed and went into the bathroom to wash him off.

"You're one lucky woman, Anna," he said.

She didn't answer, didn't turn around.

"Other men wouldn't put up with this shit you've been pulling. They'd slap you around to make sure you remember how a wife is supposed to behave. I have never hit you. I promised myself I would never ever hit a woman, not after what I saw my father do, but goddamn, it's hard sometimes to hold myself back."

Hit me, Al, she thought. Please hit me. It would give me the excuse I still seem to need although God knows why.

Twenty-two

THE NEXT DAY, Chuck was directing the cars onto the boat. He looked surprised to see Anna. The talk in the Harbor Lounge the night before must have been about her. Would she make it? Remember the time Annie Slocum had bolted? She didn't get far, did she? She'd come crawling back. Anna probably would too.

He walked along beside her as she began the slow backing down the ramp.

"You missed the big excitement. Paul Thayer collapsed last night at the Lounge. Standing right at the bar, his hand on a Manhattan."

"Is he all right?"

"For now. He's over in the hospital on the mainland. Lacey and Randy Baker did CPR on him and then Lacey went over on the ambulance boat with him. Says he thinks Paul's got some problem with his heart muscle and he wanted to be sure the doctors over there ran the right tests. Cardiomyo something. Did you know Lacey's a heart specialist?"

"I heard he was," Anna said. "How's Diane?"

"She's okay. She's there with him. The kids are staying with the Malloys and people have already started cooking. You know this place," he said. "When people are in trouble, you feed them."

She smiled. "Certain kinds of trouble."

"Where's Erin? I heard you took her along," he asked.

"She's in the truck with Al. Behind you." Dan Chester walked over to direct Al onto the boat. Al had already turned his truck around and was waiting, his eye on his sideview mirror. Erin was sitting close by the other door, her head bent over a movie magazine she had bought in the drugstore next to the train station.

"How did Daisy do?" Chuck asked.

"She flunked. Broke point twice with the guns. It was my fault. I was distracted."

"I was worried about Polly when I saw she was gone too, but I figured you must have taken her. Particularly Polly," he added.

"I couldn't leave her behind," she said, and they locked eyes.

"You okay?"

She lowered her forehead to the wheel of the car for a moment and felt his hand rest briefly on her hair. He made sure to block this one small gesture from Al's line of sight with his body.

"I really thought I would make it," she said. "But he was onto me the whole time."

"I'm sorry, Anna. I would have helped if you'd asked me. Whatever you needed."

She lifted her head.

"I would have missed you," he muttered in a low voice. "Terrible."

Al honked the horn and leaned out the window of his truck. "Hey, Chuck, stop flirting with my woman," he shouted.

"We got a boat to load, Chuck," Dan said.

Chuck dropped back to the hood of the car and lifted his right hand to direct Anna into place. Yesterday, she had left here thinking she might not see any of these people again. And here she was, right back in the thick of it. For a moment, with her tires rolling across the metal deck of the ferry, she let herself imagine how much she might have missed them.

ERIN FOUND HER mother sitting on a starboard bench and slid in next to her. When Al came up from parking the truck, he nodded at them without stopping and followed Dan to the wheelhouse. Al never rode over on the passenger deck. The sheriff belonged up in the control room, riding shotgun, ready to take over at a moment's notice, Anna thought. Everybody knew Al couldn't steer this boat if his life depended on it. Suddenly he seemed so young and immature to her. Always a little boy trying to prove himself. The childishness was part of what made him so dangerous.

"We weren't coming back, were we, Mom?" Erin asked as the engine started up beneath them. She was leafing through the magazine again.

"What do you mean?" Anna was buying time. She'd been expecting this question. This was the first time she'd been alone with Erin since the mall.

"You know what I mean. All the suitcases. We were running away."

"Yes, we were, Erin. For a while at least. Until I could sort things out."

"And Daddy caught us and brought us back."

Anna said nothing.

"Like the book we read in school?"

"What book?"

"Anne Frank," she said. "We have to go back to hiding in the attic." Her voice had this dreamy sound to it as if she were telling a story to a child. Anna got goosebumps listening to her. "It would have been an adventure. I could have started all over in another school and nobody would know me. And the class would have been bigger. More kids."

"That's what I thought."

"But Daddy would have come. He would have found us no matter where we were. He always finds us."

Anna wasn't so sure anymore. On the island, Al could swagger about. He knew every person, every road, every car, every twist in the weather. But he was unsure of himself out there in the great swirl of the world. The highways and the malls and the pace of life seemed to make him uneasy. This was the first time in ages she'd been with Al on the mainland, and in the last eighteen hours, she'd watched him pick fights with everybody from the motel clerk to the toll collectors. He always fought when he was frightened. He couldn't wait to get back to the island, to put that stretch of water between him and the big world out there.

Maybe if she had managed to get away, he might have just let her go and said, the hell with her. Good riddance to bad rubbish. No, she was fooling herself again. She would have taken Erin. One of his possessions.

She put her arm around Erin and squeezed her. Even though people in the boat were watching, Erin didn't seem to mind. She didn't stop fooling with the magazine, but her body softened.

"Thanks for buying me the dress, Mom. I love it."

She would probably never wear it, Anna thought. The circumstances of its purchase would cling to the dress like a terrible smell.

It had felt like such a small gesture of revolt, but Anna had gone back into the dressing room to retrieve the purple dress from where Erin had left it, dangling from a hook. Anna had walked clear across the floor looking for a salesperson with Al following, all the while telling her in a loud voice what he thought of that dress and teenagers growing up too quickly because their parents didn't discipline them. Erin had trailed along miserably, trying to look as if she didn't belong to these two people.

Anna had finally located a salesgirl who became so flustered by Al's ranting that she punched the wrong buttons on the cash register and had to start over again.

When the check was ready, Anna had dug into the pocket of her jeans and handed over two twenties.

"So where did you get that, I wonder—" Al began.

Anna had whirled around. "Al, shut up," she said, her voice raised just one notch, the kind of voice a teacher develops in a classroom, the kind of voice useful with dogs. It was not a scream. It was a controlled order. Each word was clipped off at the end. The person speaking expected to be obeyed, had been obeyed before, saved this voice for times like this.

Everybody had frozen. The salesgirl had looked around for a security guard. Erin stepped behind a rack of pants. But Al did it. He'd shut up. For that one minute, he'd stopped speaking and the silence had lasted all the way down to the parking lot where he'd made Erin get in the truck with him for their trip to the hunting test.

Sunday morning Al showed up at the community center. He'd already ordered Billy and Chuck onto the job and he'd rounded up the Tremayne boys and poured some hot coffee down them. They were next to useless, but if nothing else, it would keep them out of trouble for the day. He'd been thinking about calling in some of the other construction workers on the island. Times were slow and he knew they'd come in a flash because they needed the work, but he'd been holding off. He'd cut a few corners here and there. Small ones, nothing real bad. The Tremayne boys didn't know one end of a hammer from the other and he could count on Chuck and Billy to keep their mouths shut. But he could never be sure about the others. They'd just as soon steal the work from him and if it got around that everything wasn't up to code, well, he couldn't trust them. Of course he was pretty sure they did the same thing on their jobs, but at times like these, it was every man for himself.

Billy kept pressing him to call off the St. Patrick's Day party. They only had six days to finish up and they were way behind. But whenever Al was tempted to do it, he remembered the town meeting, the way people had swiveled around to look at him, the things they'd said. That's our money Al Craven is socking away, and we don't have a community center to show for it. He's four months late on our project so how come he can finish those summer houses so fast, come in right on schedule. And now that everybody thought Dr. Precious Lacey had saved Paul's life, there was talk of replacing Al as sheriff. Randy Baker maybe. Or Jim Sullivan. Someone who could keep it together. Bullshit. The last thing he needed now was to tell people they had to hold their party back down in the moldy basement of the Catholic church. He'd be damned if he was going to do that.

"You're still not finished with that circuit box, Billy? Christ, what is taking you so damn long?"

Billy put down his tools, walked over and rested a hand on Al's shoulder. Al didn't like to be touched, never had, especially by a man. He shrugged it off. Derry Tremayne was close by, pretending to tape some Sheetrock, so Billy kept his voice low. "Al, wiring a circuit box when you're running eight outlets and four switches off each breaker is a little complicated, if you get my drift. Never mind that you're working with cheap Taiwan shit, that aluminum Romex wiring. Never mind that you decided to skip the junction boxes—"

Al cut him off. "Shut up, Billy," he said. "We've been over all that before. You're sounding like a goddamned broken record."

Billy still didn't move. His staring made Al uncomfortable. What was wrong with the man? They'd done jobs like this before. Chuck poked his head around the corner at the sudden silence.

"Hey, Chuck," Al called. "You got any problem with the way this job is being wired?"

"I'm not the electrician," Chuck said. "Billy is." He slid back out of sight.

Al rolled his eyes. "Cowardly little shit." He knew Billy didn't think much of Chuck either, but Billy still didn't speak. "You wanna quit on me now, Billy? Wanna do that? Go right ahead. I'll make sure you never get another job on this island. You know I can do that, don't you?"

"Maybe, maybe not," Billy said. "People are talking, Al. They're saying you've lost it."

Al wanted to hit this man so bad that he could feel the energy pumping right down into his fists. But he hung on to himself. That was the last thing he needed to do right now, beat the shit out of his one good worker. Chuck had a bum knee and he could do rough carpentry work, but not much else. At least, I can count on him to shut his trap, Al thought. Chuck was nothing but a frightened little man. Right now Billy looked like a different story.

"All right, Billy, you give me the next five days, you make sure this place is ready for inspection on Friday, and I'll make it worth your while."

"You bribing me, Al?"

"I'm paying you overtime for this one. Just look at it that way."

"I'll see," Billy said. He stood there, thinking it over. The man needed money, Al knew that. He had a bad gambling habit. He was still paying off the debts from a turn at the casinos last fall. Stupid fool decided he was on a roll and had pulled money right out of his credit line from one of those teller machines and pissed it all away that afternoon. People are so stupid, Al thought. Half the money he had, he didn't even keep in the bank. It was stashed all over the place, down in the safe in his office, over at that house he owned by the fort that didn't get rented this winter. Places nobody knew about, but him. He didn't trust banks.

"So?" Al said.

"I want to be paid soon as I'm done," Billy said. "In cash. Got that? When's the inspector coming in?"

"Friday, noon boat."

"Then I want the money before that boat whistle blows. Don't be late, Al," Billy said. "Make sure of that."

"You threatening me?"

"Yup. That's what I'm doing," Billy said as he walked away. "I'm threatening you."

THIS TIME OF year, when spring tiptoed slyly back onto the island, Sam hated the hours he was trapped in the classroom. Everything was happening so fast and he wanted to be there. The kids knew that in March and April, they could count on at least one field trip a week. Down in the swampy areas behind Starfish Beach, the bright green leaves of the skunk cabbage were already poking their way up through the dark rotting compost of last year's leaves. The ospreys would start coming back to their nests any day now, and Sam spotted a woodcock on the rutted back road that ran across Shelter Field. The wind was still biting, and many mornings, they'd wake to frost on the grass, but underneath the earth was stirring.

The spring peepers had been singing for a couple of weeks and near Middle Field, the male toad had started its chorus. This meant he had already established his breeding territory and was singing to the female to join him. Lucky toads. They had no roads to cross, only a few yards to the brackish tidal meadow behind the wildlife preserve. But the salamanders were usually the last to cross. They could be buried as deep as two feet beneath the surface. Every free moment, Sam patrolled the road by Cattail Marsh, lifting rocks and leaf litter and poking around. For a week, ever since the ground had softened, he'd had the older kids up digging holes for the salamander traps.

On the Wednesday before St. Patrick's Day, he put up volunteer sheets on the post office bulletin board as well as in the two grocery stores and the thrift shop. *Date to be Announced. Pray for Rain,* the signs said. *Bring your flashlights and your tents. All-Night Vigil.*

"Why rain?" Maggie asked. They were standing side by side in his kitchen, baking bread for the St. Patrick's Day party. He was teaching her how to knead.

"The road has to be wet so the salamanders' skin doesn't dry out while they go over. Wait till you see. They'll come up to the edge of the pavement and cluster there until it's wet enough to cross."

"So how do you stop all of them at once if a car is coming?"

"We drop a black plastic barrier. They head left or right and fall into the buckets we've buried in the ground. Then we carry them across later when the coast is clear. "

"Don't they dry out in the buckets?"

"Not if it's raining hard enough. Later on in the month when the big crossings are done, I have people sign up just to check the buckets, once late at night and once about six in the morning. You don't want the predators to get to the salamanders before we do."

"You mean a fox might come along and scoop them out of the buckets," she said. "Like me with my spoon in the ice cream containers."

"Exactly like that," he said.

"What an operation. Did you figure all this out yourself?"

He shrugged. "Trial and error. And a little help from my herp friends up and down the coast. We naturalists keep in touch. All right, now it's time to put the dough in a bowl to rise."

"I don't want to. I love the way it feels." Her voice sounded dreamy as she turned the dough, pressed it, floured, turned again.

"If you play with it too long, the bread comes out tough," he said.

"How long does it rise?"

"An hour." He slid his arms around her from behind and lifted the dough away.

"No, don't take it away. It's mine, I'm going to miss it."

He kissed her cheek. "Don't worry, you'll get it back in an hour. Meanwhile, I'll keep you company."

"What do we do when it's risen?"

"Punch it down."

"Poor dough," she said as his hands slid up under her blouse and cupped her breasts. "What if I don't want to punch it?"

"Then it won't rise again," he murmured, grinding his hips into her backside.

"Dough isn't the only thing rising around here," she whispered. "I'm going to get flour on you."

"Feel free."

Later, when they had made love and rolled away from each other to stretch, Sam pulled her body back across the bed to him. He wanted their skin to touch in every possible place, from her head tucked against his shoulder to their legs twined around each other. She had grown restless in the last days. He could feel it.

"I wish you could come with me to the auctions," she said.

"I will if the major crossings are done. But I won't know until the last minute."

She pulled away a little to study his face. How would he feel in those big rooms, surrounded by designer clothes and the buzz of people trading shop talk? How would she feel to have him there?

"I called Woodworth today," she said. "He was surprised that the survey would be done ahead of schedule."

"He hasn't seen you at work the way I have. With a house to assess or a table to restore, you're a regular force of nature."

She propped herself up on one elbow. "And you don't like that?"

"The opposite. It turns me on to see all that fire in you."

"I'm going to have to leave soon, Sam. The calls have been coming in from clients."

He ran a single finger down over her naked breast. "I know that," he said. "And will you be back?"

"Of course, I'll be back. There's more furniture to ship out and—"

"I don't mean that," he said. "I want to know if you'll be coming back to me."

She put up her hands as if to ward him off. "Don't, Sam. Please don't—"

"You once told me the house in Philadelphia never really felt like home," he said quickly. He'd been stockpiling arguments. "It was just a place to stay between trips."

She rolled away from him and stared at the ceiling. "It's not that. I've lived my whole life traveling light and in this one winter, I've suddenly got so much baggage. The memories of Nan, her house with all its problems, the people on this island."

He got out of the bed and began to dress. "I thought of myself as more than baggage," he said coldly.

"That didn't come out right."

"Maybe that's why Nan left you the house," he said. "To teach you about baggage. It can be comforting. It can hold you to the earth and slow you down."

She closed her eyes.

"You told me once that Nan carried your history," Sam said.

"Exactly. And look what happened to Nan."

"She was seventy-three years old and she died." He leaned over close with a hand planted on either side of her shoulders and spoke in a barely controlled voice. "If you keep yourself so walled off from people, Maggie, just to be sure they don't leave you, then you'll miss out on everything. That's no way to live."

Her eyes popped open and she stared at him. "What if I don't know any other way," she said quietly.

"You and I have a history now. You don't build histories with people if you are always on the run."

"But how can I be sure?" she whispered.

"Of what?"

"Of you. Of myself. Of what will happen between us."

"You can't," he said as he straightened up and walked to the door. "It's as simple as that. You have to take a chance."

She dressed slowly and followed him downstairs. He had put her mound of dough out on the counter and was working on his. She slid her arms around his waist and rested her forehead against his back. She could feel the bumps of his spine through his cotton shirt. She could smell the faint scent of hot cloth from the iron he must have used this morning. She squeezed tighter, but he did not respond. She went cold with fear.

"Sam, let's go back upstairs."

"That might solve the problem for the moment, Maggie," he said without turning. "But not for long."

He punched his fist into the dough over and over again in a solid methodical way. When he had flattened his mound of dough and kneaded it into a neat pile, he started in on hers. She felt the muscles in his back roll up and down with each movement of his right arm and finally she let go and stepped back from him. This is how he will get over me, she thought. By concentrating fully on the task at hand, on whatever work is before him.

She hooked Kasha to her lead. The dog was slow, her way of questioning this change in pattern. They left the house by the front door. Maggie closed it quietly behind her.

Twenty-three

ON FRIDAY MORNING, Al paid off Billy and Chuck in cash as usual. Chuck put the envelope away without checking it, but Billy stood there and counted out the money one bill at a time.

"You're early, Al," he said. "That noon boat hasn't even blown yet."

"So you keep your end of the bargain," Al said.

"I have," Billy said. "Place is wired, Sheetrock is taped, and the paint is just about dry, isn't it, Chuck?"

Chuck was gathering up his tools, pretending not to hear the two men. He could feel the tension in the air as hard as a wall. You could have leaned against it if you had to.

"And you keep your mouth shut," Al said.

Billy shrugged and walked away. Chuck followed behind. They both knew Al liked to be left alone when the inspector came.

"So how bad is it?" Chuck asked as they loaded their trucks.

"You know how bad it is. It's the worst piece of shit job he's done and as usual, he's going to get away with it. It makes no goddamn sense to nickel and dime a job that way. He probably turns around and pays it all back to the inspector."

"I doubt it. Al always figures things the best way for himself."

Billy slammed the tailgate of his truck. "I'm taking Jimmy off island tomorrow. You're not going to catch me at that party."

"Why?"

"In case the whole thing goes up. Too much load on the system and it might even blow out the panel box. Running the fridge and all that electrical equipment for the band." He shrugged.

"We should tell people, then."

"What, are you suddenly getting all moral on me? Why the big change? You've heard me bugging him about the circuit breakers for weeks. And the junction boxes. He's counting on me to shut up because he paid me enough and because the asshole knows I need the money and I need the work." Billy took a step closer to Chuck. "And he's counting on you to keep your mouth shut too? You know why?"

Chuck grunted.

"Because you always have and you always will. That's why."

WHEN CHUCK WALKED into the Harbor Lounge Friday night, the place was in full swing. When the days grew longer, people started coming out of their houses, like animals out of hibernation. There was a lot of excitement about the party the next night. The women had taken over the community center the moment Al gave them the word, and they planned to be down there most of the night hanging the decorations. Al was sitting in the center of the crowd at the bar and his voice was louder than usual.

Chuck moved in quietly and took a seat at the end.

"Beer?" Jim Sullivan asked.

"Nope. Just a coke."

"You and Paul," Sullivan said. "Pretty soon we'll have to turn this into an AA meeting."

Chuck glanced at the trail of glasses scattered down the length of the bar. "I wouldn't worry about it, Jim. It won't be happening any time soon."

"Doctor told Paul he has to knock off the stuff. Some problem with his heart muscle. Other than that, the man seems fine. Right as rain. What's your excuse?'

"Don't have one," Chuck said. "Didn't think it was required."

Lila called for Jim and he moved to the other end of the bar to talk to her. The jukebox was playing "I Can't Get No Satisfaction" and everybody knew Randy Baker put that one on. It was his favorite song, and it meant he was starting to get over Ellie. Some of the men were riding Al about the Tremayne boys. Dan Chester straddled the bar stool next to Chuck.

"So, Al," Dan called, and the place quieted. "I see Billy Slade went off island this afternoon. Says he won't be back tomorrow for the party. How come?"

Al shrugged. "How the hell do I know? I don't baby-sit my workers. I've got enough trouble with Bo and Derry. Figure Billy's a grown man. He can handle himself."

"Bet he's gone to the casino," Henry Willard said.

"Bet he has," Al said, and gave Henry a friendly punch in the arm. "The man's got a serious problem with the tables. A worker like that you never pay until the end."

"I don't think he's gone off to gamble," Chuck said, his voice raised just loud enough to attract attention. "He took Jimmy with him."

"That doesn't mean anything," Al said, draining his glass. "From what I hear, he's taken that boy lots of places he shouldn't have."

"He told me he's never gonna let his boy in that community center," Chuck said and, head tilted back, finished off his Coke too. The room was still now, listening. The two men did not turn to look at each other, but stared straight ahead and talked to the air.

"Why'd he say that?" Paul asked from the other end of the bar.

"Because he did the wiring and he knows the place isn't safe."

"Shut up, Chuck," Al said in a low voice. "You're just a little chicken shit who doesn't know anything. Nobody wants to hear from you."

The bar stools scraped. Suddenly the song on the jukebox ended and the silence felt even bigger than before. The men on this island had never paid much attention to Chuck. They laughed at him behind his back and sometimes in front of him, and they handed him their tickets when they drove off the ferry as if he were some machine set up at the end of the boat ramp. The way the crowd was listening to him now felt good, better than any beer in his bloodstream.

"What are you talking about, Chuck?" Lila made her way up to his end of the bar. She was picking up glasses and refilling as she went.

"Well, if you start up on the roof, you'll find lousy shingles, no roofing paper, and the plywood is only half inch, not the three quarter that was in the specs. But that's not so bad. It'll probably hold up until the next hurricane."

"What about the wiring?" Randy asked from his place by the jukebox.

"I'm just telling you what Billy told me. Aluminum wire instead of copper, wrong gauge, no junction boxes, too many outlets and switches running off each breaker. He says with too much power going through there, the panel box could blow right out. And Lord knows, tomorrow night, that place is going to be hopping."

Al stood up. The swift snap of his legs tipped over his stool, but nobody moved to pick it up. He started to walk down the line toward Chuck.

"Funny that the building inspector didn't say anything," Al said. "This is his third trip over and he didn't find anything wrong."

Chuck was still staring at the mirror which hung above the cash register. Al was moving toward him, but he didn't turn around. All the years he'd been waiting for this, he knew what was coming now, but he didn't see any reason to offer Al his face.

"You've been paying off the inspector for years, Al," Chuck said. "We all know that."

Al turned then and looked at the others for a moment as if making up his mind about something.

"Are you all going to leave your cement asses on your stools and put up with this faggot? Let him dribble on like the drooling little fart that he is?"

Still nobody moved.

"What if he's telling the truth, Al?" Randy asked.

That question seemed to tip Al over the edge, and he went for Chuck, dragged him backward off his stool with one motion. But Chuck had been waiting for this move and he jabbed Al in the gut with his elbow just before he lost his balance. Al grunted in pain and doubled over Chuck, who came back up from the floor slamming punches at Al's skinny pale face while he had the chance. He hit like a boy, over and over again, flailing around, not waiting to time his punch or even aim it. Al put his hand up to shield his face and backed off a little, as if he intended to stand on the side and watch this display for a while. Chuck followed, still punching, a fist to the chest, one on the shoulder, another on the face. And then one came back. Just one perfectly timed punch that landed on Chuck's cheek, at the edge of the bone crater that held his eye. Chuck went down.

Lila'd had enough. She marched around the bar with her favorite weapon, the cast-iron frying pan she used for french fries, and stepped between the men. The pan was still hot, and scalding grease dripped off one side onto the wooden floor. She planted herself, one leg on either side of Chuck's body, and he scooted back, holding his face in one hand.

"Leave off, Al," Lila said. "Right now. You know my rules about fighting in the Lounge."

Al put his hands up in the air. "Hey, Lila, no way I'm messing with you and that frying pan. Looks like Mr. Montclair has learned his lesson anyway. It's a pity to keep beating up on a little bag of bones like that. How about it, Chuck? You finished telling lies for the night?"

Chuck used the wall beside the jukebox to help himself up. Once he was standing, he felt the eyes on him again. His head was pounding as if the blood was rushing to the eye on some kind of rescue mission. "They weren't lies, Al," he said. "You know that. I know that. And I bet I've got everybody here wondering."

"You okay, Chuck?" Paul asked.

"Yup. I'm okay. No thanks to any of you." He checked his face in the mirror above the bar. " 'Spect I'll have a black eye tomorrow. Same as Anna did a few weeks ago. Funny thing. You hang around Al too long and you're liable to get hurt."

Al was off the stool again, but Randy and Jim grabbed him by the upper arms and held him.

"Listen, Chuck," Dan asked. "If things was so bad up there at the hall, why didn't you warn us before?"

Chuck shrugged. "Because Al here is my boss and I need the work and—"

"And because you're a little chicken shit," Al said.

"He's right," Chuck said. "I'm a little chicken shit. But this time Billy Slade is worse than me. At least I warned you all."

"Get out of here, Chuck," Al snarled. "The sight of you makes me sick." The men were still holding on to him though they'd loosened their grip.

Chuck kept out of Al's reach on his way to the door. He turned back one last time. "Wouldn't take your kids to that party tomorrow night, boys. That is if you give more of a damn about your own flesh and blood than you do about mine."

AL WAS SITTING at Lauren's kitchen table when she got home from decorating the community center.

"This is a surprise. What happened to you?"

"Nothing," he said, grabbing her ass when she brushed past him. "Why do you ask?"

"I don't come home every night and find a man sitting in my kitchen."

"So tonight you're the lucky one," he said.

She dumped two shopping bags filled with green and white crepe paper on the table and stretched. "God, my shoulders hurt. I've been up that damn ladder for hours."

"I like a woman who isn't scared to wear tight jeans," he said, coming up behind her and taking the two cheeks of her ass in his hands. "Even when she shouldn't."

"What do you mean by that?"

"Nothing in particular. I don't remember you being so touchy, Miss Lauren Root. Root," he said again with a sharp laugh. "How would you like me to put my root inside you?"

"You know, Al, I'm really beat tonight."

"Yeah, well, so am I." His voice shifted into a snarl. "I've had a hell of a day if you want to know, so do us both a favor. Don't blow me attitude. I've had people giving me shit all day and I don't need to hear any from you." He was holding her hips and grinding his body against hers. "This feels good, doesn't it?"

"Not really," she said. "Stop it, Al."

"Goddammit, Lauren," he roared, and with one sweep of his hand, he cleared the kitchen table. The salt and pepper shakers flew off in one direction, but they were made of thick restaurant glass and rolled away intact. The bags sailed across the room and hit the near wall. Green and white paper unfurled haphazardly back toward them across the spotted linoleum. "What are you going to do, now? Run upstairs like my wife does and lock yourself in the bathroom?" He sank back into her kitchen chair and put his head in his hands. "Don't you start with me, Lauren. You have no right to start with me."

She took her time cleaning up the mess he had made. He went on mumbling to himself, rubbing his hands over his mouth so that she could not make out much of what he was saying. It wasn't just that she was tired. Sex energized her, recharged her battery. No, it was that the man sitting at her kitchen table revolted her. She liked men when they swaggered around, and cast their spinners far out beyond the surf, and drove their trucks too fast around corners so the lumber resting in back slid without warning from one side to the other. Al always used to be that kind of man. What was sitting at her kitchen table now did not bear looking at. Now he was blubbering about everybody turning against him. She cut him off. She didn't want to hear it.

"Al, you'd better go home now." She touched his shoulder and pulled quickly out of the way when he reached for her. "Go on. You'll feel better when you've gotten some sleep," and it was the nurse talking, not the sexy woman he was accustomed to, the one who went for his fly almost before the door had closed behind her.

When he stood up, his chair dug a shallow scrape in her new flowered wallpaper. She grimaced, but said nothing. Just get him out of here, she thought.

"Come on, Lauren," he said. "At least you can give me a kiss. There are lots of times you wanted to do more than that with me." He took her by the upper arms and began to pull her toward him, and then he saw that expression of disgust in her face, he saw her giving in just because she thought it would get rid of him faster. He had seen that look before from his wife. Too goddamn many times.

"Don't you look at me like that," he cried. First he tried to shake the look off her face, but it didn't change. She rattled around in his arms, her head bobbing back and forth, but she was still waiting for him to get it over with.

The saliva was rising in his mouth. He took a breath and spat at her before he pushed her away from him. The glob of spittle lodged on her cheek and began to slide slowly down toward her jawbone. She backed away from him, slapping at her cheek with her fingers to get it off until she could find the dish towel. She rubbed her skin hard, in that same spot, over and over again as if to wipe away some kind of contagion.

"Get out of here, Al. Don't you ever come back here again, do you hear me?" Her voice had dropped to a low warning growl and he backed away from her toward the door. "You are never going to get near me again. That's it, Al. You've gone over the edge. You're a pathetic, disgusting man. Do you hear that? You disgust—" He slammed the door on her words and slid across the crusty patches of snow to his truck.

AL ROAMED THE island all night. He checked his rental house and moved the various stashes of cash he kept there in the winter to different locations. He went through his office and made sure it was locked up tight. He drove by the doctor's house a couple of times, slowly, letting his lights sweep across the living room windows. Finally he came to rest for a while, parked across the street from Chuck's apartment on the second floor of an old beat-up fort house. The lights at Chuck's stayed on most of the night and once or twice Al saw a shadow cross from one side of the front room to the other. Probably putting more ice on that black eye of his, Al thought. Hope it hurts like hell, you little asshole. What in God's name got into you? When did you decide to become a big hero? Till the day you died, you were going to be a scared little man who would keep his mouth shut, a man who would be sure to run at the first sign of trouble. I could always count on you to tuck your tail between your short little legs and scuttle away. Like a crab. Now I can't even trust you to do that. What has gotten into everybody? First Anna and now Chuck. Even Lauren.

At five in the morning, Al drove his truck around to the community center. He parked it down the street near the firehouse, walked back, and let himself in through the kitchen. When he flicked the switches on the wall by the door, the blaze of lights blinded him for a minute and he blinked a couple of times to readjust. He switched the lights on and off a couple of times. They worked just fine. Slade was an asshole.

He strolled around the main room, checking the paint in places to see if it had dried. The women had outdone themselves. Green and white crepe paper, braided together, hung in big loopy trails from one side of the long low room to the other. The tables were set up with white paper tablecloths and big flowerpots stuffed with fake moss and cardboard shamrocks. The high school rock group was going to play, and they'd already begun to set up their equipment. Tangled wires were strewn about the floor, snaking their way between the speakers. It would be too loud, Al thought. He'd have to do something about that, as usual. What did they call themselves? Some ridiculous name like the Twisted Seagulls.

That damn Irish doctor would probably think this was all just for him. But the St. Patrick's Day party had been a tradition on the island for years. It was the last big time they had to celebrate before the summer people started to come back. By April, the Friday afternoon boat began to fill up with those suburban station wagons, wood-paneled cars loaded down with flats of perennial plants and brand new sporting equipment. The wives would come on the three-thirty, the men would bring the second car down for the late boat. We put on our summer faces, Al thought. Diane smiles at everybody in the post office, and by July, we're dodging blond kids in white tennis shorts. I've got to spend half my nights down at White Beach policing the teenagers' beach parties and fielding phone calls from worried parents up island who've just got in from a round of cocktail parties themselves to find their kids have taken the car and all the beer in the fridge. Never mind. They knew they could count on me. After these last few months, the summer people and their nonsense would be a relief. Lacey would be gone. He'd make sure Chuck moved on. He settled himself down at the edge of the main room with his back propped up against the south wall. I'll get things back to normal around here, he thought just before he dozed off.

ANNA AWOKE IN the middle of the night and stretched her legs cautiously, feeling for the warmth Al's body gave off and trying at the same time not to touch him. When she realized he was not in the bed, she started up and made her way across the hall, her heart pounding. Erin was sleeping, curled against the wall in a ball. Alone.

His truck was not in the driveway. Three in the morning. She crawled back into bed and lay awake for a while, listening for noises. The next time she opened her eyes, it was dawn and the dogs were starting to bark. Chuck was meeting her at the east end at six-thirty, a few minutes before they expected the hunters. Al was still not home, and she puttered about the kitchen quietly so as not to wake Erin. She let herself imagine for a moment that she was a woman living alone with her daughter. It was what she had dreamt about when she thought of them settled in some small town on the shores of Lake Erie. When you lived with a man who never left you alone, who slid down next to you on the bed when you kissed your daughter good night, who yanked open the bathroom door just when you thought you could breathe easy for a minute, who decided what you should eat and wear and say and think, you were always focused on what that man was going to do next. It was never safe to be simply a mother and a child spending time together, eating breakfast or watching a movie. You were always waiting, listening, holding your breath a little. No wonder Erin has asthma, Anna thought as she packed her daughter a sandwich for lunch.

MAGGIE WOKE EARLY Saturday morning. She'd spent the last few days preparing to leave. The survey had been mailed off to Woodworth with her final bill, and she'd called Jerry Slocum to tell him she wouldn't be able to continue the furniture repair course. Yes, the kids could certainly raffle off the table and chair they'd already finished.

She lay on her back in the middle of the double bed, her arms and legs spread like a snow angel, touching nothing but cool sheets. She hadn't seen or talked to Sam since she'd walked out of his house three days ago. It felt like weeks. So many times since that night she'd filed away some tidbit of news or an idle thought to tell him. And he wasn't there to tell. She longed to feel the palms of his hands against her cheeks, the teasing tickle of his skin, the whisper of his breath on her neck.

But whenever she closed her eyes to summon him up, all she could remember was the rigid wall of his spine turned away from her face, the rhythmic punch of his fist into the dough. What was it he had said so many months ago now about action being the only solution to despair. "Well, in that, we are alike, Sam," she said out loud as she kicked away the covers.

Home was Kasha, she told herself in the shower. Home was an airplane over the Atlantic. Home was the dim and musty storage basements of museums and the impersonal hotel suites that held no history for her. Home was contained inside the four walls of herself. It began and ended with her. It always had before. On the island, this winter, she'd let down her guard, and now it was coming back to haunt her, the way she always knew it would. If you cared too much about someone, you got hurt. It was as simple as that. She'd let Sam Matera get too close and she would have to pay for it.

She needed to get off this island, away from all the places where he might turn up. The school, the grocery store, the post office. And away from this house, from the navy blue bedroom, and the porch where they first met, and the battered kitchen table where they'd sat so many nights in the shadowy flicker of candlelight. She could put this house on the market in the spring after all. Why not? The furniture would be pretty much cleared out, and if Chuck didn't get to the roof, she could always drop the price and sell it with the leaks.

She pushed a chest in front of the dog door before she fed Kasha. The dog turned her nose up at the food and as soon as she saw the suitcases in the front hall, she whined and scratched to be let out. Maggie gave her a quick walk around the house on the check cord, then locked her inside again while she loaded two chairs into the car.

Chuck had come by the day before to help her with the Pembroke table.

"Didn't think you'd be going off so soon," he said.

"Auction season," she said.

"Well, you're going to miss the St. Patrick's Day party at the center. That's probably just as well."

She didn't ask what he meant by that. Now that she was trying to untangle herself from the island, it was better not to know what was going on.

"When will you be back?"

"I'm not sure," she said. "Can you take the other pieces in the workroom down to the morning boat on Monday? I've arranged for the shipper to pick them up on the other side that afternoon."

"Sure thing."

"Get one of the other men to help you and send me the bill. I don't want you hurting that knee."

"Think you'll make it back for the salamander walk? Sam is really in his element then. You wouldn't want to miss that."

"I doubt it, Chuck."

He didn't ask her any more questions after that.

The eight o'clock boat didn't take off for another hour and she could pull up at the last minute. Nobody else would be leaving the island, especially Saturday morning of the big St. Patrick's Day party.

Enough time to make herself some oatmeal.

ANNA WAS ON her way out of the driveway with Whistler and Daisy kenneled in the back of the station wagon and her new black hat on her head when Kasha came loping up the road.

"Damn," Anna said as she rammed the gearshift into park. Kasha trotted around to her side of the car and barked.

Anna opened the door and caught her by the collar. "What are you doing wandering around, you silly dog? Maggie was supposed to be keeping you in."

The husky shoved her head against Anna's hand.

"I can't leave you here for Al to find. I'm already late. Wish to God it wasn't Ben Murch waiting for me. All right, I'll help you in. You'd better behave yourself."

Kasha picked her way across to the passenger side of the seat where she curled up with her nose touching her tail. Her eyes rested on Anna, who took the turn onto the main road. In the back, the two vizslas stirred about in their cages at the sound and smell of Kasha, but they settled down with a word from Anna.

"Chuck can drive you home once Murch is out in the field," she said.

Kasha loved the motion of the car. She'd already closed her eyes.

MAGGIE HAD MADE the final trip to the car when she walked through the house calling for Kasha. There was no sign of the dog. Back in the kitchen, she got down on all fours and checked under the chest. It had been moved aside, only a few inches, but enough for the dog to get out. Kasha could flatten her body and squeeze under anything.

She walked around the house twice, calling. "Damn you, Kasha," she yelled. "Come here. You're not going to do this to me again."

She started down the road in the car with her window open, her breath making clouds in the cold air. The sound of her own voice came back to her, lonely and sad. It reminded her of the last time she'd done this with Sam. "Please, Kasha, please. I want to get away from here. Now that I've made up my mind to go, don't make me stay."

The ferry horn blew. The boat was pulling into the dock. She only had twenty minutes or so to get down there. If she missed this one, the next boat wasn't until noon.

She headed up to the Cravens'. The dogs in the kennel started barking at the sound of her tires in the driveway, but Kasha didn't appear. There were no lights in the house, no cars in the driveway. Probably down at the center already. Or at the Rocky Point for that first watery cup of coffee.

She turned the car around and sped down the island road as fast as she dared. Maybe the dog had circled back to the house.

"I'll give you until the noon boat and then I'm leaving without you, Kasha. This time I mean it."

BEN MURCH HAD brought only one friend this time, a short dark-haired man with a moustache who stood off to one side, his gun broken, a cigarette in his hand.

"Good morning, Mrs. Craven," Murch said. He insisted on calling her Mrs. Craven. Although she supposed he meant it as a mark of respect, it made her feel like a servant. "Is Montclair coming?"

"We agreed to meet up here. I expect he'll be along soon." But Anna was surprised. Chuck was usually early, always on time.

"What are you going to do with the husky?" Murch asked. "I don't want that dog riling up Whistler, throwing him off."

"Kasha's old and quiet. She won't bother us."

"I didn't know you owned a husky."

"It's a friend's dog," she said as she lifted the tailgate of the car and released Whistler. He jumped down and circled eagerly, trying to pick up the scent of pheasant. Murch greeted the dog, ran his hand over its rump. Whistler took off in one direction and Anna whistled him back. She slung the bag for birds over one shoulder, adjusted the pistol in her holster.

"What's that for?" Murch asked.

"I'm trying to break a dog who's shy of gunshot."

"Hard to change those habits."

"Yes, it is. Okay we're ready to go when you are."

They moved out into the field. In the car Kasha pulled herself up and peered through the front window watching Whistler. She barked once, then again. Shooter jumped up in his kennel and joined in.

Anna dropped back to the car. "Down, Kasha," she ordered. The dog glanced at her briefly, then back at the field. She settled down on the seat. "Stay," Anna said, and moved up again.

Still no Chuck. She hoped he'd remembered to put the birds out this week. His absence this morning was so out of character that she wondered. What a joke that would be, she thought, and allowed herself a smile. Ben Murch out here chasing after nothing but wild birds left behind by the less aggressive hunters.

Murch tossed a handful of grass up to find the wind. "Get on," he said, and at the command, Whistler began to cast from side to side, nose to the ground.

Twenty-four

Five men pulled into the driveway of the center within minutes of each other. Seven A.M., Paul Thayer had said on the phone. They got out of their trucks, slammed the doors, and nodded to one another, slapping their arms and cursing the weather. A front had moved in overnight, and the temperature had dropped back into the twenties after a couple of spring days. Randy Baker brought coffee and the hot steam from his cup made a cloud in the air. Jerry Slocum pulled a crowbar out from under the front seat of his car. Gus Tremayne and Jim Sullivan were both carrying toolboxes. When they had assembled themselves, everybody stopped for a moment and looked at Paul.

"So, Paul," Jim said. "I hope this is a good idea."

"I'm game," Gus said. "I don't trust Craven as far as I can spit. He'd cheat his own mother if it put money in his pocket."

"You know what I told you all on the phone this morning," Paul said. "We're just making sure. We'll open up an outlet or two and look for junction boxes. If there's any problem there, we'll move on to the panel box. Somebody can go on up and check the roof. It's easy to lift a shingle and see about roofing paper without disturbing too much. Doctor says I've got to take it easy so I'm going to let you guys do any heavy work."

"How about the studs?" Gus asked.

"One thing at a time," Paul said. They nodded in agreement. "All right," he said. "Let's go."

AL AWOKE TO the sound of car doors slamming and voices. For a moment, he couldn't remember where he was. His back was stiff and his throat dry and sore from the paint fumes. It must be the women, he told himself. They were certainly starting early. He struggled to his feet and was leaning against the wall, running a hand through his hair when the front door opened.

The men filed in one after the other and stood around gaping at the decorations. It took them a minute to notice him.

"What's this?" Al said.

They didn't answer for a minute.

"Hey, Al, " Jim finally said to fill the silence. "You guarding the place?"

"Looks like I need to."

Paul stepped forward. "Al, listen, we've been discussing this thing and we're just going to make sure that everything's done right here. You know, we've all got kids and Chuck's talk last night got us thinking."

Al ignored him. "So, Jerry, what are you planning to do with that crowbar?"

"Open up a wall here or there."

"That's going to look real pretty for the party tonight," Al said.

"We don't give a shit whether it looks pretty or not." Gus put down his toolbox and flipped the latch. "Let's just say we've appointed ourselves inspectors for the day."

"If everything's fine, we'll put it back together ourselves," Randy Baker said. "You can't have any problem with that."

"We all know why you're doing it, Randy," Al said. "You've been gunning for my job all winter."

Randy shrugged. Mr. Woodworth had been in touch with him a couple of times.

"Hey, Al, if there's nothing wrong behind these walls, what's your problem with us looking?" Paul asked.

They had him. They knew it and Al knew it too. "So long as you clean up the mess behind you. My bid didn't include people coming in and ripping open the walls once I was signed off on the job."

Gus told Jerry Slocum to find the breaker box and cut the electricity. Randy handed out the tools and the men spread out along the walls to the various outlets.

"We'll do one at a time," Paul said. His voice echoed in the high rafters. "That way we make as little mess as possible."

"You're going to look like fools when you try to explain this to the women tonight," Al said. But nobody paid him any attention. Suddenly, they were acting as if Al wasn't even there.

"Electricity's off," Jim called from the kitchen.

Jerry took a screwdriver to one of the switch plates.

"Listen, boys, I may have cut a few corners here and there," Al said, talking fast. "Nothing bad. Nothing dangerous. It was Billy's fault, really. He was taking so damn long and you guys were all over me to finish this thing. Once the party's over, we can fix it up."

The men waited. Nobody noticed Al, who had started backing toward the kitchen door. Jerry dug around some more. "No junction box here. Gus, come look at this wiring. I can't tell one gauge from another."

The men gathered around Jerry while Gus pulled a couple of wires out from the wall. "Sixteen gauge," Gus said after a while. "It should be twelve."

"Al's gone," Jim said. "Out the kitchen door."

"All right," Paul said. "Let's open up one or two more outlets to be sure. Gus, take a look at the wiring from that breaker box. Jim, you get the ladder off my truck and go check the roof."

Dennis Lacey was not surprised when Lauren left him a message that she wouldn't be in the clinic that morning. He figured that as head of the decorating committee for the big party, she had other things on her mind. He unlocked the door to the waiting room at nine. Miss Yola was the first to arrive. She needed a prescription refilled and had lost the original bottle. He'd teased Miss Yola all through the year about taking business away from him. There were some people on the island who would go to her for her root tea long before they'd come to him. She liked flirting with him.

"Could you come back Monday, Miss Yola," he said. "I hate to go through Lauren's desk. She knows where everything is."

"I suppose so. I've got a few pills left. I was downtown so I thought I'd stop in. Lauren's going to be busy today."

"She was hoping to finish that decorating last night," Dennis said. "I guess that was impossible."

"Oh, you haven't heard," Miss Yola said, and her eyes widened. "The party's been moved back to the church basement."

"Why?"

That hooded look dropped over her face, the one Dennis was so familiar with. The island people keeping their own secrets. It was warring with her desire to be the first with the story. She decided to tell.

"Paul Thayer went over to the community center this morning. Broke into the walls. Lifted some shingles off the roof. Things are not up to code. The place is a firetrap."

"I hope Paul Thayer didn't do any heavy lifting. I warned him to take it easy."

"He took a bunch of the men with him."

"So who's responsible? Billy Slade?" Dennis stopped. "No, of course not," he said as the full irony of the situation hit him. "Al Craven. The sheriff."

"So, they're looking for volunteers to move the tables back over to the church. And redecorate. We've got to take everything down and put it back up again."

"Maybe the party should be put off till next weekend."

"I don't think so," Miss Yola said as she picked a piece of lint off the shoulder of her dark coat. "Would be bad luck. We'll manage. The island always pulls together at times like this. Lauren's already over at the church. I'm going there now."

"Can I give you a ride?"

"Don't be silly." The church was just up the hill from his office. "You stay here and doctor. I'll be fine. It's good for me to move this old body around."

When Sam showed up to open the museum, he was surprised to see Erin waiting for him on the steps.

"Hi," she said, looking as if she'd been sitting there every Saturday morning since the fall.

"Hello you. You're early. Did you bike down?"

"I hitched. It's too cold to bike. It gets my asthma going."

"You should have called me. I would have come to get you. Your mother must be up island with the hunters."

"Last weekend until next October. I think she's glad. She doesn't like the shooting part. Just the training."

"Me too. I don't like the shooting part either. But she knows that." Sam hunched his shoulders in his jacket. "I don't like the way this cold weather has come back. It's going to put off the salamanders."

"The maculatum," Erin said as she trailed him inside. She loved the sound of the Latin names. "They'll go back under their rocks and wait some more."

"That's right."

The museum smelled musty, the way it always did in the winter. Summertimes, when it was open three afternoons a week and all day Saturday, the breeze aired it out a little. The phone started ringing as soon as Sam flicked on the lights.

"It was ringing before," Erin said. "I heard it when I was waiting."

Sam took the call in his office while Erin set her backpack down at the front desk. She lifted the set of keys off the board and opened up the two back rooms, the one on the history of the island and the other on the archaeological digs carried out in the last five years. Erin had never been on one of those digs, but two years ago she'd found a harpoon tip made from a swordfish bone. She'd been over at the Malloys' playing with Nina the day they were digging up the septic tank. The backhoe turned over a big pile of white shells, and they had called in Mr. M. He'd said it was a shell midden, a kind of garbage heap, where the Mohegan tribe had thrown away the things they didn't want anymore. Mr. M. had been very impressed with her find, and she remembered the adults gathering around to turn the bone over in their hands. The archaeologist from the mainland had told her later that it was an extremely rare artifact from the Middle Archaic period. She was the first human to have touched it in six thousand years. She'd been mad she couldn't keep it. It sat here now in the corner glass case next to some arrowheads. At least her name was printed on the label.

The exhibits were covered with dust. She found the rags under the counter in the front room, gave herself a shot with the inhaler, and began to clean.

"It's pretty bad, isn't it?" Sam said from the door of the room. "I haven't kept up with the housekeeping. Been too busy with other things. The ospreys will be coming back any day now, so I've been watching their nests. The seals are getting active. And I'm way behind on the herp atlas cards. There's a whole pile of them on my desk. I'm glad you came in, Erin."

She kept on dusting, her back to him.

"How have you been?" he asked.

"Fine. I'm writing stories on the typewriter now," she said. "Maggie gave it back to me."

"Good for you. You've always gotten good marks in English, haven't you?"

"I'm not going to hand these stories in. I don't want anybody to read them. Just me."

"I understand," Sam said. "I won't tell anybody."

"Not even Maggie."

"No, not even Maggie."

Throughout this whole conversation, Erin continued to talk to the glass case, and Sam was not eager for her to turn around now. He didn't want the conversation to come to rest on Maggie. Apparently, she'd told Jerry Slocum that she wouldn't be able to teach the Tech Ed class in the spring term after all. Sudden work assignments. And Woodworth had called Sam to say how pleased he was with the architectural survey. She was wrapping up all the loose ends.

So many times in the last three days he'd had to talk himself out of calling her. Signs of spring were popping out everywhere. The wintering finches had begun to sing and yesterday, when he was stacking wood, he'd spotted a long-tailed weasel, its white winter coat already tinged with brown. The otters were fishing in Beach Plum Cove, and he'd heard the male and female barred owl calling to each other near the nesting box in the wilderness preserve. There was so much Sam wanted to show her.

He was grateful to the spring for distracting him. Some nights he was out until two A.M. with the Q beam, patrolling the road for spring peepers and the very first toads, the earliest crossers. If Maggie had been sitting up in bed waiting for him, her curly hair falling across her pale freckled shoulders, he would never have been able to make himself stay out so late.

Erin reached into the back of the case and picked up her harpoon bone to dust.

"Can you hold down the fort here for an hour or so," he said. "They're looking for people to help move the tables back up to the church basement."

"The party's not going to be at the community center?" At this piece of news, Erin turned around.

"Apparently not. Some problem with the wiring." He left it at that. Gus Tremayne had filled him in on the real story, but there was no reason to tell Erin.

CHUCK HAD TO have put out the birds because by noon, Murch and his buddy had bagged twelve pheasants. Whistler performed well, and the owner was pleased with his behavior, but Anna was distracted. Twice, she'd had to return to the car to quiet Kasha, whose howling had stirred up Daisy. Where in God's name was Chuck?

"Mrs. Craven, we're going to break early for lunch," Murch said. "We'll expect to start again at one-thirty sharp."

"Will you want to work with Whistler again?"

"Let's try that new young dog. But bring Whistler back. And for God's sake, get rid of that husky."

Anna kenneled Whistler and took off first.

"Kasha, my girl, you and men have a problem. You're going to have to do something about this." Kasha was sitting up now, her snout out the window, her head turned to catch the smells. Anna was taking the curves in the road a little faster than usual and the dog had to constantly re-adjust her footing to the swerves of the car. "I'm going to water these two in the back and then get ahold of Maggie. Damn her and Chuck. What in God's name is going on on this island? Where is everybody?"

She turned into the driveway and her eye went first to the place where Al always parked his truck. He's not here, she thought, with the same rush of relief she'd felt hundreds of times before. Those few extra minutes before she had to go back on guard always felt precious to her.

She watered all three dogs, kenneled the two vizslas, and put Kasha on a short check cord while she went inside to the bathroom and the phone. If she couldn't raise Chuck or Maggie, Anna would have to drive the dog back down island herself. And she didn't have that much time.

LATER, WHEN SHE was going over it again and again in her mind, she wondered whether the flushing of the toilet covered some noise he'd made. But then she remembered the door of the truck standing open and the motor still running with the gearshift rammed in park, and she wondered that she'd heard him at all. She didn't hear him, she told herself. She had sensed him the way an animal feels danger, the way she always knew in her gut when Al was close by. Kasha's howl was the first noise she heard, and that took her outside on the run.

He was standing on the far side of the dog, and he'd already hit her once, maybe twice. The piece of fresh milled lumber was raised over his head again. Kasha had backed off as far as the check cord would allow her to go. She was crouched and snarling, her back to Anna, her fur standing straight up all the way from her tail to her neck.

"You goddamn, mother-fucking wolf."

Anna drew the pistol and shot into the air. When Al looked up, she said his name once and her voice was calm, sure, instructive. The teacher's voice. "Get away from her right now."

"The hell I will."

She took three steps closer to Kasha with the pistol held out in front where Al could see it very clearly. He watched as she flipped open the barrel and shook the blanks out onto the ground. Slowly, he lowered the piece of wood until it dangled from one hand.

"What are you doing?" he asked.

She didn't answer, but slipped the live bullets from the left-hand pocket of her jeans into the carriage and flipped it closed with her thumb. She took another step now with both hands on the pistol.

"You wouldn't dare," Al said. "You wouldn't dare shoot me."

"Get away from the dog, Al."

"Anna, you're crazy," he said. "You've gone nuts."

She didn't bother to answer.

At that moment, Kasha lifted her head and howled again, and Al jumped the way he always did at sudden sounds. "You fucking bitch," he screamed, and he swung the piece of wood in a wide arc so it caught the dog in the right leg and she went down, nose into the dirt. All Anna had time to do before she pressed the trigger was to lower the gun from his chest to somewhere below his waist. She did not know where the bullet had gone until Al grabbed for his right thigh and crumpled slowly, tumbling over himself, screaming in a high-pitched wail, a sound she had never heard a human make before. As Anna ran for Kasha, she saw that he was not hurt so bad that he couldn't roll himself away until he was out of the dog's reach.

It was her fault, she thought. That last slam with the wood. She should have shot Al earlier. She should have.

Dennis Lacey was closing the clinic for the day when the phone rang, and he hesitated before answering it. What if this was Louise Grimes wanting him to come check her father yet again? He'd been there twice this week. It would just mean another useless trip to the peninsula, where the old man would be sitting up in his rocking chair with the afghan around his shoulders, eyes on the television. "Well, his breathing sounded funny," Louise would say.

He picked up the phone. "Clinic."

"It's Anna," the other voice said. "You'd better come quickly."

"What's wrong?"

"Kasha's here and she's badly wounded."

"I'm not a vet, Anna."

"I know that. But you can sedate her so we can move her. We'll need the ambulance boat. And Al is hurt too."

"Al?"

"I shot him."

DENNIS WAITED UNTIL he was making the turn into the Cravens' driveway before he put out the call for the EMTs. He knew right then that he was thinking of saving Anna, that he cared more about keeping her out of trouble than anything else. The only way he'd be able to do that was to be the first witness on the scene.

He found her crouched over Kasha, bathing the dog's wounds with water. The dog appeared to be dead, and Dennis knew she must be in pretty bad shape because if she had any strength, she wouldn't allow a human being near her. Not even Anna or Maggie. Al was sitting up a few yards away, screaming at his wife, a string of curses hooked together like a chain. He was holding his leg in both hands the way you would hold a log you are about to throw into the fire and every so often, he looked down at himself and began to rage again. Dennis approached him carefully. He took off his jacket and made a pillow for the man.

"Lie back, Al. I need to take a look at that."

Al rotated himself around by digging the boot on his good leg into the dirt and pivoting on his rear. "She's crazy, you can have her if you want to, Doctor. I don't want her for another minute."

"Anna," Dennis said. "The others will be here soon."

She lifted her head and looked across the dirt-packed distance between them. "It's my fault," she said in a clear, quiet voice.

"Crazy bitch," he yelled at her over his shoulder. "You and that dog should be locked up together."

"If I had shot him sooner, then he wouldn't have gotten Kasha that second time—"

"Give me back that gun, you bitch," Al raved. "You took it from me. You couldn't hit a tree at five feet."

"What are you saying, Al?" Dennis asked.

"I was cleaning it for her," Al croaked. "This woman can't even clean her own pistol. I always do it for her. Damn thing went off."

Dennis crossed over to Anna.

"You have to sedate her," Anna said. "Before we move her."

"I will. Where is the gun?" he asked.

She nodded at it, but with her hands cradled around Kasha's head, she made no move toward it. The dog's eyes were closed. The rag in the bowl next to Anna was red with blood.

Dennis leaned over and picked it up. He wrapped the pistol in the extra folds of his wool sweater and tried to wipe off the prints. Would there be an investigation? Did he dare give Al the gun to get his fingerprints on it? Should he unload it or would that make things worse? His head was spinning.

"Bring that over here," Al croaked.

"I'll keep it for now," Dennis said as he slid the pistol carefully into his pocket. "Don't want anybody else hurting themselves." The firehouse whistle had started up and the first truck was already careening into the driveway. By the time Dan Malloy loped over to them, Dennis was ripping Al's pant leg apart.

"We'll need a Sager splint," Dennis said without looking at the other man. Al put his head back on the doctor's jacket and closed his eyes. The pain seemed to be registering at last.

"The ambulance is on its way," Dan said. He had hunched down behind Al's head and was already wrapping a blood pressure monitor around the man's upper arm.

Dennis found a small hole in the upper thigh, some swelling at the site, already some bruising. It looked as if the femur might have shattered. A pin would be needed. "Can you feel this, Al?" He pressed various places on his foot and the pulse under his ankle bone. Al nodded. "And here?" Al nodded twice more. "Good."

"What happened?" Dan asked.

"Shooting accident. Al was cleaning Anna's pistol and it went off."

"Jesus, Al," Dan said.

"Hell of a thing," he muttered, his eyes still closed. Dennis was sure he knew what Dan was thinking. Anna's pistol was normally filled with blanks. Where'd the live ammo come from?

"What's wrong with the dog?" Dan asked the doctor, and their eyes met for the first time.

"Not sure yet," Dennis replied. "I'm dealing with the humans first. We're going to need the ambulance boat."

"Paul's already down there revving it up."

"Somebody has to call Maggie Hammond," Anna said, and the two men turned in the same instant to look at her. "Right away."

Two more cars came up the driveway, and there was the sound

of slamming doors. In the island tradition, the first on the scene issued the orders. "Call Maggie Hammond," Dan yelled over his shoulder to Jerry Slocum. "Tell her to meet us at the boat. Her dog's been hurt. Where's the ambulance?"

"It's coming," Jerry said. "Henry's driving."

By now the cars were piling up at the end of the driveway, so Gus Tremayne appointed himself traffic cop to make sure there would be enough room for the ambulance to get through. In the distance, they could hear the wail of its siren as it made its way up from the garage behind the firehouse. A couple of men gathered around Al and stared down at him. Dennis left him and went over to Anna. He judged the body weight of the dog to be about forty pounds and gave Kasha a shot in the rump. At the prick of the needle, she lifted her head and growled weakly, but settled down soon enough.

"Anna," Dennis said, hunched down close to her. "In a minute we can lift her onto a stretcher. Are you all right?"

Anna looked him directly in the eye. "Yes," she said. "I know what I've done if that's what you mean. I'm not temporarily insane. I shot my husband because he was beating an innocent dog that I had tied up. I could have killed the man, but I lowered the gun just in time. That sounds pretty sane to me. How about you?"

"Have you heard what Al is saying?"

"Of course."

"Just let him say it for now. Off island. In the hospital. You were in the house. You didn't see anything. You heard the gun go off."

She seemed to be weighing his words.

"Anna, you have Erin to think about."

This registered. She nodded. "Chuck never showed up this morning," she said. "Someone needs to go down and check on him."

"He and Al got into a fight at the Lounge last night. From the tales I've heard, Chuck has a bad black eye. He's probably nursing his pride and his face at the same time."

"I don't care. I need him to cover the dogs. Someone's got to explain things to those two hunters up island. Erin's in the museum with Sam. Ask someone to drive Miss Yola down there to be with Erin."

"Of course. If Sam's got his radio on, he will have heard the call come in. I'm sure he's covering. Most of the men were moving the tables from the community center back over to the church."

"Why?"

"Long story." Dennis got to his feet and motioned to the men to bring another stretcher.

"It isn't the first time we took a dog over on the boat," Henry Willard said as he and Jerry lifted the sedated husky.

"I'm glad you put her to sleep, Doc," Jerry said. "I've seen those teeth. Wouldn't want them sunk into my forearm."

"She won't bother you now."

Anna walked ahead to get into the ambulance. Al had already been slid inside, but she waited until Kasha was settled back there too before she got in the front seat. Dennis would ride in the back with the two patients. In the boat there would be more room.

THE RADIO CRACKLED again. Sam was waiting for more news before he told Erin anything. He had set her to work in the historical room filing newspaper clippings. It was as far away from all the noise as he could put her. So far she seemed oblivious to the goings-on, even with the wail of the siren a while ago.

"Port Six to Port Seven. Sam, come in." It was Randy Baker's voice.

"I'm listening."

"We've been trying to raise Maggie Hammond, but nobody can find her. Have you got any idea where she is?"

"Nope." He didn't offer any more information.

"All right. We're not going to hold the boat any longer. Anna will make sure her dog gets to the vet over there. We've already put in a call to him, and Lacey will take Al into the hospital. Somebody's driving Miss Yola down to help you with Erin. Then I think you'd better find Miss Hammond and let her know about the dog."

"What do I tell her? What in God's name went on up there?"

They both knew everybody on the island with a radio was listening in. There was a long pause and Sam was about to press his talk button again when Randy's voice came across, slow and thoughtful.

"For now, just tell her the dog had an accident. We'll sort the rest out later."

Twenty-five

ERIN KNEW SOMETHING was wrong the moment Mr. M. appeared in the doorway with Miss Yola right behind him. She looked at their faces, first one and then the other.

"What happened?" she asked in a calm voice that reminded Sam of her mother.

"Your father's had an accident," Miss Yola said as she crossed the room to where the girl was sitting. "He was cleaning the pistol your mother uses to train the dogs and it went off. He's all right, but your mother and the doctor have taken him over in the boat to the mainland hospital."

"They may not be back tonight so you're going to spend the night with Miss Yola."

"Who shot him?" Erin asked.

"Nobody," Miss Yola said. "The gun went off."

"Was my mother there?"

Sam and Miss Yola looked at each other. "We're not sure who was there at the time, Erin," Sam said at last. "But she's with your father now. On the boat."

"Would you like to come on home with me now?" Miss Yola asked. Erin had turned back to the pile of clippings.

"Not yet," she said. "The museum doesn't close until five."

Sam drew Miss Yola into his office. "Can you stay with her? I've got to try and find Maggie. I know she must be out looking for Kasha."

"Certainly. You carry a chair into that room for me and I'll just settle myself down."

"What do you think went on up there?"

"I think Anna shot him," Miss Yola said, keeping her voice low. "She's good with that pistol. Very accurate. And the man certainly deserved a bullet in his leg, if not some other places. You heard what happened at the Lounge last night?"

Sam nodded.

"Apparently he showed up at Lauren's house afterwards. She said she threw him out."

"And the center," Sam said. "Sounds like Al went over the edge."

"Certainly does. Now maybe this island will shut him down. The man is a menace, but you know it don't count so much when it's just women he's hassling. Men are never going to stop beating up on women until the other men don't put up with it anymore." She shrugged. "But you know that."

"Al was pretty stupid to waste our money," Sam said. "After all the years it took this island to raise it . . ." his voice trailed off.

"Nobody ever pretended Al Craven was a particularly smart man. Thank God. If he'd been smarter, he'd have covered his tracks better and we might have been stuck with him for even longer. Now we have to make sure he leaves all of us alone. Especially Anna and that girl."

"Erin seems calm," Sam said.

"Wouldn't you be? She's got this one night when she's not going to have to be sitting upstairs in her room waiting and listening. For something bad to happen, someone to start another fight. At least now it's happened. For this one day, the waiting is over."

You sound like you know what you're talking about, Sam thought.

"Go on and do your job. I don't envy you telling that girl her dog's been hurt."

"I don't either."

"Just make sure somebody comes back for us. I need to get home to my own baby dog before too long."

"I'll put the word out on the radio."

It took him a while to find her. Randy Baker called on the radio to say her car had been spotted, half off the road by the wilderness preserve.

"She didn't take the time to park it any which way," Baker's voice said. "The back's all filled with stuff. Looks like she's taking a trip."

"Where are you now?"

"Coming down island just east of the driving range. Had to find those hunters Anna was working with. They were pretty burned up. Assholes."

You're closer to the preserve than I am, Sam thought. Why don't you tell her? But he knew they were counting on him to give her the news, keep her calmed down. God knows what she would do when it dawned on her what had really happened, what none of them was saying out loud. In his rampage, Al had messed with everybody. Women and children, men, dogs. He checked his watch. Forty-five minutes till the next boat.

"She's going to want to get to Kasha as soon as she can, Randy. See if Dan will hold that three-thirty boat for us."

"Done." And a second later, "Good luck, Sam. Don't let her go off all half cocked."

I know the message I'm supposed to be getting across to her, Sam thought. You don't need to remind me.

MAGGIE WAS TRYING to be methodical, but she couldn't remember now which path she had taken when she first came into the preserve. Did she turn left or right to go around the pond?

A while ago she'd heard the wail of a siren. Back in Philadelphia, she didn't even think twice when the sirens went off. Last fall when she first arrived, the noon whistle, the fire alarm, and the ambulance had all sounded the same to her, but now she knew the difference. This siren followed the noon whistle by only a few minutes and it had to be the ambulance itself, because it was moving up island. Who could it have been? Maybe old Wilfred Hines finally collapsed. Or that girl, the waitress in the Rocky Point who looked as if the baby was going to pop out of her any minute, maybe she'd gone into labor. Within minutes, everybody with radios would know. Some of them would already be gathered down at the yacht club dock where they kept the ambulance boat. Some would be there to help, others to look. She caught herself wanting to know too.

"Oh, Christ, Kasha, come on now." Her voice was hoarse from calling out, so she clapped and whistled for a while. One more turn before she went back to check with Anna Craven again. Then she heard a voice calling her name. It was Sam, and she yelled back her location.

He came up quietly, the way he always moved in the woods. She was expecting him from one direction, but he surprised her with a tap on the shoulder from the other. She jumped and turned.

"Sorry."

"I thought you were coming from there," she said.

"Path I know. It cuts across the bottom end of the little pond."

They were looking at each other out of the corners of their eyes. How could you feel so comfortable with a body and then between one day and the next, you flip to these careful words and hooded looks?

"Your car's all packed."

"Kasha's missing. I was trying to make the early boat and now I've missed the noon."

"We found her," Sam said. "Come with me." He took her by the hand and led her back toward her car.

"Where is she? Where'd you find her?"

How to say this, he wondered. He'd been practicing, but nothing sounded right. "She's with Anna, actually. Over on the mainland. If we hurry, you can probably catch the three-thirty. Good thing it's Saturday. Extra boats."

"The mainland? What?"

"Anna found her hurt and took her on the ambulance boat."

"Oh my God, how bad is she?"

"The doctor has sedated her and they've both gone over with her. We've been looking everywhere for you."

He glanced back to see how she was doing and saw a look of such despair and terror in her eyes that he stopped his headlong rush down the path for a moment and pulled her against him as if holding her would shut down that look. He felt her body let go and melt against him, but only for an instant. Then she twisted away to get a good look at his face.

"What happened to her?"

He wanted to lie. But he knew that soon enough she'd find out whatever the truth was and there'd been enough lying already.

"I don't honestly know, Maggie, but from the sounds of it, she had a run-in with Al."

Without another word, she broke away from him and began to sprint for the car. He kept up with her and at the last minute he ducked around her and slid into the driver's seat.

"Get in the other side," he said. "I know every curve on this road. I've told them to hold the boat, but Dan can't keep it waiting forever."

She looked as if she was going to argue, then changed her mind and scrambled into the passenger seat. She reached out to pull the door closed as he made the U-turn. The slam of her door caught a handful of dried winter brush and ripped it away from its roots as the back wheels splayed sideways, then found their grip.

He slid the radio off his belt with his free hand. "Portable Seven to Port Six. Come in, Randy."

"I'm listening."

"Get down to the ferry will you, and try to convince Dan to hold that boat. I've got Maggie and we're headed down the island road. We'll be there in fifteen minutes."

"I'll do my best."

Sam lay the radio on the seat between them.

"I'll kill him," she said. "Don't let me near Al Craven ever. I'll take a gun and shoot him."

"Sounds like Anna already has," he said in a quiet voice, his eyes glued to the road.

"What?"

"Dennis Lacey took them both over. Al Craven with a bullet in his leg on one stretcher and Kasha on the other."

"Is Anna all right?"

"From what I hear."

"And Erin?"

"She was with me. She's very calm, almost as if she'd been expecting something like this. I've left Miss Yola with her so I could find you."

"That poor kid."

"By the way, nobody's talking about what really happened. Al says he was cleaning Anna's pistol and it went off. That's the official story."

"He what? Why?"

"I expect that after the mess down at the center and Anna running away from him, you know, he just couldn't face it. Face everybody knowing that his own wife had put a bullet through his leg."

"What about the community center?"

He took his eyes off road for a moment to glance at her. "You've been out of the loop, haven't you?"

"Lost my best source," she said, staring straight ahead. Her arm was braced on the dashboard to steady herself for the sharper curves.

He took the road past the Catholic church and the left-hand turn that wound around the edge of the golf course and White Beach.

All the while, he told her as much as he knew about Chuck and the fight in the bar and what the men had found out when they poked a few holes in the walls of the center that morning.

"What will come of all this?" she asked.

"Al is finished here. I expect they'll make Randy Baker the sheriff. And figure out a way to make Al pay for redoing the center. That shouldn't be hard. We all know he's got the money. He owns a rental house down by the ferry. Wouldn't be surprised if we move him in down there. Have it fixed up real nice when he gets home from the hospital. He's an island man. The family's been here for at least three generations."

"You mean they'll never kick him off the island," she asked.

"No. But he might move of his own accord. After a while. It won't be much fun living here like a ghost."

"And what about Anna? And Erin?"

"I expect he'll leave them alone after this. Wouldn't you? Your wife has shot you in the leg and the whole island is watching you."

"And nobody will press charges. Not Chuck or Anna."

"Maggie, Al is the one who would be pressing the charges. He was the one who was shot."

"Or me," she said coldly. "Kasha was hurt too."

He kept his eyes on the road.

"And what about all of you?" she asked. "You're the ones he robbed."

"We'll get our center. We have our own way of taking care of things." He made the last turn by the school and raced down the road the wrong way, honking his horn. The boat was still there, but the metal ramp had been hoisted. Chuck waved and drew a circle in the air indicating that Sam should line the car up to back on. "They managed to hold the boat for you," Sam said. Chuck trotted up to the window. His eye was purple.

"Take it straight back till I tell you something different."

"That's quite a shiner you've got there," Sam said. "You should be proud of it."

"I am," Chuck said. He ducked his head in the window. "Anna called, Maggie. She's with Kasha at the vet." He handed her a piece of paper. "I wrote down the directions."

"How is she?" Maggie asked.

"Hanging in there," Chuck said. "She's a tough old dog, that Kasha. She'll pull through." But they all knew he was talking more out of wishful thinking than information.

Maggie put her hand over her mouth and fought to keep the tears back from her face at least until she was alone. They came anyway. Embarrassed, Chuck dropped back to his usual directing position, and Dan Chester barely gave him time to get the car backed against the port bulkhead when he ordered the crew to raise the ramp and cast off.

"You're coming with me?" Maggie asked Sam.

"I was planning on asking if that's what you wanted. Either way it looks like I'm getting a ride on the ferry."

The boat steamed out between the two rows of pilings. As it hit the swells of the open water, the deck rocked gently under them. They didn't get out of the car. Maggie couldn't face anybody. "I hate this place," she whispered. Now her tears were running down over her hand, which was still clamped over her mouth, and Sam searched through his pockets for any decent Kleenex or rag, but came up with nothing. He finally found a mashed tissue box under her front seat and handed it to her.

"You're just as guilty if you stand on the side and watch, you know," she said. "Let things happen to people and dogs and buildings and you don't step in and do something to change them."

He didn't answer, didn't try to stop her. Like her tears, he figured this all needed to come pouring out of her.

"This damn island is so scared. Every one of you is scared that something or somebody will come over here from the mainland and ruin your little paradise. Some paradise. People get beaten up and nobody does anything." She screamed these last few words and Sam imagined that up above on the deck, people could hear them even through the closed windows of the car.

"You're just like them, Sam. You may have lived here only a few years, but it's wearing off on you."

"I don't beat up dogs and people."

"I don't mean that. But you don't stand up and say no, stop, you can't do this."

"Wrong," he shouted back. It felt good to have his words banging around in the small closed space. "I do stand up. I stand up for the ospreys and the salamanders. For all the animals. And the plants and the marshes. That's my way of standing up. And I stand up for the people when I can, when it's my business. At least I don't jump on a boat and run away."

"I am not running away. This is not my home."

"Well, why can't it be? Why can't it be your home?" He sat back and stared out the front windshield. "I know why. Because there are people here you'd have to get connected to. You'd have to care about them. You couldn't just lose yourself in the crowd the way you do in your big cities."

They sat in silence for a minute. He spoke again. "Everybody on this island has been looking for you for the last two hours. Anna Craven practically carried Kasha on the ambulance boat. Tell me, in your precious Philadelphia, what would they do if you called an ambulance for your dog? We held this ferry for you. Upstairs in the cabin, the people are wondering if you're all right. No, Maggie Hammond, we're not perfect. We're regular human beings. We gossip and lie and keep secrets and love and hate and spit in your eye if you look at us funny. And we don't trust people from the outside easily. But we jump when the siren goes off and take chances when somebody's in trouble and make food for each other and keep an eye on each other. It's not because we're morally upright human beings. It's just because there's this circle of water around us that forces us to be that way." He took a breath and the anger went out of his voice. "I thought you would stop running. Keep that house. Make this the place you land when you get off those planes from Europe. Come home here to me after your trips. I want you in my life, Maggie." He gently laid the back of his hand against her wet cheek.

She stayed very still, pressed against the door. At last she took his hand in her own and squeezed it once before she put it back in his lap.

"What you're asking me to do, Sam, sounds so simple to you. After all, you're right, my life wouldn't change. I could get rid of the house in Philadelphia and fly home here to you. It's not the logistics. It's the fear. It's as elemental as if I asked you to come and live in the city with me. You could do it, physically. But it would kill you to be away from this island. For me, the running has become second nature. For so long, it's all I've known to do. I'm terrified of what would happen to me if I stopped. "

He said nothing.

"Remember what Nan said," she whispered. "It's in my blood."

He couldn't stand to be this close and not be allowed to touch her.

"I'll go and pay Chuck," he said.

"I'm so sorry, Sam."

He got himself out of the car as fast as he could.

"On the house," Chuck said as he waved Sam's money away. "How is she?"

Sam just shook his head by way of answering. He didn't trust himself to speak.

He made his way between the few seated passengers out to the bow and stayed there as the boat made its wide turn, docked, and disgorged the cars from its belly. Hers would be the first off and he knew that if he looked over his shoulder, he'd be able to catch a glimpse of it between the boat ramp and the train tracks. But he didn't. He simply stared out across the gentle swells of the sound to the red brick lighthouse and beyond that, to the hazy horizon, where halfway through the trip home, the distant gray form of the island would start to take shape.

Twenty-six

THE WEATHER ON the island in late March, early April, was always unpredictable. Winter blew away on a sudden spring breeze, then rolled back in days later, just when you thought it was truly gone. One day, you could wake up to crocuses unfurling, and the next morning the ground was sparkling with yet another hard frost.

The oystercatcher was one of the earliest and most dependable harbingers of spring, and Sam sighted one on White Beach the twenty-third of March, even though the temperature had dropped to nineteen degrees only two nights before. The weather warmed steadily from then on. The salamander walk was a required field trip for all science classes in the school, and every day in class, he reminded the kids to get their gear ready for the first rainy day. His tent and a rain slicker were stowed behind the seat of his truck.

EVERY YEAR AT this time, Sam pinned a yellow sheet of paper up on the post office bulletin board. "Spring Sightings," it said. Underneath, people noted the date, the place, and the species. It served as a diary of the island, and this year, people seemed to be trying to outdo each other. In a few days, Sam replaced the single sheet of paper with a full-length legal pad, and the notations grew longer. Patrons of the post office checked the list first before they'd go to the window to conduct their business, and Diane Thayer overheard many a conversation about other people's entries.

March 22. A pair of barred owls have moved into the nesting box in the Wilderness Preserve. J. S. Jerry Slocum had been given the job of clearing the paths in the preserve. Al Craven had done it last year.

Same day. Three of the seven osprey nests on the island are already occupied. W. S. Billy Slade had been taken on by the utility company to help with the winter clean-up around the lines on the eastern end of the island. "My dad can see right down into the nests from his cherry picker," Jimmy Slade told Mrs. Thayer.

March 23. Otter tracks in the mud around Mink Pond. S. M. Sally Malloy went on the seventh-grade field trip that week.

March 24. Wood frog (Rana sylvatica) heard at edge of vernal pond behind Chincoteale. E. C.

"My, my, aren't we fancy?" Annie Slocum said to Diane. "Rana sylvatica. Vernal pond."

"Erin is working at the museum again," Diane said. "Anna says she knows all the proper names for the species."

"Well, the poor thing. It's good she's got something to distract her what with everything else that's been going on."

March 25. A woodcock, scolopax minor, is spotted on the road by Shelter Field. H. W. Henry Willard was a long-time birder.

March 27. Oystercatcher, Chincoteale Beach, E. C., A. C. Erin and her mother must have taken the dogs down for an afternoon run.

March 28. Oystercatcher again. Chincoteale. D. L.

"D. L. Who's that, Diane?"

"Everybody's been asking. Dr. Lacey, of course."

"Oh, right."

April 1. Two robins on the field next to the school parking lot. Betsy Thayer, the full name in careful block letters.

"That's dumb. Everybody knows robins. They're nothing special."

"I don't care. I saw them. They're a species too."

"She's right, Patty. Leave her alone."

The thermometer hit the high forties three days in a row and every afternoon after school, Sam checked the edge of the road at the usual crossing spot. Under the rocks, the salamanders were moving around, but they were waiting for rain.

Gus Tremayne flagged down his truck near the post office one morning. "I saw one of your lizards up there yesterday afternoon," he called. "Just sitting on the side of the road."

"They're actually salamanders," Sam said.

"That's right. Never can remember that name."

"Did you carry him across?"

"Nope. Figured I shouldn't mess with nature."

"This warm weather is bringing them out, but the road surface has got to be wet. Pray for rain."

Gus grinned. "You pray for rain, Sam. I'm praying for this dry spell to hold so I can finish the Woodworths' roof before they come up for Easter weekend. We'll see who wins."

After a day of heavy fog, a light rain began to fall the Friday evening before Easter. The timing was terrible. The summer people would be pouring off the six o'clock ferry and then again at nine because Dan Chester always ran a late ferry on holiday weekends.

Sam put out the word on the radio, then to the kids, then beat it up island to check. It took him only a few minutes of scanning back and forth across the newly wet surface with his Q beam to pick them out. Two peepers were halfway over. He pulled his truck across the road to stop any traffic and jumped out to carry them the rest of the way. A crowd of salamanders was gathered on the woodland side. Three had started across.

Headlights signaled the approach of a car, but it pulled over to the side when Sam waved with his light. There was the slam of doors.

"Have they started?" Paul Thayer called. He'd brought the whole family.

"Yup," Sam said proudly as he spotlighted the first three.

They stood in a circle and watched for a moment in silence. The black backs of the wiggling creatures were lit up with two irregular rows of yellow-orange spots. Their skin glistened in the light.

"They're so slimy," Patty Thayer said.

"I like them," whispered her little sister, Betsy, who had hunched down to watch with her thumb still in her mouth.

"Looks like they're racing," Diane said.

"It's the males going over to establish their breeding ground," said Sam. "Best spot gets the most women. Sort of like the land rush. Wouldn't you be in a hurry yourself?"

"Sam," Diane said. "Please."

"Let's time them," said Patty. "We'll have salamander races. Mine's the one on this side."

"That's not fair," said Betsy. "Yours is already in front."

Sam pulled a pack of herp survey cards out of the pocket of his slicker and handed each of them three cards and a pencil. "Pick out your favorite salamander and fill out a card," he said. "Make sure you don't double up so we have an accurate count."

"All right, girls," Diane said. "I'll take the slowest one. Shine your light over here, Patty, so we can write. The cards are getting wet."

"They picked a bad day," Paul said as he checked his watch. "The six o'clock ferry's just unloaded. The first of the summer people will be headed up island any minute now. I'll direct traffic till Randy gets here."

The first cars were filled with volunteers who pulled over to the side of the road and lined up neatly, one behind the other. People spilled out with tents, cookstoves, flashlights, ponchos. For once, nobody seemed to mind the weather. The night was warm, almost fifty, and without the rain, the salamanders wouldn't be crossing. Somebody was posted at the eastern end of the road to stop anybody who might be coming down from the other end of the island. Nobody could remember whether Gus was still up there working on the Woodworth house, hammering in the last shingles. The Woodworths were due in on the nine o'clock boat.

Sam got the older kids to unload the buckets and the black plastic barrier from the back of his truck. They slid the plywood covers off the freshly dug holes and dropped in the buckets, six on either side of the road. One spring, after they dug the holes for the buckets, Sam hadn't thought to cover them. The amphibians had started moving in a light rain and some of them fell into the holes. In the morning when the rain stopped, the predators found breakfast waiting for them. Sam didn't know exactly how many he lost, but his counts were down that year. He was furious with himself over that slip-up. Everything in nature was carefully synchronized. You thought you were helping, but you could so easily make a mess of things.

"I'm here," said a voice at his elbow, and he looked down to find Erin. She was wearing a yellow slicker and her backpack. Under the hood of the slicker, she had a light strapped to her head.

"Where did you get that light?" he asked. "It's perfect. It's the kind miners use."

"Mom ordered it for me from a catalog. She's got a tent. We're staying the night this year. So where do you want me?"

"Up front. The Thayer family are marking the first crossers, but I need you to make sure everybody fills out their herp cards. Did you bring the clipboard?"

"Right here." She'd tucked it under her slicker to keep it dry.

He took a quick look at the headings. "Just be sure to get down the species, the size, and any comments on specific ones. Mark down two crucifers for me. I carried them across when I got here."

"Did you fill out cards on them?" she asked sternly.

"Not yet. But I will. I promise. Better get on up there."

ERIN MOVED THROUGH the crowd passing out the blue cards and the tiny sharpened pencils from the right pocket of her slicker. She liked being the one in charge. Even the grown-ups were asking her questions about what to do.

"Does it hurt the salamanders to pick them up?"

"No," she said. "Just make sure your palms are moist."

"Can I put Jimmy down on the card as my other observer?" Brian Griffen asked.

"Sure," Erin said. "Include his address."

"Where'd you get that dress?" Patty Thayer asked. "It's new."

"My mom bought it for me in the mall."

"Your mom bought you that? It's really short." She was clearly jealous.

"I know," Erin said. She had black leggings on underneath to keep her legs warm.

"Why're you wearing a dress?"

Erin shrugged. "It's a party. A salamander party," she added before she moved away to the next person calling for a card.

WHAT WITH THE dark and the rain and the sudden glare of headlights, Randy didn't notice the man making his way up along the line of parked cars until he was a few yards away.

"Randy," Al said. He was walking slowly, a cane in his right hand. "I'll take over now."

"No need, Al," Randy said, keeping his voice light. "I've got this under control. You'd better rest that leg."

"The hell I will," Al said. "This leg is just fine."

Some of the men closed in behind Randy.

"Al, go on over to the side," said Paul's voice.

"Hey, Derry," called Gus Tremayne. "Find one of those folding chairs, will you? Al needs to sit down. You got an umbrella, Al? This rain's coming down pretty hard. You want to stay dry. Man in your condition."

Al saw the faces of the men lined up behind Randy. The light from the cars picked up their expressions clear enough. They were all looking around him and above him and on either side of him like they had other more important business going on right now. He was just somebody they needed to move along out of the road.

"Damn you all," Al muttered, "you're not going to get away with this."

"Bo," Gus called. "Help the man over to the side, will you? Your brother's got a chair waiting for him."

"Don't you dare touch me," Al told Bo, and the boy raised his hands and backed away, with a sly grin on his face.

"Whatever you say, Mr. Craven. Whatever you say."

The men stood and watched as Al stumped off through the misty rain past the growing line of cars, past some people setting up their tents on the side of the road and others unloading food from the backseats of the cars. People looked up when he went by and a few called a greeting, but their voices were hesitant, and they turned quickly back to their business. The group of men stayed clustered behind Randy until Al's truck door slammed and his engine started up.

"The man's got nerve," Paul said. "You can say that for him."

"How's he like his new digs?" Jim Sullivan asked.

"You should have seen his face when we drove him home from the ferry," Gus said. "The place looks okay. He's got all that leftover furniture from his parents that he makes the summer renters live with. If it's good enough for them, then it's good enough for him."

"And Anna sent over some stuff."

"Is he leaving her alone?"

"Chuck says he hasn't gone near her."

"Don't think he'd dare."

"All right, you guys, give me some room," Randy said. "Sam," he called over his shoulder. "Can we let these first cars through?"

"Nope, not yet," Sam yelled back from the edge of the road. "I need a few more minutes." He grabbed the bullhorn out of the front seat of his truck and jumped up onto the tailgate. "All right everybody, stop right where you are." The crowd in the road froze. "We don't want anybody stepping on something by mistake. Now each one of you pick a salamander or a peeper. Put up your hand if you've got one." A bunch of hands went up. Some arguing broke out among three boys at the eastern end of the road. "No fighting. Don't worry, there are enough for everybody." Diane Thayer settled the dispute.

"Are you ready?" Sam asked. There was a murmur of assent. "Does everybody have a herp card to fill out?"

"I don't," called Sally Malloy.

"Me either," said another voice.

"Get your cards from Erin," Sam announced as Erin moved through the group.

"Hey, Sam," Henry Willard called out. "This is Montague. I remember him from last year." The crowd laughed.

"You're probably right, Henry," Sam said. "Some of these salamanders have been around longer than most of you kids. Now all of you, make sure your hands are wet, pick up your amphibian and carry it across the road."

There were the usual squeals and grunts from the crowd. It was always this way with the first carryover of the night. After a couple more crossings, nobody would even notice the wet skin of the salamanders against the damp palms of their hands. Some people took their time, others rushed across. Betsy Thayer was whispering to hers through a crack in her cupped hands. Jimmy Slade dumped his unceremoniously in the wet leaves on the other side and tore back across the road to get there before his friend Brian.

Sam whistled through the bullhorn again. "As soon as you've taken them over, clear the road. We've got some cars that have to go through. Boys, drop that plastic barrier. Henry, shine your light down the road to be sure we haven't missed any. Okay, there's one. Jimmy, you can take that one."

"Hold up, Sam, there's something over here," a voice called out, and with his Q beam, Sam picked out Anna in her cowboy hat, hunkered down on the road. Erin walked over to look. "Crucifer," she called out and made a note on her clipboard. "Okay, Mom's got it."

"For everybody's information, a crucifer is a spring peeper," Sam announced through the bullhorn. "We call it that because of the X-shaped marking on its back. If you adults have any questions about the proper species names to put on the cards, just ask the kids. They all know. Boys, when you lift that plastic again after the cars have gone through, be sure you check the buckets."

"Sam, I've got six cars lined up back here," Randy called.

Sam swept the road one more time with his light. It was clear. "Okay, Randy. You can let the first group through."

HOLIDAY WEEKENDS LIKE this one, Island Foods always stayed open late so that people could stock up on groceries as soon as they got off the boat. Randy figured there would be at least three waves of cars per boat, depending on how many checkers were working the lines down at the store and how many owners were organized enough to do their food shopping on the other side. The second group began to build pretty soon after they'd given the road back over to the amphibians. The first car in line looked familiar to

Randy, but he couldn't quite place it until the driver rolled down her window. It was Maggie.

"Hey," he said, "how are you doing?"

He sounded glad to see her. "Fine, Randy. I don't want to go through. I just need a place to park."

He pointed his flashlight over to the side of the road. "One good place left over there," he said, showing her. "Don't pull too far off though. It gets pretty muddy this time of year."

"Thanks."

"How's Kasha?"

"She's in the back." Randy peered in and the dog lifted her head at the bright light. "She's getting better, but it's taking time."

"Hard to see her in the middle of all that stuff. You're pretty loaded up back there."

"I gave up my lease in Philadelphia. There's a van coming up Monday with the rest."

"So you're going to be staying," he said.

"It looks that way."

"That's good. We heard you'd been in touch with the real estate agent about selling the place."

"I changed my mind," she said. She wondered if they'd been taking bets on her down at the Lounge. She wouldn't be surprised. "It turns out there were some things up here I couldn't live without."

"Things?"

"Well, people actually."

"Lucky people." He grinned.

"How's the crossing?"

"It's going pretty well, I guess. How'd you hear?"

"I called Anna this morning. She took a look at the weather report and made a pretty good guess."

"She's up ahead there with Erin."

"Sam's a busy man." She gazed past Randy. Her hands were shaking a little and she tightened them on the steering wheel. When she first rolled down the window, it had shocked her to hear the intimate and intensely familiar sound of Sam's low, easy voice booming out through the bullhorn. It was as if he were making love to this entire crowd of people. This same voice had whispered in her ear all through those long winter nights when they should have been sleeping. Time after time in the last weeks, she had woken with a start and reached for him, certain that he had just spoken to her. "I want you in my life, Maggie," he had said on the boat. Even in that moment, with his hand on her cheek, she had tricked herself into believing she could keep on running. But it had proved impossible.

"Don't know which he's having a harder time controlling," Randy said. "The people or the salamanders. 'Spect he'll be glad to see you." His voice was kind.

"Don't tell him I'm here," she said. "I want to surprise him." Randy nodded. He held the car behind her with an upraised hand while she made a U-turn and slid into the parking spot. She got out and leaned back against the door of her car to watch.

Sam stood with his feet planted on the truck bed, using the Q beam the way an orchestra conductor wielded his baton. People were calling out questions and his calm voice floated back and forth above the commotion. The rain hood had slipped off his head and his dark hair glistened in the passing flashes of light. At one point, he jumped down from the truck to help Miss Yola fill out her card, then swung himself back up again in an easy fluid leap. Underneath the slicker, which he hadn't bothered to zip, his favorite gray corduroy shirt was tucked into jeans. Early one February morning Maggie had woken to the sight of him cross-legged at the end of the bed, sewing the second button on that shirt before he left for school. People greeted her and she smiled in return, but they saw that her attention was focused on him and they let her be. She held herself still and watched him and waited.

Later on, they would have all the time they needed. Later on, she would step out of the shadows into the line of his light, and when he saw her, he would put down the lamp and the bullhorn and jump off the truck and start toward her, and as soon as their bodies met, he would gather her up in the circle of his arms in front of the whole island, and neither one of them would give a damn who was watching. And she would know for sure, deep in her bones, what it felt like to come home.

She was putting that moment off. She could wait. For now, he belonged to the salamanders and the spring peepers and to all these people milling about in the road, calling to him. They counted on him the way she did, to talk them through the night, to help them find the safest way across the road.

RANDY PUT A hand up to stop the next group of cars.

"What's going on here?" a voice demanded. Randy shined his flashlight on the man's face.

"Hello there, Mr. Davidson. Nice to see you."

"Hi, Randy. You the traffic cop these days? What happened to Al Craven?"

"I've taken over for now. We decided to give Al a break."

"What's this all about?"

"You'll be able to drive through in a minute. As soon as we get the word from up ahead. The yellow-spotted salamanders are crossing the road. We're making sure they get to the other side safely."

"Looks like a party."

Randy straightened up and glanced around. "I guess you could say that," he said. "Sort of one big crazy island party."

FROM HIS VANTAGE point on the truck, Sam turned for a moment and looked back down the road to where the tents were going up. Two fires had been started, and he smelled hamburgers. There was the slam of doors, the call of voices as more year-rounders arrived and greeted each other. The crowd along the edge of the road had whooped and hollered when the first eight cars went through and the people inside had waved back through the windows with puzzled expressions on their faces. You couldn't blame them, Sam thought as he gazed down at the scene in front of him. The salamander-bearers were moving about on the road like dancers in some strange pagan ritual. They dipped and weaved, they poked one another on the arm and pointed proudly to their own particular crossers, they leaned over and hurried their charges along, then scribbled on their cards and called out to Erin for another. The rain had become a fine mist and from all directions, the beam of flashlights bounced off the slick surfaces of wet ponchos and damp faces and off the black plastic barrier when the older boys dropped it at Sam's signal. Above the noise, he could make out the distant, but reliable blow of the fog horn in the waters off Stony Point and from another direction, the irregular clang of the buoy bell as it rose and fell with the waves of the ebbing tide.

For this one moment, without any hesitation, he loved every one of these people who, on a rainy spring night, were willing to help him stand watch over the salamanders as they made their slow, moist, precarious way across the road to their breeding ground in the marsh.